The Purple Pashmina

by Anita Levine

Acknowledgements

This book is dedicated to all the people who've taken the time and effort to identify, then live the life that truly fulfills them.

Special thanks to Walt Giersbach and the Writers Circle, the first to hear this story and bolster its energy, and mine, with their encouragement and feedback.

Thanks also to Jan Bentley, Betsy Strauss. Jenn Blum, Adele Polomski, Alice DiNizo and Linda Bonneau, who read the book at various stages of its development and provided some useful feedback, Natalena, who created the cover art of my dreams, and Mercedes Leo, computer guru extraordinaire!

And to Jane Nirella and Dr. Carl Calendar, a big thank you for setting me on the path.

With much love to my family, always.

Prologue
Memorial Day Weekend

I glanced at my watch, the Rolex my husband Rich bought me for our 30th anniversary a few years ago. "He's still not here."

My friend Jessica picked up two glasses and pointed to the wine on the table."Red or white?"

"White."

She poured me a glass of Chardonnay. "He'll show up sooner or later, always does."

"Not always. Remember that Soho show last Easter?"

"Just that once." She smoothed the long, colorful flared skirt she'd worn today. I'd always loved her sense of style.

"Look at all the people who did show up." She gestured around the room. "To judge from all those yellow *Sold* tags? They're buying your artwork, too."

I looked around and realized she was right. My first art show in Brook Haven was a success. Scheduling it the same weekend the beaches opened wasn't my idea, but it seemed to be working out.

"I was so impressed when they invited you to do this show," Jessica went on.

"It was Chloe's idea. She took care of all the details." I hadn't been as proactive with my career as I used to be. I knew why, too, but facing it? Difficult, right now.

Jessica sipped her wine."Chloe's been your artist's rep for a long time, hasn't she?"

I nodded. "Twenty-five years."

We helped ourselves to some grapes and cheese, standard-issue art show fare, as I admired Brook Haven's elegant new Cultural

Center. Like everything else in this upscale New Jersey shore community, it was a testament to good taste.

"Perfect weather, too." Jessica topped off her Pinot Noir as we surveyed the crowd. Lots of people were interested in the signed, limited edition prints Chloe and I began to do last year. We'd started out with print editions of 15 of my paintings. Today, I was glad to see a decent-size crowd gathered around my all-time favorite, the one I'd done when I'd spent a week in North Carolina's Outer Banks two years ago, a moonlit beach with sandpipers, gulls and egrets silhouetted against phosphorescent ocean waves under a silver-blue moon.

Jessica indicated the small crowd around it. "Looks like that's their favorite."

I nodded. "I'm glad we did those prints. They can get my work out to a lot more people." My paintings had sold at prices that started at $1900 and had gone as high as $4500 last year. When Chloe suggested signed and numbered prints we could sell in the two to three hundred dollar price range might be a good idea, I'd agreed, just like the I always do when it comes to her suggestions. Despite the fact that Rich didn't want me to sign on with a dealer as small and unknown as Chloe, all those years ago, our relationship has worked out so well, I've never looked back.

"Tomas is so sorry he couldn't be here today." Jessica's significantly older husband Tomas was resting today after some difficult medical tests this week. I admired the way she met the challenges his age presented. At 88, he was almost 40 years older than Jess. They loved each other deeply, though, enough to make their marriage work.

My marriage was a very different story. “I wish Rich would show up on time, for once.” I sipped my wine. "He said something about meeting a client." I glanced at my watch. He was almost 45 minutes late.

Jessica frowned. Rich has never impressed her. "Looks like Chloe needs you."

I turned to see Chloe, waving me over to meet the reporter and photographer who’d just arrived.

Twenty minutes later, the reporter concluded his interview with questions about my plans for the future as the photographer took photos, some of which, she promised, would appear in the Weekend Arts section of the *Brook Haven Banner*. “We’ll make sure there’s a link to your gallery, too,” she told Chloe.

“How wonderful! Thanks so much." Chloe’s chunky turquoise and silver jewelry jangled as she smoothed her flowing, hand-woven Ecuadorian tunic. She waited until they went off before she turned to me. “Great turnout. Half the town must be here.”

Everyone except my husband. “I’m glad.” Having moved to Brook Haven a little over a year ago, I wasn’t sure what kind of response we’d get. But not only had lots of people shown up, they were buying enough of those prints and original paintings to make my show a success.

I looked over at Helen Adkins, another of my Brook Haven neighbors. She was talking to Harvey Malden and Cliff Richardson, the high-profile gay couple who ran the Haven Players, Brook Haven’s award-winning amateur theater company. I was glad they’d invited me and Rich to their annual Halloween bash last year even though I was sure it was Rich they’d had in mind. But I still enjoyed the great food, costumes, games and all that laughter.

The party would've been perfect, in fact, if not for this strange, well, darkness I'd felt that night. It made no sense, when everyone seemed to be having such a good time. Nor had I mentioned it to Rich, who never gives any credence at all to my intuition even though it's been right on target, at times.

I looked up to see him coming in with my next-door neighbor Wendi. Was she the client he'd had to meet? Probably. They came up and gave me identical air kisses.

"Sorry we're late." Rich didn't volunteer any more information and I knew better than to ask.

"Glad you could make it." If Rich caught my sarcasm, he didn't react.

I turned to Wendi, who was smiling. From the looks of her red, red lips, she'd just refreshed her makeup, too. Her perfect size two body was clothed, today, in a well-cut sky blue designer sheath that made it clear that she took care of herself, as she loved to tell everyone. All the time. "What lovely paintings, my dear, and what a wonderful turnout!"

As if you mean it. "Thank you."

"I can't wait to take a look around," she added a little breathlessly. Had her time with Rich had been more than a business meeting? Would I ever find out?

Don't go there—concentrate on the show!

"I think I'll join you." Rich smiled. Two more of those lame little air kisses and they went off, talking softly to each other. Wendi adjusted the purple pashmina she was wearing over her dress so that it lay perfectly across her body as they headed for the area where my limited edition prints were displayed.

Wendi continued to adjust her pashmina as she and Rich made their way through the show. A cashmere pashmina at the end of May didn't make sense to me, but Wendi wore those big, dramatic body scarves everywhere. This one was purple with silver embroidery in an intricate Celtic knot design. Beautiful and pretentious. Almost as beautiful and pretentious as Wendi.

"I hate those goddamn pashminas," Jessica murmured. "Though I've got to say the design is nice. Must've cost a fortune," she added.

"I'm sure." I looked at Wendi again. She and Rich were playing Art Critic now, commenting softly, if not quite softly enough, on my work as they crossed slowly to the wine and cheese table. I was picturing Wendi dead, that purple pashmina wrapped around her neck, when a tall, good-looking man in black jeans and a blue v-neck knit shirt close to the same color as his amazing crystal blue eyes came up and extended his hand.

"I wanted to tell you how much I like your work. I'm Jason Connolly," he added, his smile crinkling the corners around those great blue eyes.

I smiled and extended my hand. "Amanda Warren." His hand was big and strong and felt a little calloused, too, as we shook. *Jason Connolly.* I'd heard that name before but I couldn't place him. He wasn't what you'd call handsome, exactly. Compelling, that was more like it. Tall and dark, big, muscular and macho, with those crystal blue eyes and a smile that made me a little warm.

"Your paintings? They just, I don't know, give me a feeling of peace, the same kind of feeling I get when I walk in the woods…"

My heart beat faster as I pictured him walking in the woods. With me.

"Know what I mean?" His voice pulled me back.

"Yes. Thank you," I remembered to add as I smiled and felt myself begin to blush, something I've always done and always wished I didn't.

He smiled back. He was about my age, maybe a little younger. I was glad I hadn't had too many issues with my 55th birthday last month.

A little over a year ago, Rich and I moved from the house where we raised our daughter Katie to Brook Haven Acres, a brand-new, super-upscale gated community on the central New Jersey shore. Rich had loved the Acres as much as I'd hated it when we'd toured the elegant model homes.

"That print with the ocean, the blue moon and those egrets? Terrific!" Jason Connolly's voice brought me back again. It was smooth and deep and just as, well, delicious as he was—enough to make me wish Rich had never shown up.

"Thank you." I repeated. I would've loved to come up with something more clever, but when I looked in his eyes? My mind went blank.

"Have you lived here long?" he asked.

I shook my head. "We moved down from Oakwood last year."

"Do you show your work up there, too?"

I shook my head. "I started out in Soho, in New York."

"Soho? They've got great galleries there!" He smiled. "I lived in the city for 10 years." He stopped smiling, then. I wondered why.

"I showed all my work in Soho till Chloe opened a second gallery in Chesterton, near Short Hills." I pointed to Chloe, who was writing up a sale, as I ran his name through my mind again. Jason Connolly, New York City. Who was he?

He gestured around the room. "Really, I like all your paintings." Had his smile just segued from warm to hot or was it only wishful thinking?

Whatever it was, I felt my heart, and a few other strategic body parts, heat up, a feeling so intense, it was hard to keep my voice cool and calm. "Thank you." I pointed to his favorite. "I did the original when I spent a week on the Outer Banks down in North Carolina a few years ago." I smiled as I remembered the ten days I'd spent down there, blissfully alone with the beach and the ocean.

"The Outer Banks? I love it down there."

A kindred spirit?

We talked a little more before he excused himself. Fifteen minutes later, I watched as he handed Chloe his Amex. He didn't take the picture with him, though. Had he asked her to hold it? Probably. I wondered why, as I watched him turn to leave.

Alone. Was he married? Not that it mattered, when I was, to Rich, standing by the windows talking to Wendi right now. They joined me a few minutes later.

Wendi adjusted her purple pashmina to display it as attractively as possible. "Congratulations, dear. Your show is a huge success." She smiled charmingly, no surprise there. No one worked a room like Wendi. “Wonderful, the way your little hobby is paying off!”

Art is my life, not my hobby, and it's been paying off, paying well, these past 25 years. I wondered how I could say that when Chloe came up to us. “Amanda’s been one of our top-selling artists for more years than I can count.”

Wendi nodded as she looked down her nose at Chloe, a neat trick when Wendi stood 4’11,” compared to Chloe’s 5’6.”

“Rich mentioned something about your little gallery.” She turned to him. “Where did you say it was?”

“Soho,” he replied.

“We started out in Soho, but I opened a second gallery up in Chesterton last year,” Chloe managed a smile.

“I buy all my artwork on Madison Avenue, at Soames and Bentley. Perhaps you’ve heard of them?”

"Of course." Soames and Bentley was a major presence in the art world, with galleries in Manhattan, Los Angeles, London, Paris and most every other major city in the world. Rich wanted me to sign on with them when I first started out.

A year of two before I signed with Chloe, he also insisted we buy the artwork for our first home at their Madison Avenue gallery. He’d just made Junior Partner at Duncan Fitzgerald Kaufman, the big Manhattan law firm where he'd worked for 31 years. “We’ll be entertaining important people. We need pieces by artists they’ll recognize.”

Pieces we’d bought at Soames and Bentley, relegating my paintings to the upstairs bedrooms.

Where else would someone like Wendi buy her artwork?

"Amanda and I so enjoy the Soho art scene," Chloe was saying as I tuned back in.

Jason Connolly does, too. I pictured him, big, strong and compelling, in those great jeans that molded every perfect inch of him, with eyes the color of clear Caribbean waters.

"Right, Amanda?" Chloe was asking me now.

The vision of Jason Connolly faded quickly. "I loved starting out in Soho." In fact, I'd loved it enough to decline Soames and Bentley's half-hearted offer to "try me out." I began to say something about that when Wendi cut me off.

"Soho is much too left of center for me, but I'm glad you're happy there."

"Yes." Less than brilliant, not that it mattered. The only opinion Wendi cared about was her own . Someone came up with a question for Chloe, then, and she went off, leaving me with Wendi. And Rich.

I glanced at her pashmina and imagined it in my hands. I was wrapping it around her neck, squeezing it tight, watching her eyes bug out as she struggled for her very last breath on this earth...

"I thought we'd go to the Garden Gate tonight." Rich glanced at Wendi, who nodded. It was Wendi's idea. I knew that because she was a vegetarian, the most vocal one in the civilized world.

"I so adore the Garden Gate." Wendi smiled sweetly.

Thai was my favorite. I pictured Golden Siam, a good Thai restaurant in town. Since this was my day, shouldn't we go there? "I was thinking Golden Siam."

Wendi frowned daintily. “I’m afraid I had dinner there the other night.”

I thought about it. Rich and Wendi could go to the Garden Gate while I had Thai with Chloe or Jessica. That’d make me happy. Thai with Jason Connolly would make me even happier. I couldn’t help but picture that scenario, until I realized the women he’d have dinner with would probably be younger, single-- beautiful.

“Amanda?” Rich's voice brought me back.

“The Garden Gate? Fine.” *Not!*

“Please don’t pout,” he said quietly.

Deny I was pouting? Why bother?

Chapter One
Three Months Later

"Ohmm..." *Breathe deeply. Go with the music, go with the flow.* Not easy this morning. I'd gotten up at 6:30, early for me. I'd taken my time getting dressed. I was wearing my painting clothes today, black yoga pants and an incredibly soft teal blue organic cotton tee-shirt. But it was still so early, Rich hadn't left for the office.

I opened my eyes as I heard Rich in the kitchen. Might as well get up, go in there and have another cup of coffee.

"Good morning." I glanced at our new single cup coffeemaker, Rich's latest have-to-have. If we still had the old coffeepot, I could pour myself a cup right now.

"I can't believe this!" He pointed out the window, upset.

I wished for that coffee as I looked outside. Someone had run over our decorative Pampas grass, the grass I'd hated from the first. Judging from the deep, ugly tire tracks that'd gouged out whole sections of our once-picture perfect lawn, someone else hated that stuff as much as I did.

Rich frowned. "I called Security. They said they'd come out this morning. You will be home?" We both knew it wasn't really a question.

I nodded. *I'll be here to paint, not deal with Security.* I chose my issues carefully, with Rich, these days. "I wonder who could've done it." I popped a French vanilla cartridge into the coffeemaker. Rich was the one who'd insisted we plant that Pampas grass after Wendi'd planted it in front of her house and all the other couples in her Inner Circle followed suit.

I looked up. He was checking his watch, a Rolex that cost almost as much as our first house. "I'm late." He picked up his sleek designer attaché and headed out, leaving me to deal with the Pampas grass, Security, maybe even the police. I'd planned to get back to my painting today, but it looked like I'd need to put it off. Again.

I took his coffee cup from the table and put it in the dishwasher as I heard him start his Mercedes SUV. He claimed to be semi-retired these days, but he still wasn't home much, no problem for me. He'd told everyone he was leaving Duncan Fitzgerald Kaufman to cut back on his hours. "I'll lease a little office down here, limit my client load and take some time to enjoy life."

I'd questioned it then, but a few weeks later, I knew he didn't mean it. I also wondered why he'd gotten so many phone calls, his last few weeks at the firm. He'd seemed nervous, too, when they came in. Was there a problem?

"A problem? Don't be silly."

But my intuition is seldom silly. And it was saying yes, there was a problem. Which made me wonder why Rich really resigned. I knew he'd always wanted to become a judge. Did he think he could make more contacts working here on the Jersey shore? He'd been socializing with Edgar Robertson to that end, a Columbia Law School classmate who'd been a judge for ten years now.

"Arrogant bastard, but a strong network always pays off," he'd say after a round of golf at the country club with Judge Robertson. No surprise there. He'd always sought out connections with people who could help him get where he wanted to go. Which I couldn't believe was into semi-retirement.

The reason it didn't surprise me when the hours he worked in his upscale office in a new building with floor to ceiling windows overlooking Barnegat Bay turned out to be just as long as they were when he'd commuted into the city. No problem for me. I got used to that a long, long time ago.

***

Rich had been gone almost an hour. I was sitting on the floor in my semi-authorized meditation space in my semi-authorized artist's studio, both in the three-season room, as they called it here in Brook Haven Acres. I was meditating again, trying to get in touch with the Universe to clear the creative block I'd been fighting for months, now. I needed to start painting again.

"Ohmm…" I chanted, as the sound of the garbage truck rumbling down the street broke my concentration. It was recycling day and I'd promised Wendi I'd put her recycling can back in her garage.

Odd, the way she'd asked me directly this time instead of relaying the message through Rich. "I've got a Shelter by the Sea meeting down in Brigantine tomorrow. I would so appreciate your doing this for me, dear."

"No problem." If there was anything that made me hate her a little less, it was her work with Shelter by the Sea, an organization that ran shelters and provided counseling and support for domestic abuse survivors.

There's a little bit of good in the worst of us and a little bit of bad in the best of us, my mother used to say. Despite all those visions of strangling Wendi with her purple pashmina, I tried to keep that in mind whenever I had to deal with her.

"Recycling? Such a bother." She sighed dramatically.

"No problem," I repeated.

Today, in my studio, I stood up slowly. I hadn't reached the meditative state I'd hoped for, but I still couldn't get up too fast. I didn't want to trip over my easel, the one I used to paint, when I—used to paint. I hadn't done much since my show three months ago, but I would get back to it, as I kept telling Chloe whenever she called.

I headed out to our garage, an oversized two-car garage with all the bells and whistles: custom shelving, a cedar-lined storage closet, a sophisticated wine chiller, all the accoutrements of the good life, Rich liked to say.

My artist's studio should only look this good, I thought as I headed over to Wendi's, where the recycling truck had just stopped in front. Two men were getting out, now, walking over to her designer recycling can.

Wendi had given a party last Sunday, a *soiree,* as she called them. That meant her recycling can was full, the only reason she'd put it out. Recycling was mandatory in Brook Haven but Wendi considered herself above the rules. I knew that by the way she conducted herself when she held court at the Acres' Women's Club meetings, meetings I attended once a month when I should've been painting.

Rich's idea.

"I know how much you resent Wendi—"

"I don't resent her." *I hate her.*

“But we both know her heart is in the right place. Think of all the time and money she gives to the Shelter.”

"The shelter is a good cause," I agreed. Grudgingly.

“You have your responsibilities and I have mine. We’ve discussed this before, more than once,” he went on.

We’ve discussed it much too often, not that I said that. Rich loves to spell out my responsibilities. It was at the worst when I stopped freelancing as a commercial artist so I could move on to the kind of painting I’d always dreamt of doing.

“Not that I object to the time you spend on your little paintings.” He’d patted my shoulder condescendingly that day before he went on to tell me how he really felt.

Which boiled down to what he perceived as my unwillingness to be the kind of wife he expected me to be. He completely discounted the way I’d taken care of him, our daughter Katie and the house even as I’d worked 35 to 50 hours a week as a freelance commercial artist, designing everything from hardware packaging to print ads for jewelers, banks, plumbers-- and every other kind of business known to man.

Looking back, I wasn’t proud of the fact that it'd taken me more years than it should’ve to move on. I was 26 that year, so overwhelmed with the responsibility of raising Katie, running our household and being a freelance artist, fighting with my husband was the last thing I wanted to do.

But I finally succeeded in standing up for myself, trading freelance art for painting by the time I was 30. but I still continued to do my best to go along with his other wishes, over the years, making an effort to do the "little things," as he called them, the things he wanted me to do to be the kind of wife he wanted me to be.

As far as responsibility went, I was so responsible it was stifling me. I knew, deep down, it was high time to break out of that prison. I just needed a little more courage, I told myself as I went off to my first Women's Club meeting.

I hate those meetings and I hate her more, I thought as I watched the garbage men struggle to lift her recycling can. It was heavy even when it was empty. I knew that because Rich insisted on buying the same can, one so stylish, it had everything but a Versace label.

"Heavy sucker," one of the men grumbled. They both frowned as they positioned themselves on either side of the can, counted to three and picked it up and turned it over, not without difficulty.

They gasped when a big purple lump fell out and landed on the curb. I took a deep breath before I moved a few steps closer, close enough to see that it was a purple pashmina. Wrapped around—Wendi?

"Holy—" The first man stepped back. The other one took out his phone and entered a number as his partner turned and saw me there.

I pointed to the big purple lump. "My neighbor? She, um, asked me to bring in her recycling can." A lot for me to say when I was in shock, but he just nodded and took a few more steps away from the purple pashmina--and the dead body underneath it.

I retreated to my garage quickly and as the first police vehicles arrived, not to check on our ruined Pampas grass, either, that was for sure! I looked at the landscaping Rich had been so proud of. I was asking myself why anyone would've wanted to destroy it when the flashing lights of yet another Brook Haven PD vehicle brought me back as it pulled up to the curb.

Far from old-fashioned black-and-whites, Brook Haven's Finest drove top-of-the-line Mediterranean blue and white SUV's with a trendy ocean wave design, one that proclaimed exactly how upscale a community we are.

I've never cared much about status but I love the fact that Brook Haven is only eight miles from the ocean. Summers are tough, with the tourists, but we deal with it. That's what I was thinking when Jessica came over and pointed to Helen, standing on her porch across the street with her husband John, watching the action.

How did Helen feel about that purple lump on the curb that was probably, well, Wendi? Happy or something like it, I suspected. She hated Wendi, a feeling that had to do with the Haven Players, the theatre group they'd both belonged to. Jessica didn't know Wendi too well but she didn't like her, either.

Jessica's husband Tomas felt the same way about Wendi. Tomas had fought the Nazis in the Czech Underground in World War Two when he was barely into his teens. After it ended and the Communist regime took over his country, he'd managed to escape by crawling across the Czech border under barbed wire and machine gun fire in 1951. It'd taken him a few more years to reach the United States, where he'd met and married his first wife Dawn, had a daughter and worked hard enough to finance a nice retirement, one that'd enabled him to ask Jessica to marry him 14 months after Dawn passed on.

"Take a look at that!" Jessica pointed to the purple pashmina-wrapped lump still lying on the curb. "Wendi? I always said she was nothing but trouble."

She won't be trouble anymore. That's what I would've said if I was sure it was Wendi's body under that pashmina. Two men in white suits were pulling it back, now, just enough for me to see it really was Wendi. And she really was dead.

"What happened to your Pampas grass? I know how much you hated that stuff, but vandalism?" Jess was asking me now.

"Someone ran it down. Rich called Security, but now, with the police here?" I shrugged my shoulders. Clearly, the Great Pampas Grass Incident would not be their top priority.

"Rich called Security?" Jessica put the same edge on his name she always did.

"C'mon, Jess, he's not that bad."

She rolled her eyes.

"I could never have become an artist without his support."

"So? He could never have become a big, important lawyer without yours."

He saved me, that night in college, something I'd never told Jessica, or many other people. *I owe him. I always will.*

"About your Pampas grass..."

I glanced at it. "I don't know why Rich insisted on putting it in."

"Seriously?" She pointed to Wendi's Pampas grass.

"Whatever. They won't investigate today."

"They do look busy." They were loading Wendi's body, wrapped, now, in a plain black body bag, into the back of a plain white van.

It took off a few minutes later. I thought of the woman I'd loved to hate, super-attractive, undeniably bitchy and totally indestructible, so I'd thought. Dead, her body wrapped in her purple pashmina and stuffed into her Versace recycling can. A chill ran down my spine as I remembered how I'd imagined wrapping that same pashmina around her neck and squeezing the life out of her petite, too-perfect body.

Somebody beat me to it. What to say: goodbye and good riddance? Harsh, but Wendi was the neighbor from hell. She'd made me crazy from the day she'd moved in and pressed her spare key into Rich's hand. "Just in case," she'd murmured softly, seductively.

In the months that followed, she'd thrown herself at him whenever she got the chance. It wasn't personal, I told myself. Wendi threw herself at every man she met, including Harvey, the gay guy from the theater group and Cliff, his husband.

"If a man's standing upright and breathing on his own, Wendi will put the moves on him," Helen liked to say. Wendi didn't put any moves on Helen's husband John, though, a retired accountant and a very nice guy, but not much to look at unless you liked men who wore their pants halfway up to their shoulders.

Jessica was laughing now. "And here they say only the good die young."

I knew I shouldn't laugh with her but I couldn't help it. I'd disliked Wendi intensely. Now that she was gone…

She can't come on to Rich anymore.

Jessica and I were both laughing, now-- was it glee, nerves or something darker? I wasn't sure, as John and Helen crossed the cul-de-sac to join us. Being on a cul-de-sac cost extra, but

Rich insisted it was worth it. I went along just like I always do.

The house of my dreams is one by the ocean. I pictured a quaint little cottage where I could look out at the ocean while I painted, walk along the beach when I needed to relax and fall asleep to the sound of the waves rolling in, breaking and rolling out again. But Rich thought a gated community was the only way to go, the pricier and more exclusive, the better. Security was another concern, he said, not that the Acres' eight-man, eight retired man, security staff had stopped someone from running over our Pampas grass. Or murdering Wendi.

The cost of a house by the ocean was another factor, he insisted even though I knew we could well afford it. But the past, my past, persisted. I let him win that battle the same way I've let him win every battle, in the 30-odd years we've been married.

"Hard to believe she's really dead." Helen frowned as she watched the action next door. She looked upset. Strange, when I knew how much she'd hated Wendi.

Helen is an acquired taste. After spending 38 years as the executive assistant to the CEO of multinational giant Allied Financial, she never quite got over the habit of managing things. She frowned as she watched the police—until she turned and noticed the Pampas grass. "I see you finally worked up the courage to get rid of that stuff."

Not! I was about to say that when Jessica cut in. "Someone vandalized their property. Security was supposed to come out, but now?" She shook her head as she gestured next door.

Helen nodded as her husband John put his arm around her. “Wendi Willis, dead. Who could've imagined it?”

Everyone who knew her. Not that I said that. I glanced at John, dressed, this sunny September day, in a yellow striped knit shirt, faded olive green Bermuda shorts and freshly-polished white sneakers with black socks.

No Rich Warren. No Jason Connolly, either.

Jason Connolly. After the show last May, I’d looked him up on the Net and found out, remembered, really, he’d been a decorated NYPD detective until he’d fumbled the ball on a big society homicide, making a mistake that ultimately allowed the killer to go free.

Demetria Margolies Grasso, 67, heiress to the Margolies shipping fortune, was alleged to have been murdered by her 35-year old fifth husband Tony. According to the articles on the Net, Jason Connolly made the mistake of searching their Sutton Place penthouse with a warrant that failed to cover all the bases, one that'd enabled Tony to appeal a verdict that would’ve resulted in a life sentence with no chance of parole.

According to the media, Tony offered to put Jason on his payroll, at that point. When he refused, Tony tried to have him killed. I was glad when I'd read that Tony left the country a few weeks after the trial and hadn't been seen or heard from since.

The good news? Jason was still alive. The bad news? It cost him his job. The case was so high-profile, it took me hours to find the item about his subsequent move to Brook Haven, where two years later, he was a lead detective.

It'd been three months since I’d met him but I couldn’t get him out of my mind. Not that I didn't know why. He was an attractive, macho, once-famous crime fighter who loved my paintings, at least my prints, a man who'd never replace me with name-brand artists, Soames and Bentley artists.

Would he?

"I can't believe the way those garbage men dumped her body on the curb." I couldn't believe Helen was smiling, as she pointed to the spot where Wendi's body had ended up.

"They just went to empty her recycling can. They didn't know what was inside." *They didn't know she was inside…*

"When that purple pashmina fell out, with Wendi's body underneath it..." Jessica smiled.

Helen nodded. "Someone offed Wendi. Sorry it wasn't me."

We went on to share a moment of silence that had nothing to do with respect before I pointed to the two uniformed officers checking Wendi's property. "She really is dead." Not that I'd meant to say that out loud. No matter how I felt about her, how we all felt about her, she was still a human being, at least on a good day.

"I hated those pashminas she always insisted on wearing." Helen frowned.

"They were just as pretentious as she is, I mean, was," Jessica agreed.

"I wonder how she died. You think she was strangled?" I asked.

"With her purple pashmina, then stuffed head first into her garbage can? Looks that way," Jessica observed.

Helen took a deep breath. "There is a God!"

I was about to say, well, something when John cut in. "Hard to figure out who might've done it. There were so many folks who would've liked to see her dead."

"Including me. Not that I did it," Helen added quickly. "Though I can't say it never crossed my mind." She sighed softly. "I starred in every Haven Players' production till she moved in."

"And wrapped herself around Harvey Malden, the fool." John shook his head.

"Not like everyone doesn't know he's gay. He and Cliff got married in Vermont the week after it became legal." Helen sighed.

"But that one?" John pointed to Wendi's house. "Threw herself at him anyway."

"At rehearsals? She'd hang on his every word. One night, I even saw her pat his thigh." Helen looked scandalized.

I frowned. "Strange." Very strange, not that I cared about her relationship with Cliff or Harvey, the way she'd always come on to Rich.

"One thing's sure, if there was anyone who liked her? I never heard about it," Jessica said.

Wendi's friends Paige and Monica liked her. They proved it every time they dressed like her, went to the same hair and nail salons she did and mimicked her every move. Rich liked her, too, something I didn't want to think about right now.

Rich was an intelligent, successful lawyer allegedly moving into semi-retirement when Wendi moved next door. After that, five or ten minutes with her and I could almost see his brain cells turning to mush. There were times when I wanted to do something about it. But I never did, probably because on some level, I still believe I owe him. That's what I was thinking when Jessica's phone rang. She took the call, then turned to us. "Tomas needs me."

We nodded as she went off and a tall, rugged-looking man wearing faded jeans and a well-worn brown leather jacket over a pale blue oxford shirt that complemented his blue eyes perfectly came over. He looked familiar, as he flashed his gold detective's badge. "Amanda Warren?"

Jason Connolly.

"Jason Connolly. We met at your show last May, if you remember."

Remember? I couldn't get you out of my mind. Not that I said that. "Memorial Day weekend?"

He nodded, indicated Wendi's house and frowned.

She really is dead. Not that I needed to confirm it. Hadn't I just seen her body land on the curb? "Investigating?" *Dumb question.*

He nodded. "Looks like a homicide, as I'm sure you must realize."

I struggled to come up with a response, not that he was waiting for one. "Did you happen to notice any suspicious activity around here this morning, or maybe last night?" He glanced at my Pampas grass. "Looks like you had a problem here yourself."

I nodded. "We called Security. They're supposed to come out."

"Why don't you let us take care of it? Might be related." He made a note of that, then turned to Helen and John. "Did either of you see or hear anything unusual?"

"Nothing, really." Helen's voice was so soft and sexy, I almost expected her to bat her eyes at him. Not that I didn't understand why.

John shook his head. "I didn't see anything either. If you'll excuse us?"

He nodded. "I may have some questions for you later." They turned to go, then, leaving us alone.

"Would you, um, like to come in?"

"I planned to stop by later to get a statement from you. But if you should think of anything, Miss Warren, or is it Mrs.?"

"Call me Amanda."

He smiled ever so slightly.

"I didn't realize anything was wrong till I went over to take in her recycling can. She asked me to do that because she had this meeting in Brigantine, near Atlantic City? There's this charity organization she works, I mean, worked with."

He checked his notes. "Shelter by the Sea?"

"Right."

He flashed me another smile, a real one. Had he meant it to be that sexy? No matter, he stopped smiling quickly as he turned to go back to Wendi's. I knew I should go in, but I couldn't take my eyes off him as he told two uniformed officers to check my lawn and a third one to deal with the CBC news truck that'd just pulled up in front.

So much for security, in our exclusive gated community.

I kept watching Jason Connolly, a man who knew how to take charge, a man you could rely on, one who was also sensitive enough to appreciate art, my art. Not like Rich, who was always pushing me to get more active in the community. Sad to say, I'd caved in, at some point, when I'd joined the Women's Club.

I flashed back to the Women's Club meeting a few months ago, chaired by Wendi, as I turned to go back inside.

Chapter Two
Four Months Ago

"The April meeting of the Women's Club will come to order," Wendi wasn't yelling, exactly. She just had a very loud voice. Strange, when she was so tiny. Wendi stood 4'11" and weighed 85 pounds or so, a perfect size two, as she never failed to tell anyone who'd listen. I'd never been fat, but I did go from a size six or eight in college to a ten or twelve after my daughter Katie was born. If I was okay with it, Rich was not. I knew that whenever he spouted the old cliché: "You can never be too rich or too thin."

But you can be too obnoxious. I almost said that once or twice. I didn't see anything wrong with my size, not when I'm five foot nine. But I realized, one day, that while size ten or twelve may've been acceptable at one time, it had morphed into *big* when I wasn't looking.

Rich was a Junior Partner at Duncan Fitzgerald Kaufman that year. I was doing freelance commercial art from home and taking care of Katie the day I went to his office and saw it: women were getting thinner. Most of the women who worked at Duncan Fitzgerald Kaufman were size six or less. And the higher up the ladder they were, the thinner they got, so that all the senior partners' secretaries and paralegals were built pretty much like Wendi.

Wendi, who always looked perfect. Her voice was as big as her presence, too, when she chaired those Women's Club meetings, playing queen, a role she loved almost as much as she loved to flirt with every man on her radar. Almost as much as she loved to flirt with Rich.

It didn't surprise me when Rich insisted we see her last play, *The Glass Menagerie.* Wendi didn't play queen in that one. She played the decades younger Laura Wingfield with a Southern accent so convincing, I felt sure she'd been born somewhere south of the Mason-Dixon Line.

I never confirmed it. Wendi refused to say word about her past. "Don't dwell on the past, always look forward," she'd say if anyone asked where she was from. That night on stage, she stayed firmly in the present as she played the ingénue the same way she did everything—shamelessly.

It was the same night the director, Harvey Malden, made this huge fuss over her and her performance, while Cliff Richardson, his tall, handsome, silver-haired husband looked on, frowning the same way I did when Wendi threw herself at Rich.

"Ladies? Come to order!" Wendi flung her pashmina around dramatically, a cranberry red one with metallic gold accents that day. Why did her pashminas bother me so much? *Concentrate on the meeting*, I told myself. Not easy, with Wendi in charge.

I've always been all right with women's clubs. I was glad when I found out this one also functioned as the Acres' Sunshine Club. In addition to sending flowers to the bereaved, get well cards to the sick and fruit baskets to people with a happy event to celebrate or a tragedy to mourn, the group also did fundraisers for Shelter by the Sea and other non-profits.

But I hated the way Wendi ruled the group absolutely, the reason it was the last place I wanted to be that day. The reason I drifted off, back to 1970, the year ***it*** happened.

***

Freshman year at Forestville University. Forestville was my father's dream school, not mine, but I wasn't complaining. When we'd driven up there six months before I was set to begin freshman year, I couldn't help but admire all those stately gray stone buildings arranged around perfect green lawns dotted with aged-to-perfection Vermont shade trees. A dream school, an expensive one, too. It was only the college fund my grandparents set up for me, along with some scholarship money I'd managed to accrue, that'd enabled me to attend.

"You'll meet the right people there," my father said one night as he sipped his first home-from-the-office martini the day I got my acceptance packet. "And they have a wonderful art department. I think," he added.

Art was my favorite subject in high school even though my grades were almost straight-A across the board, something I didn't need to work too hard to achieve. A good thing when I didn't care much about my other subjects. Art meant so much to me, I knew even then that it was destined to be my life.

Whether I was working in charcoal, watercolor, acrylic, oils or pencil, I was happiest when I was drawing or painting. I was even happier when people liked my work, especially my mother.

My father worked too many hours and drank too many martinis to pay much attention to my artwork. He sold telephone equipment to companies in Manhattan, then came home to our modest four-room apartment near Van Cortlandt Park, a safe, pleasant, middle-class Bronx neighborhood. Martinis helped him unwind, he said. Having enough liquor on hand was never a problem for dad. His long hours and natural salesman's charm ensured that he made good money. But he always managed to spend it faster than it came in.

He spent money that way because he came from money, he said. He'd grown up in elegant Pelham Manor, a tiny suburb just north of the city. He loved to tell us how his parents lost the Family Estate in the Crash, when he was eight years old. But his childhood home didn't look like an estate to me whenever we did one of our drive-bys in our 1958 DeSoto. It was a nice house, but by the time I was 11 or so, I knew how much dad loved to embroider the truth.

"Would've gone to Forestville myself, if not for the Crash," he'd say, the reason he didn't think twice about my college of choice. His choice.

"It'll be wonderful!" my mother echoed. I loved my mother dearly, but she never failed to affirm everything my father said. She'd been working in Saks Fifth Avenue the day they met, when he'd come in to buy some new shirts. It was love at first sight.

His parents were not happy with his choice of a *poor shop girl,* as they called my mother, a poor Jewish shop girl at that. Dad's family was Episcopalian and proud of it. But he didn't let that stop him. My parents eloped to Maryland six weeks later. His parents were horrified—until they found out my mother was pregnant. They adjusted their attitude quickly, then, enough to welcome me into the family when I arrived six weeks sooner than the requisite nine months. I was a senior in high school when I found out they'd adjusted it enough to provide me with a college fund.

Forestville impressed me even more the first day of orientation, when I met Rich Warren, the senior leading my group. A little taller than me, he was just, well, skinny. With his floppy sandy brown hair, big brown eyes and shy smile, he seemed pleasant, too. But his thick-lensed, horn-rimmed glasses were enough to make me clear on the fact that he was a nerd. He was old, too, at 22, five years older than I was.

But it was hard not to like him. His enthusiasm for Forestville was contagious. We all felt good about the school that day. I dismissed him quickly after that, as I met, then began to date a few new guys, my first semester.

Rich was in his first year of Forestville's MBA graduate program that year. He lived off campus and worked as Freshman Class Advisor, the reason I went to see him when I was in danger of failing Calculus, a required course. When he suggested I sign up for Peer Tutoring, I didn't hesitate.

I was glad when my tutor Danny McNally turned out to be a big, friendly ex-football player enrolled in Forestville's graduate math program. "I was headed for the pros till my knee got ripped up in this big play against Villanova," he told me one morning as he pointed to his scar. It was easy to see— he wore shorts no matter the weather. But he was a good tutor, so good, I managed a B-minus on my Calculus final. Danny was quick to invite me for drinks, to celebrate.

I shook my head. "I'm only 18." I was legal in New York that year, but in 1970, you still had to be 21 to drink in Vermont.

"My friend and I have an apartment in town. Who'll know?" He winked, then. Sexy...

"I guess it'd be okay." I wouldn't drink much, in light of the liver problems my father had recently begun to have. I'd worked hard for that B-minus,. I deserved to celebrate. And it was a party. Maybe I'd meet someone new, someone special.

Danny wrote down his address, a big old Victorian that'd been divided into apartments. "Saturday, nine o'clock. If you know any other girls who wanna' come? Bring 'em along."

I asked my roommate Denise but she said no. "That guy Danny? He's got a reputation."

"How do you know?"

"Rich Warren, the Freshman Advisor, he told me."

I pictured Rich then shrugged it off as I put on my new black miniskirt and a red v-neck sweater. It'd been a long semester. I deserved some fun.

I was disappointed when I got there and found 20 people, mostly boys, crammed into the tiny apartment. The music was blasting but there was no room to dance. Was that why everyone was drinking, making out or both? "You didn't bring any other girls?" Danny looked disappointed.

I shook my head. "I thought..."

He grinned. "That's okay, honey. You're all the woman I can handle." He hauled me up against him, then, and kissed me, a kiss that tasted like my father's martinis smelled. I pictured all those martinis, thought about dad's liver problems and felt a wave of revulsion come over me.

"Stop!" I tried to push him away but he was so big and strong, I felt like I was pushing concrete. Had he even heard me, with the music blasting?

"Stop!" I repeated as he pulled me into his bedroom. Paneled in dark wood, it smelled like sweat and dirty gym socks. I glanced at the double bed, where the sheets hadn't been changed in a while. "Let me go!"

I screamed when he didn't, not that anyone could hear me over the music. I tried not to panic when he threw me down on the bed and got on top of me. I pushed at him ineffectually as he pulled at my sweater. When he slid his hand under my back to unhook my bra, I screamed as loud as I could.

He was pulling his pants down when the bedroom door slammed open. I managed to sit up enough to see—Rich Warren? "Get out of here right now or I'm calling the police." He sounded bigger and more authoritative than I would ever have believed. Danny thought so, too, apparently. I knew that when he got off me and pulled his pants back up.

Rich pointed to the door. "Out!" He waited till Danny left before he asked if I was all right. I wanted to say yes but I couldn't seem to say anything. He pointed to the ceiling. "My bedroom's right upstairs. Not the first time this has happened. One of these days? I will call the police."

I picked up my sweater.

"I'll turn around while you get dressed," he told me quietly.

A nice gesture when he'd already seen me half-naked. "You'd really call the police?" I asked over my shoulder.

"If I did? They'd call your parents. How would you feel about that?"

I thought about my father's health problems and shook my head.

"It's not your fault."

"I know, but if you hadn't heard me…" *He would've raped me.* I was dressed, now. He came a few steps closer.

"I can drive you back to your dorm, if you'd like. I have a car."

I thought of being alone with a man, any man, and shuddered. Rich seemed all right, but after tonight? I shook my head.

"We can still call the police."

"No." How to say it? "He didn't, y'know, go all the way."

"Good."

"And as for my parents? It's complicated."

He smiled. "Always is."

I felt a little better when I followed him out of the bedroom and through the living room, deserted, now.

The party was over.

***

Rich asked me out a few times before I said yes, because of what he'd done for me. *You owe him.* I'd tried to get over that feeling, but the memory of the night Danny had almost raped me wouldn't go away.

We saw ***Butch Cassidy and the Sundance Kid*** on our first date. I loved Paul Newman, Robert Redford and the great story line, but I still couldn't stop thinking about Danny, enough so that it felt almost like Danny was right there with us, when we stopped at the local ice cream parlor afterwards.

Rich told me a little about his childhood that night. "Nana Kate raised me after my parents were killed." They'd been on their way to Nantucket when their friend's small private plane went down. "I was staying with Nana in her apartment in Brooklyn that week. I never went home."

"I'm sorry." I pictured Sheepshead Bay, Nana's neighborhood. Near Manhattan Beach, it was a long subway ride from the Bronx, but I'd been there a few times with my friends.

"Nana didn't have much, but she always said I was so smart, she knew I'd make something of myself."

"I guess she was right. I mean, you are going for your MBA," I replied.

He nodded. "Getting ahead is important to me." I was glad when he asked me some a little more about myself, and my art. He'd seen two of my pieces hanging in the Fine Arts Building lobby. "Art's not my thing, but I liked them. Really," he felt the need to add.

"Thank you." I wondered if he meant it. I looked up as our waitress came up and gave Rich the check. Should I take care of it? Probably, after the way he'd saved me. But when I looked up, he was paying her.

Next time, I told myself, assuming there was a next time. He was pleasant but bland, I thought as he kissed me gently on the lips, a kiss that tasted like the vanilla ice cream he'd just had. "Vanilla's my favorite," he told me as I savored my Rocky Road.

Rich was just as boring as vanilla. If he asked me out again, I'd say no. There was a good chance he wouldn't, though, I thought. We didn't seem to have much in common. A long weekend was coming up, too. I'd promised my parents I'd come home.

"I'm going home for the weekend, too," Rich said when he called to tell me what a great time he'd had. It was great for me, too. No choice but to say that, just good manners. He was a nice guy who'd saved me from being raped. Now he was offering me a lift home in his 1962 Buick Skylark.

***

"When I make it big? I'll buy myself a nice car," he said on the way home. "A Thunderbird, maybe even a Corvette."

I looked at him. Hard to picture him in a hot car. He'd filled out a little, but he was still thin and he still wore those thick horn rims. A big black Mercedes Benz passed us, then-- the perfect car for him. "I can see you in a Mercedes Benz."

"Really? They're so expensive."

"No problem, when you make it big."

He brightened when I said that, looking as happy as a kid at Christmas, a holiday I suspected he celebrated. I confirmed it when he told me he'd been born and raised Presbyterian, as he carried my overnight bag upstairs. I'd made a point of telling him he didn't have to, but he just shook his head. Hard to argue the point when he'd just, well, saved me...

Chapter Three

Rich charmed both my parents that day. My mother was impressed with his manners, my father with the fact that he still attended services at an established Presbyterian church in Brooklyn a few times a year.

Their approval might've been one reason Rich and I got a little closer that weekend and began to date when we got back. He still didn't set my world on fire but he was so kind and thoughtful, I felt like there wasn't anything he wouldn't do for me.

"I'd like to kiss you goodnight, a real kiss, if that's all right," he said after we'd been dating for a few weeks.

Odd. Goodnight kisses generally happened by themselves, in my experience. I hesitated before I said yes. If his kiss was not the stuff of romance novels, it wasn't unpleasant.

"You'll never have to worry about Danny again, by the way, not unless you plan to transfer to Penn State," he told me a few days later.

"Penn State?" I'd never reported the "incident," as Rich called it, but the next girl Danny tried it with had called the police and pressed charges.

"Danny managed to worm his way out of it. Then he left town."

"That's good." I was grateful he'd left, grateful to have Rich in my life, too, I thought. That's why I let him go a little further the next week. As time went on, I didn't stop him when he began to caress my breasts under my bra, something that made my heart race and my emotions surge. Looking back, it was probably hormonal but at the time, I felt sure it was love.

By the time he drove me home at the end of the year, I'd almost convinced myself I loved him.

I found a waitress job that summer in a little café at the edge of Greenwich Village. Rich had secured a back office intern position at Duncan Fitzgerald Kaufman, a prestigious Park Avenue law firm. Three weeks in, he began to go running in Central Park with a few of the younger lawyers after hours. "Running is trendy," he said. "And the better you look, the easier it is to get ahead." The reason he started working out at a gym near Nana Kate's apartment.

I still hadn't met Nana Kate but he'd told me a lot about her. "She'll be 68 next month but she still won't retire." He frowned. "Working full time at Macy's, she has to take the subway into Manhattan, then she's on her feet all day. Not good."

I finally met her unexpectedly a week before we went back to school. Rich and I had gone to Macy's to update his wardrobe. He'd built his upper body that summer to the point where he needed new clothes. "They have to be trendy," he said. "I need to look the part if I want to get ahead."

I had to agree. The way he dressed had never thrilled me. We decided to start at Macy's, where we'd check out their men's department, then see how much of that look we could put together at one of the 14th street discount department stores, stores that carried closeout merchandise from their pricier uptown counterparts.

It didn't take me long to find the line of men's clothing I liked best once we got there. I'd never been into labels, but I knew he needed name brand clothing this year. I started off with a Hart Schaffner and Marx three-piece suit. I liked the Geoffrey Beene men's line, too. There were a few other designers I liked almost as well. With luck, I thought, we'd be able to find them on at a discount.

We were on our way out when Rich pressed the ninth floor button. "Nana Kate works in the children's department."

"You want me to meet her today?" Most guys I knew gave their girlfriends some warning before they met the family.

"You're always saying how much you want to meet her."

After I've had time to get ready. But if Rich had a clue how I felt, he didn't acknowledge it as he looked around, spotted her, smiled and waved.

Old and *tired* were not the way I would ever have described Nana Kate. "Call me Katie, hon.' Everyone does," she said, then gave me a hug before she reached up and patted her hair. Dyed a shade of red that did not occur in nature, it was styled in a big, heavily teased beehive updo. Far from the conservative outfits my mother favored, Katie's dress was a brightly-patterned sleeveless sheath with a stylish boat neckline and a skirt that ended a few inches above the knee. "I found it at Orbach's. It's a copy of that new Italian designer, Pucci? Ever hear of him, honey?"

I nodded. I'd seen his designs in *Seventeen Magazine.* I couldn't decide if I liked them. "They're really, uh, different." Very bright and cheerful— nothing I'd ever wear to meet my boyfriend's grandmother.

She went on to tell me how she'd had her daughter Deb when she was 17. Since Deb was only 20 when she'd had Rich, Katie became a grandmother at 37. "Me and Richie went everywhere together, the playground, the zoo. We went shopping together, too. Always had a ball, right, Richie?"

Rich looked embarrassed as he nodded. "We wouldn't want to keep you from your work."

"Don't worry about it." Katie smiled. "I'm meeting Harold for drinks after work." She turned to me. "Join us--you'll love Harold."

Rich frowned. "Sorry, we have other plans." We didn't, but I wasn't about to contradict him. If he didn't want to have drinks with Nana and Harold, I felt sure he had his reasons.

"You don't drink," he pointed out on the way to the subway.

"I could. I'm legal, here in New York."

He just frowned. He didn't say anything else about it until we got off the subway. "I don't like Harold."

"Why not?" Katie was so nice, I couldn't imagine not liking her boyfriend.

"He's younger than she is."

"How old is he?"

"63."

"And she's, what, 68?"

He hesitated. "She's my grandmother! She should act her age."

I thought about my mother, who'd turned 50 last month. She'd been acting like an old lady ever since. Not that she'd had an easy year, with dad in and out of the hospital, but I hated to see her age that way.

"You think it's okay that she's dating a younger man?" he was asking me now.

Better than rolling over and playing dead. "You met my mother."

He smiled. "She's lovely, a real lady."

An old lady. “She’s aged a lot this year, with my father’s health problems.”

Rich nodded before he changed the subject. “Katie will be home late tonight. That'll give us some time alone, know what I mean?” He leaned over and kissed me.

“We haven’t had much of that.” But we had spent a weekend together last April in Stowe, Vermont. We’d been seeing each other a few months and I was a week away from my 19th birthday when Rich asked how I’d feel about taking our relationship to the next level, sex. I knew he was afraid I’d say no, maybe because of the way Danny'd tried to “force me into it,” as he put it.

“He would’ve done it, too, if you hadn’t heard me scream.” I’d told him that a few times. It'd taken a while, but I felt like I was over it. And up at school, all the other girls were having sex with their boyfriends. A weekend in Vermont sounded romantic, too, the reason I didn't hesitate before I said yes.

We headed over to Stowe that Friday. “They've got all these great resorts up there. You’ll love it.” He was right about that. Stowe was lovely, and the resorts looked great, too. Not that we stayed in one.

“Too expensive,” he said as he checked us into the generic chain motel where he’d reserved a room. But he did take me to dinner at Mountain House, one of the top resorts' restaurants. It had a big stone fireplace and tall, arched ceilings. He ordered steak. I was about to order lobster tails when I saw how much they cost. I settled on chicken glazed with lemon and white wine. After dessert, he made a point of showing me the bill, almost $60 just for the two of us.

We went back to the motel after dinner, where *it* happened. We'd been doing *everything but*, as the other girls called it. That night, I almost convinced myself our motel room was special as we held each other, kissed, cuddled, and went from there. Rich took it slow, asking over and over if I was all right.

"I'm fine." Just, well, not ready. But he didn't ask me that as he slipped on a condom and entered me. Not too bad, I thought, until he finished right around the same time I was getting started, 12 minutes after we'd begun.

"You were really a virgin."

Why was he surprised? "Yes."

"Sweet…" He held me close.

I sighed. I was probably the only virgin on campus, the reason I knew that good sex should take more than 12 minutes. Mention it? I was relieved when he spoke first. "It'll be better next time. You were probably thinking of Danny."

I shook my head.

"You're sure?" He sat up. "It felt like there was something stopping you from, y'know…"

I didn't. "What?"

"Getting into it."

Hard to get into anything in 12 minutes, not that I said that.

"There are a few things you could've done, y'know, to make it better," he went on. If we wanted to have good sex, we were both responsible for doing the right, well, things, he went on. "A threesome might be nice," he added, smiling.

"A threesome? You mean—"

"Not now. Maybe sometime."

Maybe never, especially not when sex tonight had been so, well, unimpressive. But later, when he talked about my responsibilities and mentioned that threesome fantasy again, I was young enough and innocent enough to wonder if I should go along. He'd saved me from Danny. I owed him. I always would.

***

By the time June rolled around, I'd succeeded in putting that weekend out of my mind. But I couldn't help flashing back to it, that day, as he unlocked the door to Nana Kate's apartment. It was furnished in a lovely art deco style except for her queen-size bed. It was beautiful, I thought, with its headboard upholstered in pink and white silk in a watercolor-style paisley pattern. A matching bedspread and lots of plump little throw pillows complimented the look.

"I love it," I murmured as we headed for his room, with its navy blue and green plaid bedding and curtains, small student desk and academic award plaques on the walls.

He frowned as I sat down on the narrow bed. "I don't usually let anyone see her room."

"Why not?"

"It looks like a goddamn bordello." That got my attention. Rich didn't curse often but he looked angry, now, as he began to unbutton his shirt.

What to say? Since I had no idea, I decided to help him get that shirt off. He smiled. His anger had passed by the time we got in bed and I began to make a conscious effort to do the things he expected. It detracted from my own pleasure, but if he thought that was the way sex should be, I felt like I needed to go along. He'd saved me. I was beginning to think he loved me, too, despite the fact that my level of responsiveness between the sheets still didn't make him happy. I'd work harder at being the woman he wanted me to be, I told myself. It would work out, in time.

"You were a little better tonight," he said as we got dressed.

What to say? Nothing.

***

Sophomore year. I filed my art major and Rich began the final year of his MBA. Everyone thought of us as a couple this year. I was proud of his new image, too. He'd continued to fill out over the summer, and we'd found lots of great designer clothes for him on 14th Street before we went back to school. He was a different man this year, well-built, well-dressed, confident.

He hadn't said he loved me, but he had told me how beautiful I was, how talented, how clever. I still didn't seem to make him happy in bed. I hoped that would come in time.

And it made me happy, after my first on-campus solo exhibition, when he said he loved my paintings. "I'm so proud of you, so lucky to have you in my life." He took me in his arms, then, right there at the show, and kissed me. Not a great kiss, but it looked good. I knew that when everyone stopped and stared. Maybe he was right when he said I wasn't responsive. Maybe there was something wrong with me.

A few weeks later, Rich told me a little more about Nana Kate. "I do love her. The way she took care of me and always praised me? Made a difference for sure!"

"But?"

"You met her. I'm sure you can understand why I never brought my friends home."

"Never?"

"The other kids always made fun of her."

"Really? That's so cruel."

"Kids can be cruel." He took my hand. "It wasn't all bad, though."

She loved me with all her heart, that's what I expected him to say.

"It forced me to realize that if I wanted something, I'd have to go out and get it myself."

I was about to ask what he meant when he went on. "I knew I'd have achieve my goals by myself." He smiled. "I developed a way to do that, too a system, one that works."

A system? I began to ask him more about it when he reached for me and we started to make love, the same kind of just, well, mediocre love I'd come to expect. I didn't ask him more about his mysterious system until later. "You started to tell me about your system?"

He smiled. "You're such an innocent."

I wasn't sure if that was good or bad until he kissed me again. A decent kiss but it wasn't enough to get me off track."What kind of system?"

He stood up and began to get dressed. "Nana Kate is a good woman, but she never made a smart move in her life."

I shook my head, confused.

Rich sighed. "She's had lots of boyfriends, all losers. None of them asked her to marry them, either," he added.

"She's very independent. Maybe she doesn't want to get married." Katie had been widowed at 35. According to Rich, she never said much about her marriage. Maybe it was bad...

"She should've gotten married. Women need husbands."

Including me? Like most of my friends, I assumed I'd get married someday and have kids. Not that I'd ever give up my painting.

"Then there's her job," he went on.

"She likes working at Macy's. She gets a discount, too." Not a big enough discount for Rich to buy his clothes there, but it was still a good thing. Wasn't it?

Rich shook his head. "She's been a salesgirl for 20 years now. Never made buyer, or even department manager."

Maybe she didn't want to be a buyer or department manager.

"She never tried."

I thought of my mother, who'd been a salesgirl before she married my father. He'd supported her after that, financially, if not emotionally, psychologically and in all the other ways that count.

"As for me? My system will help me achieve all my goals. It's simple," he went on. "First, I keep my goals in mind every minute of every day."

I thought of Machiavelli, a devious Italian Renaissance politician we'd studied in World History. Rich sounded, well, Machiavellian right now. Had he always been this way? Had he been hiding that part of himself, all this time?

"You've been a big help. Encouraging me to work out, helping me pick out those great new clothes." He smiled and put his arm around me. "You're the best."

Except in bed. No matter, I still wanted to know more about his system. I was about to say that when he went on.

"You don't think I got those advisor positions by accident?" He smiled. "I made a plan and stuck to it. I joined the highest-profile clubs and organizations on campus and worked my way up."

What made an organization high-profile, and why was it so important? I took a deep breath before I asked him.

He sighed. "The biggest, most influential groups on campus are the ones that can put and keep me on-track to make the best connections." He sat up a little taller. "It's not what you know, it's who you know. Nana Kate is proof of that. She never made a single good connection in her life."

Chapter Four

But she loved and cared for me all those years. If that's what I expected him to say, he proceeded down an entirely different track.

"My system is working, working well. I've made some excellent connections these past few years. My internship at Duncan Fitzgerald Kaufman is just one example."

"You got that job through a connection?"

He nodded. "The Young Republicans' President, Tim Fitzgerald, Jr."

"You never told me."

He wasn't about to tell me now, either, apparently. Or give me any more details about the junior Fitzgerald. "This year, with my new look? It'll be even better." He didn't want to brag, he went on. "But all the groups I belong to will pay off, and pay off big in the future." He touched his horn rims and frowned. "Contact lenses, that's next," he murmured. "As soon as I have the money."

"Contact lenses, why?"

He never told me. He leaned over and began to nuzzle my neck and whispered how beautiful I was, how talented, how sweet— almost enough to take my mind off the fact that the last thing on my agenda was joining clubs or organizations. I'd never been a team player. All I wanted to do was paint.

But I also wanted to be with Rich. So whenever I had issues with all the groups he belonged to, I'd remind myself of his issues with my reluctance to join any groups. A few months later, I almost convinced myself that the way we each felt about that issue was one way we balanced each other.

When I told him that one night, he was quick to agree. That kind of balance made us soul mates, he said, a declaration that thrilled me almost as much as if he'd said he loved me. Enough for me to give him my favorite painting, a couple walking on the beach together under a starlit sky.

That declaration, along with our almost-passionate lovemaking that night was thanks enough, I told myself. He still hadn't said the words. I had my doubts, too, when I saw the way he'd propped my painting on his desk. If I'd expected him to frame it and hang it on the wall, I realized, at some point, it wasn't about to happen.

But I didn't let that bother me over the next few months. The sex got a little better and Rich began to concentrate on the things he could change about me, the Bronx accent he helped me lose, a few clubs and organizations he finally convinced me to join. But I still wore my long skirts, big, handmade jewelry and hand-dyed peasant blouses instead of the trendy designer clothes he favored. I was glad when he seemed to be okay with that.

He finally got those contact lenses, too. I never asked where he'd gotten the money. I couldn't deny how pleased I was when he lost the horn rims. With his new look, and the body he continued to work on at the Forestville gym, he was getting more attractive by the day.

He began to choose his own designer outfits that year, too. The labels he chose were even more expensive than the ones I'd selected. Nor did the fact that there were no discount stores in Forestville stop him from buying them. I couldn't understand how he could afford all those designer slacks, blazers, shirts and ties, so many, his closet was full. Nana Kate sent him what money she could but I felt sure it wasn't enough to buy all those new clothes.

He finally volunteered a little information the night he showed me the new suit, shirt and tie he planned to wear to a Young Republicans' dinner that night. "I took over the treasurer position, remember?"

I nodded. The Young Republicans wasn't a group I'd ever join, but *live and let live* was something I'd always believed in.

"The kid who was treasurer before me? They kicked him out because he was a homo," Rich went on.

"He was gay?" More than a few of my male artist friends were gay. Other than the fact that they seemed to enjoy life drawing classes a lot more than I did, homosexuality didn't pose a problem for me. "They thought his sexual preference would affect his ability to keep the books?"

He didn't answer me directly. "These are the Young Republicans we're talking about. They were thrilled when I agreed to take over as treasurer. It's grunt work, and rich kids? They don't like grunt work."

I nodded, but I still didn't realize he'd taken the money from their treasury until he spelled it out for me. "I borrowed it. I'll pay it back. With all the money those guys get from their parents? They'll never notice."

"I still don't understand why you felt like you needed a new suit. With all those designer clothes we bought last summer—"

"You just don't get it."

I guess not.

"Those clothes were on 14th Street for a reason." He paused, for effect. "They were old goods. Dated."

"Maybe a little," I agreed. *How much difference does it make?*

"If I want to keep up? I need to wear trendy clothes."

Hard to believe this was the same man who'd saved me from Danny that night. "You took money from the treasury so you could buy new clothes?"

"I borrowed it." He smiled. "Because I can."

Machiavellian for sure.

"I'm a lot smarter than those guys," he went on. "I could drain their goddamn treasury and they'd n ever know."

I got it. And hated it almost enough to confront him. Looking back, it shames me to admit I never did. But he'd done so much for me the night he'd stopped Danny. And now, for whatever reason, I wasn't ready to let him go.

He never told me if he returned that money or not. I managed to convince myself he did but looking back? I doubt it. He continued to dress impeccably that year, something he had to do in order to work his system, and socialize with the "right" people, the same ones he called his friends. As for my artist friends, I managed to convince myself, at some point, seeing them on my own time was enough.

As for our relationship, Rich and I were together whenever he didn't have a meeting or another commitment. He belonged to so many groups, I could barely keep track. Every time he volunteered for another position, I knew it would take that much more time away from me, from us. A mixed blessing, but whenever I wondered if it could be time to walk away, I remembered that horrible night with Danny.

I decided to work on the feeling that I still owed him. Then maybe someday I'd come up with a way to get out of the relationship.

***

A year later, Rich and I were still together, the reason it shouldn't have surprised me when I found myself pregnant two weeks before the end of junior year. I'd qualified for, and managed to finance a semester in Italy. Rich, meanwhile, had completed his MBA and found a nice position with Duncan Fitzgerald Kaufman. His friendship with Tim Fitzgerald, Jr. notwithstanding, it'd still taken two interviews, but they'd finally offered him a well-paying entry level marketing assistant job at the big, prestigious law firm.

His system was working, he told me gleefully as we celebrated by spending the night in a room at the world-famous Plaza Hotel. He'd taken me to dinner at Trader Vic's, one of the Plaza's pricey restaurants. He wore Geoffrey Beene that night; I wore my first designer dress, a basic black, boat neck A-line by Sonja Sanchez, a trendy new designer. The dress cost an unheard of $110.00, but Rich wanted me to buy it so much, he insisted on giving me half the money to pay for it.

Worth every penny, he declared as we shared an appetizer: steak, chicken and vegetables on flaming skewers, perfectly seasoned, absolutely delicious. The perfect couple eating the perfect dinner, I thought as I ate—carefully. No way did I want food stains on my first designer dress.

Later that night, I did my best to be more responsive in the luxurious king-size bed we shared. Not easy, when I kept wondering where he'd gotten the money to pay for half my dress, dinner at Trader Vic's and this fabulous room on the twentieth floor with a sweeping view of Central Park.

Not that I asked him.

I told him about my semester in Italy over breakfast the next morning in the legendary Palm Count. I was crushed when he said he didn't want me to go. I debated it long and hard, that week, before I made the decision: I would not change my plans. I held on to that idea, and the visions of my wonderful semester abroad until the day the college infirmary nurse called me with "some sensitive information," as she put it: I was pregnant.

I wanted to blame him: *he didn't want me to go so he got me pregnant.* But I knew I'd been a willing partner. There was also a baby, our baby, to consider. I did my best to accept the situation for what it was. Two days later, I told the program administrator I couldn't go-- the same day Rich drove up to Vermont to ask what I planned to do.

"We're going to have a baby." Hard to say it calmly, with all those hormones beginning to just, well, rage.

I was shocked when he rolled his eyes. "It's not a foregone conclusion. There are options."

Options? "You mean abortion?" Abortion had been legalized last year. I liked the idea that women had the right to choose, but in my case? Rich and I had created a new life together out of love, or at least what I'd believed in my heart was love.

"Nana Kate had two abortions in Puerto Rico, where it was legal. Nothing to be ashamed of," he went on.

"Two abortions?" Another shock, not that he noticed.

"These days, you can do it right here in Vermont. I checked," he added.

"An abortion, after I gave up Italy…" *For you and our baby.*

"You can always reapply."

After he told me he hated the idea of my going abroad? I was so angry, I began to tremble. I clenched my fists to try to get it together. "I didn't get pregnant alone."

"I know, and I'm prepared to do the right thing. If you refuse to terminate—"

I didn't reply. I couldn't.

"I'll do the right thing," he repeated. That was my marriage proposal, a far cry from any romantic scenario I might've imagined. The wedding arrangements progressed quickly after that. Rich directed them the same way he'd directed everything else in our relationship.

The ceremony took place three weeks later in St. Thomas, a United States territory that didn't require any special permits. It was a tiny wedding, just Rich and me, Katie and my parents. If it was a far cry from the wedding of my dreams, it was still exciting—my first airplane flight, my first trip to the islands. It was wonderful, I told myself, glamorous, too, almost enough to make up for the fact that I'd need to drop out of college, at least for now.

"Nana Kate hasn't been feeling well. I wanted her to stay home, but she insisted she wanted to be there," Rich told me on the plane.

I wanted to know more about her health problems, but he looked so upset, I decided to ask her myself when we got there. I was glad Katie and I had gotten close, but it was hard not to love her.

I didn't get time to speak to her before Rich and I exchanged our vows on a lovely white beach in a quiet cove with gentle turquoise waves lapping against the shore, a setting so romantic, I could almost believe our love was strong enough to see us through.

Rich was perfectly dressed, in his new Armani suit. If I wondered where he'd gotten the money to buy it, I knew better than to ask. My gown was Priscilla of Boston, but far from buying it at an exclusive bridal salon, it was last year's model, a sample I'd found on 14th Street and managed to have cleaned and pressed in time for the wedding. It was a beautiful gown, enough to make me feel like a beautiful bride. The fact that I had the good taste--and dumb luck--not to be showing yet was another plus.

I'd almost convinced myself everything would be all right by the time we reached the café where we'd be having lunch. Rich's firm had made the arrangements; the owners were Duncan Fitzgerald Kaufman clients.

We were toasting the wedding, and our future together, with a nice bottle of domestic champagne when Katie clutched her chest and slumped down in her seat. I glanced at my father. He was going pale. Was he going to pass out, too? I hoped not, as the ambulance arrived to rush Katie to the hospital.

***

"We have to get her home," Rich told the head hospital administrator the next day. They'd stabilized Katie after her heart attack and planned to keep her another few days for observation before they discharged her.

Something that was not going to happen, if Rich had his way. He made phone call after phone call—at $36 a minute—to Katie's doctor in Queens, the airlift service he'd hired to fly her back to New York City and Duncan Fitzgerald Kaufman, to keep them in the loop.

"Don't be foolish. I'll be fine right here," Katie insisted. But Rich didn't care. He'd made arrangements for her to be taken to Columbia Presbyterian Hospital, the best in the city, he said. He'd be flying up with her while I flew home with my parents.

Not the best way to begin married life.

"I'm so sorry, honey. Newlyweds should be together," Katie said softly as they came in to prepare her for the flight.

"Just get better, Katie." I leaned down and gave her a hug.

"If anything happens to me—"

"With Rich in charge?" I shook my head and managed a smile.

"He'll do his best. Always does. but—"

"What is it, Katie—tell me."

"It's just, the baby? If anything happens, I'll be watching over your baby."

What to say? "Nothing's going to happen. You'll be fine." But privately, I decided if anything did happen to her, I'd name the baby after her. I was almost about to tell her that when she closed her eyes, her alarms went off and a code team rushed in with a crash cart.

I watched from the doorway as they worked on her but I knew she was gone. Rich didn't get there until it was over. He'd been at the airport taking care of the paperwork. I told him what happened before the doctors could, my first act as a married woman.

It did not bode well for our future.

***

Our daughter was born seven months and two weeks later. I wanted to name her Katherine, after Katie.

"Too old-fashioned," Rich insisted.

We settled on Kaitlyn, a name that suited our blonde, blue-eyed baby girl perfectly. She was beautiful, too, so beautiful, no one commented on the fact that at 8 pounds, 7 ounces, it was unlikely she was premature.

Rich had had his heart set on a boy, as he'd told me repeatedly the last few months, but I was glad when he put a good face on Kaitlyn's arrival the first time he held her in his arms, hours after she was born.

"Kaitlyn, that's a beautiful name. We should always call her that, no nicknames."

Katie. I want to call her Katie. Something I would've said, if it didn't involve bringing up Nana's death.

Kaitlyn didn't last long, though. She was eight months old the first time she tried to say her name. "Kay-teee…" From then on, like it or not, she was Katie.

Rich and I were living in Beachville, New Jersey, the small town on the central New Jersey shore he'd decided was the right place to live. A few of the top partners from his firm lived there, too, in luxurious homes right on the ocean. That was the reason he'd signed a one-year lease on a tiny caretaker's cottage two blocks in from the bay before I ever had a chance to see it. "I had to act fast. There were three other people who wanted it, too," he explained.

It was a long commute to New York, over an hour each way, but Rich took it in stride. I did my best to accept it. We were close enough to the boardwalk for me to put Katie in her stroller and enjoy nice long walks, when the weather was good. But I missed my friends and family. My father's hospital stays were getting more frequent, too, as his cirrhosis got worse.

But the little cottage was charming, even if the antique heating system and vintage appliances left a lot to be desired. It was crowded, too, with Katie's crib and changing table in the living room. We'd kept her in our bedroom her first night home, but Rich had been quick to move her out when her crying kept him awake.

The cottage felt homier after I hung up some of my paintings, even better when Rich said he liked them—enough to motivate me to put a portfolio together and begin to show it at Manhattan advertising agencies on days when my mother could come down to watch Katie. She couldn't do that often, though, in light of my father's liver problems.

But several agencies liked my work enough to offer me freelance assignments. In fact, I got so much work over the next few months, I was thankful when my parents decided to move to New Jersey to be closer to me and the baby. I was even more grateful when my mother offered to watch Katie three days a week while I worked from my home office, a secondhand drawing table I'd set up in the same corner of our bedroom where I'd first put Katie's crib.

I didn't know how much of a factor that was in Rich's decision to apply to law school.

Enthralled with law, and the money he saw Duncan Fitzgerald Kaufman's lawyers earning, he was thrilled when he did a little research and saw that a few of his MBA credits would give him a step up in Business Law.

He applied to three law schools, all of which accepted him. I wasn't surprised when he chose Columbia University Law, the most prestigious, and expensive. If I was worried about how we'd pay for it, he was not. "All kinds of grant money out there," he said. "And I can always apply for a student loan, if need be."

The need for loans did not arise, however. Rich turned out to be just as good at applying for grant money, some of which he secured by stretching the truth, as he'd been at Forestville, where he'd manipulated everything to his advantage through all those club and organization memberships.

"You just have to put the right spin on it," he explained as he completed one grant application after another. In the end, he qualified for enough grants and scholarship money to cover his tuition and all his expenses. With my freelance art assignments generating enough money to pay the bills, we were set, he told me one night as we discussed the future. His future.

"Three years from now? I'll be a corporate lawyer," he said as I rocked Katie to sleep.

Rich didn't see Katie and me as much as I would've liked. Law school was turning out to be a lot like college. He took too many credits and belonged to lots of clubs and organizations, groups where he volunteered for officer positions, preferably those with access to the treasury. I didn't have time to consider the possibility that he might still be "borrowing" funds, but in the back of my mind, I was afraid he was.

He also spent eight to ten hours a week with his study group. Study groups were invaluable, he'd say whenever his study buddies called, something that seemed to happen whenever we got a little time together. I forced myself not to complain when he had long conversations on the phone with Amy, the study buddy he spoke to most often. They talked three or four times a week. And when he wasn't on the phone with her, he talked about her. A lot:

"Professor Markson told Amy he'd give her an A if she slept with him. I said she should report him."

"Amy's boyfriend got this great job offer in Baltimore. He says either she goes with him or they're through. It's so unfair!"

"Amy's parents can't afford to come to graduation."

I don't want to hear it. I would've loved to say that but I didn't say much, whenever he told me more than I wanted to know about Amy. That was how determined I was to fulfill my responsibilities as his wife, responsibilities he liked to spell out whenever he found the time to come home.

It took a while, but I almost convinced myself I was okay with Rich, his ambitions, our anemic sex life, even Amy. He was going to law school for our future, wasn't he? Nor did I ever find any evidence to prove there was anything more than studying going on between Rich and Amy.

"The workload's horrendous, but it'll all be worth it," he told me one night toward the end of his first year. I'd just gotten Katie to sleep, a good thing, with three deadline projects on the beat-up drawing table in the bedroom that still served as my office.

"You'll be a lawyer and I'll be—" *A mother.* I wanted another child. I was averaging 40 hours of paid freelance art work every week, generating enough money to cover all our expenses. I loved my work, but I adored being a mother. "Wouldn't it be wonderful to give Katie a baby brother or sister? You'd be thrilled if it was a boy."

Rich nodded but he didn't say anything more. I didn't rock the boat that night, either, because even after all this time, I still felt like I owed him. I sighed and slid a little closer to him until he stiffened, my cue to move back to the spot where he felt I belonged.

A metaphor for our marriage.

"Plenty of time to have another baby after I finish law school." He kissed me lightly on the cheek. Sex with him had never been the best, but it was almost non-existent these days. I missed it, but Rich didn't seem to care, or even notice. And doing commercial art full-time while taking care of Katie took so many hours and so much effort, and he got home so late that by the time we went to bed, we were both exhausted.

"After you finish law school."

Chapter Five

As time went on, Rich began to acknowledge my ambition to be a full-time artist, however grudgingly, while I continued to try to be the wife he wanted me to be. The sexual part of our relationship returned slowly. It was not as frequent or passionate as I would've liked, but like everything else, I accepted it as our lives continued down increasingly different paths.

Nor did we ever have another child. As close as I am to Katie, that still makes me sad. It never bothered Rich, though, even though he and Katie always had their differences.

Katie and I stayed close even after we moved 30 miles away. She lives three blocks away from the house where she grew up. Her husband Andrew is the Assistant Chair of Social Sciences at New Jersey Coastal University. She stayed home with her five year-old son Corey, too, as Andrew believed she should.

I was glad she didn't get married until she'd graduated college, *Magna Cum Laude.* It upset me, sometimes, that I'd never graduated myself. On the other hand, my freelance work did enable me to create some form of art, enough to make me happy.

Katie was never interested in art, or any of the subjects Rich thought she should major in. After she graduated high school, he expected her to prepare for a career in teaching or nursing, neither of which appealed to her, not when she had her heart set on a business degree. I was proud of the way she stood up to him.

Nor was she pregnant at her wedding, a big, traditional affair she and I planned down to the last detail. Andrew and Katie seemed happy enough until last September when Corey started kindergarten and Katie decided she wanted to go back to school for her MBA. I didn't expect Rich to support that idea. He didn't disappoint. I was surprised, though, when Andrew refused to pay her tuition, a minimal expense, in light of his position at Coastal.

"You'll still need money for books, to say nothing of childcare," he reminded her.

His attitude upset me. "We could co-sign a loan," I suggested one night.

I wasn't surprised when Rich shook his head. "Katie's a mother. That should come first," he replied in his best courtroom tone of voice. I went along, because I still felt like I owed him, after all these years?

I was glad when she finally managed to get Andrew to agree to let her take two of the four courses she'd need to get into Coastal's MBA program. They wouldn't count if she went to another school, but she didn't let that stop her. She enrolled immediately, afraid he'd change his mind.

A possibility that upset me almost enough to defy Rich and give her the money. Rich has always had his way in our marriage, with the single exception of my trading freelance work for painting.

Brook Haven Acres is just another example of Rich getting his way. That and the Women's Club. Rich was the only reason I joined, something that made me hate Wendi even more.

As for the way Rich felt about her, that was just a little more salt in the wound. I realized how special she was to him a few weeks after she moved in. Like Amy and a few other women he'd been close to over the years, he made a special effort to be charming whenever he saw her. And when she wasn't there, he talked about her frequently, just as he'd done with Amy and a few other women I could think of, if I let myself go there.

"Wendi had her heart set on her stepdaughter Steffi working with her at Shelter by the Sea," Rich made a point of telling me one night. "But Steffi's just not interested. It's breaking Wendi's heart."

Nothing can break her heart. She doesn't have one. Not that I said that.

"Wendi just got the lead in the new Haven Players' production," he said a few nights later. "But it's hard for her to do her best, with Harvey and Cliff fighting all the time."

Over her? Strange.

"The contractor Wendi hired to do her closet took off with $7000. I offered to help her file suit." Something he couldn't have done if he was still a partner at Duncan Fitzgerald Kaufman, not that I cared. At least that's what I told myself whenever I wondered how close Rich and Wendi really were.

***

I was thinking about Rich and Wendi again when the sounds next door pulled me back. I pushed the verticals aside enough to see what was going on. Four police vehicles were parked in front and five or six plainclothes and unformed officers, including Jason, were taking photos and measurements and talking on their phones.

Two other uniforms, a man and a woman, were checking my ruined Pampas grass, to try to find out who vandalized my property? More likely, they were hoping to find evidence that'd help them figure out who'd murdered Wendi.

Murder. I was making a mental list of all the people who would've liked or maybe even loved to see her dead when the phone rang. I checked the caller ID. It was Chloe. I'd promised her more paintings. I wasn't sure why I hadn't followed through. Laziness and procrastination came to mind, but I've never been lazy, not when it comes to painting. No, this creative block, the same one that'd set in right around the same time we'd moved to the Acres, went deeper than that.

"Chloe, I meant to call you." Could she tell I was lying? I hoped not.

"I just wanted to check in and see how you're doing on those new paintings we talked about. I still have a few pieces from the last show, and a good number of prints, too. But you know the drill: the more we have, the more we can sell."

I so want to paint. I wish I could. "Everything's going fine. I plan to finish a few new paintings soon." I sighed softly as I pictured the six paintings she still had in stock, the ones that hadn't sold, along with the two new pieces I'd somehow managed to complete. I'd driven them up to her gallery in Chesterton myself, hoping that would motivate me to keep going. I was crushed when it didn't work, a problem that had everything to do with Rich, Wendi and the Women's Club. If only I hadn't agreed to join.

The day I'd gone up to Chloe's gallery, I also noticed she still had one limited edition print of my favorite painting, the same edition she'd told me had sold out. Had Jason changed his mind? I took a deep breath and asked her.

She shook her head. “His divorce was delayed and the condo he planned to buy? It fell through.”

“He’s divorced?”

She nodded. “In the process. He expected it to be final three weeks ago, I think." She shrugged her shoulders. "I haven’t heard from him in a while.”

She put one of my new paintings on her worktable, then, looked at it and smiled. I smiled right along with her. The fact that Jason was single cheered me a lot more than it should’ve. I was married. I'd stay that way, too, until I worked up the courage to put the past behind me and walk away.

“I’m putting together a group show a few weeks before Christmas. I’d love you to be part of it, but I'd need at least four or five new pieces, more if you can manage it.”

Was that the motivation I needed? I hoped so, as I told her I was in and promised her more paintings, pieces I hoped would help me reclaim my art, and my life along with it. If I could only follow through.

I heard more vehicles pulling in next door as we said goodbye. I went in the dining room and looked outside again. Jason Connolly was giving directions and the others were following them. *A man who knows how to take charge.* That’s what I was thinking as he turned and glanced my way. I did my best to ignore the shivers of excitement that ran down my spine.

Stop! I stepped back quickly—and pictured the last Women’s Club meeting. Third Wednesday of the month, one to three PM. Two hours that felt more like a week, a month...forever.

***

“The July meeting of the Women’s Club will come to order,” Paige said. I hoped she was the one who'd be moderating today. Her voice was softer than Wendi’s. She was a lot more laid back, too, enough to make me feel better about being there till she bowed, slightly, as Wendi came in and took her seat at the desk in front of the Acres’ meeting room, a big room decorated in a style Jessica liked to describe as *Sistine Chapel meets the Home Improvement Outlet.*

Wendi’s desk, a big, Italian provincial affair, was at the same level as the rest of the room, but it always felt like she was sitting above us, the queen surveying her dominion. Was it her theater experience, I asked myself as Paige passed out today’s agenda, a list of residents who might be of interest to the club. Might be. Wendi made the final decision. Forceful, on her part. She was even more forceful when she was planning a fundraiser for the shelter, something she did several times a year.

It’s a good cause. I tried to keep that in mind whenever Wendi made elaborate plans for her next fundraiser then delegated all the work to the rest of us.

“First item of business.” Paige’s voice was strong enough for the group of women sitting in back and chatting, a group that usually included my neighbor Helen, to get quiet, not fast enough for the Queen, who glared at them.

They looked away, looked down, looked anywhere but at Wendi, who glanced at Paige and nodded slightly.

"Peggy Morrison, 141 Sycamore Drive? She lost her husband Sean to prostate cancer last month."

"How old was he?" Wendi demanded.

"85 last month. Peg gave him that big party in the clubhouse, remember?"

The women in back nodded. Wendi didn't react. No way would anyone's 85th birthday party ever be of interest to her.

"85? What, did she expect him to live forever?"

I was gratified to hear the horrified gasps from the back. I knew Wendi'd heard them, too, not that she cared. "I know, let's send a nice little plant."

Fran Thompson raised her hand and stood up, not easy, with her arthritis. "Everyone should get the same size plants and flower arrangements. Anything else is just not fair!"

Her back of the room buddies all agreed. I was almost about to join them when I looked around and noticed how silent the rest of the room had just become. Rich was fond of telling me how much he needed me to get along with everyone now that he was running for Association President, a decision that'd surprised me.

"Why would you want to do that?" I asked.

He smiled. "Because I can."

Shades of Forestville. And Machiavelli.

Wendi was sighing dramatically as I tuned back in. Fran was still standing, waiting for the Queen to speak.

Wendi sat up taller. "We discussed this at our last meeting. "You do remember our last meeting, don't you, dear?"

“Of course I do.”*You little twit!* I knew that’s what Fran was thinking. I wished she’d say it out loud.

Wendi orchestrated a moment of silence, then, debating the best way to dismiss Fran and her objections. Helen would’ve handled it better but she wasn't here today. “I know I should go to meetings and keep the Devil from her evil ways. But it’s getting so old,” she commented over iced tea on her porch the other day.

Back at the meeting, I knew Wendi was glad Helen wasn’t here. She cleared her throat importantly. “After we discussed this last time, *ad nauseum*, I might add, we all agreed that people who make the biggest contributions to our community should get the most recognition.”

Fran began to reply when Muriel Honeycutt stood up. “I move we take another vote. All residents should be treated equally.”

Support from the group in back was stronger this time. Wendi still managed to ignore it. “Next item, Paige?”

“Hold on,” Muriel repeated. “We need to take a vote.”

Wendi tapped her pen on the desk impatiently. “Would anyone here care to second Muriel’s motion?” *Would anyone dare to second her motion?* That's what she really meant.

My hand went up pretty much on its own. “I second that motion.” Wendi narrowed her eyes and glared at me. I felt my cheeks heat up and considered running out of there and never looking back.

“Amanda seconded the motion,” Muriel chimed in.

"I move we take that vote right now," Fran said.

Wendi looked her in the eye. "We will finish the items on our agenda first and take the vote before we adjourn." Not a suggestion, it was an edict. That was clear to everyone, especially Muriel, Fran and me. Muriel and Fran hesitated before they sat down, and my heartbeat slowly began to return to normal.

How does she do it? If I knew, I could do anything, quit the Women's Club, clear that stubborn creative block, leave Rich.

"Next item on the agenda, Eric and Gloria Martin," Paige intoned as I thought back to the Haven Players' production of *The Glass Menagerie.* Paige had played the supporting role in that one, too, Wendi's mother.

"They move into Harmony House next week, the assisted living residence on the highway," she went on. A hush fell over the room. Nursing homes were the worst, but assisted living implied the beginning of the same kind of decline that could bring you that much closer to, well, death.

"Assisted living?" Wendi didn't look up from her notes—her shopping list, her social calendar? Whatever it was, I felt sure it had nothing to do with the meeting. "I know, we'll send a nice little card,"

The murmurs from the back got louder, but one look from Wendi and silence prevailed. What a bully! Why couldn't anyone stand up to her? Why couldn't I stand up to her?

Because Rich is running for Association President and, like it or not, we're still married.

"Next? Pete and Monica Gardner. Their daughter just had twins." Wendi announced that one herself. Pete and Monica were charter members of her Inner Circle. I detected that slight southern accent again.

Where did she come from and why does she insist on keeping it such a secret, I asked myself as she went on about Pete and Monica, an attractive, trendy couple, trendy enough to have gone on this African safari last year with Paige and her husband Jim.

Home now, Pete and Monica wore designer clothing accented with unique handmade African accessories. The two couples also drove high end SUV's and lived in the biggest model, the one with granite countertops, en suite master baths with double sinks and oversized whirlpool tubs, along with the deluxe three-season room with a fireplace. The same model as Wendi's.

The same model as ours.

The fact that they were Wendi's friends sealed the deal. "Pampered Baby makes some wonderful gift baskets. We'll get one out to them ASAP," Wendi was saying now.

"Those baskets cost over $100!" It was another friend of Helen's, Denise Wetherill, objecting this time. Her back of the room buddies agreed. Loudly.

"Spending all that money on one resident? Totally unfair!" Muriel added.

Wendi just shrugged her pashmina-clad shoulders and turned to Paige. "Send the basket." She looked up, then, directing her deadly glare towards the back of the room as Paige made a note of it.

A few more items and Paige moved to adjourn when Denise, Muriel and Fran reminded her about the vote. "Amanda seconded the motion, remember?" I blushed when Frannie mentioned my name and Wendi glared at me again.

Madame Chair sighed dramatically. "Okay, Fran feels that everyone should receive equal recognition. Not the way we've always done it…" She frowned.

Muriel stood up. "Hold on, we need to discuss it!"

Wendi glanced at her watch. "There's someplace I need to be. It will have to wait."

Someplace she needed to be? Lunch with friends, shopping at the mall, an assignation with my husband? I didn't have a clue as she stood up and adjusted her pashmina. "I move that we put this vote off until next time," she said.

No one was surprised when Paige seconded that motion. Could I afford to object? Could I afford not to? I was debating it when everyone began to file out. I'll never come back, I told myself. Not till Wendi's been dethroned. Or murdered.

Looking around, I saw lots of other women who felt the same way. I joined Helen's friends in the clubhouse lobby. Denise spoke first, as she shook her head and indicated Wendi's desk, in the meeting room. "If only she wasn't Chairperson."

Muriel nodded. "If only she wasn't—"

"Alive." Fran shook her head and started to take it back, but in the end? She just laughed.

"It'd be easy to kill her. If someone wrapped one of her goddamn pashminas around her neck. Tight—" I couldn't believe I'd just said that out loud. Not that I hadn't pictured myself doing it, but I'd never, ever planned to tell anyone.

I was relieved when they laughed, more so when Fran patted me on the back and Muriel smiled. I'd do it myself if not for my arthritis."

Enough to set off another round of laughter.

***

I was watching the news that night as I ate dinner alone, just as I did most evenings. Rich claimed to be cutting back his hours but I knew better. Between the clients who'd come with him from the firm, not as many as I would've expected, and all the community groups and committees he still belonged to, he seldom got home much before eleven.

His schedule stopped bothering me a long time ago. I used that time to paint, for one thing. Really, I would've been painting that night if I wasn't so blocked.

I pictured Rich, who was still—who knows where—and sighed. He had it all, as far as I could see. Three weeks before the big 6-0 and he was still attractive. Charming, too, when he wanted to be. Add distinguished and financially secure to that equation and it was no wonder my suspicions made sense.

Not that I'd ever followed him or gone through his things, a decision I made right after he passed the Bar. Study-buddy Amy had just found a job in Baltimore, where she'd be living with the same fiancée who'd given her that terrible ultimatum, in Rich's view. I was writing a check for the phone bill when I noticed 14 calls to Baltimore, some of which had lasted as long as 45 minutes. I'd confront him, I decided, until I realized Rich could talk his way out of anything.

That was when I decided I was too busy to waste any of my precious spare time on suspicion. As a wife, mother and working freelance artist, there were never enough hours in my day. I was raising Katie pretty much alone even as I completed one freelance commercial art assignment after another. I always met my deadlines, too, my job back then, even if Rich didn't see it that way.

"I'm glad these little jobs make you happy." That was how Rich perceived my work. Thirty-odd years later, he could still be condescending when it came to my art. Really, he never treated my work and the money it brought in with anything close to respect.

I was particularly appalled by his attitude after I finished a big textbook project, anatomical sketches that drove me crazy but paid enough for me to book the Greek Island cruise-tour I'd promised myself ever since I'd given up my semester in Italy. Convincing Rich to take ten days off to go with me was so hard, I was almost about to book a single cabin when he finally backed down.

Despite all his attitude, I was thrilled the day I picked up our tickets. I could hardly wait to sketch the windmills of Mykonos, the steep, terraced hills of Santorini and all that other wonderful Greek island scenery I'd seen in travel magazines and cruise brochures. The fact that I never actually did it still makes me angry.

"Why would you do sketches, when photos are so much more accurate." We were flying to Athens first class, at his insistence, when he made that pronouncement. I hesitated, then agreed. I didn't do any sketches that week but I did shoot 14 rolls of film.

I promised myself I'd turn my best shots into paintings, but I seldom had time to do my own artwork back then, before computers replaced me, providing cheap and attractive, if distinctly non-original artwork for the kinds of advertising projects I worked on. A good thing, I told myself. The new technology would free me up to do the kind of painting I'd always dreamt of.

Something that never would've happened if Rich had his way. As soon as computer graphics came in, he urged me to go back to school to learn the new technology. "You can combine it with a college degree," he added pointedly. I'd never gone back to college, as Rich liked to remind me from time to time.

Oh well.

"Just imagine, Internet websites," he exclaimed a few days later. "You'd be part of a whole new frontier. You just have to go back to school."

A few days later, at his insistence, I went down to his office to check out this brand new phenomenon even though really, I wanted out of the art-for-hire business. He was earning good money now, enough for me to stop freelancing.

He didn't see it that way. Now that Katie was in school, it was time for me to get a "real" job. He said that so often, it took me almost a year to work up the courage to tell him I had no intention of learning computer graphics or ever getting what he'd perceive as a real job.

I planned the way I'd say that carefully. "I've decided to paint full-time, and do my own art," I told him one night over crème brulee, his favorite dessert, one I'd served him after his favorite main dish, meatloaf, oddly enough. Not that he ever ordered meatloaf at any of the gourmet restaurants he frequented. Not that they'd have it on the menu. Secretly, though, he loved it.

"I guess you could try it, see how it goes," he conceded around a mouthful of the rich dessert. I was so shocked I didn't know what to say, *Thank you*? Not the message I wanted to convey. No matter what he thought, no matter how much I still thought I owed him, he was my husband, not my boss

I appreciate it? Too submissive. "Okay," I replied as he finished his dessert, stood up and headed for the spare room he'd designated as his home office. "I'm working on a nasty divorce. All this paperwork," he added as he went upstairs.

I didn't bother to reply, not that he would've cared, or even heard me. He was spending so much time at work, I didn't know why I felt the need to tell him anything. Honestly, there wasn't any way he'd know if I stopped freelancing, not unless I told him.

I heard him on the phone as I cleared the table and tidied the kitchen. Rich spent lots of time on the phone. With clients? That's what he said, but I thought it was strange, the way he spoke to many of them so late at night.

That's what I was thinking when he emerged around 11 and began to tell me about his new intern. "Maggie Parsons? She's really something." He talked about her often. It didn't bother me as long as I had my painting, I did my best to believe that. But deep down, I couldn't help but suspect she meant more to him than an intern should.

Concentrate on your painting. You don't know what's going on between them and you never will. That strategy worked for a while. I was thrilled, too, that I finally had time to transpose some of those Greek island photos into sketches, then paintings.

I'd managed to enjoy the trip despite the way Rich insisted on leaving the tour group a few times a day to make outrageously expensive transatlantic calls to his office. To talk to Maggie Parsons? I forced that question out of my mind and concentrated on how much I loved those Greek island paintings instead.

Chapter Six

The Greek island paintings pleased me even more when I sold nine of the fourteen paintings I exhibited at a local street show Rich didn't want me to do, a show that turned out to be a lucky one. That was where I first met Chloe. As soon as she saw my paintings, she invited me to show my work at LiveArts, her tiny new gallery on a side street in Soho. That offer felt so right, I accepted it then and there.

"You did what?" Rich's face turned a vivid shade of magenta. "I told you, I have a colleague who's representing Merrill Soames in a big lawsuit." He paused, waiting for me to reply? "Merrill Soames. Of Soames and Bentley, the biggest and best, in the art world?"

"I know that." Soames and Bentley represented name-brand artists, promoting and selling their work in upscale galleries all over the world. They were too big and conservative for me, something I did not share with Rich that night. But it didn't surprise me when he continued to remind me, over the years, I could've been a name-brand artist, a Soames and Bentley artist, if only I'd made the right decision.

An assertion that made no sense, in light of the other career paths he'd had in mind for me. If I had gone along with his wishes, I'd still be doing print ads, brochures and websites.

I never succeeded in convincing him that Chloe was the right rep for me, a feeling she confirmed when I sent her slides of my work, including a painting I'd done of the Mykonos windmills at sunrise. I was thrilled, a few days later, when she called to say one of her clients had just offered to pay $1800 for it. I loved that painting so much, I could hardly bear to part with it. In the end, it was the way Rich continued to push Soames and Bentley that motivated me to let it go, then finish 12 more Greek island paintings over the next eight months. When Chloe sold them all, I knew my intuition was right on target. Chloe was the best rep I could ever have chosen.

I showed all my paintings at LiveArts after that. I started out with group shows and worked my way up to one-woman exhibits. Chloe was always happy with the results. I was making money, too, so much that Rich stopped complaining right around the same time the exposure I'd gotten in Soho began to generate invitations to show my work in New Jersey.

I was almost about to sign on with the New Jersey gallery Rich thought best when Chloe decided to open a second gallery across the river. When she asked to represent me exclusively, I agreed. I've never regretted it. Our agreement helped her establish herself in Chesterton, a lovely little town close to the mall in Short Hills, a top-notch New Jersey location.

I felt sure my agreement with Chloe was another step in the right direction. Much to my surprise, it wasn't long before Rich accepted it. He never involved himself in my art again, something that should've made me happy. But every time he was late to one of my shows—if he bothered to show up at all— it hurt. I tried to ignore it. Better to focus on how much Chloe and I have done for each other, the reason I had to find a way to do her Christmas show.

If only I hadn't agreed to use the three-season room as my workspace because Rich hates the mess I make when I paint. Since he doesn't spend enough time at home to go in there, I never understood what difference it made.

He also complained if dinner was late, on the rare occasions that he came home in time to eat it. But his biggest complaint was that my art took time he'd rather I spent promoting our position, his position, at the Acres. Easy enough, he said, if only I was willing to commit to help Wendi raise more money for Shelter by the Sea.

I wouldn't have minded doing that except for fact that working for the shelter always involved being with Wendi. I planned to tell him that, too, the night he informed me he was running for Condo Association President and assumed I'd provide help and support.

Since I had no desire to fight with him, I agreed to help when I had time. The next day, I stopped painting completely. He was glad when I promised to try a few of the other clubs in the development.

I checked out three or four of them over the next few weeks but found them all so cliquey, I felt like I was back in junior high. Wendi may have been the highest-profile, most obnoxious power broker at the Acres, but she was far from the only one. The fact that the Women's Club supported a good cause clinched the deal. I'd stick with it, at least for now.

"Wonderful! Wendi is looking forward to seeing you there."

Right!

It wouldn't kill me to keep going to Women's Club meetings to support the Shelter. The upside? Rich stopped complaining. The downside? I never got back to painting.

Not that Rich's opinion should've mattered, at that point. I knew I should've gotten over that horrible night Rich had saved me, and the feeling that I owed him, a long, long time ago. These days and nights, I spent so little time with Rich, I couldn't help but wonder what he was doing when he wasn't home. But whenever I let myself speculate about it, these odd, prickly sensations would begin to run down my spine, the reason I chose to let it go.

Probably a mistake, when ever since we'd moved to the Acres, all those strange little sensations had Wendi's name on them. She's dead, I reminded myself as a cute young newscaster named Chip, with broad shoulders, well-styled dark brown hair and perfect white teeth reported the story on TV. "Breaking news, now, from Brook Haven Acres. The body of Wendi Willis was found in front of her house this morning…"

Found in front of her house did sound better than *dumped on the curb by two garbage men.* He went on to show some recent photos of Wendi, all flattering. The woman never took a bad photo in her life, apparently. The camera wouldn't dare!

"BHPD Detective Jason Connolly has not released the cause of death as yet." Why did I feel so sure she'd been strangled? My heart began to race as I pictured that purple pashmina wrapped around her neck. Someone had shared my vision, apparently. Whoever it was? I wanted to shake their hand.

Bad idea. Bad…

"The Brook Haven PD is investigating with help from the New Jersey Major Crimes Division. Anyone with information is asked to call this hotline…"

Jason said he'd be back to take my statement. Our crushed Pampas grass came to mind. Was it related in any way to Wendi's murder? Would they ever find out who'd done it? How soon could I plant my pink, white, red and yellow rosebushes?

Questions I set aside as I pictured Jason. I couldn't wait to see him again. I smiled and wondered what I could say. The unvarnished truth? *Wendi was so obnoxious and controlling, everyone hated her. Really, I hated her enough to fantasize about strangling her with one of her pashminas. Not that I did it, despite the fact that I'm almost sure she was sleeping with my husband.*

Not smart. Nor was I the only one who'd had that particular fantasy. Who'd wanted her dead, who hadn't?

So if and when Jason Connolly came around, I couldn't say much, not unless I wanted to be a person of interest, as they call the suspects on all those TV cop shows.

Since Jason was in charge, maybe he'd send one of his subordinates to take my statement. The fact that he'd have subordinates was enough, then, to send a bolt of heat down my spine as, almost on cue, the doorbell rang. I got up and crossed to our top-of-the-line front door with its hand-wrought leaded glass inserts and looked through the side panel to see who it was.

My heart began to race when I saw Jason—flashing his badge. "Jace Connolly. May I come in?"

I opened the door and looked into those crystal blue eyes, enough to make me just, well, tingle in parts of my body I'd overlooked, lately. He was wearing the same leather jacket and jeans he'd worn at the scene. He looked just as good, too, good enough so I almost forgot to invite him in.

I gestured him inside then watched as he filled the entryway with his presence. The scent of a nice, woodsy aftershave drifted around him as he followed me into the living room.

Where I'll have my way with him.

Didn't I wish! I felt myself blush as I got warm all over. "Would you like some coffee, or maybe tea?" *Tea? Big, strong, macho men don't drink tea.*

He shook his head as he sat down. "Is this a good time? I wouldn't want to interrupt your painting. "

In this house? "No problem."

He nodded and looked at me with interest, enough to make me blush some more. If he noticed the way my cheeks were pinking up, I was glad he wasn't saying anything about it. "I'd like to begin with a few questions about the victim."

I nodded. *I'll tell you everything--except the way I fantasized about killing her myself.*

"How well did you know Mrs. Willis?"

Well enough to hate her. Not that I could say that, either. I struggled to clear my mind enough to consider my options. Background information, that'd be safe enough

"She is, I mean, she was a widow. Her second husband passed away just before she moved in, 13 months ago?" My voice sounded shaky even to me. I wished Jason, Jace, as he'd just called himself, didn't have this effect on me. Every inch of me.

A feeling that probably wasn't mutual. I could tell by his posture he was making a conscious effort to keep things formal between us. He glanced at his notes. "The victim, did she ever give you a key to her house?"

Tell him she did? *He'll find out anyway and strictly speaking? She gave it to Rich. God, I hope he didn't murder her!*

Rich, a killer--crazy! "She gave us her spare key a few days after she moved in. Just in case, that's what she said." My voice trailed off, guiltily? I hoped not. I was relieved when he didn't react.

"Did you ever use it?"

"No, but my husband did, once or twice." *A week.* I frowned as I pictured Rich and Wendi together. I got so upset, then, my hands started to tremble. I shoved them in my pockets and hoped he wouldn't notice.

"And Mrs. Willis, did she have problems with anyone in the neighborhood?"

She had problems with everyone in the neighborhood, something else it'd be best to keep to myself. "She, um, chaired the Women's Club. Oh, and she belonged to the Haven Players, too." *Where my neighbor Helen despised her after she pushed her out by sleeping with one of the gay directors,* something that sounded bizarre even to me.

"What can you tell me about the Women's Club?"

"We support Wendi's pet charity, Shelter by the Sea? It's near Atlantic City, in Brigantine."

He glanced at his notes and nodded. "We're checking it out."

"To make sure they're legitimate?"

He shrugged his shoulders. "We just need to cover all the bases." He frowned. "This club, do they do anything else?"

I nodded. "It also functions as the Acres' Sunshine Club. We send cards, flowers and fruit or food baskets to people who are sick, or celebrating special occasions."

He made a note of it. "And the victim, she chaired that group, correct?"

"Yes." It was hard not to feel good about the way he'd just called Wendi *the victim*, but I gave it my best shot.

He glanced at his notes again. "The Haven Players and the Women's Club? Unlikely breeding grounds for murder."

Murder. A chill ran down my spine. "How was she killed, exactly?"

"Sorry, we can't release that information."

I felt sure someone strangled her with her purple pashmina. Would I ever find out? "I was just thinking, I mean, her purple pashmina—"

"Pashmina?" He looked confused.

"That big purple body scarf? It's called a pashmina. She wore them all the time."

"I see." He made a note of that before he looked back at me. "Do you know if any of her friends, or anyone else she might've known, owned a hunting knife?"

I shook my head. "I don't think so." *You have beautiful eyes.* I imagined myself telling him that. He'd smile seductively, then he'd kiss me. I felt this very potent heat begin to build deep inside me as I imagined it.

"In terms of her friends and associates, can you think of anyone who might've had a reason to kill her?"

So many, I'd have to make a list. Not that I could say that, either. I wondered what I could say when Rich came in. He was wearing a good designer suit with an ivory oxford shirt, but he'd taken off his tie and opened his top shirt button, two things he never did. He looked tired, too. Strange, when he's always needed just a few hours' sleep to function—at warp speed—the rest of the time. But tonight? He looked exhausted. What did it mean, I asked myself as Jason--Jace stood up and introduced himself.

“Such a terrible loss,” Rich gushed as I tuned back in. That was odd, too. I hadn’t seen him get this emotional since Nana Katie died.

“Everyone loved Wendi! I can’t imagine who would’ve wanted to do her harm,” he added.

What about her stepdaughter Steffi? As soon as Steffi found out it was Wendi who’d inherit the bulk of her late father’s estate, Wendi had become the enemy. They’d made up, at some point, but I felt sure Steffi would’ve loved to see Wendi dead. Say that or keep it to myself? I began to speak when Rich shot me one of his smooth, subtle Lawyer Looks.

I took a deep breath and went for it anyway. “You might want to speak to Wendi’s stepdaughter Steffi. She and Wendi didn’t get along.”

“Till recently,” Rich cut in. “They’re fine now," He added smoothly, too smoothly?

Jace made a note of it while I considered the fact that Steffi was a certified personal trainer, physically capable of doing the deed.

“The stepdaughter claims she was out of town that day, but we’ll check it out,” Jace was saying as I tuned back in. I remembered seeing Steffi in town the day before the murder. I was debating whether or not to tell him that when Rich asked Jace if he’d had a chance to take a look at our Pampas grass.

He nodded. “We took some samples and sent them to the lab. The tire tracks were made by a Lexus SUV. Upscale vandals, unless the vehicle was stolen,” he added.

Rich nodded. “How soon will we be able to repair the damage?”

"Any time you'd like." He stood up and handed us each one of his cards. "If you should think of anything else, please give us a call."

Rich assured him we would as he went out. I went back in the kitchen. I'd just finished my dinner when Jace rang the bell. I wasn't hungry, but I had a craving for dessert. I pictured the fresh raspberry tartlets I'd picked up at the Upper Crust, the best bakery in town. Have one or not? I didn't usually eat dessert if Rich was home, not when he was always comparing my size ten to Wendi's size two.

He might stop, now that she's dead.

I looked at the bakery box on the counter longingly. The Upper Crust was such an elegant bakery, even Wendi shopped there. Not that she ever allowed sugar to pass through her lips, but always the perfect hostess, she kept Upper Crust goodies on hand for her guests.

I began to open the box when Rich came in and sat down at the kitchen table. Ignoring my raspberry tartlet, he got right to the point. "This murder will put a dent in my campaign."

What campaign?

"Wendi promised to help me with the Condo Association election, though I can't imagine anyone would vote for Ed Cullen. A retired CPA?" He shook his head.

"Everyone seems to like Ed," I ventured. "His CPA background could give him an edge, too. People want to keep their expenses down." Here at the Acres, low fees would enable them to take ski trips, escorted tours, cruises, even African safaris, like Paige and Monica and their husbands. Although they did get a discount. Paige's husband Jim was an escorted tour packager, one reason Monica and her husband

Pete, a successful insurance broker, may have decided to join them.

As for the other residents, no matter how much money they had, it was theirs to spend as they wished. And the less they needed to pay in HOA fees, the more disposable income they'd have, not that I was about to say that.

"Ed drives a Lincoln Town Car, for God's sake. A geezer car," he added. "Though I will say at least it's not a Lexus. He wasn't the one who vandalized our property."

Ed, are you for real?

Rich frowned. "That detective? I don't think he had a clue."

That detective? I can't wait to see him again. I finished my tartlet and glanced at the stove. "There's shrimp scampi. I can heat it up."

"Shrimp? You know I'm allergic." He wasn't allergic to shrimp until he met Wendi, who said she broke out whenever she ate shellfish and was paranoid about the mercury content, too.

Rich was heading into his bedroom now, the master suite, as he called it. He'd change into one of his designer running suits, for comfort rather than to actually run. He didn't need to run, not when he worked out at Heavenly Bodies at 6:30 AM five times a week.

Heavenly Bodies was the best health club in town. He'd invited me to join with him when we first moved down here but I declined. I didn't want to spend any more time with him than I had to, for one thing. I also thought it would take too much time away from my painting. That wasn't what I told him, though. I said I'd rather walk on the beach, the truth, even if I seldom take the time to do it.

Rich worked out with a personal trainer at least once a week. Steffi was a trainer there. Did Jace know that? Assuming he did, would that make her a person of interest? Had Steffi ever worked with Rich? I didn't think so. He mentioned his trainer's name often enough for me to know it was Bill.

I remembered the dorky kid Rich had been the first time I met him. Thousands of workouts later, he'd stayed in shape. I began to tidy the kitchen as he went into the den, sat down in the recliner, turned on the TV and tuned it to the news. He muted the sound when I joined him. He still looked upset. "What's wrong," *Dumb question.* Wendi…

He frowned. "Tonight's meeting ran late. Greg Barton? That man loves to hear himself talk. It was after eight by the time we wrapped up. We all decided to grab some dinner at that Italian place, Santelli's? I told you about it."

You promised to take me there, too. Santelli's had made *Jersey Life Magazine*'s Top Ten restaurants list for the past five years. I was almost about to ask when he planned to take me there when I thought the better of it.

An hour later, in the kitchen, I watched as he flipped through the mail, separating bills from junk mail, then tossing the junk mail only after tearing it into little pieces. He stopped long enough to open the envelope from the Haven players and take out two tickets.

"*The Man Who Came to Dinner,* starring Wendi Willis and Burt Davidson." He looked almost like he was about to cry. Strange. I'd never seen him cry, not even at Nana Katie's funeral. I debated what I could say: *maybe we'll get a refund?* I didn't think so.

“A pity about Wendi,” he murmured as he ripped up the envelope, tossed it and fixed himself a vodka tonic. “You didn’t call me. I had to hear about it on the radio.” He looked at me, accusingly? “She lived right next door.”

Where you visited her and slept with her, too, most likely. "With all those police cars, and the coroner's van, it was just so hectic." I waited for him to reply. Nothing. “A couple of news trucks showed up, too. Crazy.” I still would’ve phoned him if I thought for one minute he'd take the call. Rich seldom took my calls. Because he was busy with other women?

I’d never found any evidence to prove he was cheating on me but I couldn’t help but imagine him and Wendi in bed together. Was that because he always came home so late and never asked what I’d been doing-- unless I’d been messing up the three-season room with my painting?

Something I needed to do. Something I would do. *Stand up for yourself!* I had the perfect excuse, too. A few more paintings and I could be part of Chloe’s next show, not that I planned to tell Rich about it, certainly not tonight.

He’d gone back into the den, where he was watching a basketball game, from the sound of it. I poured myself some Merlot and took a few sips. I frowned as I heard him turn up the volume. Rich only watched news or sports. That’s why we had three TV’s, his, mine and a just-in-case spare.

They were all HDTV’s, but the one in the den was the biggest, at 60 inches. Way too big for the den, but that was the size Rich decided to buy. No point in arguing or room for negotiation, not when he’d made up his mind.

I heard him switch over to the news as I poured myself a little more wine."A new development in Brook Haven, the upscale community on the central New Jersey shore," the announcer was saying as I watched from the kitchen. "Cliff Richardson, Director of Brook Haven's award-winning Haven Players, announced that the company will cancel all performances for the next three weeks due to the death of Wendi Willis, the murder victim who starred in so many of their productions."

Enough for me to join Rich in the den. "Cliff Richardson." He murmured the name softly, almost reverently. Strange, when he'd always been such a homophobe. But the first time Wendi'd invited Harvey and Cliff to one of her soirees, much to my surprise, Rich had been okay with it. *If gays are all right with Wendi, they're all right with me.* Was that how he'd felt? Not that he'd explained himself that night. Not that he ever did.

Why were Cliff and the Players so important to him? Could whatever relationship he had with Cliff and Harvey be related to Wendi's murder? I supposed it was possible. If only I could find out more.

He started to speak when the phone rang. No question whose job it was to answer it. The day he first made partner was the same day he informed me it was my job to answer the phone.

"Amanda?" It was Jessica. She sounded upset. "Tomas is having trouble breathing. You think you can come over?"

"On my way." I grabbed my jacket and glanced at Rich, still engrossed in the news. Thinking about Wendi? One thing was certain, I thought as I went out. Assuming he did sleep with her? No way would I ever find out.

Chapter Seven

Two hours later, Tomas was in the ICU and Jessica was debating whether or not to let them hook him up to a respirator. We'd discussed it with the resident, not that we had much confidence in him. He didn't look old enough to be a doctor. "If Mr. Masek makes it through the night? He could recover."

Thanks for the positive attitude, kid.

"Lots of new drugs out there," he added.

"Tomas would never want to be on life support." Jessica frowned. "We were going to draw up living wills, but he hasn't been well."

"You don't have living wills?" Rich would be horrified. *To hell with Rich!* Where did that come from? Did I mean it?

"Tomas has always been so vital," Jess was saying now.

"Your call, Mrs. Masek, but you need to decide ASAP." He began to go on when his phone rang and he turned away to take the call.

"What would you do?" she asked me.

"If it were Rich?" *I'd let him die.* "I guess I'd choose life support, see what happened."

"It's just, Tomas? He always said he'd never want to be a burden."

Since I had no idea how to respond to that, I was relieved when the resident ended his call. Jessica took a deep breath. "Can we hook him up tonight and see how it goes?"

He nodded and handed her some papers."If you'll sign these papers, I'll call upstairs."

Should I call Rich? I checked my watch. It was 11:15. He never went to bed much before one and he always slept with his phone on the nightstand so he wouldn't miss any calls. In fact, he'd gotten so many calls in the middle of the night, when Katie left for college, I moved out of our bedroom and into hers. We've slept in different rooms ever since. Not great for our sex life, not that sex with Rich ever rocked my world.

Focus, Amanda! I needed to be here for Jessica, who was frowning, now, as she debated whether to stay with Tomas or go home, as the doctor suggested.

"You can only see him 10 minutes every hour, and if there's any change in his condition, they'll phone you," I pointed out.

She hesitated.

"We'll be 10 minutes away," I went on. " I'll stay with you, too. Then we can come back in the morning." Privately, I hoped we didn't have to come back sooner. I liked Tomas. I wasn't ready to say goodbye. I glanced at Jessica, who looked a lot less ready to say goodbye than I was.

"I guess…"

I phoned Rich 20 minutes later from her house. No answer. *At least he's not with Wendi.* I glanced over at my house through Jessica's kitchen window and saw the glare of the TV through the verticals. Telling her I'd be right back, I headed over there.

And found him asleep in his recliner, something else he never did. As for the phones, our land line was in the cradle across the room and his cell was nowhere in sight. Strange. "Rich?"

He looked confused as he opened his eyes. Was this the same man I'd seen give legal advice on the phone at two in the morning? "What time is it?"

"After midnight."

"You've been at the hospital all this time?"

Nice that you noticed. "I would've called, but you looked so tired."

"Damned meeting…"

Forget the meeting, you were thinking about Wendi, and how much you loved her.

"How's Tomas?"

"He's in the ICU. I told Jessica I'd stay with her, in case they call."

Rich nodded, stifling a yawn. "He's, what, 85?"

"88. We celebrated his birthday last month, remember?"

He nodded. "Hope he kept his will up to date. His daughter? She seemed a little grabby to me that night."

Trust Rich to go right to the subject closest to his heart, money. Not that I planned to discuss Tomas' daughter, or anything else with him right now. "I'll call you in the morning."

He nodded and yawned again, a full-out yawn, something else he never did. *He and Wendi were lovers, I'm sure of it. No surprise, after the way she wrapped herself around him at the Holiday dance and flirted with him every chance she got.*

If I could only find out for sure.

You wouldn't care if you were painting. That's what I was thinking as I packed a few things and tried to focus. I felt almost like my old self until I went back in the den and saw him, asleep again in the recliner. The TV was still on, still tuned to the news. I wished I could talk to Jessica about it, but tonight? I didn't think so.

***

3:12 AM. Jessica was dozing in her recliner and I was lying on the sofa as a Magic Mop infomercial played on TV when the phone rang. She opened her eyes as I got up and answered it. "I'm afraid Mr. Masek has taken a turn for the worse." The voice at the other end of the line was soft and gentle. "Mrs. Masek should come in."

"On our way." I glanced at Jessica. She was wearing the same clothes she'd worn to the hospital, as was I. She paled as she stood up and I gave her a hug. In her driveway a few minutes later, I looked over at my house. The TV was still on. Was Rich still asleep in the lounger?

How much did I care?

***

"He opened his eyes, kissed me and said goodbye." Jessica bit her lip to keep from crying.

"That's so sweet. You know how much he loves you." *Loved you.* I couldn't bring myself to say that. Not that it mattered, as upset as she was.

"Then he took a deep breath, and—" She shuddered, then burst into tears. I put my arms around her and wished I could do something more to ease her pain.

"I was such a mess when Tomas and I reconnected after all those years. Dennis had just taken off with Tara, after he left me with nothing. I was thrilled when Tomas offered to help."

Jessica's 13-year marriage to her high school sweetheart Dennis had begun to unravel when his company outsourced his IT job to India. Unable to find another job, Dennis became depressed but refused to get counseling. “Why would he, when he could sleep with that little slut next door?”

Tara, the girl Dennis married two years later, was their next door neighbor’s mother’s helper that summer. That September, the minute she turned 18, she and Dennis packed up and took off for San Diego, only after he'd emptied all his and Jessica’s joint bank accounts.

“I was devastated. Then when my father was diagnosed with cancer? I fell apart. Tomas came over one day to see my dad. He still lived across the street. When I remembered how good he was with money, I told him what happened and asked for his help. I was so happy when he agreed to help me.”

A year later, six weeks after Jessica’s divorce became final, Tomas and Jessica were married, three years after Tomas’s first wife’s death. That should’ve been long enough for his daughter Grace to accept the marriage--and Jessica. But maybe because she missed her mother, more likely because she was five years older than Jessica, who would now inherit half Tomas’ estate, Grace and her family, Grace & Company, as Jessica called them, never did.

“What should we do next?” Jess was asking now.

“Funeral arrangements. Do you know what he would’ve wanted? Is there a church…”

She shook her head. “We haven’t been to church in a while. A funeral home, that'd be best.”

I nodded. “I went to this service at Thompson Brothers last year. It was…” I struggled for the right word. "Dignified.” I waited for her to respond, but she didn't say a word. “Or we could wait till his daughter gets here. Oh, and you’ve got to call her.”

“Can you do it? She’s always so mean to me.”

“I’ll get her on the phone, but you need to be the one who tells her."

She hesitated before she nodded, then began to cry again.

“I’ll take care of it.” I gave her more tissues. “Everything will be all right,” I murmured, even if I had my doubts, lots of them.

Grace lived in Asheville, North Carolina, near her three grown children, their spouses and her seven grandchildren. Tomas had just become a great-grandfather for the third time. He and Jess planned to fly down to see the new baby as soon as he felt up to it. Sad...

Jessica gave me Grace’s number as soon as we got home. I was relieved when the call went to voicemail and I left a message. When Grace called back about an hour later, I listened as Jessica told her about Tomas. Grace responded angrily enough for me to hear every last, bitter word.

Jessica ended the call quickly. “She’s coming up tomorrow. I wish she wouldn't. She still thinks I’m this fortune hunter. And now, with the funeral arrangements?” She sighed. “What was the name of that funeral home again?”

“Thompson Brothers.” Wendi was the one who'd always said it was the best. With two dead husbands, I guessed she’d know. “It's just across the highway from the clubhouse.” The same over-decorated clubhouse where Wendi'd ruled, the clubhouse I never wanted to set foot in again. *You don’t have to, if you just get back to your painting.*

Jessica frowned. "Are you okay?"

No! "I'm fine. Why don't I fix us some breakfast, then we can shower and maybe take a nap." I knew I needed a nap. I looked at the clock. It was 7:45 AM. I glanced out the window, not surprised to see Rich's SUV gone. Where did he go this morning, a meeting, an appointment, an assignation? With whom, now that Wendi was gone? I was relieved when I realized I was too tired to care.

***

It was almost two by the time we got to Thompson's. The dignified brick building was only five years old, but with its stately white columns and perfectly landscaped grounds, it looked like it'd been there forever.

Today, that dignified exterior belied the mayhem inside: Wendi struck again! I heard the yelling and screaming as soon as we went in. I looked down the hall and saw Steffi screaming. Who'd ticked her off? Paige or Monica, I decided as they came out of one of the offices, careful to keep their distance.

"I was her stepdaughter!" Steffi screamed at them as the funeral director, a quiet man in a well-cut dark suit, came out and positioned himself between them.

"Really? It took you almost a year to see her after your father died. That's why she designated us to make her final arrangements," Monica replied coolly, as Paige watched as quietly and unassumingly as always— until Monica gave her a little poke.

Paige stood up a little taller. "She put it in writing, too."

Monica nodded. "As we said before, if you tell us your preferences, we'll listen. No promises," she added.

"My *preferences* are very simple--I want you to butt out and leave the arrangements to me." Steffi wasn't screaming now, she was moving in on them. The funeral director was the first to back off, Paige followed quickly. But Monica stood firm, as she took out her phone and entered a number, to call her husband? Her lawyer? The police? I was about to find out when Steffi knocked the phone out of her hands.

"Why don't we step into my office and discuss these matters privately?" the funeral director suggested. I was thankful when they began to follow him into one of the private offices. It looked like Steffi was going along until she stopped, turned and took a swing at Monica, who ducked barely in time to miss a black eye. The funeral director frowned. "Please don't force me to call Security. This way, ladies."

Monica hesitated before she went into his office. Paige trailed behind as Steffi stopped, to pull herself together? I wondered if she was planning to take a swing at Paige as I watched her catch up to them. I was relieved when she didn't. But she did draw herself up to her full 5'7" as she followed them inside.

She looked every inch the successful personal trainer, too, slender but well-toned, as she smoothed her designer cotton sweater and coordinating linen slacks. I recognized the ensemble as Sonja Sanchez, the same upscale designer Rich had chosen for me. Sad to say, I'd stuck with that label all these years.

How close was Rich to Steffi? Had he slept with her, too? Not if Wendi had anything to say about it. That's when it hit me-- Steffi was strong enough to strangle Wendi, move the body, even stuff it into her designer garbage can, probably without breaking a sweat. If only I could be sure Wendi had been strangled. If only Jace would tell me...

I pictured him as the front doors opened and he walked in. He was wearing a black shirt today, with light blue jeans that fit like they'd been custom made. He looked, well, wonderful, I thought as he came up to me. "Amanda?"

Had his eyes just softened or was it wishful thinking? "Jace. Hello…"

He smiled, then looked confused. "I thought you said you weren't that close to the victim."

I indicated Jessica, who'd taken a Xanax with her coffee this morning and still looked, well, tranquil. "Jessica's husband passed away last night."

He turned to Jessica. "I'm very sorry for your loss."

She nodded tearfully then bolted for the ladies room. He looked after her and frowned. "It's never easy." He shook his head.

I resisted the urge to take his hand. Or kiss him. "You thought I was here for Wendi?"

He nodded. "She was your next door neighbor. I was also wondering if you or your husband might've thought of anything else."

My husband? Tell him how Rich was so upset, he was totally out of it last night? I pictured him asleep in his recliner, minus his ever-present cell phone. I felt sure, now, he'd been Wendi's lover. "Wendi and I? We didn't have much of a relationship."

But Rich did, Talk to him, if and when he gets back to normal. He was a lot closer to Wendi than I was. I wished I could say that.

"I'm sorry." Jace repeated.

I nodded as he went off. *If only he wasn't so special. If only I wasn't so—married...*

Jessica came back, then. I was about to try to say something reassuring when a dignified, impeccably dressed man approached us. "Good afternoon, ladies. How may I assist you?"

His voice was deep and soothing. Jessica began to reply when I looked up and saw Jace standing by the door to the office where Steffi, Paige and Monica were meeting with Wendi's funeral director. Jace frowned as Steffi started yelling again but the funeral director didn't miss a beat. "Why don't we discuss some of the options in my office?"

Jessica hesitated. "My husband's name was Tomas, Tomas Masek. His daughter Grace will be here tomorrow. Maybe we should wait?"

"We could discuss a few options today and finalize the arrangements tomorrow," he suggested. Jessica hesitated before she nodded and he gestured us down the hall to his office. We were almost there when the door across the hall flew open and Steffi rushed out angrily, followed by Monica and Paige, who both looked upset. I caught a glimpse of Jace, watching them quietly from the end of the hallway.

"She wanted to be cremated!" Steffi was just, well, shrieking.

"Oh, did she tell you that telepathically? She must've. You never came to see her." Monica waggled her fingers in Steffi's face. Courageous, on her part.

"She killed my father for his money and now you're going to bury her in some solid gold coffin?"

"It's Honduras mahogany, dear. Wendi would've liked it. Style was important to her," Paige added quietly.

"A Hefty bag, that'd do it for me." Steffi took a few steps closer to them. I was relieved when she turned away and rushed out the door.

Our funeral director ignored it completely as he escorted us into his office, held Jessica's chair and offered us coffee from his single-cup coffeemaker.

What was it with those things?

Jessica shook her head while I wondered if Jace was still here and what he was doing. Had he found any clues as to who'd done the deed?

I tuned back in as the funeral director began to discuss Jessica's options. I tried to focus, but I couldn't stop thinking about Steffi's father. Had he died from natural causes, or, evil as Wendi was, had she helped things along?

If only I could ask Jace what he'd found out, if only there was the slightest chance he'd tell me.

"Perhaps you'd care to see our burial beds?" It took me a moment to realize the funeral director was referring to coffins, laid out attractively in the Slumber Room, according to the big, elegant bronze placard on the hand-carved maple doors. Jessica was staring at those doors, now, paralyzed with fear? Grief? Exhaustion?

"Maybe we should wait till Grace gets here," I put my arm around her shoulders and steered her away from the Slumber Room. I looked around. Jace was gone. Where did he go and what was he doing? I wished I knew, as I drove her home.

***

We should never have gone to Thompson's. I realized that the next day when Grace arrived with three of her children, two of their spouses and five of her grandchildren. She made all the arrangements, shutting Jessica out completely.

The arrangements for Wendi's funeral, scheduled the same day as Tomas,' were going on in the next room, with no raised voices today. No, everything was quiet as Jessica and I sat in the lobby waiting to find out about Tomas' arrangements.

I looked down the hall and noticed that Paige and Monica had brought their husbands along today, as reinforcements? Not a bad idea. Jace wasn't here today, either. I debated phoning to tell him what was going on, until I realized nothing was happening that'd help him or anyone else figure out who'd murdered Wendi.

Steffi, Paige, Monica and their husbands were calm as they came out--and it occurred to me that Pete and Jim were both strong enough to have done it. I pictured the hunting knives they'd brought back from that African safari and shown off at Wendi's last soiree. Important? How could I find out?

Pete and Jim had both seemed to like Wendi well enough, but there could've been some secrets there, too. And Pete was an insurance broker. What if he'd taken out a policy on Wendi and decided to cash in on it? Maybe he'd asked Jim to help him. *They could've done it together.* They were crossing to the front door, now. Steffi was holding back tears. Paige and Monica were comforting her.

How did that happen, I asked myself when the funeral director we'd met with yesterday came out with Grace and two women who could've been her daughters. They thanked him before they went out, walking right past us without a word. It was the funeral director who told us Tomas' service was scheduled for 11 AM Thursday, with only one day for the viewing.

"Tomas had so many friends. I would've done two days." Jessica burst into tears.

I helped her over to the plush green sofa, grabbed the box of tissues on the end table and put it in her hands. "It'll be all right." I wished I could believe that.

"May I offer you a latte?" the funeral director asked softly. Jessica shook her head. "If there's anything else?" But he didn't wait for a reply before he turned and headed back to his office.

"Maybe I will have a latte. With one of those cookie things, what do they call them?"

"Biscotti. I'll get it." I went over to the coffee bar and asked for two lattes, then selected two biscottis before I sat down. Jessica chose the chocolate one and nibbled at it as she sipped her latte, finishing it off with another Xanax.

She seemed calm enough as we left Thompson's. I pulled into in my driveway when we got home and suggested she join us, me, really, for dinner. She was quick to agree. I debated cooking something but decided on takeout from The Main Street Grill, a restaurant in town that delivered.

Jessica was asleep on the couch by the time my chef's salad and her lemon-garlic chicken arrived. Maybe it was the scent of the garlic that woke her, but I was glad when she got up and began to eat her first meal since last night. Was it only last night Tomas passed on? It felt like forever.

I was making us two cups of coffee when Rich came in. I looked at the clock-- 8:15, early for him. I debated asking if he'd had dinner, but I knew he'd tell me if he needed anything. He'd never had any problems with that!

He was preoccupied tonight. I knew that when he nodded vaguely in my direction and headed for his bedroom. He came out wearing one of his track suits a few minutes later, then picked up his keys. He didn't tell me much till he was almost out the door. "Steffi needs a copy of Wendi's will."

"Why would she ask you?"

"I redid it a few weeks ago. I told you." He frowned.

He hadn't told me, not that I planned to make an issue of it. I glanced at Jessica, who'd dozed off again. I pictured Rich and Wendi discussing her will together, then. In bed. I sighed as I put the dishes in the dishwasher. Why did I feel so sure they'd been intimate?

Why didn't I see it?

I considered Rich's strange behavior last night and the way he'd just lied to me and wondered again if he could possibly have been involved in her murder.

Whatever went on between the them? It had nothing to do with you. If they had been together, it was about them. Not the first time Rich cheated on me, either, I'd put money on that! Visions of a few of the other women who'd been important to him, over the years, flashed before me.

Study buddy Amy came first, followed by Janice, his administrative assistant his first year at the firm. A petite blonde, she could barely type or take dictation. Maggie Parsons, the super-hip law intern whose model-perfect good looks belied the brain Rich always described as sharp as a steel trap, was next. Eleanor Barry, Katie's wedding planner, followed. Then there was our realtor Debbi Mangione, and Heather Burke, the decorator Rich said we had to hire. Had to hire or had to have?

Where had I been all that time? Staying home, painting— stuck in a bad marriage.

No more! I put on my jacket and headed over to Wendi's, to confront him? As much as I would've loved to do that, talking to him first to try to find out more about who could've murdered her made a lot more sense. Knowing I could call Jace if I came up with anything that might help him ID the killer was another reason I kept going. He'd asked for my input. If I could find out something, anything important, I could call him, maybe even see him again.

Chapter Eight

I was glad to see that some of the yellow crime scene tape had been removed, as I opened Wendi's door, went in and looked around. Inside, it felt as if she was still alive, like she'd be home any time now, and find Rich sitting on her sofa looking over her legal papers. Several copies of her will were spread out on her coffee table, a thick, smoked glass tabletop mounted on a signed Nigel Blakeley bronze worth almost as much as Rich's gold-and-diamond Rolex. I wondered who'd inherit it.

Rich looked up from her will and stared into space, oblivious to everything, including me. Not like him, not at all.

I'll bet he loved her. That made sense. Wendi was a lot better suited to him than I was. They could've furnished the perfect home, moved in the top social circles, taken exotic vacations…

"Amanda?" Rich looked confused when he finally noticed me there. What to say:

I'm here to accuse you of adultery.

I know you wanted Wendi more than you wanted me.

When are you planning to leave me, you evil bastard?

Calm and reasonable, that'd be best. "You never told me you revised her will."

"Of course I did. You were probably out there meditating or something."

I shook my head. "I only meditate when you're not home."

"Why, because you're ashamed of it?" He laughed, but it had nothing to do with humor.

"Tell me why you're here, going over her will, or—" What? I wished I knew, not that it mattered. He was never at a loss for words.

"She gave me her spare key a few days after she moved in. Surely you must remember that."

I nodded. "And you put it in a drawer, not on your key ring."

He raised an eyebrow. "My fob? I put it on my fob after she suggested I use it when I came over."

"Oh, how often was that?" I was headed for disaster, here, that or divorce. I still didn't care.

You don't file for divorce if your husband's an attorney. Something I forced myself to block out as I watched him lean back on her white leather sofa. He closed his eyes for a moment, long enough to come up with another lie but not long enough for me to grab a copy of the will. "Wendi was my client. So confidentiality applies, here, something you should know by now."

Wendi was more than a client, a lot more.

"I called the nursery, by the way. You need to set a time for them to put in our new Pampas grass."

I took a deep breath. "I did call, to order the rosebushes I'm putting in."

"Rosebushes? Our landscaping needs to make a statement."

Statement be damned! I almost said that, but it didn't matter. I'd plant those rosebushes whether he liked it or not. "That grass was ugly beyond belief." I heard the anger in my voice but I didn't care. Fighting with Rich felt good, especially when he was so broken up over Wendi's death. That's what I was thinking when the doorbell rang.

Rich answered it for once, giving me time to grab a copy of her will and shove it down the front of my shirt. I looked up, surprised to see Jace, wearing black jeans and an oatmeal-colored Irish fisherman knit sweater tonight, looking good enough to…

Don't go there!

"Just doing a drive-by when I saw the lights on." He flashed me a warm smile, barely giving me time to smile back before he turned to Rich, who extended his hand.

"Detective Connolly," he said in his best courtroom tone of voice, one that made it clear, Jace was the last person he wanted to see.

Jace would probably want to know why I was here, too. "My husband had an important phone call. I just came over here to tell him." It sounded like a lie even to me, but it was the best I could do. Rich never went anywhere without his cell phone. Not that Jace knew that, necessarily.

Not that he wasn't smart enough to figure it out. I glanced at him and tried to read his reaction, but the only thing I noticed was that he hadn't shaved since this morning. His face was shadowed, a rugged, very sexy look.

"A phone call?" Enough to force my attention away from his, well, face.

Rich nodded. He looked sincere or something like it. "Correct."

I let my breath out slowly. Rich had just covered for me. I couldn't imagine why, but I was okay with it. Jace pointed to the papers on the coffee table. "The victim's will?"

"Yes." Was there any way he could possibly know one copy was missing? Of course not. "Wendi asked me to make a few changes last week. Steffi called tonight with some questions.

As Wendi's attorney, I need to be there for the family at this difficult time," Rich added, his voice emotionless.

Her attorney, is that all you were? Not that I asked. I was glad when Jace focused on Rich and asked him why he wouldn't have checked the copy of the will in his files.

A computer glitch, Rich replied, too smoothly. Could Jace tell he was lying? Hard to decide, as he moved on, asking Rich how often he'd used his key and if he'd ever lent it to anyone else.

I wasn't surprised when Rich replied with a question of his own. "Why would I do that?"

Was Rich a person of interest? Maybe. Jace stood up taller and gestured around the house. "We're not quite finished here. Perhaps we could continue this discussion elsewhere?"

"Our house..." I ignored the way Rich was frowning at me.

Jace nodded. "That'd work."

Rich hesitated before he agreed, considering the legalities? Whatever he was thinking, a few minutes later, we were sitting at my kitchen table, the only one we ever used even though Rich insisted on moving our formal dining room set, too.

For myself, I would've put my studio in the dining room and put in a nice, big skylight. I pictured it, a studio I could use all year round, one where I could paint and draw— life drawings? I recalled the embarrassment my one life drawing class caused me, back in college. But if the subject was Jace, it would be different. So different, I began to get warm all over just thinking about it.

Jace was sipping his cup of gourmet coffee, now. I'd just as soon drink the regular stuff, but the day after Rich first made partner, he'd begun to insist on freshly ground, gourmet-label coffee.

I glanced at Jessica, still dozing on the couch, as Jace spoke. "I realize you can't discuss the details of her will, but if you could share anything that might help us ID her killer…" Was this the third time he'd asked or the fourth?

Rich nodded. "As I said before, Wendi is survived by her stepdaughter Steffi. There are also bequests to her favorite charity and a few close friends."

"And that's really all you can tell me?" His crystal blue eyes darkened, turning a shade or two closer to purple. Periwinkle, I decided. *I'd love to draw this man!* I pictured him posing for me, under a skylight big enough for me to admire every detail of his body. His very big, very male, very nude body.

"Attorney client privilege." Rich's voice brought me back abruptly. "Hard to believe she's gone." He frowned. "Terrible…"

Does he mean it, I wondered as her will, still tucked under my shirt, shifted. I pictured it falling out, landing at Jace's feet, humiliating me beyond belief.

"Can you tell me why she changed her will?" Jace ventured.

Rich shook his head. "Sorry."

Jace frowned. "If either of you can tell me anything about her relationship with the Haven Players, that might also help."

I began to suggest he talk to Helen when Rich cut in. "Everyone knows how close she was to Harvey and Cliff." He glanced at me for confirmation. Like I'd know?

"Cliff was so upset when I spoke to him today," Rich went on.

Rich spoke to Cliff? Why?

Jace nodded. "Anything else you can think of?"

Rich shook his head and stood up, Jace's cue to do the same. I felt the will shift again and hoped he'd leave quickly.

"Anything we can do to help, Detective." Rich's tone of voice struck the perfect balance between *goodbye* and *good luck.*

Jace stood up and nodded. "I'll be in touch." A promise or a threat? I wished I knew, as he smiled slightly in my direction and turned to leave.

Jessica opened her eyes and stretched when she heard the door close. "I'll walk Jessica home," I told Rich, relieved that walking her home had nothing to do with him, Wendi or Jace. Not that he heard me, not when he'd already turned on the TV.

I stopped in my bedroom and tucked Wendi's will between my mattress and the box spring. Jessica and I were almost out the door when the house phone rang. It was Katie. "Mom? Thank God you're there! Andrew is just being horrible!" I frowned as I heard her begin to cry.

"Calm down. Tell me what happened." I pictured the little girl she used to be as her tears subsided.

"Andrew says he'll leave me if I go back to school."

An ultimatum, I thought as she started crying again. Rich chose that moment to come back in the kitchen and shoot me one of his famous pointed glances.

"I need to call you back. Give me a few minutes, okay?" I hated to put her off, but I was not about to talk to her with Rich in the room. I felt even worse when she kept crying. "I'll call you back," I repeated before I ended the call and picked up my keys.

"Who was that?" Rich asked.

"Helen." I was thankful when he nodded, never thinking to ask why she'd called. No surprise there-- Helen was as negligible to him as Wendi had been important.

I glanced at the phone. What if he checked the caller ID after I left and found out it was Katie? For the first time in too many years, I was thrilled to realize I didn't care.

***

The longer I talked to Katie from Jessica's house, the less I liked Andrew. Nor was I surprised when she told me how Andrew kept talking about Emily Wakefield, a student whose dreams did not include graduating *Summa Cum Laude,* apparently. She'd just switched her major to Sociology, Andrew's subject—because she wanted him? Katie felt sure that was the reason.

Let her have him. I so wanted to say that.

"Then, when I asked him about this receipt I found in his pocket from the Brook Haven Inn? He accused me of prying into his private affairs. It just fell out when I took his jacket to the cleaner's. I told him that, but he got so angry."

I felt torn between pointing out that the receipt had come from the best hotel in town, one I wouldn't have thought Andrew could afford, or providing some real help. Real help quickly won out. I couldn't take her pain away, but thanks to the money I'd earned over the years from my paintings, I could finance her MBA. "I'll wire the tuition money into your account first thing in the morning." If she had an account Andrew couldn't touch. "Do you have an account in your own name?"

"Of course. You were the one who told me to do that just in case, remember?"

"This does look like a just in case situation."

"Oh yeah," she replied, then gave me the account information. "Thank you so much, mom. I'll pay you back, too, every cent."

"Don't worry about it. Go for your MBA. Full time," I added. If only I'd been that assertive with Rich.

"Full time? That'll be the best!" I could almost hear her smile. "I'm still upset about Andrew, but the MBA? It means so much to me."

More than Andrew?

"As for Andrew, he can be such an arrogant fool! Right now? Emily can have him."

Good thing he's not a lawyer, and you can file for divorce. But that was my problem, not Katie's. I told her I loved her, ended the call and turned to Jessica, who'd dozed off again. Tomas' funeral was scheduled tomorrow at 11:00. Wendi's service was scheduled at noon.

***

Double funerals, double trouble. It was a beautiful morning, too, no day for one funeral, let alone two.

"I'll go to Tomas' service with you, then we'll both go to Wendi's repast," Rich informed me when I got back from Jessica's last night. If he'd checked the caller ID, he didn't mention it.

No reason for me to go there either, especially not today.

I'd been exhausted last night but I'd still managed to take a quick look at Wendi's will, scanning it for her gold Rolex and the Nigel Blakely bronze, both of which she'd left to the Shelter. Maybe she did have a heart, I thought as I stifled a yawn. I'd read it all tomorrow, I promised myself as I put on my nightgown, brushed my teeth and crashed.

I checked to make sure her will was still where I'd left it as I put on my new Sonja Sanchez little black dress. It cost a small fortune, but looking my best would help, today.

I wasn't surprised to see Rich was wearing a new Armani suit, tie and shirt. He'd settled on Armani right after he'd made Partner. He'd stuck with it ever since. I watched as he gazed at himself in the rosewood-framed three-way mirror he'd insisted we put in the walk-in closet in the master suite, a closet almost as big as the bedroom in the Beachville cottage where we'd lived when we'd first been married.

"Armani makes a statement, just like your little Sonja Sanchez." He smiled into the mirror.

I thought about Jessica. "Jessica asked me to go to Tomas' repast."

"I don't understand why you insist on spending so much time with her," he replied without taking his eyes off his reflection.

You don't understand much, when it comes to me. "There'll be lots of people at Wendi's repast." Really, I had no idea how many people would be there to honor her memory. I glanced at Rich. Did he hear me? Hard to tell, as he adjusted his tie.

"Wendi's friends are our friends, too," he said when he finally turned to me.

Seriously?

"Monica and Pete, Paige and Jim? We see them all the time."

I'd never see them if it was up to me.

"I drew up Wendi's will, too," he went on.

And slept with her. Often. I'd hated Wendi. Jessica was my friend, and what with Tomas' daughter Grace giving her such a hard time, she needed me. I began to explain that to him when he cut in.

"You're always there for Jessica. She lives right next door."

So did Wendi, unfortunately. "For now." Jessica had already told me she was thinking about moving to her vacation home on North Carolina's Outer Banks. She was still upset about the way Grace & Company took over the funeral arrangements, too. "Tomas' daughter Grace cut her out of all the funeral arrangements. She's so upset."

"The daughter will be gone tomorrow and I'm sure Jessica will inherit most of his estate." Rich glanced in the mirror and smoothed his lapels.

"We don't know that for sure." Would he ever stop admiring himself in the mirror?

"I'm sure, absolutely certain Tomas protected her."

"Maybe, but—"

He finally turned to face me. "She had to know he'd go sometime. She'll probably stay here, too. It's a great community," he added, because he was running for Association President? The election was next week. I was gratified to realize I couldn't care less.

The prospect of Jessica moving away, on the other hand, made me feel like crying. "I hope she stays on."

He picked up his keys. "She's coming into lots of money. She might want a bigger place or maybe one by the ocean." He checked his appearance one last time, making it clear how little Jessica and her wishes meant to him.

"If you're thinking she married him for his money—" *You're wrong.*

"He was, what, 79 when they got married? And she was 35?"

"He was 78. She was 36."

"Why else would she have married him?"

Because she loved him. Not that there was any point in saying that. Women like Jessica have always rubbed Rich the wrong way. As a lawyer working his way up in the firm, he'd represented too many women who'd married wealthier older men for their money, then divorced them. Litigating those cases had hardened him to the point where he felt nothing but contempt for younger women who married older men, including Jessica, apparently.

Will you ever work up the courage to put the past behind you and walk away? Sometime, maybe. Not today. I checked my makeup carefully, to buy some time to work up the courage to tell Rich I'd be going to Tomas' repast? *You go to Wendi's repast, I'll go to Tomas'* That's what I was almost about to say when he turned on the TV, tuned to a local news channel.

I was surprised to see Jace onscreen wearing an attractive, if visibly non-designer suit and tie, being interviewed by a blonde who could've been a cheerleader back in college. I frowned. Why would he look at me twice when he could have Miss Rah Rah News? Not that it looked like he was interested in the perky blonde, the way he held himself. Stiffly. Professionally.

He is the lead detective on the case, I reminded myself. *It's just business.* I was probably just business, too. I knew that, but I couldn't help but imagine what it'd be like to be more than that to him.

"We've heard speculation that Wendi Willis was murdered by one of her neighbors at Brook Haven Acres. Any comment on that, Detective Connolly?"

Jace squared his shoulders and shook his head. "Sorry, Samantha. I'm not at liberty to say." He smiled, then, turning on some charm for Miss Rah Rah News. How good could he make a woman feel when he turned it on full-force? How good could he make me feel?

"I can't imagine anyone here did it." Rich shut the TV and checked his Rolex as I checked mine. We were 10 minutes late.

***

No one said much until we were in the lobby after Tomas' funeral.

"The police questioned Cliff about Wendi's death. I can't imagine why they'd think he had anything to do with it," Helen told me quietly. She and John were here today, along with 30 or 40 other neighbors, including Ed Cullen, Rich's election opponent.

"Everybody knew Harvey liked Wendi a lot better than Cliff did, but murder?" Helen shook her head. While I remembered how much Wendi had relished replacing Helen in the Players' production of *Macbeth.* I flashed back to the night she'd bragged to her friends when she'd found out it would be she, not Helen, who'd be playing the lead.

"Helen as Lady Macbeth? Get real!" She threw her head back and laughed. "She's much too old for Lady Macbeth, too old for anything." Rich and I were at one of her soirees that night, along with four other couples including Paige and Monica and their husbands. Helen and her husband John hadn't been invited. Nor had Wendi invited Jessica and Tomas.

And that night, her comment about Helen, no matter how arrogant, selfish and judgmental, was also the most interesting moment of the evening-- enough to arouse my curiosity about the Players. I checked out their website the next day and found out the company had been established ten years ago. Helen, who'd lived in Brook Haven all her life, was a key member of the group from the beginning. I scanned her reviews. Lots of them--she'd played the lead in so many of their productions.

Cliff had directed her in those roles until last year, when he'd taken a leave of absence to meet with a Hollywood producer who'd optioned one of his screenplays. Harvey took over in his absence, directing his first production right around the same time Wendi joined the group. He was the one who'd replaced Helen with Wendi, strange, in light of the stellar reviews she'd always gotten:

Helen Adkins sparkled as the Unsinkable Molly Brown last night.

Helen brings a brilliant combination of love and pathos to the role of Willy Loman's wife, making the Haven Players' production of "Death of a Salesman" an unqualified success.

Kudos to Helen Adkins for her right on-target portrayal of Mama Morton in "Chicago."

"Grace didn't say a word to me about the repast arrangements. The funeral director, he was the one who told me." Jessica's voice brought me back to Thompson's lobby. "You are coming to the repast?"

"Rich insists I go with him to Wendi's. I'm so sorry."

"Can't you come without him?"

"I wish I could." A sigh escaped me. "There'll be lots of people at Tomas' repast," I gestured to the crowd in the lobby.

"Like Grace & Company? They hate me so much, I don't even want to go."

I looked around. "John and Helen will be there. Ed Cullen, too." I was glad they were going. She needed all the support she could get. I felt terrible that I wouldn't be there to give it to her.

"Grace never accepted me. Now, with her children and grandkids here…" She gestured to the other side of the lobby, where Grace and her family were talking to each other in hushed, private tones, excluding Jessica completely.

"I'll stop by after we get home." *I'm sure it will be fine,* I would've added—if I believed it.

Chapter Nine

Wendi's funeral was running longer than Tomas.' There were more flowers, too. But I was surprised that there were fewer people at the service. Paige and Monica were sitting the front row. Monica was sobbing, her husband Pete comforting her. Paige, on the other hand, just looked numb. Steffi had come with a friend who could've been one of her Heavenly Bodies' colleagues. She looked great in a deep purple dress I'd spotted at Saks last week. Beyond that, the expression on her face gave nothing away.

Cliff Richardson was here, too, with a few other people from the Players. Harvey was nowhere in sight. Strange, when Helen made a point of telling me how Harvey had pretty much worshipped the ground Wendi walked on.

There was also a group of women I'd never seen before. They ranged in age from 20 to 70 and were not particularly well-dressed. Shelter by the Sea women? Probably. There were a few more couples from the Acres, too, but all in all, the chapel was only half-full.

At the podium, the funeral director began to speak. No one seemed surprised that it was he who led the service rather than a clergyman. Everyone knew how much Wendi hated organized religion. "Ministers and priests? Hypocrites, every last one of them! All they care about is power, that, and the money they make," she'd say.

I tuned back in as the hapless funeral director delivered a eulogy that left little doubt about the fact that he'd never met the deceased, lying in state in the elegant Honduras mahogany casket behind him. He didn't speak long, but I felt like I'd been there forever by the time he invited anyone who wanted to share their memories of the deceased up to the podium.

I was surprised when Steffi went first. "My stepmother and I faced some big challenges when she married my beloved father. I'm glad to say we'd put that all behind us before her untimely demise," she intoned.

Untimely demise, did she really just say that? And when did they put all it behind them? I couldn't remember ever seeing Steffi visit her.

"Looking back," Steffi went on, "I'm grateful to have known Wendi. She taught me so much." She smiled sweetly as I wondered what Wendi really taught her-- how to seduce other women's husbands, how to inspire loathing and hatred at Women's Club meetings, how to offend and alienate people enough for one of them to strangle you?

I flashed back to the sight of Wendi's body, dumped unceremoniously on the curb, as Paige went up to the podium. "Wendi was not only a great friend, she was also the foremost trendsetter in our community. We'll all miss her so much."

Her voice was soft, calm and even. If she was really that upset about Wendi's death, it didn't show. She began to go on when her husband Jim shot her a warning look and Rich frowned. Why would Rich care, unless—what? I'll think about that later, I told myself as Paige wrapped up. "God bless, Wendi. Rest in peace," she added emotionlessly.

A woman in her 60's from the Shelter was next. She thanked Wendi for her dedication and support before she went on: "Mrs. Willis set a fine example for our clients. She was living proof of how much you can grow, and how much you can help others after surviving domestic abuse."

Wendi survived domestic abuse? When and where? I had no idea. Neither did anyone else at the service, to judge from the dead silence as the woman returned to her seat.

More silence, then, before the funeral director cleared his throat and looked around. A few moments later, Monica picked up the slack, speaking softly about Wendi and crying daintily over her demise.

Rich didn't speak, another surprise. I wasn't sure why it mattered. It just seemed important, somehow. Paige's husband Jim was speaking when everyone heard the unmistakable sound of a cell phone ringing. Cliff stood up and went out. Was it Harvey who'd called him?

I thought about Cliff and Harvey's relationship with Wendi. They'd always appeared to be the best of friends. Strange, when Wendi never made a secret of the fact that diversity was tough for her. Did she overlook their sexual orientation because Harvey gave her the parts she wanted and the exposure she craved? That's what I was asking myself as I spotted Jace, wearing the same dark suit he'd worn on TV, standing in the shadows, and trying to catch my eye? Maybe not.

Back to the service, which didn't end for another 22 minutes. I was thankful when everyone began to file out. Jace was still there, in that same dark corner, as we went out. I wondered how many people noticed him there.

No one but me, I concluded when I got outside. But I was still glad I'd taken the time to put on my new makeup. I'd just gotten my hair done, too, ash blonde with highlights.

The good news? He'd caught my eye and smiled, slightly, as I'd gone out. If I could just come up with something, anything I could tell him. Did he know how Wend replaced Helen in the Players? Did he have any idea how much Helen hated her?

Helen's friends felt the same way about Wend, too. Was it one of them who'd murdered her, then stuffed her body in her recycling can? Unlikely but not impossible.

Not that I'd want to cast suspicion on Helen, either. Despite her controlling ways, her heart was always in the right place. I'd never forgive myself if she became a person of interest.

I could call Jace if Wendi's will revealed any clues. I might even get to talk to him at the repast, assuming he was there.

I've got to find a way to call that number on his card, his private number. I segued from *private* to *intimate* instantaneously.

***

A half hour later, Rich handed his car keys to the parking attendant at En Pointe, the elegant private restaurant at the Eastpointe Country Club, the club Rich insisted we join so he could play golf with Edgar Robertson, the Columbia Law school classmate who'd succeeded in becoming a judge. He didn't play with Robertson because he liked him. Rich's network was just as important to him now as it had been back at Forestville.

His business, not mine, I told myself as we went into the elegant restaurant overlooking Barnegat Bay. If En Pointe's award-winning regular menu was expensive, their catering menu was outrageous. But dining here was worth it, according to people in the know, including Rich.

A formally attired maitre d' directed us into a big banquet room with floor to ceiling windows overlooking the bay, an oak-beamed ceiling and a big stone fireplace. Rich made a point of telling me how the repast had been scheduled so coffee and dessert would be served at sunset. Good food, an open bar and a lovely sunset. Perfect, like everything else in Wendi's life? Considering the way she'd ended up face-down in her garbage can, I didn't think so.

I looked around, surprised to see how small the crowd was, the same 30 or so people who'd been at her service, half of them from the Shelter. I would've expected a bigger turnout for En Pointe, if nothing else. Rich was seating us, now, with Paige and Monica and their husbands. I checked my watch. 3:27. Assuming he was right about the dessert-and-sunset business, the repast would end around 5:30.

Two hours and three minutes. I'll manage somehow, I told myself as I noticed Jace lurking in a dark corner behind the bar, one so far removed from the crowd that Rich, getting our drinks, didn't seem to notice him there. Moments later, he came back with a martini for him and a vodka cranberry juice for me. "Here you are, darling."

Darling? Playing attentive husband today? "Thank you." Vodka would help. If I could finish it fast enough, I could hit the bar myself and maybe talk to Jace. If I told him my suspicions, he might tell me something in return, something that could bring me that much closer to figuring out who'd murdered the woman so many of us loved to hate.

Reading Wendi's will tonight would help, too, I thought as a server came up with a tray of hors d'oeuvres and I helped myself to a miniature Greek spinach pie. I popped it in my mouth as Rich waved me back to our table. I glanced at Jace, watching me guzzle hors d'oeuvres? He flashed me a smile, a real one this time. Did he care whether I was eating or not? Was his divorce final yet? How much did it matter? Whatever, I smiled back.

"Here we are, dear." Rich held my chair. It was next to Pete, who smiled at me. I smiled back and stole another glance at my Rolex. 3:48. The repast would last forever.

They were setting out the food now, an elegant buffet that looked delicious. But it was hard to concentrate on the food when all I could think about was Jace. I looked around, then, and noticed Steffi. Seated at another table, she wasn't saying much as she sat next to the same man who'd escorted her to the funeral and some of the Players, including Cliff but not Harvey.

Where was Harvey? I wished I knew. It was then that I noticed how mellow everyone was, because of the liquor? Maybe. Whatever the reason, no one was ever this mellow when Wendi was alive.

I glanced out the window as a server came up to remove my plate, a small plate. "Small plates, how trendy," Paige had exclaimed a few minutes ago. Everyone agreed, then began to discuss their small plate dining experiences.

You'd be at Tomas' repast if you'd stood up to Rich. A sigh escaped me. I was glad my tablemates were too busy discussing small plates to notice. I glanced at Jace, leaning on the bar right now. I wished I could go over there and talk to him, something I couldn't do, not with Rich sitting next to me. I glanced at him as he nodded in response to something Pete said.

If you can't work up the courage to get away from him for five minutes, how will you ever get out of this travesty of a marriage!

Nothing else to do but go up to the buffet, then, and fill another, well, small plate. The food was delicious, but it wasn't bringing me any closer to Jace, still at the bar.

Ninety endless minutes later, the sun began to get lower in the sky as the servers put out coffee, tea and trays of desserts that looked delicious. I glanced at the bar, where Rich was getting liqueurs for our coffee. Jace was nowhere in sight.

I frowned as I waited at the buffet for the server to slice a chocolate mousse torte that looked yummy. But he stopped abruptly when two ministers in clerical garb burst into the room. They were upset about the liquor, that was the first thing they said, shouted, really. Then they began to yell and scream about all the other *ungodly goings-on.* "Just like Winona to desecrate our Lord God this way," The older man exclaimed loudly. He spoke with a distinct southern accent. That seemed important, even if I couldn't figure out why.

"Who are they?"

"What are they doing here?"

"I can't imagine Wendi actually knew them."

I tuned out those voices and concentrated on the men, planning their next move right now. I thought about what they'd said: *Winona. Ungodly. Desecration against our Lord God...*

Wendi's real name must've been Winona and of course she'd come from the south. The religion business was a tougher call. Wendi hated organized religion. If these two knew her at all, surely they'd know that.

The manager was coming in now, the two parking valets behind him. The guests began to back away from the dessert table as the three advanced on the clergymen, who were going behind the bar, to grab liquor bottles? Yes! They had the bottles in their hands when the bartender stopped them--not before the younger man grabbed a second bottle, on that looked like scotch. He was lifting it over his head, poised to throw it into the elegant mirror behind the bar when the parking valets came up. One took the bottle from his hands, then the other wrestled him to the floor.

The guests froze in place as the manager took out his phone. He was about to enter a number when Jace stepped out of the shadows, two uniforms behind him. They were the ones who cuffed the clergymen and read them their rights. The crowd's reaction began at a murmur but quickly gained momentum. Moments later, everyone began to leave.

Who were those two? Since it was clear they'd known Wendi, aka Winona, she must've been born down south. Was either of them the abuser the Shelter woman referred to? Did Jace know? Was there any chance he'd tell me?

"I'll get your coat," Rich was saying as I tuned back in. The sky was a rich shade of indigo by the time we went out to wait for the car. Despite Paige and Monica's careful planning, we'd all missed the sunset.

I watched as a Mediterranean blue-and-white SUV pulled away, the clergymen inside. *It's none of your business,* I reminded myself. But I couldn't stop thinking about what'd just happened as Rich and I got into his SUV. He'd just started the engine when Jace came up to Rich. "If we could have a word with you?"

Rich hesitated before he shut the engine, got out and followed Jace back inside. Not sure what else to do, I went in, too. They went into the manager's office, then, leaving me in the lobby. There was deep red velvet-covered sofa that looked comfy, but it had been a long day. I wanted to go home and read Wendi's will, too, every word of it. There was also Jessica to think of. I'd promised her I'd stop by.

I sat down on the sofa and settled in. I had no idea know how long Rich would be in there, but this time, Jace flashed me a smile, a real one. Not much, but it was definitely, well, something.

I decided to call Katie. She felt better now that I'd wired her the tuition money. "Dad called. He said he thinks I need an attitude adjustment. He even offered to pay for counseling." I was glad when I heard her laugh. "If he had his way, I'd be teaching nursery school or working as a nurse in some hospital. He's just so clueless." I could hear her anger, not a bad thing. If only I'd gotten angrier myself, angry enough to put the past behind me and walk away.

"Mom? Are you there?"

"Sorry." I hesitated. "I'm glad you majored in business. And as for your MBA, you're an adult. Your father has nothing to say about it." I took a deep breath. "I can't tell you how glad I am that you know it's not you who needs the attitude adjustment." *It's your father, and your dirtbag husband, too.* Not that I said that.

"Thanks. It's great to know I can count on you. But dad sounded so sure of himself."

He's delusional. Something I would've said if she didn't have her own issues to deal with. "He's a lawyer. They always sound sure of themselves." A nervous laugh escaped me. I felt better when she began to laugh with me. "Don't worry, honey, it'll all work out."

Rich came out as I was saying goodbye. He looked tired and what-- relieved? Jace followed. The way was frowning, I could tell he knew something I didn't.

I did my best to remain cool and calm as Rich and I got back in the SUV. "Didn't have to wait for the car." He smiled as if nothing had happened. Denial? Secrecy? I was too tired to go there. *Concentrate on Wendi, and her will.* With luck, it'd provide some clues.

We drove home in silence. I was exhausted. I didn't remember my promise to Jessica until Rich pulled into our driveway and I saw the two cars parked in front of her house, late-model sedans that looked like rentals. Grace & Company, no doubt. Harassing her. I should go over. I would go over, if I wasn't so tired.

"I guess you'd like to know what went on with that detective." Rich took off his tie.

"You were in there a while."

"In this case? Truth really is stranger than fiction. Those two clergymen are wanted."

"By the police?"

"The FBI. They're ministers of a little congregation in western Kentucky. Nominally," he added. "But really? They're terrorists."

"Terrorists?"

He nodded. "They hate African-Americans, Jews, Catholics, Muslims--everyone." He frowned. "And don't even ask how they feel about gays. They also believe a woman's right to terminate her pregnancy should be against the law, even in cases of rape or incest. Last but not least? They'd love to bring back prohibition."

Radical, but everyone was entitled to their opinion. "It's not illegal to feel that way, is it?"

"No, but burning down abortion clinics and assaulting a hospital administrator? That'll get you time behind bars."

"They did that?"

He nodded. "They definitely set the fires. The threat against the administrator hasn't been proven yet. The victim spent almost ten days in the hospital," he added.

What were they doing at Wendi's repast and why had Jace asked to speak to Rich? By the time I turned to ask, he'd gone into the den. I hesitated before I followed. "Any idea why those guys showed up, and why they called her Winona?"

"Winona was her legal name. She told me that when we drew up her will."

Of course he knew more about Wendi than I did. "I can understand why she'd change her name. But those men, were they related to her?"

He hesitated. "In a manner of speaking. The older man was her ex-husband. She was 16 when they got married, an arranged marriage that lasted a little over a month."

"Wendi told you that?" *While you were in bed with her?*

"It came up when I saw her birth certificate and marriage certificates."

"Three of them, including the minister?" Not that I'd meant to say that. Not that it mattered. Rich didn't react. Water under the bridge, now that she was dead?

"She'd just turned 16, the age of consent in Kentucky, the year her father arranged the marriage."

And handed her over to a much older, over-the-top minister, a man responsible for hate crimes? "Who was the younger man?"

"Connolly thought he might be Wendi's son, but neither of them would talk. I can't imagine Wendi would've abandoned her son," he added, frowning.

I can. What I couldn't do was condemn her without proof. A son? Hard to imagine. "You think that man could've abused her?" That'd explain why she'd devoted so much time and money to Shelter by the Sea. Hard to imagine anyone abusing a woman as strong as Wendi, but she was only 16 when she'd married him.

Rich shrugged his shoulders. "She never said anything about abuse." He turned the TV on. I was about to ask him why Jace called him in when he turned up the volume and I let it go.

I could still read Wendi's will, all of it, tonight. I made a show of yawning. "I need to call Jessica before I go to bed." I knew I could count on Jess' name to turn him off. True to form, he just nodded as I headed for my bedroom, aka the less-than-master-suite. I went in and slipped the lock into place as quietly as I could, even though there was no way he could hear much, over the TV. I lifted the corner of my mattress, then, and found—nothing. The will was gone!

Rich knew, somehow, that I'd swiped a copy of her will. He'd come in here, found it and taken it back.

What now? I wracked my brain as I lay down without changing my clothes, washing my face or brushing my teeth. Minutes later, I was asleep, dreaming of Wendi, crawling out from under the purple pashmina on the curb outside her house, pulling out a big, sinister-looking knife and smiling as she stabbed Paige and Jim and Pete and Monica.

They were all lying there, dead, when she turned to me and raised the knife. I looked for help, but the street was deserted. She was about to stab me when I opened my eyes, shaking and sweating. I managed to calm myself enough to change into a nightgown and doze off an hour later. But it was still early when I woke up, 5:30, according to my bedside clock.

It was dark out as I showered, got dressed and went into the kitchen, where I brewed myself a single cup of gourmet coffee, hazelnut today. I took it into the three-season room, cozy, when I lit the fireplace. The gas fireplace was the feature I loved best about this house. All I had to do was flick the switch.

I didn't think I'd be able to meditate, but I gave it a try. Ten minutes later, when nothing happened, I picked up a drawing pad and began to sketch. Rough sketches of Wendi, Jessica, Tomas and Jace came up on the first few pages, followed by the two ministers and Harvey and Cliff. There was a pattern here, maybe even some clues. All I had to do was figure out who had the strongest motive and how it'd all gone down. Daunting? Yes.. Impossible? Probably.

I still had to try. I closed the pad and took a notebook out of my desk drawer. Not much, but it was a start. I heard Rich getting in the shower as I began the list. Steffi was first. Her demeanor at the funeral was so different from the way she'd acted at Thompson's a few days ago, I had to wonder why. She was physically strong, too, strong enough to strangle Wendi with that purple pashmina. The police hadn't released the cause of death yet, but I felt sure she'd been strangled.

It was a shame I hadn't gotten the chance to read the whole will but from what I'd seen, she'd left the most valuable items to the Shelter. Steffi, Paige and Monica may have gotten something. If they hadn't, they'd all have motive, assuming they knew she cut them out.

I sighed. Helen came next. She'd hated Wendi and she loved to take charge. But Helen was 71. She was in good health, but she wasn't particularly strong. She had a loving husband, too, along with three grown children and their spouses and six grandchildren who visited her every week. I didn't want it to be Helen who'd done it but I couldn't rule her out either.

I considered Cliff and Harvey, then. Again, knowing if Wendi had left them anything would've helped. Helen knew them a lot better than I did. I could ask what she thought. I made a note to talk to her before I moved on to the two clergymen, Wendi's first husband and the son she may or may not have abandoned.

Assuming that early marriage had really only lasted a month, it was unlikely the younger man was her natural son. But again, I guessed it was still possible. If she did abandon him? That'd give him a powerful motive for murder.

I needed to find out more about those two, and why they'd come up here. Best if I could find a way to talk to one or both of them. I'd have to find out their names first, but Brook Haven was a small town, There'd probably be something about the incident and their subsequent arrest in the *Banner.* Easy enough to check the website. I made a note to do that.

Rich came next. Hard to believe he'd do anything violent, when he could file a lawsuit to even the score. And even if he and Wendi had been intimate, she could also have been intimate with one or more of the other men in her Inner Circle, including Pete and Jim. Good-looking and successful, they would've appealed to her every bit as much as Rich.

As for their wives, I'd never trusted women like Paige and Monica, who cared more about outward appearances than what was inside. Murder? Unlikely, but far from impossible.

"Amanda, you're up?" Rich was dressed for the office and God knows what else. I smelled the coffee. He was in the kitchen. I tucked the notebook under a chair cushion and joined him there. It was 7:25, late for him. That's what I was thinking when the phone rang. I glanced at the caller ID. It was Jessica.

"I can't believe I was stupid enough to invite Grace & Company over after the repast. The minute they got here, they started taking all these things, our things. God, I'm an idiot!"

"You had good intentions." I waited for a reply. "You want me to come over?"

"That'd be great, if you're sure it's no problem."

"Not at all." Not quite the truth, but I wanted to help, especially after I'd missed Tomas' repast.

I went into the kitchen to tell Rich I was leaving but he was gone. No goodbye, no kiss on the cheek. How long had that been going on?

Forever, give or take a few years.

Chapter Ten

Something was very wrong, I knew that the moment I walked in. Jessica's living room looked almost like she was getting ready to move. Grace & Company had come over last night and taken mementoes, as they'd called them. They'd eaten lots of cake and cookies, too, to judge from all the dirty dishes in the sink.

"I can't believe this!" She gestured around the living room, where I noticed many of the framed family photographs were gone. The only ones that remained were photos of Jessica and Tomas, Jessica and Tomas and me and Rich, Jessica and Tomas and—Wendi? When was that taken? I would've asked her, if she wasn't slumped on the couch, her head in her hands.

The living room tables looked a little bare, too. So did the two etageres where Jessica displayed her crystal, including the Waterford service for eight Tomas bought her when they'd stopped in Shannon on the way back from their honeymoon in Paris.

Her art glass collection had been depleted as well. Jessica loved art glass, enough for Tomas to buy her signed, hand blown paperweights, dishes and vases as gifts for her birthdays and other special occasions. "The Waterford and your art glass, what happened?"

"Grace & Company, that's what happened! I knew I should've asked them to leave." She gestured around the room and shook her head sadly.

I should've been here for you . "I'm so sorry I didn't come over. I was just so tired."

"Not as sorry as I'm going to be, according to Grace. She said Tomas would've made me sign a pre-nup for sure if he'd had his faculties. Imagine, thinking he was losing it!" She started to cry.

I sat down and took her hand. "C'mon, Jess, we both know Tomas was fine, mentally. Rich thought so too," I added.

Jessica frowned. Nothing about Rich has ever impressed her. "She's going to challenge the will. I don't know what I'm going to do."

"You'll call your lawyer and let him deal with it. It'll be fine," I assured her. "I'm here for you, too. Anything you need…"

She shook her head. "Incompetent? I can't believe she'd say that about her own father—while she was busy taking our things."

She started to get up but I gestured her back down. "I'll make coffee."

"I could use something stronger. They didn't take the liquor." She managed a smile. I nodded sympathetically, made her a cup of coffee and hesitated before I added a half-shot of brandy.

I glanced at the étagère again as I put the bottle back, then took another look at that photo of Jessica, Tomas and Wendi. They looked so happy, it must've been taken when Wendi first moved in. There was a tall, lean, silver-haired man in the background, Cliff? Could be. A short, dark man stood next to him. Harvey.

I glanced at Jessica, glad to see that she was settling down. I pointed to the photo. "Do you remember when this was taken?" *You have to remember. I need something, anything I can tell Jace.*

She stood up and went to look at it. "I guess it must've been taken when Wendi…" Her voice trailed off.

You have to remember! I have to see him again. If I didn't, I'd still have Rich in my life. Not enough, even if, on a real and very deep level, it still felt like I owed him.

Jessica sat down and began to sip her coffee. "This is the best coffee! Can you make me another cup?"

I sighed as I made it-- minus the brandy. I was glad when she didn't seem to notice. I pointed to the photo again. "Do you remember when this was taken?" *And why you and Tomas looked happy to be with Wendi?*

She got up again and looked at it closely. "Oh yeah! We were at this benefit for the Haven Players, it was right after we moved in. That was the first time I met Wendi. She seemed okay that night. She just kept talking about that shelter."

"Shelter by the Sea?"

She nodded. "Although she did flirt with some of the men. Not Tomas, though."

I smiled. "Lucky for her!"

Jessica smiled back. "Looking back, I imagine she would've been all over him if she had any idea how much he was worth."

I pointed to the two men in the background. "Cliff and Harvey?"

She nodded. "Cliff was leaving for California that week. Harvey was going to take over as the Players' director. Tomas and I both thought Harvey was a little arrogant. We thought it was strange, too, the way he seemed enthralled with Wendi, especially after he made of point of telling us how he and Cliff were married."

"You thought there was something going on between him and Wendi?"

She nodded. "Tomas thought so too. She just kept throwing herself at him. She'd touch him when they talked and he'd touch her right back. He even kissed her."

"On the lips?"

She nodded. "They made a date, too. Pete and Monica had invited her out on their boat. When she asked Harvey if he wanted to come along, he said yes."

"What about Cliff?"

"He didn't look happy, but he was leaving for LA the next day." She began to go on when my phone rang. I looked at the caller ID—*Brook Haven PD*. Jace?

My heart began to race when I heard his voice, even though he was all business today. "We need to take a formal statement. Can you come down to the station?"

I'd love to. "Anything I can do to help."

"Good. See you in a little while."

I turned to Jessica and smiled.

"Your detective?"

I felt myself blush. "C'mon, Jess, I'm a married woman."

"Until you work up the courage to stand up for yourself and walk away."

I heard myself sigh as I headed for the door.

"You go, girl!" she called after me.

I pulled into the Municipal Complex parking lot 15 minutes later, thrilled to be part of an honest-to-goodness murder investigation. And the fact that the victim was Wendi? Icing on the cake!

***

"Your husband said client-attorney privilege prevented him from giving us any information about the victim's will. We're working on a subpoena, but it could take a while." Jace was wearing a suit and tie again, today. I noticed the outline of a shoulder holster under his jacket as he stood up and made me coffee from the single cup coffeemaker on top of his file cabinet. The fact that he had one surprised me, but I was glad when the coffee turned out to be almost as good as the gourmet blends I used at home.

Tell him I stole a copy of her will and hid it in my bedroom? If I did, I'd also have to tell him how Rich had stolen it back. I couldn't decide what to do when he sat down and looked me in the eye. "This isn't procedure, but if your husband ever discussed the will with you, or if you happen to know anything about it, it could help." I was glad when he broke eye contact long enough to take a few sips of his own coffee. I sat up taller as he set the cup down and visibly, well, stiffened, moving into formal mode. It made sense, when we were in his office, his cubicle, really, but I couldn't help but imagine what it'd be like if he ever relaxed with me. *Don't go there.*

"Amanda?" His voice brought me back to his cubicle, my coffee, those crystal blue eyes.

Focus! "Rich never discussed her will, but I did manage to, um, steal a glance at it at Wendi's house the night you stopped by."

He hesitated. Did he know I stole a copy of her will? "And?"

I took a deep breath. "She left her gold-and-diamond Rolex and the Nigel Blakeley bronze to the shelter."

He glanced at his notes. "Shelter by the Sea?"

I nodded. "The bronze is quite valuable."

"I thought it looked like an original Nigel Blakeley." He made a note of it, then looked back at me and relaxed a bit. "Y'know, I could've sworn you were hiding something under your shirt that night." When he looked me in the eye, I felt like he could see right through me. I was relieved when he smiled.

He knows, and he's not going to arrest me. I struggled to for a reply. "I didn't realize I was that transparent."

"Not rocket science." He smiled. "Hard to believe your husband didn't notice."

He must've, he stole it back. "I was going to read it that night in my bedroom, but I was so tired, I just looked it over. The, the next day? It was gone."

He made a note of that, too. "You husband may be smarter than you think. My ex..." If I'd expected him to go on, he stopped speaking abruptly and shook his head.

Interesting, but all I could think about was Rich. Whatever else he was, he'd always been smart. How could I ever have believed I'd get away with it? Not that I'd say that to Jace, who'd gotten over that reference to his ex, apparently, and was looking at me intensely, sending out all this—energy, energy that didn't feel like it had anything to do with the murder.

"You read it in your bedroom? You and your husband don't sleep in the same room?"

How great is your need to know? My breath caught in my throat. I had no desire to lie to a police officer. "Rich used to be a Senior Partner in this big Manhattan firm…"

He glanced at his notes. "Duncan Fitzgerald Kaufman?"

I nodded, and wondered how much he knew about the firm, and the real reason Rich had left. I wished I could ask.

"You were about to say something about the firm?"

I nodded. "He got all these late-night phone calls. He always insisted on taking them, too. I never got a good night's sleep. So I moved into my daughter's room when she went away to college."

He nodded thoughtfully. "And you stayed there even after he left the firm."

What does that have to do with the case? I was almost about to ask him until I thought about Duncan Fitzgerald Kaufman again and the real reason Rich might've resigned. Did Jace know? Would he tell me?

In this universe? I don't think so.

"So, the reason you sleep in separate rooms?" His voice brought me back.

I shrugged my shoulders. "I need my sleep."

He nodded, while I asked myself how he felt about the fact that I slept alone, assuming he had any feelings about it at all. Not that he'd tell me that, either.

Time to change the subject. "I don't know if you can tell me—" I hesitated. "It's just, I wonder if you'd spoken to Harvey and Cliff, the men who run the Haven Players. Wendi was close to both of them, closer to Harvey, I think."

"We plan to talk to them, not that I should be telling you that." He hesitated. "We haven't located Malden yet. The fact that he's been reported missing will be public information later today," he added.

"Harvey's missing?"

He nodded, glanced at his notes again and looked back at me. "Any other questions?"

Lots of them. "No, but I thought you might want to talk to Helen Adkins, my neighbor? She was with the Haven Players from the beginning. She starred in many of their productions, too."

"Till the victim moved in and pushed her out. She told me about it when I interviewed her."

I should've known. "She, um, thinks Wendi got those parts because she and Harvey were…"

"Intimate?"

I nodded.

"We're exploring that connection, too. We're also taking a close look at Richardson, who was here in town the day of the murder with no alibi, something else I shouldn't be telling you." He reached out and patted my shoulder. His touch radiated heat, heat that worked its way out and down and just, well, all over. And when I looked in his eyes, he was smiling, leaning in closer, about to do—what—when his phone rang.

He took the call quickly then turned back to me, all business again. "The last time we spoke, I asked if the victim had any enemies. Your husband came in at that point. I'll ask you again. Whatever you can tell me? It could help."

I debated telling him everything I knew. *Do it!* "Remember John, Helen's husband?"

He glanced at his notes and nodded. "No fan of the victim, or your husband's, either."

"Rich?"

"He said something about irregularities he'd found in your association's financial statements. Since your husband is treasurer…" He shrugged those broad, well-muscled shoulders. I stared at them, stared at him...

"John thinks Rich skimmed money from the treasury?"

He answered that question with one of his own. “What do you think, is it possible?”

When he’s been skimming money from treasuries ever since his Forestville days? Absolutely! “He'd have no reason to do that. Financially? We’re fine.”

“We're also looking at the fact that your husband held the victim in such high regard.”

Something I didn't even want to think about. "About Helen Adkins? Some of her friends..."

He smiled. “Mrs. Wetherill mentioned your little fantasy when I spoke to her.”

I felt myself blush. *Making love with you?*

“Something about wrapping one of the victim’s, what'd you call them, pashminas around her neck? She wore them often, apparently.”

I nodded. “I was kidding. I could never, like, murder anyone.”

“I don’t believe you could." He hesitated. "But you didn’t like the victim, did you?”

“No.” My heart began to pound.

He sat back and stretched. Slowly. Deliberately. “You’re no killer, I know that. Your neighbor Jessica told me how shocked you were when you realized whose body it was on the curb. But you might want to be more careful about what you say in the future.” He smiled. “You never know when it could come back to haunt you.”

“I never thought—I was just kidding,” I repeated.

He patted my hand then, enough for me to feel all that heat, his heat, again. “Don’t worry, you’re not a person of interest.” He raised an eyebrow. “Yet.” Cop humor? I hoped so.

"Glad to hear it." My heart began to race as he moved in closer and smiled, enough to make me feel like I was going to melt.

"Meanwhile? If you think of anything else—"

"I'll call you." *I so want to call you.*

He sat up taller, moving back into formal mode. "Just don't forget, the victim was murdered. In cold blood. The person, or people who did it are dangerous. They're still out there, too." He leaned in a little closer. "Be careful."

"I understand." *But I still want to try to find out who did it.*

"If you come up with anything, anything at all? Call me. But keep your distance, as I said. You don't have the training or authority to apprehend anyone. I'll repeat: we're dealing with a killer here, maybe more than one."

"I understand."

"Good." He stood up, thanked me for my time and began to escort me out. He patted my shoulder again as he opened the door and held it for me, sending more of that same heat down my spine.

He wanted my help, but he'd also warned me to keep my distance, the last thing I planned to do. That's what I was thinking as I unlocked my car and got in. It was a Beamer, the car Rich believed I had to have. For myself? I'd just as soon drive a Toyota, or maybe even a plain old Chevy. I spotted Steffi going into the station as I began to pull out.

Why is she here? How can I find out?

I remembered what Jace said: *keep your distance.*

Seriously?

***

A few hours later, I was watching the news while I made dinner when Chip came on again. "A new development in Brook Haven, New Jersey, where Harvey Malden, 44, co-founder and director of the Haven Players, Brook Haven's award-winning amateur theater company, has just been reported missing. Malden disappeared two days ago."

I sat down and let my breath out slowly. Was he missing or just, well, dead? Wherever he was and whatever happened to him, I felt this sudden need to do something. I was trying to figure out what when the phone rang.

It was Monica, oddly enough. "Rich's phone went to voicemail. If you could give him a message?" She didn't wait for a reply. "About the election? Just tell him Paige and I have it covered."

"I'll tell him," I was about to ask what she meant when I heard another phone ring in the background and she ended the call. *Give him a message?* How long had I been playing messenger, housemaid, cook, everything but wife?

Too long.

Rich didn't react when I told him what Monica said, but he was surprised when I asked what she meant. "Don't worry about it," he replied. "Oh, and thanks," he added as he took off for the clubhouse, murmuring something about a meeting. He gave me a quick kiss on the cheek as he went out. That's when I realized I couldn't remember the last time he'd done that.

Time to walk away. Since I didn't know when, if ever, I'd work up the courage to file for divorce, I set those thoughts aside and forced myself to focus. Rich would be gone an hour or two tonight, but he'd be at work all day tomorrow. Giving me time to go through his things for one reason and one reason only: to help find Wendi's killer. If I found anything important, that'd also give me an excuse to call Jace, too, and maybe even see him again.

You never went through anyone's things before--why now?

I never knew anyone who was murdered before. Nor have I ever met a man like Jace. Two reasons I didn't feel guilty as I began to search his drawers, closet and nightstand the next day.

I had no idea what to expect, making it somewhat exciting until I checked my watch. It was 11 AM. I'd been at it for two hours, now, and I hadn't found a thing. *Is his life really this boring or did I miss something?* I debated giving up, then thought about my motives: *why didn't you do this the first time you suspected he was cheating on you?*

I was too busy with my art.

Don't you wish!

I frowned. I hadn't been nearly busy enough with my art these days. I'd done a few shows and sold some pieces, along with a good number of those limited edition prints. But I hadn't come close to painting as much as I used to, as much as I wanted to.

I sighed. If only Rich didn't make it so hard, always saying how much he hates the mess. It took a while for me to realize the mess he meant was more than physical.

Emotional, spiritual, unpredictable, art is all those things. Nothing is ever certain, or even a given when it comes to art. Was that the real reason it was always so hard for Rich to accept the fact that painting is and will always be my life, no matter how he feels about it?

Not that it mattered, not when I was the one who agreed to limit my creative time, substituting Women's Club meetings and other activities important to him when all I really wanted to do was paint. He'd saved me from rape, back in the day. I owed him. How much longer would it take before I could mark that debt paid in full?

Since I couldn't answer that question right now, I put it aside. *Think about Wendi. And the murder.* I hoped finding out who'd killed her and where Harvey fit in, assuming he fit in anywhere at all, would clear my mind enough to get back to my painting. As if to affirm that thought, it was then that I noticed the small key in back of his nightstand drawer. I was reaching for it when the phone rang.

It was Rich. "I won't be home till late. Don't wait up."

I never do. Something I would've said, if I wasn't so busy going through his things. Not that he waited for a reply. Nor did he ask what I was doing, a good thing, under the circumstances. I put the key in my pocket, then noticed an envelope in back of the drawer, a pale blue greeting card-type envelope.

An *I love you* card? From Wendi?

Even she wouldn't dare, would she? I waited for my heart to slow down before I ran my fingers over the flap. It wasn't sealed, but it'd been sitting in the drawer long enough to stick. I was trying to pull it apart as gently as I could when the phone rang again.

It was Chloe, this time. "About your new pieces, how soon do you think they'll be done?"

"Soon. The painting's going great," I lied. "I'm hoping to finish them by the end of next week." I was also hoping she believed me. I knew how much I'd been slacking off, but my art? It still, well, mattered. A lot.

"Oh, I meant to tell you, the guy who bought that print, Jace Connolly? He came in two weeks ago and bought two more. That reminded me, we need to do a few more runs. It'd be great if you could do some new paintings we could transpose into prints, too."

"No problem." But really, all I could think about was Jace. "He bought two more prints?" It wasn't a question, I just wanted to hear her say it again.

"Yes, now you know the drill. Time to get to work!"

I promised to do my best before we ended the call and I got back to work-- on the blue envelope. It was almost open when the phone rang again.

This time, it was Jessica. "Hal, my lawyer? He got a letter from Grace's attorney. She's officially challenged the will. I need to meet with him today." She hesitated. "It's the last thing I want to do, but I don't have a choice."

I offered to go with her and hoped she wouldn't say yes.

"Thanks, but I'll be fine. The way Grace & Company dissed me over the funeral arrangements, then came over here and started taking our things? I need to take care of this one myself."

"I understand."

"I also thought I'd go down to the my place in North Carolina for a few weeks, unless Hal says I need to stay here," she added.

I wished I could go with her. I'd stayed at her beach house twice and loved every minute.

"I'm so glad Tomas put that house in my name. They didn't get all the Waterford, either. Half the stems were in the wine cellar that night." She hesitated. "You can come with me to North Carolina, I mean, if you want to."

"I'd love to go, if I didn't have that show coming up." I went on to tell her how I'd promised Chloe enough new paintings and limited edition prints to make it a success.

I couldn't help but think how wonderful it would be to get as far away from Rich as I could. But I could not, would not set my art aside. Nor did I want to leave Jace, not that anything was happening there, except in my imagination.

"Remember how I talked about moving down there someday and opening my own little boutique or café," Jess was saying as I tuned back in.

"Yes." The first time she'd mentioned it, I'd begun to think about my own dreams and desires: *Where would you go and what would you do if you could be wherever you wanted to be and do whatever you wanted to do?*

Beyond my painting, I still wasn't sure. But I was getting closer. I knew that as she elaborated on her dream, one that might soon become reality. We went on to talk about other things, then. We spoke for such a long time, I was almost surprised to see the pale blue envelope in my hand when we said goodbye.

Chapter Eleven

I finally got it open, only to find a smaller envelope inside, one with a window, the same kind they send with bills. Not that we paid our bills by mail. Rich and I didn't have many credit cards, but we paid them all online.

They were all in both our names, too, except Rich's personal Amex, the same one he'd applied for right after he passed the Bar. I perked up a bit when I found his current Amex statement folded neatly in the second envelope, my first meaningful find today. I looked it over carefully.

His credit line had grown substantially, that was the first thing I noticed. He'd started out with a plain old Amex; this one was Platinum. I didn't doubt he spent enough to qualify for the elite card. I also felt sure he believed at a soul-deep level he was entitled to Platinum. Entitled to anything and everything he wanted, including money from the Acres' treasury. Including Wendi.

My heart began to beat faster as I went over the statement. The first few charges looked like business lunches. I saw some other charges, too, for office supplies, a tie and a pair of Italian loafers from an upscale Manhattan men's boutique.

The next charge, an overnight stay at Ocean Winds, an upscale resort just north of Atlantic City, was the first shock. He'd paid for a room there on a Thursday night two weeks ago. Strange. I was sure he'd come home that night. It might've been late— I stopped keeping track of that kind of thing years ago. I looked at the statement again. The room, a suite, cost $395.

Imagine what they'd charge for the weekend.

Not the point, I told myself as I spotted another hotel charge, this one from the Borgata, one of Atlantic City's newest, most upscale casino hotels. That suite, the following Tuesday night, cost $375. I was trying to process it when I flashed back to the day Wendi asked me to take in her recycling can because she was going down to Brigantine. Had she planned to go there to meet Rich? Was there any way I could ever find out?

Think.

I looked at the statement again. Rich had gone down there two afternoons or early evenings, paid for two suites and never said a word about it. Then he'd hidden the statement in a pale blue envelope in the back of his nightstand drawer. I frowned. He wasn't there for the ocean view, he was there to fool around. If only I could prove Wendi had been with him.

How, I asked myself, until it occurred to me maybe they hadn't been alone. Assuming all, or even some of Wendi's Inner Circle buddies had been there, too, what were they doing--as if I didn't know! I tried to calm myself as I went into the kitchen, put on water for tea, ran a few more scenarios through my mind and came up with—nothing.

A few minutes later, I fixed my tea, sat down at the kitchen table, took out the statement and kept reading. It didn't take me long to spot the $467.89 charge from Jamison Davies, a women's clothing boutique at one of the other casino hotels, the same boutique where Rich didn't want me to shop.

"Their merchandise is so cheap and flashy. They're overpriced, too," he pontificated one night when we were down there for one of his business dinners. I noticed a cute little beaded evening purse in their window that night. I was about to buy it when Rich saw it and shook his head.

I pictured that purse as I saw the next charge, $1423.55, at one of the casinos' jewelry stores. No description, but I'd checked Rich's rosewood jewelry box this morning, the one I'd given him for our first anniversary. I hadn't found anything new. Whatever he'd bought? It wasn't for him. Or me.

I imagined myself driving down there, going into the jewelry store and demanding to see their security tapes like they did on TV. Something I could do, if I had that kind of authority.

Jessica might have some ideas. I wished she was home. I glanced across the street at Helen's house. Her daughter Elaine's minivan was parked in front today-- the grandkids were there. I took some deep breaths to center myself then realized I had two choices: drive myself crazy or paint.

It wasn't till I saw Jessica pull into her driveway that I realized I'd lost all track of the time. I glanced at my wall clock, a fanciful mermaid with a sparkly fishtail pendulum that swung back and forth. I'd picked it up on the Outer Banks the last time I stayed at Jessica's beach house. Rich hated it on sight, the reason it was here in my studio, where I'd been painting almost three hours, now.

A good thing. If I could finish enough new pieces for Chloe, maybe I could meet Jessica in North Carolina. I packed up and wondered if I should call Rich to see if I could find if he was in his office or just, well, somewhere else.

Till I realized even if he answered the phone, something he seldom did, I'd still have no way of knowing where he was.

I was relieved when the phone rang and Jessica's name was on the caller ID. "You think you could come over?"

***

Ten minutes later, we were sitting at her kitchen table.

“It's like this: Tomas included Grace & Company in his will, but now she's claiming he didn’t leave them enough.” Jess frowned. “I know exactly how much he left her and her kids and grandkids. Believe me, it was more than generous. I don’t want to give her anything, but Hal said it'd be better to negotiate than end up in court.”

“Makes sense.”

“Not to me, but he was Tomas’s lawyer for over 20 years. He trusted him and I do too.”

“You plan to stay here till it’s over?”

She shook her head. “Hal said it'd take a while and I really need to get away.”

I wish you weren’t leaving. “I understand.”

“You plan to tell me what’s wrong or are you going to make me guess?”

I shook my head and started to deny it, but I knew she wouldn’t believe me. I frowned as I handed her the Amex bill. She looked it over then looked up at me. “He spent over $2000 in Atlantic City and you had no idea?”

I hesitated before I nodded.

“But if you weren’t there with him..."

“Wendi was, most likely. I was thinking Harvey and Cliff and Paige and Monica and their husbands might've been there, too.”

"The whole Inner Circle?" She whistled softly. "I know, we'll follow him one day, see where he goes."

"What if he sees us?"

"In my car?" She shook her head. Her gold Camry was the best blend-in car I knew of.

"I wish I had some authority, you know, to question people. "

"Like they'd really remember customers who were there a few weeks ago?"

"They probably all have security cameras."

"Which they'd be oh-so-happy to let you see." She rolled her eyes.

I frowned. I knew she was right.

"We'll follow him, and--I know-- we can take some pictures, too. Then, when you file for divorce, you can prove he was unfaithful. I found out how important that was the hard way. I had to hire a detective to prove Dennis was cheating on me."

"You knew he was cheating. I don't know anything, here, not for sure."

"Don't you?"

"I suspect he was, but proving it?" A sigh escaped me.

"I saw the way Wendi used to throw herself at him. I don't know how you stood it. When you file for divorce…"

Tough to file for divorce when your husband's an attorney. I began to try to explain that to her when she cut me off. "You can't give up! All we have to do is to find an attorney he can't intimidate. I know, I'll ask Hal. It's worth a try."

I nodded, then ran the Atlantic City business through my mind again. One suite in a pricey hotel north of Atlantic City, another at the Borgata. Factor in one trip to Jamison-Davies to buy flashy, overpriced clothing and another to a jeweler to buy—diamonds, emeralds and rubies, for all I knew. For Wendi, I felt sure of that. Was there any way I could ever prove it? "How soon can you speak to Hal?"

"I'll call him first thing in the morning." She took my hand. "You and me? We're powerful women, and together? We can do anything."

I so wanted to believe her, but it was hard, especially when I suspected it was just a matter of time until she moved away.

We never did follow Rich, as it turned out. Jessica called me later that night. She'd decided to take off for the Outer Banks in the morning. "I need to get away."

"I understand." *Not!*

***

I was glad when she phoned me from North Carolina two days later. I'd been doing my best to ignore Rich, not hard, as I focused on the paintings I'd promised Chloe and kept trying to figure out who'd murdered Wendi.

I couldn't help but wonder what Jace had found out and how I could see or even just talk to him again. I was still curious about where Harvey had gone, too, and what might've happened to him.

Rich didn't seem to miss me, either, no surprise there. If he'd noticed the envelope in his nightstand drawer was slightly awry, he hadn't said a thing about it. Nor had he said anything about the key I'd found and hidden in my purse.

I tried not to think about all the ways he'd betrayed me, but a few days later, I got so angry

I decided to clean the garage. Crazy, in light of those paintings I'd promised Chloe I'd finish, but I hoped it would help get all those images of Rich and Wendi out of my mind.

I kept picturing them in those pricey hotel suites as I began to go through some cartons on our steel shelving units--until I saw it, a big, curved-blade knife with an African design that looked familiar. It was one of the hunting knives Pete and Jim brought back from Africa and showed off that night at Wendi's house. What was it doing in my garage?

My hands trembled as I went inside, found Jace's card and phoned him. A few minutes later, two uniformed officers arrived. One of them slipped on a pair of latex gloves before he took the knife and put it into a paper bag while the other one looked me in the eye. "You touched it, didn't you?"

It wasn't really a question. I was about to remind him that it wouldn't be out in the open if I hadn't touched it when Jace came in, wearing black jeans and a pale blue denim shirt today, his well-worn leather jacket over it. "I thought I'd come by and take a look," he said, his demeanor a little more relaxed than it'd been the last time I'd seen him. He looked around as I admired the cut of those jeans, his broad shoulders, and, when he turned to look at me, his smile. He was coming over to me now, putting his finger under my chin and lifting it, compelling me to look him in the eye.

"It's going to be okay," he said softly, staring at my—lips. Too soon, he turned away, slipped on a pair of gloves, took out the knife and looked it over. "Could be important," he told the uniformed officers, then, "Why don't you let me take it from here."

I was relieved when they turned to leave. I glanced at the street. Helen and John were out. With Jessica away, the block was deserted. So deserted, a chill ran down my spine. Not that I needed to worry, with Jace there. He squared his shoulders and held up the knife. "Didn't you tell me Pete and Jim had knives like this one?"

I nodded. "They brought them back from that African safari they took. One had a straight edge, the other a curved blade. They showed them off at Wendi's one night." Wendi's group showed everything off, all the time. Not that I could say that without sounding like a whiner. Or a bitch.

"You hated her." This time, when he looked me in the eye, I knew he could see right through me.

I hesitated. "Yes."

"You have no idea what this knife is doing here either, do you?"

"I can't imagine."

"Someone hid it here, obviously. Since this is your garage and you didn't do it, that'd seem to leave your husband."

"You think Rich may've had something to do with the murder?" My heart began to pound as I considered that possibility, not for the first time.

He let his breath out slowly. "I'll tell you something we haven't released to the public, but you need to keep it to yourself, understood?"

"Wendi was strangled, wasn't she?"

He hesitated before he nodded. "That thing she was wearing, what'd you call it?"

"The purple pashmina? I saw it, when they dumped it, I mean, her, on the curb…"

He sighed softly. "There's something else, too-- strictly confidential."

I nodded.

"Someone slashed that pashmina. We took some fibers. If the same fibers turn up on this knife, or if we find any fingerprints? It may help. Meanwhile…" He leaned in closer, then, close enough for me to catch that woodsy scent—his aftershave, or was it the soap he used?

I pictured him in the shower and began to get warm all over. I forced myself to breathe. The last thing I wanted to do was-- react, no matter how good he smelled. He was moving in even closer, now, close enough to kiss me. I was relieved, and disappointed, when he shook his head and stepped back. "Did you ever use this knife?"

"I didn't even know it was here."

"That does leave your husband."

"You think it was Rich who slashed her pashmina?"

"I don't know, but I hope we can find out."

"It's just, I can't imagine him doing anything violent. If he had a problem, he'd take it to court."

He nodded thoughtfully. "Let me bring this in, see what they find."

"Good."

"Glad you approve." He smiled. He didn't look like a lead detective when he smiled that way. He looked like a man. Enough for me to smile back.

"You're smiling."

I nodded. "It's just, you look…" *Like you want me.*

He raised an eyebrow.

"You're glad I found the knife, aren't you?"

He shrugged his shoulders. "New evidence? Always good."

I took a deep breath. "You have time for a some coffee?"

He checked his watch and nodded. I got even warmer as we went inside.

He spotted the papers I'd left on the table as soon as he sat down, the copy of the Amex bill I'd made before I put the blue envelope back in Rich's drawer, one of Rich's old date books and a few other things I wanted to take another look at. "You've been busy."

What could I say? "I had some time."

"So you thought you'd try to ID your neighbor's murderer? I warned you—"

I held up a coffee cartridge. "French roast?"

He nodded. "You really need to stay out of this, Amanda."

I loved the way he said my name as I slipped the cartridge in. "I can't imagine Rich's Amex statement has anything to do with the murder. If I thought it was important, I would've called you. I called when I found the knife," I pointed out.

"Gotta' be grateful for that." He stopped smiling. "I just want you safe."

He cares what happens to me. "I appreciate that, but—" The coffee maker beeped. I took out his cup and put it on the table with milk and sugar.

He nodded his thanks. "*I can take care of myself.* Is that what you were going to say?"

"I've been taking care of myself for a while now."

"I'm sure you've done a fine job of it, too. But this is murder we're talking about." He stirred milk into his coffee. "Okay, now that you know the victim was strangled …"

I tensed, but he didn't seem to notice as he gestured me to sit down. "Care to tell me what else you found?" He indicated Rich's papers and the date book. "You must've thought these were important," he added when I didn't reply.

I hesitated. "It's just, all our bills come here to the house except Rich's Amex. It's an elite card," I felt the need to add.

"Gold?"

"Platinum."

He nodded slowly.

"That bill goes to his office. So when I found it in an envelope in the back of his nightstand drawer—"

"You thought you'd take a look?"

I considered trying to justify the fact that I'd gone through his things, then just, well, moved on. "There were these two charges for hotel rooms, suites, really."

"You didn't know anything about them?"

I shook my head. "Rich comes home every night. Late, sometimes."

"How late?"

"Late enough so I don't wait up. But he never said a word about taking rooms at any hotel. I couldn't help but wonder—"

"What he was doing there and who he was with?"

I hesitated. "They were suites, as I said. Expensive ones." I handed him the statement.

He looked it over. "The Borgata? You're sure he didn't say anything about it?"

I shook my head. "He may've come home late that night..." *He always comes home late,* something I had no desire to tell him. I focused intently on his coffee cup to try to hold back the tears. I was horrified when I began to cry anyway. He stood up, looked down at me, then helped me to my feet, put his arms around me and kissed me.

You shouldn't be doing this.

Why not? After all these years with Rich? I deserve it...

He pulled away. "I'm sorry."

I'm not. "It's just—"

"What?"

I responded to you in a way I never responded to Rich. How could I say that, I asked myself as the doorbell rang.

"Don't answer." He breathed those words in my ear and kissed me again.

"Amanda, are you okay?" Helen called out. Loudly.

"Be right there."

Jace stepped back, away from me and frowned. "I never should've…"

But I'm so glad you did. That's what I was thinking as I opened the door for Helen, the last thing I wanted to do.

A half-hour later, the three of us were sitting at my kitchen table discussing the case. Helen fingered the key I'd found in Rich's drawer. "You're sure you never saw this before?"

I nodded, then turned to Jace. "Any way you can find out what kind of key it is?"

He held his hand out and Helen gave him the key reluctantly. She hates to rescind control. "It doesn't look like a safe deposit key, but I guess it could be," she said as Jace slipped it in his pocket.

"I'll take it in, see what they find." He stood up and turned to me. "You think your husband will notice it missing?"

"I doubt it but even if he did? I don't think he'd tell me. I've never gone through his things before," I added.

"Never?"

“Never.” I was glad when he flashed me a smile, then nodded in Helen’s direction before he turned to go out. Not much, but along with those kisses? It was more than enough.

Helen looked after him and smiled, then turned to me. “Took you a while to answer the door. What were you doing?”

I was debating what to say when she spoke first. “Don’t tell me you were kissing that sexy hunk.”

I smiled. “Okay, I won’t tell you.”

“High time! You can't be getting anything from that husband of yours.” She smiled. “If you ask me, no one deserves a big, handsome, macho guy like that detective more than you do.”

Since I had no idea what to say to that, I was glad when she went on. “Back to the murder, or murders—”

“Murders? You think Harvey--"

She nodded.

“Do you have idea what could've happened to him?”

She frowned. “I'm sure I wasn’t the only one who didn’t like him. And I've got some other ideas I didn’t mention to your hunky detective.”

“Hunky, yes. Mine?” I shook my head. “I’m a married woman.” *At least for now.*

“Whatever.” She got up and fixed herself some tea. “Okay, we've established the fact that Wendi was involved with your husband. I’ve got a feeling she and Harvey slept together, too.” She frowned. “And in light of who, and what that woman was? God only knows who else she slept with.”

I had to agree. We considered some possibilities until she checked her watch and suggested we go over to her house. “John will be home soon. He and Ed have put in all this time auditing the books." She frowned. "They still haven’t found much."

We were sitting at her kitchen table a half hour later, sharing a plate of oatmeal chocolate chip cookies. I shouldn’t have been eating them, but Helen’s daughter Elaine bakes the best cookies. Just one more, I told myself as I helped myself to another one, tasted it and closed my eyes. Heavenly.

“Amanda?” Helen was looking at me, waiting for me to say—what? Wendi and Harvey, that's what we were talking about. “You think the two of them might’ve been together?”

She nodded. “I think it started not too long after he and Cliff came back from Vermont.”

“Right after they got married?”

She nodded and helped herself to another cookie.

“You're saying Harvey might not be, like, one hundred percent gay?” Something that'd seriously affect his relationship with Cliff. I began to say that when she cut in.

“Cliff never said anything to make me think he’d caught them in the act. On the other hand, everyone knew he didn’t like Wendi.”

“They did?”

She nodded. “One night? I overheard Cliff tell Harvey he was crazy to cast Wendi as Lady Macbeth. That part was mine until he replaced me with her, if you remember.”

Hard to forget, when you keep telling me about it.

“There’s more to that story--you'll love it! Wendi’s house, her bedroom, specifically...”

"Don't tell me, her king-size bed opens up to accommodate large parties?"

Helen laughed. "It wouldn't surprise me. But the day Harvey told me he was replacing me in that part? He asked me to drop my copy of the script off to Wendi."

"Wasn't that a little insensitive?"

She nodded. "Harvey's an all right director, but a man with his people skills wouldn't last a minute in the corporate arena. Not much tact, a lot less sensitivity. Strange for someone who claims to be an actor."

"Harvey? I didn't realize…"

"He just did a few supporting roles off-Broadway. He only got to direct was because he was Cliff's, what'd they call it? Life-partner. A life-partner who cheated," she added.

"Hard to believe it happened right after they got married."

She shook her head. "Straight or gay, men are men, and Harvey? He fooled around."

"With Wendi?"

"She wasn't the only one. He liked them young, pretty and preferably blonde. Wendi was older, but she took such good care of herself. She threw herself at him, too. Harvey was never much to look at. He had to be flattered."

"Makes sense."

"The day he asked me to drop the script off at her house? I saw this hidden compartment she'd had built into the walk-in closet in her bedroom. I don't think she intended me to see it, but when I got there, she was putting something inside. I couldn't tell what," she added.

"Interesting." Interesting enough for me to try to get hold of Rich's key so Helen and I could go in and see what Wendi had hidden in there. If whatever we found had anything to do with the murder, what a coup it would be to tell Jace about it.

I pictured myself calling him. He'd come out to investigate. Maybe he'd kiss me again. My heart begin to race as I pictured it. *Stop! You're still a married woman. You shouldn't...*

"I know we shouldn't, but..." Helen's voice brought me back.

Breaking and entering. That's what we'd be doing if we went to Wendi's and tried to get into that secret compartment—after Jace pretty much ordered me to stay out of it. But the prospect of uncovering Wendi's secrets was so tantalizing, how could I pass it up?

When I looked up, Helen was worrying at her lower lip. "I wouldn't think of going into that closet, except—"

"What?"

"I hated that woman. Not enough to murder her," she added quickly. "But I've always been curious about what made her tick."

"You think the answers are in her closet?"

She smiled. "I think it's worth a try."

Chapter Twelve

Seven-thirty the next evening, Helen and I unlocked Wendi's door and slipped into her house. We both had flashlights, but we didn't turn them on till we were inside her big walk-in closet.

The block was quiet tonight. Jessica was still in North Carolina, Rich wouldn't be home till later and John was at the clubhouse with Ed, working on the books again. I put it all out of my mind as Helen tapped the wall behind Wendi's custom-made shoe rack, one that still held 40 pairs of her size four and a halves, Pygmy shoes, as Helen called them.

"Look at that!" I watched as this little panel slid open then knelt down next to her as she reached in and took out six DVDs in hard plastic cases bound with a rubber band. She held them up triumphantly. "Paydirt!"

Fifteen minutes later, we were in my three-season room, where the two new paintings I'd promised Chloe were almost finished. Our spare TV was in there, too, along with a DVD player I seldom used. "Are they numbered?" I asked as I put my flashlight back in the drawer Rich had designated as its proper location.

Helen nodded. "Wendi was nothing if not well-organized. Remember the Women's Club?"

"I'll never forget it."

She smiled. "Let's start with number one. You're sure your husband won't be home any time soon?"

"He never gets home this early but even if he does? He never comes in here."

"Good." She slipped the first disk in and pressed the *play* button. *Harvey, Cliff Wendi and Another Guy Together in Bed.* That could've been the title.

"Looks like you were right about Harvey and Wendi being, y'know, together."

I'm always right. I knew that's what Helen was thinking as she gestured to Wendi, wearing a very X-rated black leather bustier with rhinestones and silver studs, in the video. "What man wouldn't want a woman who was wearing that?"

I took a closer look. "Looks custom-made, too. I bet it cost all kinds of money." It was hard to come up with something to say that didn't have to do with the activities going on in the DVD, ones that also involved some, well, specialty items I'd never seen up close before: leather g-strings, handcuffs padded with fur and crotchless lace panties, to name a few.

"I'm glad there's no dialogue." She pointed to the screen. "I can't believe Burt Davidson got involved with this group."

"The other guy's a dentist, really?" I glanced at the screen, where Burt the dentist was showing off his gold lame briefs right now.

"Sure is," Helen replied without taking her eyes off the action.

"But he's a dentist. I wouldn't have thought—"

"It doesn't affect his performance." She indicated a spot on the screen that proved it.

I felt my cheeks start to burn. I wished I wasn't so embarrassed, but I couldn't seem to do much about it.

"Look at Cliff. Agile, for a guy his age." Helen smiled.

I had to agree as I watched him move extraordinarily well in his satin serpent-print briefs. *Where do they get these things?* I was about to ask Helen when she spoke again.

"Mesh stockings? C'mon, Wendi, you can do better than that!"

I leaned in for a closer look. "They are metallic. And along with those spike-heel boots…"

"They do get the job done," she agreed.

I frowned. One thing to know Wendi took lovers, lots of them, apparently. But seeing her, Harvey, Cliff and Burt the dentist performing sexual acrobatics on our spare TV? Too much information! I focused on the action for a moment as Harvey joined in, before I remembered he was still missing. Where was he? Was he still alive?

"What are you thinking?" Helen demanded.

I hesitated, "It's just, I thought you said Cliff hated Wendi." I pointed to the screen. "He's not having any problems with her on the DVD." I pointed to the screen, where Wendi was taking off one of her spike-heeled boots and running the long, impossibly narrow heel down Cliff's back, driving him crazy, from the looks of it.

"He's still a man."

"A man who went up to Vermont to marry Harvey but here he is fooling around with Wendi. It doesn't make sense."

"Guess he's equal opportunity." She laughed.

I didn't join in. "Jace thinks Cliff might've lied about being out of town the day Wendi was killed."

"*Jace* told you that?" She smiled.

I felt myself blush. "It's just, he came to my show last May and bought one of my prints. I guess he must've remembered me the day they found Wendi's, y'know, body." I glanced back at the screen. The first DVD was over now, thank goodness.

"He likes your paintings? That's great!" Helen took it out and put in the next one. "Ready for Number Two?"

As ready as I'll ever be. "I guess." Moments later, we watched as Wendi, Pete, Monica, Paige, Jim and Rich just, well, kept the action going.

"Your husband's in good shape, but that necktie business? Bizarre."

A gross understatement. In the DVD, Rich was wearing one of his good designer neckties and nothing else. Wendi, Paige and Monica were taking it off, so they could do—what? I didn't want to think about that as I watched the muscles in his shoulders flex when he flipped Wendi onto her stomach. I pictured the skinny geek he'd been when I'd first met him and frowned.

"The man has some moves." Helen's voice brought me back.

"He works out at Heavenly Bodies four times a week. "

"Looks like it's paying off."

Rich insists everything pay off. "It costs $175 a month."

"That's more than John and I paid for our first apartment,"

"We paid $215 for our first place." I pictured the tiny caretaker's cottage in Beachville. A lifetime ago, I thought as Monica and Paige began to just, well, do each other. They both wore bustiers similar to Wendi's but not as elaborate. Not black, either. Monica's was taupe, Paige's pale blue. Why did I feel so sure it'd been Wendi who'd chosen those them? How had Paige and Monica felt about that?

I closed my eyes, then, and focused on my breathing. Focusing on something, anything else was easier than watching the DVD. *When did Rich morph from skinny geek to crazed sex fiend?*

"Looks like your hubby's up at bat again." Helen turned to me. "Seen enough?"

"More than enough."

She hit the stop button, ejected the DVD and slid in number three. I closed my eyes again, long enough for my cheeks to cool down. When I opened them, Wendi, Pete, Monica, Paige and Jim were engaged in some group, well, activities. A few minutes later, Steffi and Rich joined in. "I don't know that we need to watch them all," I told Helen. *I'd do anything not to have to watch them all.*

She hesitated. "I know, we'll fast forward it, see if there's anyone else." She clicked the remote, then we watched all this incredibly fast, incredibly lewd motion. As awful as it was, I couldn't look away. Nor could we stop laughing, from time to time. Nerves…

Rich didn't make his next appearance until number five, with Wendi, Paige, Monica, Harvey and Steffi. Since Steffi was Wendi's stepdaughter, did that make it incest? I debated asking Helen, but she was watching the DVD closely. Very closely, not I blamed her. She wasn't embarrassed, either. Okay with me, when I was embarrassed enough for both of us, especially now that they were bringing out those-- sex toys again. Bizarre.

"Just look at Steffi." Helen glanced at me and frowned. "Sorry. I should be more sensitive, what with Rich in the middle of things."

And doing a fine job of it, too. I almost said that, until I thought back to the summer Rich began to work out. He'd succeeded in building his body the same way he'd succeeded in accomplishing every goal he'd ever set for himself. He'd continued to stay in shape, too. I could see that as Paige and Monica began to just, well, share him, onscreen. "I never realized Rich was that, um, close to Paige and Monica." Did I really just say that?

Helen smiled. "I don't think friendship is the overriding issue, here." She looked back and the screen and began to giggle.

I didn't join in. She pressed the remote, then, stopping the DVD.

"Why'd you do that?" I asked.

Not that I didn't know, as she slipped number five back in its case."Let's move on to the next one, see if there are any other people involved."

"But we didn't finish this one."

"That's okay, I can watch it later."

I nodded, glad to see she had a little sensitivity. "I was doing okay till I saw Rich."

"With Paige and Monica? I saw how much it upset you."

I began to deny it when she spoke again. "Look, I'll watch the rest of them myself."

Great idea! "The good news? After seeing all this? I'm more than ready to talk to an attorney." Not that kissing Jace the other night hadn't given me another, even better reason to file for divorce. I couldn't wait to kiss him again.

"I'm wondering if this is the entire cast of characters, or if there could be any other people involved." Helen's voice brought me back.

"I doubt Wendi would've invited anyone outside her Inner Circle."

Helen nodded. "I have to agree. Did you notice how each DVD seemed to have its own specific cast of characters? If you want to watch the last one with me—"

I shook my head. "Not unless there's some reason you think I should.."

"No. But if you're really planning to file for divorce? Why don't I copy them on my computer? Could come in handy."

Copy Wendi's X-rated DVDs? I couldn't imagine.

Helen took my hand. "It's like this, let's say you decide to file for divorce. Not today. Maybe not ever. But if you do, we both know how much the fact that Rich is an attorney could work against you."

I nodded. "That's the reason I haven't done it."

"These copies? They'd give you leverage. Just say the word, Amanda."

"I don't know," I replied. Really, though, I loved the idea. But for some reason, it just felt wrong.

Almost as wrong as stealing those DVDs out of Wendi's closet.

Almost as wrong as kissing Jace.

"Think of it as insurance."

I hesitated. "Okay."

"My pleasure." She patted me on the shoulder. "I'll copy them tonight and keep them in my house. I'll watch the last one myself too, no problem." She stacked them neatly and slipped the rubber band around them. “We'll put them back in the morning.”

“Good.” I thought about the copies she’d offered to make. They'd give me all the evidence I could ever need to prove Rich was a lying pervert, something I didn’t even want to think about. Leverage. That was how I needed to look at it, if I wanted to stay sane.

I felt better when I realized the DVDs would also give me a good reason to phone Jace. Hard to figure out what I could say: *I heard there was this secret compartment in Wendi’s closet.*

Yes. That'd be okay. No reason to confess we’d done that B and E, taken them and watched them. No reason to tell him how I’d watched all those years of marriage unravel right before my eyes.

I was grateful I’d never have to watch them again. Time for the next step, finding a lawyer Rich couldn’t intimidate. I’d call Jessica tomorrow.

“Are you listening?” Helen pointed to the DVDs. “I said now we know why Wendi insisted on sending that $100 baby basket to Pete and Monica.”

“You knew about that? But you weren’t even there that day.”

“Muriel told me about it. So did you,” she added

I nodded. If I’d only known then, or even imagined...

“So, are you going to call your hunky detective?”

“Jace?”

She rolled her eyes. “Not Mr. Wonderful!”

I heard myself sigh. “All right. I suspected Rich and Wendi might be, like, doing it, but I saw a lot more on those DVDs than I ever wanted to."

Helen pursed her lips. "Whatever it takes to get you your freedom."

"I guess." I let my breath out slowly and glanced at the clock. It was 10:35 and Rich still wasn't home. Fine with me. Wendi was dead and Harvey was missing, but Steffi was still alive. So were Cliff, Monica, Paige, Burt the dentist and the rest of the gang.

Would they keep their sexual antics going, with Wendi dead? How could I find out? Would I ever succeed in getting out of this travesty of a marriage?

Not like you have a choice, after watching those DVDs, I told myself, then, *the debt? It's paid in full.*

"Amanda?" Helen's voice brought me back. "You want me to hold on to Wendi's key?"

"Good idea." I handed her the key. If Rich noticed it missing, I wouldn't want him to find it among my things.

She slipped it in her pocket. "John has a board meeting in the morning. I'll call you as soon as he leaves."

"Good."

She turned and left. I kept an eye on her until she got into her house. Rich pulled in as she closed the door behind her. I thought about what I'd seen tonight and made a show of yawning as he came in. "I didn't realize how late it is. I'm exhausted."

"Going to bed?" The look in his eyes made his intentions clear. We hadn't stopped having sex completely, but it hadn't been frequent, not for a long time. I knew why, too.

"I'm out of the rat race these days. No more midnight phone calls. Maybe you'd like to move back in?" He reached out to stroke my hair, then kissed on the cheek, our first kiss since—I couldn't remember when. It was all I could do not to recoil…

You need to find yourself another squeeze, now that Wendi's gone. Paige and Monica might be willing, Steffi, too, if you like them young— and built. Even Harvey and Cliff, if and when Harvey turns up and you enjoy that kind of variety. I so would've loved to say that. "Big day. I'm exhausted," I repeated.

"Oh, what'd you do all day?"

Now he was asking, now he cared? *I went through your things and found a mysterious key, along with a very incriminating Amex bill. I copied it and showed it to Jace, who came over when I found the curved-blade African hunting knife in a carton in back of the garage. He's brought it down to the station to try to find out if it's the same knife that was used to slash Wendi's purple pashmina.*

Then Helen and I used your key to get into Wendi's house and steal six DVDs she'd hidden in a secret compartment in her closet. They featured you, among others. Now? I feel like I'm going to throw up. "I did some painting."

"Painting? Now we're back to that?"

There is no we. *There never was, not when it comes to my painting.* "I promised Chloe I'd do that show."

"I can't believe she asked you to paint, what? Eight pieces? And she'll probably just sell five or six. A total waste of your time!"

You're the one who's a total waste of my time. That's what I wanted to say. What I would say, as soon as I found a lawyer. I took a few steps back, away from him. Why did he always have to put me down? Why had I always allowed it? *Danny.* I heard myself sigh. It'd happened so long ago, it felt like forever. Time to move on.

"You should be out in the community. I'm glad you finally joined the Women's Club, but there are other clubs you can join, too," he was saying as I tuned back in.

Not in this lifetime! I'm resigning from the Women's Club, too. I told you that, not that you heard me, not that you ever do. I almost said that, too, until I realized I didn't care what my pervert soon-to-be-ex thought. I headed for my bedroom, then, relieved when he didn't follow. I let my breath out slowly as I turned on the light, shut the door behind me and slipped the lock into place.

I made the decision at 3:22 AM. *I'll fly down to North Carolina and stay with Jessica for a while.* Her beach house was the perfect place to heal—and paint. Until I remembered everything else on my agenda: find a lawyer, finish those two paintings and, most important, try to lose all that rage I'd been feeling ever since I'd seen those DVDs.

I got out of bed and looked in the mirror. *Claim your power,* I told myself. *Lots of time to go down to the Outer Banks and stay as long as you'd like, a week, a month. Forever.*

Enough to bring a smile to my lips. This time, I'll really do it, I thought as I finally drifted off to sleep.

***

It was a little after 10 the next morning when I got up, made myself some coffee and phoned Jessica.

“Hal hasn't gotten back to me yet. I’ll let you know as soon as he does. I can’t tell you how happy I am that you’re finally doing it!” She began to go on when her call waiting cut in and she promised to call me back.

I didn’t tell her about the DVDs, probably because I still couldn’t believe what I’d seen. Nor did I want to dwell on the fact that Rich was— I couldn’t give his behavior a name, let alone say it out loud. I didn't imagine Jessica would understand, either. Tomas had been a wonderful husband. Even her first husband Dennis only slept with one other woman. He didn't record it for posterity, either.

She called me back a few minutes later. “I love it down here! I'm going out with a realtor today to look at some business properties.”

"Great!" I was genuinely happy for her. “Who knows? When I get down there, maybe I’ll look for a place of my own.” I pictured the beach house of my dreams and smiled.

“Oh, I’d love it if you moved down here!”

“Me, too.” Could I really do it? *Maybe.*

I thought about Helen and the DVDs after we said goodbye. We needed to put them back. I’d call Jace after we did, omitting the B and E aspect of last night's adventure--as well as the fact that we'd watched those horrors. The phone rang. This time it was Helen. “Ready to put them back?”

I was still in my pajamas, about to have my second cup of coffee, but first things first. “Give me five minutes, okay?”

“No problem. Your husband’s at that meeting, too. He's finally going over the books with John and Ed, explaining his accounting system. John thought it'd take a while.”

Good!

Fifteen minutes later, we were coming out of Wendi's back door, minus the DVDs, when we spotted the black sedan with oversized side view mirrors pulling up in front of Wendi's house. An unmarked police car— Jace's car? I confirmed that when he got out, squared his shoulders and adjusted his tie, on duty today.

"Let me do the talking. Oh, and don't look guilty," Helen added softly as she leaned over to examine the rosebushes in back of Wendi's house. I'd plant mine in front, where they'd replace that awful Pampas grass.

I glanced at Wendi's roses. She'd favored exotic colors, lavender, a red so dark it was almost black and the palest of pinks. The roses I'd chosen were much more mainstream, red, yellow, white and coral.

"Wendi loved to brag about her roses," Helen murmured. "Loved to brag about everything."

She hadn't bragged about those Atlantic City trips or the jewelry Rich had probably bought her. If she did mention them, what would I have done?

Helen touched my arm. "Look at the roses. Don't look guilty," she repeated.

I felt my face heat up as I nodded.

"Don't ever play poker." She smiled.

Rich said that, too, years ago. I've always been a terrible liar. *You need to give it your best shot,* I told myself as Jace rounded the corner and my heart began to race.

"Ladies?"

Ladies, how condescending is that?

Helen just smiled. "Detective Connolly, how nice to see you. Amanda and I were just admiring Wendi's roses. They're heirloom plants, you know. They come from seeds that are over 100 years old."

Jace nodded. "Diane, my ex? She planted heirloom tomatoes one year." He looked down at Wendi's roses and frowned. "Gotta' say, those tomatoes were nothing special." He frowned some more, then, thinking of his ex? Was his divorce final yet? How could I find out?

He was looking at me now, looking through me. Again. I forced myself to meet the intensity of that crystal blue-eyed gaze. When I did, the look in his eyes sent the same heat down my spine it had the last time we were together. Then, when he smiled at me? It was all I could do not to throw myself into his arms and wrap myself around him.

Could Helen see it? I hoped not. "Wendi said we could take some cuttings. That was a few days before she died, wasn't it, Amanda?" She turned to me, confident Jace wouldn't notice anything amiss. Wrong! The man noticed everything.

She turned to face him. "No harm in doing that, is there?"

"We're all right with it, but you need to check with the person, or people who'll inherit this house," he replied evenly.

Too evenly. He suspected something, I wished I knew what. But he wasn't giving anything away as he took out his own key, unlocked the same door we'd just locked and went inside.

"We've got to tell him about the DVDs," Helen whispered as she turned to follow him in.

"I thought we were just going to show him that secret compartment and let him find them himself."

She didn't hear me, though, not when she was already inside. "Detective? Something else I think you should see." Jace came out to the kitchen as I stood in the doorway. I took a deep breath before I joined them and shut the door behind me.

Jace looked at her. And me. "What's that?"

"Wendi and I moved in right around the same time, when these houses were first built," she began.

"And?" He was striving for patience. I could see that but Helen didn't seem to notice.

"One day? She showed me this little compartment she had built in the big walk-in closet in her bedroom. She didn't say why she'd put it in, or what she planned to put in there."

"Helen doesn't know what's in there but we thought it might be important." I managed to get that out somehow even though, deep down, I felt like nervous adolescent. But I still wanted him to know I was there.

I was gratified when his expression softened as he turned to me and I felt more of that heat, his heat. "Care to show me where it is?"

"No problem," Helen replied before we followed her into Wendi's bedroom, and the big walk-in closet. "It's been a while, but as I remember, it's down here somewhere." She pointed to Wendi's shoe rack. "She was so proud of this closet! Hired this big New York City designer to do it. She paid over $10,000 for all these custom racks and drawers. I told her she could get the same components at Hardware Depot and have a handyman put them in, but Wendi? Always had to have everything her own way."

"You're sure about this compartment?" He knelt down and looked around.

Helen nodded as he ran his hands over the wall behind the shoe rack, slid the panel open, felt around and pulled out the DVDs. He stood up, then, looked at them and shrugged his shoulders. "I'll bring them in, take a look. Thanks," he remembered to add.

"DVDs? I can't imagine…" Helen looked so surprised, I could almost believe we'd never seen them before. But when I glanced at Jace, I felt sure he knew exactly what we'd done.

What to say? "You think maybe they'll provide some clues?" *Lame.* I knew that even as the words came out of my mouth.

"I hope so."

A brief but awkward silence followed as I worked up the courage to go on. "We were also wondering about those two clergymen, the ones who showed up at En Pointe." Was there any way he'd tell us anything about Wendi's first husband and son, or possible son?

"That investigation's still open, but just between us? It's unlikely they had anything to do with the murder. I can tell you we have the older man in custody. As for the younger one, we had to let him go."

A lot for him to say, but I would've loved to hear more. "The way they spoke that day, we thought they might've been related to Wendi," I ventured.

He nodded. "The older man claims to have been married to her at one time. We haven't found any legal record of that union yet. Beyond that? I can't comment."

He's just doing his job, I told myself. He was also waiting, however patiently, for us to leave. "Thanks again for your help." He flashed Helen a tight little smile. Then much to my relief, we were out of there.

Chapter Thirteen

"I watched the last DVD after breakfast this morning," Helen whispered, back at my house. Not that we needed to whisper. No one was in my house but us. There was just something so secretive about those DVDs. As awful as they were, I couldn't deny it, watching had been exciting.

"You're not going to believe this." She leaned in closer.

Try me. "What?"

"The last one? That was the main event, as far as I'm concerned-- Paige, Wendi, Steffi and Monica. Monica was the only one who kept her panties on."

"I guess she couldn't bear to part with the designer label."

"Maybe." She smiled. "Her hot pink lace bikinis were really something. You should've seen them."

I'm so glad I didn't. "Interesting…"

"Interesting?" She shook her head. "Hot! Hottest of 'em all, if you ask me. "

What could I say to that? Nothing.

***

A half hour later, I was on the Internet.

"Did you find it yet?" Helen asked again.

"No, but I'm getting close."

"Why don't you let me do it?"

"Give me a few more minutes, okay?" I didn't want Helen to take over, but maybe it was time. We were looking for the names of the two clergymen who'd burst in on Wendi's repast then been arrested. I'd found a list of everyone arrested in Brook Haven that day, but it only gave their names. Not much help.

Ten minutes later, I stood up, stretched and gestured her over to my laptop. She sat down, did a search for the date and the word *Reverend,* then looked up and smiled. "Got it!"

I moved in close enough to read the news item over her shoulder: *Reverend Willard Bailey, 76, minister of the Holy Redemptionist Church, Brookville, Kentucky, was apprehended by BHPD Detective Jason Connolly after breaking into the Eastpointe Country Club, smashing two liquor bottles and threatening guests attending a post-funeral repast. Bailey is wanted in Kentucky for arson, alleged to have set two fires. The fires destroyed one women's healthcare clinic in Brookville and another in New River.*

"My father is innocent," said his son, Bobby Joe Bailey, 45, who was taken into custody but later released.

"What next?" Helen tapped her fingers on the desk impatiently.

I had no idea, not that I wanted to tell her that. She'd been a huge help. I never would've found those DVDs, let alone watched, and copied them without her. But I still believed this was my case to solve, something that would've horrified Jace, if I was foolish enough to tell him. I was picturing him, and flashing back to that kiss, when we heard the key in the lock. I glanced at the clock. It was 12 noon. John was home for lunch.

"It got nasty, down at the clubhouse," he said as he helped himself to a cup of coffee—no single-cup coffeemaker for Helen! "Our esteemed Treasurer showed up, confident he'll be elected Association President next week,

God help us.“ He turned to me and sighed. “Sorry.”

“No problem.” *Not when I feel the same way.*

“But Warren? He's never been one to compromise.”

I nodded. “I’ve lived with him long enough to know that.” *Too long, much too long.*

“What happened?” Helen asked.

“When we told him about the problems we’ve been having with the way he keeps the books, he claimed he’s using a new system. Assuming that’s true, Ed and I both hope it is, it still doesn't explain why all that money's missing.”

Did he suspect Rich embezzled it? It sounded that way. I couldn’t imagine why he’d do that until I flashed back to Forestville, where he’d “borrowed” money from the Young Republicans, “because I can.”

Was it that simple, or had he needed it for those secret hotel suites, the jewelry he’d bought Wendi behind my back, blackmail payments?

“First, he explained his so-called system,” John was saying as I tuned back in. “When Ed and I, two retired CPA’s, couldn't understand it, he had the nerve to tell us it was probably too sophisticated for us.”

Sounds like Rich. No reason for me to stick around long enough to hear the rest, I decided as I stood up and headed for the door. “Got to go. I'll be back for my laptop,” I remembered to add.

Helen followed me. “What next?” she whispered.

I have no idea. “I’ll call you.”

In fact, the next step came to me a few minutes later, as I reread the news item about Willard Bailey. Since he was in jail right now, I felt sure he'd appreciate a visit, along with some nice homemade baked goods.

I knew just where to get them, too. The Upper Crust.

***

Brook Haven's Municipal Complex looked like a 19th century fishing village. It was only two years old, but it was historically correct, politically correct, architecturally correct, perfect in every way, something that made sense, in light of how much it'd cost to build this testament to Brook Haven's good taste.

I was thinking how nice it looked for a complex that housed the county jail, among other facilities, as I found a parking spot and reached for the basket of homemade baked goods and other goodies I'd picked up on the way over. I had a plan. Not a great plan, but it was the best I could do.

I went in, stopping long enough to admire the glass front doors etched with an elegant wave, sailboat and jumping fish design similar to the ones on the township's police cars. Artistic unity. Brook Haven couldn't survive without it. That thought that brought a smile to my lips— until I reminded myself I was here on business, serious business.

The doors to the jail were glass, too, plain glass surrounded by heavy iron bars. Somehow, though, they still managed to look elegant.

Focus, I told myself as I approached a stern-looking woman in an enclosed, most likely bulletproof booth. "I'm here to visit Willard

Bailey?" I didn't mean for it to come out as a question, but the woman, *Eleanor Burns*, according to her name badge, intimidated me. Not that I planned to let that stop me.

Helen would've done better. I forced that thought out of my mind. I needed to find out who'd murdered Wendi and what'd happened to Harvey even if I wasn't sure why I cared so much. Because it was Jace's case? Maybe. There was also the fact that Wendi was murdered the exact same way I'd fantasized doing it myself.

Harvey's disappearance was important, too. He'd gone missing the day after the murder. That's why there'd been so little publicity. The police didn't seem to have a clue as to where he was. On the other hand, they hadn't found his body yet, either.

Back to Wendi and the fact that she'd been sleeping with Rich. That had to fit in somewhere. *Don't think about Wendi. Think about Helen.* But when I did, I just felt guilty about not asking her along today.

"Photo ID?" Eleanor Burns' voice jolted me back to the present. I hated the way my hands shook as I took out my driver's license and passed it through the narrow slot beneath the window. She looked at it, then at me. "I need to make a copy of this. Amanda Warren?"

"Yes."

She got up, copied it and passed it back. "Why are you here to see Mr. Bailey?"

"I, um, represent the Brook Haven Acres' Women's Club?" I held up the basket from the Upper Crust and managed a tight little smile.

"A Women's Club?" She frowned.

"The Brook Haven Acres Women's Club," I repeated. *High time I got something out of all those meetings.*

"I see."

I was sure she didn't but she picked up her phone, entered a number and spoke to someone so softly, I couldn't hear a word. She turned back to me, then. "Have a seat."

Fifteen minutes later, a uniformed officer opened the glass and iron bar doors and gestured me to follow him. I did my best to remain calm as I followed him down a narrow gray corridor to one of several heavy iron doors, which he unlocked.

Willard Bailey was sitting at an old, beat up metal table in the small, windowless room. He looked at me with curiosity as I went in and the officer turned to lock the door, then stationed himself in front of it.

Calm down. I took a deep breath, crossed to the table and began to give him the basket when the guard moved in. "I need to check that, ma'am." He picked up the basket and began to take it apart, not that it mattered. Each item had been individually wrapped in Upper Crust logo cellophane.

Willard Bailey watched me, wondering who I was? I smiled. "I represent the Brook Haven Acres' Women's Club. We thought you might enjoy some homemade baked goods."

"How very nice of you, ma'am. Thank you kindly." He spoke softly, with a pronounced southern accent.

Who are you and what were you doing at Wendi's repast? That was what I really wanted to know. "I, uh, noticed you at Wendi Willis' repast last week." Impossible not to notice you, when you were yelling, screaming and trying to smash those liquor bottles. "I guess you must've known Wendi?"

"Wendi?" He laughed. "Ain't that something! That was our Winona for you, always putting on airs."

Winona? "I lived next door to her. My husband and I were fond of her." He was a lot more fond of her than I was, not that he needed to know that.

"Don't imagine she ever mentioned the likes of me."

I shook my head. "We wondered if you might be-- might've been related to her?"

"You could say so."

"I see," I replied even though really, I didn't. Was he going to tell me more? He was staring into space now. Remembering what it was like when Wendi had been part of his life? Only one way to find out. "May I ask how you were related?"

He nodded but he didn't reply, not right away. Time for another approach? "We didn't realize she came from Kentucky."

"Lotta' water under the bridge since that little gal left the holler. She was 16 the year we got hitched. Wasn't but three months later she took off. Waited till I went to work that morning. Then she called Elsie next door to watch Bobby Joe. After that? She was gone! Didn't tell nobody where she went, neither." He shook his head. "Hit me hard as a ton of bricks."

"Uh, Billy Joe, was he Winona's son?" I got that question out somehow.

I was relieved when he replied. "Claire, Billy Joe's mama? She passed on a couple weeks after he was born. Winona was my buddy Dwayne's daughter. Pretty little thing. When I asked her to marry me, she said yes—to get away from Dwayne. I knew it, but I didn't care." He frowned. "I needed a wife and Billy Joe needed a mama. Looked like it was working out, too, till the day she took off."

More than I'd expected? Definitely. More than I wanted to know? Absolutely. "I didn't know..." Assuming Wendi's father had been abusive, that would explain the way she supported the shelter.

"Winona never belonged with the likes of us." He frowned. "Had to have new clothes and furniture, a new stove and icebox, too." He sighed. "Only 16, but she had to have the best."

Sounds like Wendi.

"Just the way she was. She needed some fun, too. Not much of that, in the holler." His voice broke, then. Were those tears in his eyes? I looked at the door, the floor, anywhere but at him. My father'd cried when he had too many martinis. Rich never cried.

I took a deep breath. "So you decided to come up here when you found out she'd, um, passed away?" *Passed away* did sound better than *murdered.*

"Didn't know she'd passed on. Just came to talk to her."

"Oh, what did you want to talk to her about?" Not that it was any of my business, the reason I was okay with it when he didn't respond. I kept a close eye on him as I picked up my purse. He might be extreme in his beliefs, he might even be a criminal. But Wendi, aka Winona, broke his heart and he never got over it. I thought back to Danny and Rich and I understood. I sighed as I looked at him again. He could never have murdered Wendi. I knew that for a fact.

"Abortion is an abomination against our Lord God. Satan's work! We need to end it, right here, right now!" His voice pulled me back abruptly. "Burn every last one of those clinics down, I say!" He stood up and began to move toward the door. The guard was quick to grab him, take him back to the table and gesture him to sit down.

Time to go. I pointed to the basket. "Enjoy!"

He looked up, startled to see me there, before he recovered quickly. "Thank you kindly, ma'am," he murmured.

My pleasure? It's all right? Since I had no idea what to say, I smiled and left. Quickly. I let my breath out slowly as I reached the corridor and another guard came up to escort me out.

I saw Bobby Joe coming in when I got back to the waiting area. As much as I would've liked to talk to him, his father had worn me out. *Another time,* I told myself as I turned and spotted Jessica's lawyer Hal sitting on a bench in the hallway outside the courtroom. I was glad when he gestured me over. "Jessica told me a little about your problem."

I nodded, glad I hadn't told her about the DVDs and the way Rich pretty much starred in them. "I need to find a divorce lawyer who can deal with..." Did I have to spell it out?

He nodded sympathetically, feeling sorry for me? "We all know how tough Warren can be." He handed me a business card. "I think you should talk to Teresa Fortunato. Her ex was an attorney, too. She went to law school after she got burned, when she filed for divorce. If anyone can help you, it'd be her." He began to go on when the courtroom doors opened and the bailiff gestured him in.

"Thank you," I called after him. I ran my fingers over the card. Teresa Fortunato, a woman who'd walked in my shoes, my attorney's wife designer shoes. I put her card in my purse. *The debt is paid in full,* I told myself. I was thrilled when this time, I believed it.

I stood up, then, but instead of going out, I followed the arrow on the wall to police headquarters. Could I really work up the courage to go in there and talk to Jace? What would I say? The DVDs were the big coup, and Helen beat me to it.

He'd probably watched them by now. If he had, he knew what a fool I'd been all these years. An even more horrific possibility occurred to me: what if he'd watched them with someone else and what if that someone else was a woman? My cheeks began to burn as I pictured him and a female colleague watching those DVDs together, discussing them? Laughing?

Enough to stop me in my tracks. *Everyone on the force knows all about those DVDs by now.* That's what I was thinking as I stopped in front of the locked doors to police headquarters and saw another stern-looking woman posted in the glass-windowed cubicle next to them.

I was debating my next move when I glanced inside and saw Jace stand, to escort Cliff Richardson out. Wearing a suit and tie today, he stood out among all those uniforms. He is a detective, I reminded myself as he and Cliff came out. Neither of them looked happy.

I went over to the row of vending machines on the other side of the lobby and stopped by the coffee machine. *Is there anything worse than vending machine coffee?*

Yes. My marriage. I smiled as I took out some change, then moved down to the end of the row of machines, to get as close to them as I could. I caught a few words as they spoke, not that they were saying anything I didn't know.

"Wanna' know who hated Wendi?" Cliff frowned. "As manipulative, arrogant and overbearing as she was? I'd hardly know where to start."

Jace said something I couldn't hear before Cliff went on. "That purple pashmina? Of course it's important. The other women hated those things, even her so-called friends." He frowned. "That's where I'd start. Monica and Paige? They both look good to me."

Jace nodded and went on to say something about Steffi. Cliff shook his head. Interesting. Cliff and Steffi had looked, well, close on those DVDs. Not that he hadn't looked just as close to Paige, Monica, even Burt the dentist.

"We've already taken statements from her friends," Jace was saying now.

"Wendi didn't have friends, she took hostages."

Jace raised an eyebrow as Cliff turned to leave, and I turned back to the closest vending machine and stared blankly at the neat rows of different kinds of chips. If I didn't want Jace to notice me and the way I'd been eavesdropping, I needed to put in some change. I was putting the first coin in when I felt his hand came down on my shoulder. "You don't look like a corn chip kind of girl to me."

I turned and smiled-- into his eyes. They weren't crystal blue in this light. The color was closer to the sky on a brilliant autumn day. He smiled, a smile that was too close to laughter for comfort. Was he laughing at me because of what he'd seen on those DVDs? Maybe he was laughing because he knew what a fool I'd been, to stay with Rich all these years?

"What are you doing here, really?"

I struggled for a plausible reply. "I just came down to pay my property taxes."

He nodded doubtfully. "The Assessor's office is on the other side of the complex."

How did he know that? What did it matter? "I didn't know." What next? "We usually mail them in." A decent enough recovery? I hoped so. "Do you live in Brook Haven, too?" Not that I should be asking him that.

But it didn't seem to bother him, as he nodded. "I'm renting a little condo right now, but I grew up in Haven Shores, on the bay. Then when I got married, we had this house…" He stopped speaking abruptly.

A lot more than I'd expected, but I still couldn't help but push for more. "You raised your children here in Brook Haven?" Definitely none of my business.

He nodded again. "My daughter Kim started at the University of North Carolina this fall. That was her dream school. Her grandparents live in Durham, real close by." He frowned. "What are you doing here, really?"

Since he knew about Rich and the DVDs, I couldn't say anything about that. I wasn't about to discuss my visit to Willard Bailey, either. I focused on the vending machines and tried to convince myself I wasn't lying. Wendi's murder had upset me, at lot. "With everything that's been going on in my life right now…"

"Involving the victim?"

Like he didn't know? "It's complicated."

"I've got a few minutes. Why don't we talk in my office?" He put a hand on my shoulder, then, to escort me in? Whatever the reason, I couldn’t help but enjoy the heat he always seemed to radiate, as we went in.

I'd been in his cubicle before but I hadn't noticed the small framed photo on his desk--him with a beautiful little girl with black hair and eyes the same shade as his. His daughter, I thought. There were lots of papers on his desk today, too, more than I kept on mine. Did he have a system? He must, I decided as he moved some of them aside and offered me coffee from the machine on top of his file cabinet. He put some milk in it before he put it down in front of me. He remembered how I took my coffee.

I was impressed. “Thank you.” I took a sip. Perfect.

“Now do you want to tell me why you’re here?” He managed, somehow, to sound warm, friendly and firm all at the same time, enough for me to realize how good he must be at his job. Good enough to figure out who’d murdered Wendi. Without my help.

I looked in his eyes. *He knows everything, why you’re here, how you feel about him, what you’d like to do with him...*I felt myself blush as I began to speak. “Rich just wasn’t himself when he found out Wendi was dead.” As good a place to start as any, I told myself.

He looked me in the eye. “You think he was involved in the murder, don't you?”

I know he was involved with Wendi. Although Jace would know that, too, by now. “I have to wonder if he was.” I hesitated, “You spoke to him that day at En Pointe. What’d you think?” Not that I expected he'd tell me.

He sighed softly. “He didn’t say anything that would've made him a person of interest. As an attorney, though, he'd know exactly how to answer our questions without actually telling us much."

I understood perfectly. "You suspect he may've been involved, don't you?"

"That day, we felt satisfied that he wasn't. But everything can change as an investigation goes on." He shrugged his big, broad shoulders. "So, when's your next show?"

"My paintings?" What did that have to do with Rich, Wendi, the murder or anything else?

"I love that print, the beach scene with all those stars in the sky? I put it up it in my bedroom. Helps me relax."

His bedroom. Enough to send those hot little shivers down my spine again. "Chloe said you went up to her gallery a while back."

He smiled. "I bought two more prints, one of this path in the woods?"

I pictured it, another one of my favorites. "That was the park behind the house where we raised our daughter." The house I wished I'd never agreed to sell.

"The second was this great sunset over the mountains."

"I did that one from a photo I took in Asheville, North Carolina, the Smokies at sunset from the deck at the Grove Park Inn." Too much information? Maybe.

He leaned in closer, close enough to make my heart race. "She mentioned something about another show."

I nodded. "It'll be few weeks before Christmas, in the Soho gallery."

"I've been looking forward to it."

I nodded, shocked, after all those years with Rich. A man who liked my work enough to go into the city for my next show? Wonderful!

“Tell me, where do you get your inspiration?"

I could get all kinds of inspiration from you. A sigh escaped me. “Working artists can’t afford to wait for inspiration. We just sit down and do it.” *I will sit down and do it. Really.*

“About your next show? I didn't get the invitation. I thought she had my address.”

“I can double check.” I looked around. “You want Chloe to send it here?”

"No." He took out one of his cards and wrote his home address on the back. I tried not to be disappointed when he stood up, giving me no choice but to do the same. “In terms of your neighbor's death? If you have any information you think might help, feel free to give me a call.”

“I will.” Had he found out anything more about the murder or Harvey's disappearance? If he did, he wasn't saying a word about it. Ask him? Sometime, maybe. Not now.

Chapter Fourteen

The next day, I realized that when it came to Jace, and the murder, getting involved could definitely get, and keep me closer to him. But that wasn't the only reason I wanted to investigate. I couldn't help but feel Rich had been involved. I needed to know how, and why.

The Haven Players could be important, I thought. If I went to a rehearsal or two, that'd give me a chance to see them in action and find out more about the group's dynamics. Since Helen had been with them from the beginning, it made sense to ask her to go with me.

I was grateful she'd copied those DVDs. It didn't take me long to realize how valuable they might be when I filed for divorce, something I was finally ready to do. Rich's starring role in those X-rated horrors would've been enough, but that incriminating Amex bill sealed the deal. I'd called Teresa Fortunato's office at 9:00 this morning and made my first appointment. I was anxious about the prospect of meeting with her, but I managed to put it aside. Filing for divorce was that important.

It'd been 24 hours since I'd seen Jace and gotten my hopes up, not that I mentioned that to Helen when she phoned to ask if I'd found out anything new.

Going to a Haven Players' rehearsal was my best bet right now, I thought. They met at Joyful Spirit, a small and very liberal non-denominational church on the other side of town. When I checked out their website, I was glad to see they didn't burn down women's healthcare clinics or attack people who didn't agree with them. They preached tolerance, charity, peace and environmental responsibility instead.

They also sponsored support groups for parents of children who'd died, gays, people with addiction problems and singles, among others. In fact, there were so many different meetings at the church each night, it'd be no problem to blend in.

"Neal Benson, the minister? He wanted to be an actor," Helen said on the way over. "He majored in drama at Rutgers then actually tried to make it on Broadway for a while."

"How'd he end up as a minister?"

"He had a spiritual awakening and went back to school to study theology." Helen smiled. "He's got lots of stage presence. Gives a great sermon, too."

"I guess he would! Do you and John attend services there?" I didn't think they did, but we don't discuss religion much on the block.

"John was raised Catholic. My family was Methodist, so a church like Joyful Spirit works for us. We don't go there often but we enjoy it when we do. You should come with us some time."

"Maybe." I'd been raised in the Jewish faith, even though my mother and I only went to services on the high holy days. I'd stopped going when I'd hooked up with Rich, who made no secret of how much he hated organized religion. Just like Wendi.

Hypocrites. That's what Rich called the Presbyterians he and Nana Kate had worshipped with when he was growing up. It was the same word Wendi used to describe churchgoing people and their leaders, including Willard Bailey.

"What time is it?" Helen was asking now.

I checked my watch. “7:45.” The rehearsal started at eight. I wondered who’d be there. Helen made a point of telling me how Wendi had brought some of her Inner Circle friends into the company when I spoke to her yesterday.

“Paige and Steffi are regulars. I don’t know if they’ll stay with it, now that she’s gone,” she was saying now.

I asked if she’d heard anything about Harvey.

“Not a word." She frowned. "Harvey and I were a lot closer before Wendi came along.” She hesitated. “I still would’ve expected he'd get in touch.”

“I thought Cliff would take more time off, too, with Wendi gone and Harvey off the radar,” I ventured.

“Doesn’t look that way.”

Another reason to go, to try to find out more about Cliff. Right now, I knew next to nothing about his relationship with Wendi and the rest of the gang. The more I found out, the closer I could get to finding out who’d murdered Wendi.

I was also curious about who’d shot those DVDs and why the people in them may have agreed to be included, assuming they knew they were being filmed. I also wondered how they all got along off-camera. But the most important thing I hoped to find was a connection, any connection between the Players and the murder.

Cliff could be the killer. For all I knew, he could’ve killed Harvey too. No one knew where Harvey was or even if he was still alive. I also wanted to find out why Paige and Monica had always followed Wendi’s lead. How did she do that? Had her controlling ways been enough to motivate one or both of her so-called best friends to hate her?

"Left at the next light," I was glad when Helen's voice brought me back. I spotted the church as I made the turn.

***

"They replaced the auditorium seats," Helen whispered as we sat down in back. Onstage, Cliff was directing. He looked as good as he always did. In contrast to Harvey, who was short, dumpy and dressed in outfits that looked like they came from the final sale rack at DiscountMart, Cliff was tall, slender and perfectly coordinated. Tonight, his designer tan slacks and navy blue silk shirt fit like they'd been made for him. The ivory silk scarf he'd thrown around his neck added extra panache. Unlike most men, he had everything it took to carry it off.

"Back in character," he barked at Paige. "In *Menagerie*, you were the best. But tonight—" He began to go on when she rushed off the stage in tears. Her co-star, Burt the dentist, glanced at Cliff before they went off together, chatting as calmly as if nothing happened. What did that mean?

"Let's try that scene with you, Stef," Cliff said when he came back.

"The lead? Wow, thanks!"

Cliff smiled at Steffi as Burt turned to him."Steffi? Come on!"

Cliff shook his head. "She'll be fine."

"Just look at that little slut!" Helen poked me, not gently, in the ribs. I looked at Steffi, who was wearing jeans tight enough to look painted on. Thigh-high red stiletto heel boots and a tight red deep v-neck sweater completed her look.

“Okay, so her outfit is a little over the top. But that can't come as any surprise, after seeing her on those DVDs."

“You really think she’ll do okay?” Burt was asking Cliff, now.

“I’d do better.” That from Helen.

Don’t say a word! Billie Dawn, the female lead, was the beautiful mistress of a wealthy older businessman. Steffi might be a rookie but Helen was more than twice Billie’s age.

“I'd just need the right makeup,” she added softly.

In your dreams, I thought as I focused on the rehearsal. Steffi seemed to be doing an all right job. They rehearsed for 20 minutes before Cliff called for a break. Then, before I could remind Helen to keep a low profile, she went right up to Cliff. I hesitated before I followed.

“Helen? How wonderful to see you, darling!” He gave her a hug. “Do I dare hope you’re coming back to us?”

“I’d come back in a red-hot minute if I could play Billie Dawn.”

He hesitated. “Hardly the best showcase for an actress of your depth.” He smiled benignly. He had a great poker face, something that'd come in handy if you wanted to get away with murder. He didn’t seem distraught over Wendi’s death or Harvey’s disappearance, either.

I let my breath out slowly, glad Helen hadn’t mentioned the murder.

“I just need the right makeup to play that part,” she was saying now.

He looked a little stressed as he nodded. He would look stressed if he’d been the one who’d murdered Wendi or had anything to do with his life-partner's disappearance. “We still meet Thursday nights and Saturday afternoons.”

Helen began to reply when he cut in. “I know, we'll find you a nice solid character role.”

Helen began to protest when he turned to me. “Amanda? How lovely to see you, my dear. I didn’t realize you aspired to the theater.”

Neither did I, till Wendi's body turned up on the curb. “Just exploring some possibilities.” *And trying to find out more about you.* I managed a smile as Cliff put his hand on my shoulder and I realized how strong he was, strong enough to strangle Wendi and slash her purple pashmina in two with that big, curved-blade African hunting knife. How would he have gotten hold of it? And, assuming he was the killer, how had it ended up in my garage?

“There aren’t any mature female roles in this play. ” Helen frowned.

“No reason one of the politicians can't be female,” he replied smoothly. “Just imagine, power, public recognition—the perfect showcase for a talent as big as yours.”

“I guess I could give it a try. Saturday afternoon?”

He nodded, then turned to me. “There's a good little part for you, too, if you’re interested. Four scenes, just a few lines each.”

I hesitated. “Sounds like fun.” *With Chloe’s deadline hanging over your head, are you crazy?* Maybe, but it'd be a great way to gather more information about who killed Wendi, information I could share with Jace, a perfect excuse to see him again.

Moments later, Steffi and Burt were running through their lines again when Cliff took Burt aside and spoke to him quietly--and I realized Paige had never come back.

"I have no idea why Cliff cast Burt in that part. That man? He has no dramatic presence whatsoever." Helen frowned.

"Looks like he's doing okay." *Almost as well as he did in those DVDs.*

Helen pointed to Cliff, still talking to Burt. "Maybe he got the part because Cliff likes him, if you know what I mean?"

I didn't.

She sighed. "Cliff's teeth? Look at them."

I glanced at Cliff, who was smiling now. Enough for me to see how white and perfect his teeth looked.

"Burt's a cosmetic dentist. Cliff never had bad teeth, but tonight?" She shook her head and smiled.

"Maybe he went to Burt as a patient."

"Right! And maybe he didn't have to pay one red cent."

"You think Burt's, like, gay? But he's a dentist." A far cry from an interior designer. Or a theatrical director.

"I think it's a definite possibility," she replied. "I would've expected Cliff to be more upset over Wendi's death and Harvey's disappearance, too. He's not, in case you didn't notice."

"I did. But he and Harvey? They're married."

She shrugged her shoulders. "Straight, gay or AC-DC, men are men. And sensitivity? It's seldom their strong suit."

True, except for Jace? I could hope.

***

"We didn't learn much," Helen said as we went back to my car. I looked around for Paige's car but it didn't surprise me when it wasn't there.

Helen gasped as I took out my keys. “Look!” She pointed to my front tires. “Flat as pancakes. Somebody slashed them!” She went around to check the back. “All four of them.”

I called the auto club and wondered if I should call Jace.

“If you don’t call him, I will,” Helen said as we went back into the church. “When he comes out to investigate, he can give us a lift home.”

He’s a detective, not a car service. “I guess I could call him.”

She nodded and took his card out of her purse. She was taking out her phone when I got mine out first and entered his number. She smiled. “I knew it," she said as I waited for him to answer. “You and that big, hunky guy…” She kept smiling as the call went to voicemail. I was relieved when he called me back a few minutes later and said he was on his way.

He got there about 15 minutes later. Wearing jeans and an old gray NYPD sweatshirt, I knew I’d gotten him out of bed. I pictured him there, and felt myself begin to blush. *Stop it!*

He was looking at my tires and frowning. “Cancel the auto club.”

Giving me orders? High-handed, but I was the one who'd called him. I could see how upset he was, too. “Why?” I asked.

He just rolled his eyes. “Just do it. Please,” he added, as he turned away and barked some orders into his phone before he turned back to us. “They'll be here shortly, to tow your car into the lab.”

"The police lab? You really think it's that important?"

"Could be related."

"To Wendi's murder?"

"I'm not at liberty to say."

Thanks a lot, Mr. Lead Detective!

The BHPD tow truck pulled in 20 minutes later. I watched them hook up my car and tow it away. "I'll drive you home," he said after they were done, the first good thing he'd said tonight.

"Thank you," I replied coolly--and wished Helen wasn't here. *Get over it. You're married and he's, well, pushy.* Two things that didn't bother me nearly as much as I might've expected.

We were in his car, an older silver Toyota, when he asked if we had any idea who could've slashed my tires. Paige was the first one who came to mind. "She was there tonight until—"

"Cliff criticized her performance and she left in tears," Helen cut in.

"She did look upset." I pictured her running out to the parking lot. Where she'd slashed my tires? Why?

He frowned. "It looked to me like they'd been slashed with some kind of heavy-duty knife. I don't know that it could've been done by a woman."

"Paige works out at Heavenly Bodies a few times a week," I offered.

He shook his head.

"You think it was a man?"

"It had to be a man." That from Helen. I fought the urge to tell her to shut up. Then I wondered where Rich was right now and realized I had no idea. As usual.

"You're thinking it might be Amanda's husband, aren't you?" Helen asked Jace, reading my mind?

"I'm not sure where he is tonight."

"Never is, poor thing."

Shut up, Helen!

We were at the Acres' gatehouse now. He flashed his badge, drove in and turned to me. "Call me tomorrow. I'll let you know what's happening with your car."

I nodded. Minutes later, in Helen's driveway, I told him how Cliff hadn't seemed upset tonight. Strange, in light of Wendi's death or Harvey's disappearance.

"He wouldn't be upset about Harvey, though, not when he has a new squeeze," Helen offered. "His teeth looked fabulous, too."

"His teeth?" I was gratified when Jace looked confused.

"Burt Davidson's a cosmetic dental specialist," I explained.

He nodded slowly. "He was on those DVDs, too."

I nodded. "Helen thinks he and Cliff might be involved, which would give them motive. Though everyone who appeared on them would've had motive, too."

"I knew you watched them." He smiled.

"Of course we did," Helen piped up from the back seat.

He turned to me and sighed softly. "I'm sorry you had to see that."

"It's okay." *Not!* I was still upset, but the last thing I wanted him to think was that I was weak.

I was wondering what else I could say when Helen spoke again. "Amanda took a quick look. I watched them all."

He frowned. “Me, too. I had them make copies before I put the originals back, too. We're keeping an eye on the victim’s house in case anyone tries to break in and take them.”

Good thing you weren’t keeping an eye on it the night we broke in.

“Good idea,” Helen replied.

Jace smiled. “Glad you approve.”

I was glad when Helen didn’t say anything more before she thanked him for driving us home and said goodnight. I glanced over at my house. Rich’s SUV was in the driveway and the lights were on in the den. He was watching TV-- news, sports, I was way past caring.

“Going home?” Jace indicated my house and looked at me with— sympathy? I hoped not.

“I guess.”

He hesitated before he nodded, my cue to get out. Not that I wanted to, not when I felt so safe with him. I was reaching for the door handle when he leaned across, pulled me close and kissed me, a kiss that segued from warm to hot quickly as I responded with passion, more passion than I’d ever felt with Rich. *Maybe it wasn’t me, all these years.*

I sighed as he pulled away. As much as I would’ve loved to keep kissing him, I was still a married woman. And we were parked in Helen’s driveway, where anyone could see us, including Rich, if he tore himself away from the TV long enough to get up and look out the window.

“I’m sorry.” He let his breath out slowly. “I don’t know what got into me.”

“I don’t care what got into you.” Did I really just say that?

"I kissed you right here in your neighbor's driveway."

Was he upset, about the fact that he'd just kissed me, or was it his divorce? "Your divorce was just finalized, right?" Too forward? Maybe.

He hesitated. "Yes, but we'd been separated a while before I filed."

How long? Not that I could ask.

"Three years," he murmured. "I haven't had more than a couple dates, all that time. Just not ready, I guess."

You were ready tonight. "I see."

"Do you?" He kissed me again. It was quick, this time, but just as, well, intense. And passionate. I was crushed when he let me go. "You don't want to go home tonight, do you?"

I hesitated. *What if Rich saw me kissing you,* I thought, then, *what if it was Rich who slashed my tires?*

"You think your husband might've slashed your tires, don't you?"

Reading my mind again? I nodded. "I can't imagine why."

"Anything's possible. Look, is there any place else you can stay tonight, with a friend, maybe?"

I glanced at Jessica's house. "Jessica's out of town. I have her key, but—"

"What?"

"Don't you think it's a little paranoid for me to stay at her house?"

"Nothing paranoid about staying safe." He hesitated before he took my hand. I fought the urge to throw myself into his arms and kiss him. "Amanda?"

I forced myself to meet his gaze. "I could stay there, but if Rich was the one who slashed my tires, why would he have come home tonight?"

He shrugged his shoulders. "Because he thinks he's too smart to get caught, maybe."

Sounds like Rich. A sigh escaped me. "I was also thinking about Cliff and Burt. Assuming the two of them are, y'know, involved? You think that could be related to Wendi's murder or Harvey's disappearance?"

"Do you think they're involved?"

"I don't know Cliff that well, but Helen does and she felt sure they were."

"What do you think?" he repeated.

"Cliff and Harvey went up to Vermont to get married . They always seemed close at Wendi's gatherings--she used to call them soirees."

"Figures." He smiled.

I smiled back. "About Harvey and Cliff—"

"They were together almost two years as a married couple and five or six years before that." He hesitated. "The thrill could've been gone." He looked off into the distance and frowned, thinking about his own marriage?

"I can relate."

"Yeah, me too." He hesitated before he took my hand and began to run his fingers over my wrist, then my palm, sending hot little tremors of pleasure through my body, pleasure I didn't have any right to feel. I was disappointed when he let go. "Cliff and Burt talked to each other a lot tonight. Privately," I added. "You plan to question Burt?"

"I guess I should."

"Cliff offered me a little part in *Born Yesterday,* too. I said yes." Because I thought it might help me find out who'd murdered Wendi, not that I planned to tell him that.

"I didn't realize you were interested in acting. I figured you were a full-time painter."

I should be a full-time painter. "I thought it might be fun."

He nodded thoughtfully, then looked me in the eye. "Where are you going to stay tonight?"

I'd love to stay with you. "I guess it'd be okay for me to go home."

He looked almost like he was about to kiss me again when he sat up taller and nodded. "I'll keep an eye on you till you get inside. Call if you need me, I mean it."

"I will." I got out, crossed the street and went into the house that no longer felt like home, the house that'd never felt like home, really.

The slashed tire business, that was the most important thing that happened tonight, I told myself.

I wished I believed it.

Chapter Fifteen

I heard the blare of the TV from the front door. Rich was watching the news in the den. Ironic that he should be home tonight. All the years I cared what time he got home, he was always late. Ever since I stopped caring, he'd come home early enough for me to have to see him. *You won't be with him much longer.* I'd meet with Teresa Fortunato soon. I expected it'd go well, especially in light of those DVDs.

I heard him talking on the phone as I went into the den. He looked up, startled to see me. "Got to go," he said, then ended the call quickly. Who was he talking to? Wendi was dead and Harvey was missing, but the rest the gang was alive and well.

And he'd been secretive about that call, even for him. He was getting up now, crossing the room and giving me a chaste kiss on the cheek, a kiss I couldn't help but compare to Jace's.

I forced myself not to recoil. *I'll file for divorce and find peace, serenity, maybe even a nice little house by the ocean.* I pictured a little white house with character, an ocean view and a sky-lit studio perfect for painting.

"I wondered where you were," he was saying as I tuned back in. Was there the slightest chance he cared?

No, and don't forget it! "Helen and I went to a Haven Players' rehearsal at Joyful Spirit." I took a deep breath. I needed to lie and I needed to do it well enough for him to believe me. "I auditioned for their next production. The director—"

"Cliff?"

I nodded. *You know Cliff. You made love with him on two of those DVDs.* "He offered me a part."

"You didn't take it, I hope. You don't have time, with Women's Club meetings, our other social obligations and those paintings you insist on doing."

Thanks for all that attitude! "We don't have many social obligations till the Holidays." *And maybe not then, with Wendi dead.*

"What about all those other groups you promised to try?"

"What groups?"

He sighed dramatically. "We discussed this."

"I remember. I also remember I told you, I'm resigning from the Women's Club. The show is my top priority right now." I turned to head for the kitchen, as he—exploded.

"Resigned? You never said a word!"

Oh yes I did! No reason to argue about it, though. *I hate the Women's Club.* That's what I would've said if I didn't have one foot out the door. And if they didn't find Wendi's killer by next month's meeting, I might go one more time to try to come up with more clues. "I might go to one more meeting," I murmured as I took a bottle of water from the fridge, uncapped it and took a sip.

Rich looked down at me. "We do have glasses."

When did our kitchen become formal? I almost asked him that, but he was heading back to the den, now, to watch the news, or maybe make another secret phone call. Whatever he planned to do? I couldn't care less.

***

I met Teresa Fortunato four days later and liked her right away. Anxious about the meeting, I drove down the local road that ran along the ocean from Brook Haven to Seaview Pines. I hoped it would help me relax.

I would've asked Jessica to come with me, if she was home. I could also have asked Helen. We'd gotten closer this week. She was happy with the role Cliff had rewritten for her. He'd assigned me the 10-line role of a high-profile U.S. Senator's wife. "You look the part," he said. Of course I did. Wasn't an Important Man's Wife the same role I'd played most of my life?

The *Welcome to Seaview Pines* sign brought me back. *You're really going to do this,* I didn't think her office would be hard to find. Seaview Pines is tiny, just a mile or two along the shore. I slowed down as I reached the quaint little shopping area, where I expected her office to be.

It turned out to be another mile down the road. It wasn't in an office building, either. It was one of a row of summer bungalows that'd been remodeled for year-round use. I liked the sign, too, her name in silver letters on a background the color of the ocean on a cold winter day.

My hands trembled a bit as I picked up the envelope with our tax returns, other legal papers and Rich's secret Amex statement. Helen had hidden the DVD copies in her sock drawer. I wished I'd asked her along as I went in.

The waiting room reminded me of the beach, with its bright blue and yellow color scheme, seashell accents and driftwood-base coffee table. Almost enough to ease some of that tension.

You can do this, I told myself as a short, curvy woman with curly golden brown hair came out. “Mrs. Warren? I’m Teresa.” We shook hands, then she gestured to the empty receptionist's desk. “Gina, my assistant? She's still at lunch.”

I nodded. I still felt a little shaky as I followed her into her office, where the same blue and yellow color scheme relaxed me a little, as did the fact that it was filled with an unlikely combination of files, law books and family photographs, lots of them.

“I know how nervous you must be right now, Mrs. Warren.”

“Call me Amanda. Please.”

“Okay, Amanda. Let me assure you, nerves are the norm at this point, especially in light of the fact that your husband's an attorney, like my ex.”

“Hal said something about that.”

She nodded. “We’d been unhappy for a while, but he was a divorce lawyer. Daunting,” she added as she sat down at her desk and gestured to the client chair. “It was my divorce experience that motivated me to go to law school."

“Yes, Hal said that.”

She nodded. “In terms of your divorce, I’ll do everything I can to make it as simple and painless as possible.”

I began to thank her when Gina, her assistant, came in. It didn't take me long to realize she was the grandmother in those family photos, a warm, loving grandma.

A good thing.

***

An hour later, I wasn't so sure. I also wished I'd brought someone with me. Helen would've been perfect. I was sure, absolutely certain I wanted to divorce Rich and free myself to paint, travel, live my life the way I wanted and maybe even get involved in another relationship, in time.

I pictured Jace in his jeans and NYPD sweatshirt the other night. He'd looked so handsome and rugged, and his kisses? Heavenly. *Much too soon to go there,* the sensible part of me said. I needed time before I got involved in a new relationship. But Jace was just so special.

Teresa's voice pulled me back as she began to discuss money. I hadn't considered the material side of the equation yet. No surprise there. I'd never been into material things. I'd grown up in a modest household, but these days? It was hard to remember the days when I'd needed to watch my pennies. Enviable? Maybe, but here in Teresa's office, the prospect of focusing on the monetary aspects of the settlement upset me, especially after I signed her legal agreement and wrote her a retainer check from my personal account, the same one I'd used to fund Katie's MBA.

Katie would be using that check soon to register for her MBA courses and buy her books. As for this check? I hoped it'd help me fulfill my dreams, too.

Ironically, it was Rich who'd suggested I keep the money from my artwork in a separate account. "The amount you bring in won't make a difference in our finances," he'd said. "I think you should have your own account, too, just in case."

He'd just made junior partner, something he could never have done if I hadn't supported our household when he'd gone to law school. I was still taking care of Katie and doing freelance commercial art from home, at that point, and not complaining, either.

I'd opened my own account the next day and kept it going all these years. The earnings from my artwork had accumulated nicely, enough for me to help Katie with plenty left over to cover my legal fees, that little house on the ocean and whatever else I might want or need.

"The State of New Jersey requires all assets accumulated in a marriage be distributed evenly. I expect this case to go smoothly, but we still need to spell out how much you'll need for living expenses."

I started to reply, then stopped. Rich took care of the bills, the reason I didn't know how much I'd need.

"I can help you arrive at that figure, if you'd like."

I began to panic. Could she see it? I hoped not.

"Many of my clients say they want it all." She smiled, then, enough to ease a little of my anxiety.

It will all work out. I needed to believe that. I took a deep breath. "My freedom's a lot more important to me than money."

"I understand, but you and your husband have accumulated substantial assets as a couple. Half of it belongs to you. And the fact that he's done something egregious? That can only help."

Egregious? "Something bad?"

I was thankful when she nodded. "More so, if he knew he was being filmed. You said you're not sure?"

"Right." Nor did I have any idea how I could find out.

"Assuming he did know, and in light of the fact that he committed adultery with multiple partners, 99 out of 100 judges would give you everything you ask for. Not that I think you'll end up in court," she added.

"You think he'll want to settle?"

She smiled. "He'd be crazy not to. If those DVDs ever went public? It'd destroy him."

Why didn't I think of that?

"That's why you need to decide how much money you'll need. Consider the kind of home you'd like and the lifestyle you have in mind. It also needs to be enough to cover your monthly bills, health, vehicle and home insurance, and don't forget incidentals." She paused, waiting for me to respond? "We can arrive at that figure together," she repeated. "In this case? I'm almost certain we'll get it."

I let my breath out slowly. Monthly bills, insurance, the house of my dreams and the lifestyle I wanted? Confusing, except for the house. I pictured that little beach cottage again and sighed.

"Any questions, Amanda?" she asked.

I nodded. "I've always wanted to live by the ocean. I wouldn't need a big house, but I'd love an older one with character. Oh, and a studio with skylights, too."

She made a note of it. "You'll need enough money to buy and maintain that house, along with the rest of your lifestyle."

A lifestyle that'd cost a lot less than the one Rich had always insisted on. Say that or keep it to myself?

"Why don't you go home, write it all down and bring it in next time?"

"Okay." *Terrifying!*

I was glad she looked so cool and confident. "My clients are always anxious at this point. They get over it. You will, too."

I did my best to believe that.

"Where are those DVD copies, by the way?"

"Helen made two sets. They're both at her house."

Teresa suggested I put one set in a safe deposit box and bring the other one here to her office. I ran several possible replies through my head: *good idea, thank you, I'll do that?*

"Meanwhile? I'll start the paperwork."

***

The next day, I rented a safe deposit box in a small bank in Seaview Pines, safely away from Brook Haven, and Rich. I put one set of the DVDs and photocopies of those papers in there before I drove down to her office to give her the other set.

If those DVDs ever got out, it'd destroy him. I repeated that mantra all the way down to Seaview Pines. Wendi was dead but the rest of her Inner Circle was alive and well. There were six DVDs featuring 10 people doing lewd things, so lewd, some of them might even be illegal.

I thought about the possibility of blackmail again. Was Wendi the one who'd had them shot secretly, planning to blackmail her so-called friends? Or maybe someone else had shot them,, planning to blackmail them all.

Was Jace still investigating? Probably. It was his case. How good a detective was he, in light of that fiasco back in New York City? Not that his past, or that mistake was any of my business.

Let him find the killer. Concentrate on the divorce and your painting, I told myself as I pulled up in front of Teresa's office. Freedom and a little house on the ocean with a well-lit, year-round studio space. That's what I wanted. I didn't need to find Wendi's killer to get it.

Why had I ever wanted to find the killer, I asked myself as I went in and caught the scent of amaretto. I glanced at Gina's desk and smiled when I spotted the plate of cookies accented with pine nuts and dusted with confectioner's sugar. "They smell delicious." Even more so, when I'd just had coffee this morning.

"I baked a couple of batches last night. Help yourself."

I smiled, took one and resisted the temptation to take a handful.

"My grandmother's recipe." Gina smiled as Teresa came out and helped herself to some cookies, too. "Aunt Gina bakes the best cookies!"

I had to agree.

Ten minutes later, the DVDs were in Teresa's office safe and I was back in my car.

"Don't worry, it'll all work out," she said. Despite my sadness about the end of my marriage, despite the realization that I'd allowed guilt to keep me with Rich a lot longer than I should have, despite my regrets over the fact that I hadn't painted more, I felt good. I was confident Teresa would get it done, too, enough to keep me happy—until the Association election the next day.

***

"Don't forget to vote," Rich reminded me when he came home around 11 that night. I was glad I wouldn't be seeing much of him tomorrow. He planned to be at the polls when they opened at 7 AM. After that, he'd go to his office.

"Your vote could make a difference," he added, frowning. His initial certainty that he'd defeat Ed Cullen had given way to enough doubt to surprise me. *Fiscal Responsibility First* was Ed's campaign slogan. It was neither slick nor catchy, but it seemed to resonate with the people who lived here.

Rich's slogan, *The Best for Brook Haven Acres,* hadn't gone over nearly as well. Everyone expected it to be close.

"Amanda, did you hear me? The election's tomorrow and--" Rich wasn't giving up, apparently.

"I'll vote when I get the time. I promised Chloe—"

"More paintings? Hard to forget, when that's all you talk about."

Good thing we don't talk much. "I will vote, okay?" Teresa had emphasized the importance of choosing my battles. I couldn't afford to stress out over the little things.

"Good." Rich smiled, something he wouldn't have done if he knew I planned to vote for Ed. An hour later, in the clubhouse, I realized Rich hadn't gone to work when he came up to me as I dropped my ballot in the box and kissed me on the cheek. "Smile," he whispered as someone took our picture. "My victory picture, for the media," he added as they took another shot.

I hope not!

The results weren't final till 3:00 the next day. Rich had won by 23 votes, the reason he'd come home early. "We're celebrating," he informed me. "I made reservations at that Thai place, your favorite."

My favorite, when I hadn't even voted for him? It made no sense, Not that I was complaining, I loved Thai. Nor was there any way he'd ever find out I voted against him.

"We're meeting the others in half an hour."

"The others?" My heart sank.

"Jim and Paige and Pete and Monica."

At least they'll have their clothes on tonight.

At dinner, I focused on my Pad Thai with lobster, crabmeat, shrimp and scallops, as Rich began to discuss the official victory dinner he'd planned for next Friday evening. "I reserved the Waterview Room at En Pointe, the perfect venue," he announced over the sweet rice dessert I was sharing with Paige.

"The same place where Wendi's funeral repast was held?" I asked.

"I don't see what difference it makes." He began to go on when Monica cut in.

"He said the Waterview Room, dear." Her tone of voice was even sweeter than my rice. Cloyingly sweet.

"Wendi's repast was in the Bayview Room," Paige added, looking down her nose at me. It took the edge off my dessert but I managed to finish my half anyway.

That wasn't the case the night of the victory dinner, when I couldn't eat a thing. Rich had invited more than 80 people. "Everyone who supported me," he said as the manager handed back his Amex and told him the Waterview Room was set up for 85 guests.

I could see how disappointed he was when only 56 people showed up. I was even more surprised when I saw how few of them were Acres' residents. Burt Davidson was there with his trophy wife Kayla. Rich's golf buddy Judge Robertson was there too, with his wife. Cliff was there with Steffi, but Harvey was still missing. As far as I knew, no one had a clue where he was or what might've happened to him.

"We're focusing on the homicide," was all Jace would say. I'd asked him about when he'd phoned a few days ago to make sure I was all right.

I was not glad, tonight, when I asked Rich why he'd invited all those outsiders and he changed the subject. "Why don't you call some of your friends? Jessica might like to come, maybe Helen and her husband, too."

Jessica's out of town, something you'd know if we ever talked to each other. As for John and Helen, they hate you. I would've loved to say that, but I knew it'd be better to just agree, then excuse myself to make those two imaginary phone calls.

My poker face was coming along. Now that Rich was Association President, he'd be home less than ever, too, giving me more time for my painting, the divorce, maybe even figuring out who'd murdered Wendi. I wasn't sure why I still felt such a strong need to do that, but it wasn't going away.

***

The next day, I felt confident about having retained Teresa, but I was finding it hard to dispel the sense of doom I'd been feeling ever since last night's dinner. Some of that tension eased a bit when I forced myself to paint. My next show was three weeks away. I'd shipped two more paintings up to the gallery last week. I was glad when Chloe called to say how much she liked them. "I realize this is a lot to ask, but is there any way you could do one or two more paintings?"

I smiled as I glanced at the two paintings I'd been working on, almost finished now. "I've got two more paintings right here in front of me. They'll be finished by the end of the week."

"Wonderful!"

I thought so too. Painting eased my mind these days. Oddly enough, Rich wasn't complaining, either, not that he was home often enough to complain. In fact, I saw so little of him, there was no way he'd know how I was spending my time.

I still wondered what he might be doing when he wasn't home, but when I asked Teresa for her take on it, she advised me to focus on the divorce. "Everything's right on schedule. You say your painting's going well, too," she pointed out. "As for your husband, whatever he dishes out, we'll handle it."

I did my best to believe her. I'd finally come up with the amount of money I planned to ask for and she'd completed the paperwork. I just needed to tell her when to serve him.

"Some of my clients tell their spouses they intend to file before we serve them," she said at our last meeting. "Unless there's abuse."

"No abuse," I replied, then began to wonder what constituted abuse. Rich had never raised a hand to me, but in all the years we'd been together, I'd always, just, well, mattered less than he did. My fault? Partially.

If we ended up in court, how would the judge see it? Rich did save me from rape, back in the day. And a few years later, if he wasn't passionate about marrying me, he'd done it anyway. After he finished law school and passed the Bar, his hard work and success enabled us to buy and maintain a nice house, a country club membership and good schools, a rounded schedule of extracurricular activities and a top-notch college for Katie. His earnings also gave me the option of painting full-time.

How could any judge find fault with that, especially if the judge in question turned out to be Rich's golf buddy and sometime friend, Edgar Robertson?

Not that I didn't believe Teresa, who felt sure we'd never end up in court. Thanks to those DVDs, Rich would agree to my demands and pay up promptly-- unless he managed to come up with some kind of secret attorney trump card, unlikely but not impossible, she admitted.

The sound of Helen blowing her horn brought me back. She was driving to rehearsal tonight. My car was still at the police lab.

Chapter Sixteen

I hadn't known what to expect when Jace said he'd get back to me after they'd gone over my car, but four days later, it was still at the police lab. I hadn't called him, but I still wanted to know who'd slashed my tires. I felt sure, somehow, it'd been related to Wendi's murder.

I wanted my car back for practical reasons, too. The only rental they had was a big, gas-eating SUV. I hated driving it. Time to call him, I decided the morning after rehearsal.

"I meant to get back to you, but things have been crazy down here," he said, carefully omitting what, if any of that insanity might've had to do with Wendi's murder. He did say they'd confirmed the fact that my tires had been cut more than ten times each, most likely with a knife. Unusual, he'd added. "We'll get it back to as soon as we can. Oh, and don't forget, you'll need four new tires."

"Okay." What else could I say?

"The perp, or perps? They used a heavy-duty knife."

"Like the one I found in my garage?"

"Not exactly. Your tires were slashed with a straight-edge knife. The one in your garage had a curved blade. Do you remember if the other one was a straight-edge?"

I pictured the night Pete and Jim showed them off. "Yes, definitely."

"Do you remember whose knife that was?"

I tried, but all I could remember was how bored I'd been.

"Amanda?"

"Why would Pete or Jim slash my tires?"

"No idea, but we're working on it."

Vague, but there was still something sweet about him. That was why I loved him. *Love,* when I'd practically just met him? I was still married, too, at least in the eyes of the law.

"We'll speak to them both. Whoever did it was strong. We didn't find any fingerprints or fibers, either."

"Nothing?"

"No, but from the size and angle of those cuts? Whoever did it was probably..."

"What?"

"Angry."

I pictured Pete and Jim. "I've never seen Pete or Jim get angry." Hard to imagine either of them could've done it— until I realized anyone in those DVDs would go crazy if they were afraid they might go public.

"It was not a random act," Jace was saying, now.

I realize that. "What about Rich?" Not that I wanted to ask.

He hesitated. "We'll speak to him. As for the other people in those DVDs, do you know if any of them hunt?"

"No. And really, I don't know anyone who hunts. Even that African safari Pete and Jim and their wives took? It was a photo safari."

"How 'bout Harvey and Cliff?"

"They belong to PETA. They're vegetarians, too, like Wendi is, I mean, was."

"I guess neither of them would own a hunting knife." I could almost hear him frown. "Hold on?"

"Okay." I wondered who he was talking to as I waited. And waited.

"Amanda? That was one of the techs. They're finished with your car. I can drop it off in an hour or so, if that's okay."

"That'd be great." I let my breath out slowly. I had mixed feelings about the fact that he was coming over. On one hand, I couldn't wait. On the other, I was married. There was also the possibility, however slight, Rich might come home.

I sighed as I looked out the window. Helen's Buick was in her driveway. I called and invited her over, as much for safety's sake as anything else. I was glad when she agreed. We discussed Wendi's murder over coffee and some Upper Crust cookies in the kitchen. "He asked if Harvey and Cliff hunted, you mean like animals?" She laughed.

I nodded. "My tires were slashed with a straight-edge hunting knife. I told him about the knives Pete and Jim brought back from Africa. He plans to speak to them both."

She nodded. I wished I could come up with something, anything that'd help him figure out who'd destroyed my tires and, even more important, who'd murdered Wendi. I was still wondering what'd become of Harvey, too. Not that I liked him, particularly, but it was just so strange, the way he'd disappeared right after the murder.

"What did Rich have to say about the tires?" Helen asked.

"Not much."

"He wasn't upset?"

I shook my head. "I thought that was odd, too. He's really into material things."

"And he wasn't surprised when you told him?" She hesitated. "He wouldn't be, though, not if he was the one who did it."

I frowned. "I considered that possibility, but if Rich wanted my tires slashed, he'd never do it himself. He'd hire someone." *Unless Pete or*

Jim offered to do it for free. “I wish I could remember if it was Pete or Jim who brought back the straight-edge knife.”

“And bragged about it, that's what you said."

I nodded. “Jace will talk to them. He’s bringing my car back, too. I can’t wait to return that SUV.”

“Can’t wait to see that gorgeous hunk again, either, I'll bet." She smiled. “Don’t do anything I wouldn’t do,” she added as she checked her watch and stood up. "Got to go."

Really? I might've tried to stop her, but on some level, I did want to be alone with Jace.

The BHPD tow truck pulled up 15 minutes later. I went out to meet Jace, who got out and gave me some papers to sign. I took a deep breath before I invited him in. He checked his watch and nodded. A few minutes later, we were having coffee, along with the rest of those cookies, in my kitchen. “I’m glad I arranged to keep the SUV another few days. I almost forgot about the new tires.”

“You have a place where you buy them?”

"We always go to the dealer.” Rich's idea. Time for a change? Maybe.

Jace put his cup down and frowned. “I've got this garage I use, but I guess you'd want to check with your husband.”

Not anymore. I fought the urge to smooth that frown away. With my lips. “He won't be my husband too much longer. I’m filing for divorce.”

He didn’t react, a disappointment, when I'd hoped for another kiss. *You haven’t even filed yet,* a thought that went out of my head as he stood up and moved in closer.

“I wish—” He shook his head.

“What do you wish?” Hard to believe I'd asked. Nor did I get time to dwell on that question as he helped me up, put his arms around me and kissed me, a sweet kiss that quickly segued into, well, hot.

“I wish…” He whispered that in my ear as he let me go, reluctantly? I hoped so.

What does he wish? What do I wish?

He stroked my cheek gently. “I stopped because—I mean…”

Tell me...

“You haven't filed yet, have you?”

I shook my head. “The paperwork's done, but..." *I've been wussing out.*

He let me go and sat down again. "It's not just that."

“Oh?” *Maybe it's me.*

“My track record with women...” He shook his head.

I don't care about your track record with women. “After a divorce? I guess everything, y'know, takes time."

I felt better when he smiled. And nodded. “After this is over…”

After what's over, my marriage, your doubts about your track record, the investigation? Was there anything I could do to make it happen more quickly?

“Can you drive me back to the station?” he asked at I tuned back in. “If you have time. If not, I can call someone.”

“No problem.” Not quite the truth, in light o those paintings I needed to finish, but it was close enough.

***

He pointed to a three-story building on the way back to the station. “My condo’s right there, three blocks from the Bay. I can see it from my terrace in the winter. I wish I was closer."

“I've always wanted a place by the ocean, but Rich had his heart set on a gated community.” I frowned as I remembered how I’d gone along. *No more.*

“Maybe you’ll find one, after...”

I nodded. “Teresa's keeping her eyes open.”

“Your attorney?”

I nodded. “She divorced a lawyer herself.”

“Which is important, why?”

“It’s hard to divorce an attorney. Her divorce motivated her to go law school.”

"I guess that makes sense." He looked out the window and frowned. “I’d love to live by the water, but on my salary? Not gonna’ happen.” He smiled. “Those prints of yours make my place feel better. I guess you hear that all the time.”

No. “I get some compliments, every now and then."

“Now and then? But your work's so great, I—”

“What?”

“Don’t take this wrong, but I’d love to show you where I hung them. Sometime,” he added carefully.

“I’d like that.”

“Maybe we could have dinner. I realize you’re still married—”

“It’s only dinner.” *I wish it was more.*

He was smiling when we pulled up in front of the station. Did he enjoy the ride as much as I did? I hoped so.

***

"Rehearsal was awful tonight." Helen shook her head as we drove home in her Buick. I had an appointment to get my new tires the next day at the repair shop Jace recommended. A small thing, but it was progress.

"Amanda?"

"I thought it went okay tonight."

"Not when we open in three weeks."

I knew that wasn't much time, but Cliff said I was doing fine. Everyone else had looked all right, too, at least to me.

"Steffi and Burt act like they hate each other!" Helen frowned.

"I thought that was part of the script. Billie Dawn does leave her boyfriend."

"To develop her potential. She's not supposed to hate him."

I shrugged my shoulders. Steffi and Burt had liked each other well enough on those DVDs. But these days, Helen and I both felt sure Burt was involved with Cliff, something that had to affect the production. Was Steffi jealous of Burt because she was in love with Cliff? Strange, but it was certainly possible.

"The worst part? When Steffi and Burt were sniping at each other tonight, Cliff seemed to enjoy it." *Something you didn't notice because you're a newbie.* I knew that's what she was thinking.

"I noticed the tension between them, but it's hard for me to understand how they could hate each other, after they way they, y'know, acted together on those DVDs."

"That was sex. This is life." I began to reply when she cut in. "Cliff should know better, too.

It's one thing for him to hook up with Burt, another to let it affect the production."

"Burt and Cliff are pretty open about it." They'd spent lots of time talking quietly to each other tonight, and Cliff's teeth got whiter and brighter every time we saw him. I still thought Burt was doing okay in his role. As for the way he interacted with Steffi, it could just be a serious lack of chemistry.

Whatever was going on between them, it was none of my business. Finding out more about Wendi's murder and Harvey's disappearance was the only reason I'd taken that part. I hadn't learned anything, but there was still time before my theatrical debut, and I was enjoying the rehearsals, too.

In fact, it felt like everything was going better these days. Cliff liked me in my part and Chloe expected my show to be a success. As for the divorce, it would be great if it was finalized right around the same time I found out who'd killed Wendi and what became of Harvey. Not that I really expected it to happen that way.

At least I hadn't had any more scares. No slashed tires, no one vandalizing my property. I hadn't put those rosebushes in yet, but the Pampas grass was gone. Most important, I'd finally declared my debt to Rich paid in full, enough so that I was ready to take back my life.

I checked my watch as Helen pulled into her driveway. It was 5:30 and Rich wasn't home. His increasingly longer absences gave me that much more time to paint and practice my lines. I didn't have many of them, but there was no way I'd want to mess up, my first time out.

I hadn't told Rich about those last two paintings. Really, we hadn't talked much at all, a good thing. In light of the divorce, the less he knew, the better.

Jace promised to come to my show. Now that was important! Really? I couldn't wait.

“So, how’s your daughter Katie doing?” Helen’s voice brought me back abruptly.

“A lot better since I sent her the tuition money. She started her classes two weeks ago. She has one with this TV guy. He does this financial show on one of the cable networks. Nice looking man.”

“Kevin Patterson?”

I nodded. “That’s the one.”

“John watches his show from time to time."

“I've seen it, too, once or twice. Katie’s impressed with him.”

“Good looking, charming, smart and rich, what could be bad?” She smiled.

Nothing, I hope. “Katie thinks he’s a real financial genius. She says the more she learns about money management, the better she’ll end up, if she decides to file for divorce.”

“I would've thought she'd ask your husband if she needed financial advice.”

I shook my head. “They're not close. It started when she was eight years old and wanted to take Karate lessons. He insisted she take ballet.”

“A real male chauvinist!”

I smiled. I hadn’t heard that term since the 1970's. It'd emerged right around the same time I finally worked up the courage to tell Rich I didn’t plan to get a “real job.” Not that I planned to mention that to Helen. “I’m glad Katie stood up to him.”

“I’m proud of you for giving her the money, too. Couldn’t have been easy.”

"Dealing with Rich gets easier all the time." Because he was never home? Because he and I were barely speaking? Because I was filing for divorce? Because Jace kissed me—something else she didn't need to know.

We got out of her car. "You're sure you don't want to go out to dinner with me? John has another one of those blasted meetings. He and Ed still haven't resolved those budget irregularities. You can't imagine how frustrated they are, now that they have to clear everything through Mr. Association President." She sighed. "I thought I'd go to the Main Street Grill. They have the best burgers."

"I want to finish my last two paintings and look over my lines again." And decide when I wanted Teresa to serve Rich. If there was any time left over? I'd keep trying to figure out who'd murdered Wendi.

***

"Do I have to keep living with Rich after we serve the papers?" I asked Teresa a few days later. I didn't want to be there when he got served. North Carolina came to mind, but I didn't know how much longer Jessica would be there. Nor could I get back in time for either of my shows. Not like I really had to leave, either. Ever since the day I told Rich I'd given Katie the tuition money, he hadn't been home except to change his clothes and sleep.

"I thought you couldn't get away right now." Teresa frowned. She'd been ready to serve him three weeks ago.

"It's just, I didn't think I'd have to, like, be there when it happened."

"If you want to move forward—"

"Of course I do," I replied--halfheartedly? I hoped not. I took out four tickets to *Born Yesterday* and gave them to her. I'd debated buying one for Jace, too, but I hadn't seen him since that day I'd driven him back to the station. I missed him. *I wish I could see him every day. And night.*

Teresa took the tickets and smiled. "Thanks! I'm looking forward to it. So is Aunt Gina." She sighed softly. "Thanksgiving's coming up. We can still serve him before that."

Thanksgiving was another issue. Andrew and Katie were still living in the same house, but they hadn't spoken since she'd started class. Katie, Andrew and Corey had always come to our house for Thanksgiving, but this year? It looked like we'd all need we to make some changes.

I had other commitments, too. I was glad there were only eight performances of *Born Yesterday,* four the weekend after Thanksgiving and another four the weekend after that. My role was tiny, but I was enjoying it, especially when Cliff said I was doing fine, more than he'd been saying to Steffi and Burt.

Helen had been right about the two of them. They seemed to hate each other a little more at every rehearsal. I wondered what that might have to do with Wendi's murder, Harvey's disappearance or those DVDs. I needed to talk to Jace. If only there was something, anything I could tell him.

"I asked about Thanksgiving" I was thankful when Teresa's voice pulled me back.

"Don't you think that's a little soon?"

"No, but it's your call." She looked at her desk calendar and sighed. "December 8th?"

No! I almost said that, but if I did want to move on, it'd have to happen sometime. "I guess that'd be okay."

***

Jessica was coming home Wednesday. That was my first thought as I pulled into my driveway an hour later. Rich's SUV was gone and there was a strange car, an older white import, parked up the street. Our cul-de-sac got so little traffic, I had to wonder whose car it could be as I checked our mailbox, a miniature version of our house Rich insisted we have custom-made.

I was looking through the mail when the doorbell rang. I went to the door, looked through the side panel and saw a clean-cut young man. "Amanda Warren?"

"Yes?" I opened the inner door, careful to leave the storm door latched, not that one good shove wouldn't force it open.

"Officer of the Court." He held up some official-looking papers and looked at the screen door pointedly. When I didn't unlatch it, he flashed his ID in my face. I opened it, then, and he shoved those papers at me. "Sign here, please." He thrust a clipboard and a pen into my hands, giving me little choice but to sign.

"What is this about?" I asked as I handed the clipboard back.

But he just took the clipboard back, turned and headed back to his car. I considered calling after him, but in the end, I shut the door, looked at the papers--and realized Rich had filed first. Horrifying, till I thought it over and asked myself again if he had any idea those DVDs existed. Assuming he didn't, I pictured him going ballistic when he found out about them. There were three copies, now, the two Helen had made and Jace's copies, locked up somewhere down at police headquarters.

I checked my watch— 4:45. I took my phone out to call Teresa, then glanced at Jessica's driveway before I remembered she was still away. When I checked Helen's driveway, I was glad to see her Buick was there.

With John spending all that time at the clubhouse, she'd been taking herself out to dinner often,. Slipping my phone in my pocket, I grabbed my coat, keys and purse and headed over there, those legal papers in hand. I felt stressed beyond belief as I rang her bell, but I calmed down a bit when she opened the door, gestured me to come in and frowned. "Amanda? You're white as a ghost!"

That'd be the ghost of my marriage, the marriage I should've ended before we ever moved to the Acres, before Rich pressured me into joining the Women's Club, before he got busy with Wendi and the Sex Games Gang...

***

An hour later, Helen and I were sharing a cozy leather-padded booth at the Main Street Grill, where I'd been pushing my veggie burger around my plate instead of eating it.

"I can't wait until he finds out about those DVDs!" Helen said as she polished off her burger, the real thing.

Did I switch to veggie burgers because that's what Wendi ate?

"Will you take a look at that!" Helen's voice brought me back as I followed her gaze to the bar, where Cliff and Burt were having drinks, talking quietly to each other and laughing, from time to time. Helen smiled. "Hot and heavy!"

I nodded, but really? All I could think about was my divorce. I'd phoned Teresa from Helen's house to tell her I'd been served. "No problem. We'll counter file ASAP, unless you still want to wait?"

"ASAP sounds perfect." Not that I really thought so. Not that I had a choice.

"After we serve him, I'll phone his attorney and schedule a meeting."

"We have to meet with him?"

"Don't worry. I can do the talking, if you'd like. I don't foresee any problems. Once they find out we have those DVDs, I'm sure they'll want to settle quickly."

"Okay..." I wanted to believe that but I couldn't quite get there.

"We could let them make the first move," she went on. "But taking the lead should give us some advantage."

"Sounds good." Confident enough? I hoped so.

"I'll take care of it today."

"Thank you."

Helen was there when I made that call and she was here with me now, looking at me with sympathy, even pity. "High time you divorced that man." She pointed to my veggie burger. "Eat!"

I nodded, picked up my fork and stabbed at it. I was almost about to take a bite when Helen turned to look at Cliff and Burt again. "They're practically doing it right there at the bar!" She shook her head.

I knew she was waiting for me to respond, but the way I felt tonight, I wouldn't have cared if Cliff and Burt took off all their clothes and did just, well, whatever.

"No wonder Burt and Steffi aren't getting along." Helen signaled the waitress for more coffee. "You're taking that burger home, I hope. You barely touched it."

I nodded. I knew she was right. After we finished our coffee, the waitress brought a takeout box along with the check. "Don't forget the sweet potato fries," Helen reminded me as she double-checked the bill.

While I watched Cliff and Burt, sitting in a booth on the other side of the restaurant, holding hands across the table, something that made me wonder again where Harvey was and what might really have happened to him.

***

Helen and I had discussed so many divorce scenarios over dinner, I needed to talk about something else on the way home. I thought about Cliff and Burt. "You think Burt's wife knows what's going on?"

"His little blonde trophy wife?" She laughed.

I shrugged my shoulders. "If the shoe fits--"

"Kayla has it in her closet," Helen cut in, enough to make me laugh--a good thing.

"That one? Shopping's her middle name." Helen smiled as I pictured Kayla Davidson. At 28, she was 25 years younger than Burt. A former Miss Maryland, she'd placed third in that year's Miss America pageant. Ten years later, her perfect, very white teeth complimented alabaster skin, big blue eyes, award-winning legs and breasts perfect enough to have been surgically augmented. Well-coordinated designer outfits and lots of gold jewelry completed Kayla's trophy wife image.

I frowned as I thought of Burt's first wife Nancy, living, these days, with their three teenagers in a modest house in Emeryville, the next town over. I felt bad when I'd heard Burt, Jr. had gotten caught driving drunk, one reason I couldn't help but feel a little gratified to see Kayla's man cheating on her—with Cliff.

"Truth really is stranger than fiction," I checked my watch as Helen pulled into my driveway. It was 10:35. I was glad to see Rich's SUV was nowhere in sight.

Chapter Seventeen

I was about say something about Rich not being home when Helen spoke first. “I'll bet he’s out playing with his friends.” She put the car in gear, then, and backed out of the driveway quickly.

Planning to look for Rich? I debated trying to stop her. The last thing I wanted to know was where he was and what he was doing.

I wouldn’t have minded staying there in my driveway and talking about Wendi’s murder some more. I still wasn’t sure why I felt such a strong need to find her killer, the same need I'd felt ever since the day I saw them dump her dead body on the curb. Tell Helen? Hard to decide.

“Now that we know Rich and Wendi were fooling around—”

Do you think he loved her? I so wanted to ask her that, but I let it go, along with all those images of Rich and Wendi and the rest of the gang on those DVDs. Why did it have to hurt so much? I tried to focus on my breathing, but it didn’t block out the pain.

“Are you okay?” I was glad when Helen’s voice pulled me back.

“Fine,” I lied. “Where are we going?” I asked, not that I didn’t know.

She just smiled as we turned onto Paige and Jim’s street. “No cars in the driveway.” She said, then made a quick U-turn.

“How'd you know that was Paige’s house?”

“Remember last year’s Valentine’s Dance?”

“Hard to forget.” Rich had danced with Wendi all night after pawning me off on Jim and Pete. When that got old, I sat with Helen and John, surrounded by the decorations: garish red paper hearts strung with glittery crepe paper streamers. Valentine's Day a la Junior High, as Jessica put it.

"I was on the committee. Paige chaired it. We met at her house, that over-decorated monstrosity."

"All that marble is a bit much," I agreed.

"To put it mildly."

I nodded as I pictured her hand-carved moldings, granite countertops, custom wood parquet floors and the elaborate marble mantel in the den—too much of, well, everything. "They could never have shot those DVDs at her house. All that granite and marble? Cold." Not what I'd intended to say, but it brought a smile to my lips.

We were on Pete and Monica's street now. Paige's baby blue Mercedes was parked in Monica's driveway and Rich's SUV was up the street. Helen parked in front of it, got out and gestured me to follow her.

I hesitated.

"C'mon, Amanda, don't be a wuss!"

You did promise yourself you'd never be a wuss again. I hesitated a moment before I got out and followed her to Pete and Monica's house. I couldn't deny I was curious.

Curiosity killed the cat.

Good thing I'm not a cat.

"We'll take a quick look and see what they're up to," Helen said quietly.

"We're going to spy on them?" *What if we see something awful? What if they see us and call the police? What if Jace shows up and arrests us?* Lots of possibilities, all of them grim, I thought as we got closer. I was disappointed when all we saw were Monica's designer window treatments, rose silk drapes in the living room, custom bamboo roll-ups in the kitchen, plantation shutters in the den, all of them closed. “Let’s go,” I whispered.

Helen shook her head. “We'll just go around to the back.”

“You want to look in their bedroom windows?”

She smiled. “That’s where the action is.”

What if Rich sees us? A possibility I couldn’t afford to consider. Minutes later, we were standing by the master bedroom windows, where the pearl gray drapes were open just enough for us to see Monica and Jim in bed with Paige. Monica and Paige wore lacy silk bikini panties and matching demi-bras that left almost nothing to the imagination as they made love to each other. Jim joined in from time to time as Rich and Pete watched.

Helen took out her I-phone. “I can shoot some video."

We don't have enough? I shook my head. “They might see you."

She grinned. “They’re too busy to see me.”

“Shhh! They’ll hear you!”

“Too busy to hear me.”

Wrong! I knew that when they stopped. I was relieved when Monica draped a sheet around herself before she got up and went over to the window, inches away from us. Helen stepped back quickly, pulling me with her so fast, I almost tripped over one of their perfectly trimmed hedges. She put a finger to her lips. “Shhh.”

I glared at her but if she noticed, she didn't care. She was gesturing me to get out of there. We turned and raced back to her car, stopping only when we heard Monica say, “Someone’s out there,” her voice as clear and loud as if she was standing next to us. I turned and looked back at the bedroom window, glad to see she still had that sheet wrapped around her.

But a moment later, when I turned back for one last look, I was dismayed to see Jim behind her, buck naked. I was thankful when he shut the drapes.

"Someone's out there!" That from Paige, who sounded panicky.

"We should call the police," Monica replied.

"Right!" That from Rich, who was laughing humorlessly.

"I'll go take a look," I heard Pete say.

I stopped, stood there and kept listening till Helen put her hand on the small of my back and gave me a push. "Move," she whispered urgently, enough for me to do so. We reached her car just as the front door opened and Pete and Jim came out, wearing clothes, thank goodness.

"Get in!"

I did. A moment later, I held my breath as she peeled off.

She touched my hand. "Breathe."

I felt better when I did. "What if they got our license plate number?" We were in Helen's driveway, now.

"How could they? I parked in front of Rich's SUV."

I nodded. I wanted to believe her, but if they'd managed to see us, somehow, and get her license plate number, we were in trouble. Best to believe they didn't, I thought as I glanced in the rear view mirror just in time to see Rich pulling into our driveway.

"I guess the party's over." Helen giggled.

I frowned. I couldn't believe Rich had come home after serving me. The last thing in the world I wanted to do was go in there and see him. What would I say if he asked where I'd been and what I'd been doing? Rich being Rich, he'd do his best to manipulate me into telling the truth.

"You could stay at my house tonight," Helen suggested.

"What if he comes over?"

"I'll just say you're not here." She indicated my house. "I know you don't want to go home tonight."

I nodded.

"You could also get a room at the Welcome Inn on the highway."

"I'd have to take the rental." Which was parked in the driveway next to Rich's SUV. "I couldn't arrange for new tires till tomorrow," I added as I pictured my Beamer. I'd had it towed over to Jace's friend's garage this afternoon.

I asked myself again if Rich could have any idea we'd found those DVDs, watched them, then passed them on to Jace-- after making copies.

If he found out, would he kill me, too?

Crazy, or was it? Could he really have been complicit in Wendi's murder and Harvey's disappearance? A chill ran down my spine as I opened my purse, spotted Jessica's key and took it out. "I know, I can stay at Jessica's."

"If you're sure you're okay to do that."

I nodded. "It's just--"

"What?"

"Do you think Rich had anything to do with Wendi's murder or Harvey's disappearance?"

She shrugged her shoulders. "I don't have a clue, but I don't think you should go home tonight."

What about Jace, call him or not? If he found out what we'd just done—

"Make sure the alarm system's on," Helen was saying now.

I nodded. No matter how mixed my feelings were about living in the Acres, I was grateful, tonight, that every house had come equipped with a good security system.

"I think you should call your detective, too, tell him what we saw tonight."

"Oh, right!"

"Tell him I made you do it. Yes. Blame it all on me."

You did make me do it and I do blame it all on you. I felt myself blush as I pictured telling him what we'd seen through Pete and Monica's bedroom window. "I don't think so."

"Maybe he'll send someone to keep an eye on you," Helen pointed out.

Better if he did it himself.

"He might even come over himself."

"Oh, right! Maybe he'll spend the night, too."

She grinned. "Sounds good to me! Go on, I'll keep an eye on you till you get inside. And call me tomorrow. I can't wait to hear what happened."

***

Two hours later, I felt almost safe. I hadn't called Jace, but I had checked to make sure the alarm system was on. I'd also checked all the doors and windows.

It was almost midnight and I was curled up in the guestroom bed, finally beginning to drift off when I heard the crash. I looked over at the nightstand, where my glass of water had just, well, shattered. I turned on the light and saw the shattered glass on the nightstand, the bed and the floor.

I was reaching for my shoes when I heard a loud, popping sound and shut the light. I rolled over to the other side of the bed and dropped to the floor, then waited to see if anything else would happen. It took a few minutes for me to work up the courage to go back and look at the window. That's when I spotted the two small, round holes in the glass.

Bullet holes.

Do something! I started to reach for my phone but found myself frozen in place for the second time tonight. Did Rich own a gun? Did he have any idea I was looking into Wendi's murder? Had he just tried to kill me?

Call Jace! It took longer than I would've liked to look away from the window and make that call. I was careful to stay down as I did, away from the windows.

"Connolly." His voice sounded so deep and gravelly. I knew I'd awakened him. I felt bad about that even as I pictured him in bed.

"I woke you. I'm sorry..."

"Amanda? What's wrong?"

Did he recognize my voice or was it the caller ID? What difference did it make? "I'm at Jessica's house. I thought I'd, um, stay here tonight." I let my breath out slowly. "I was in bed when I heard this sound. I turned on the light, then, and saw my glass of water shattered on the nightstand." I took a deep breath.. "Then, when I looked at the window? I saw two little holes. Bullet holes," I managed to get that out somehow.

"Where are you now?"

"Jessica's guest room. I'm on the floor. Away from the windows," I thought to add.

"Good. The doors, are they locked?"

"Yes. The security system's on, too."

"I'll call it in. Someone will be there soon. Stay right where you are till they get there. And make sure you stay away from the windows."

I started to say I would when he ended the call. A Mediterranean blue-and-white arrived a few minutes later. I made my way to the front door slowly, careful to stay as far away from the windows as I could. I was thankful when I saw the uniformed officer through the side panel, a tall brunette who identified herself as Officer Melissa Harding.

She asked a few questions before she went out to check the exterior of the house with a flashlight powerful enough to light up half the block.

Jace got there a few minutes later. Wearing well-worn jeans and an old NYPD sweatshirt, I knew he'd gotten dressed quickly. His face was shadowed, too, enough to make him look—dangerous, dangerously sexy. I was about to apologize for waking him when Melissa came back and showed him the two empty shells she'd found outside.

Someone just tried to shoot me. Rich, I know it was Rich. The image of Rich trying to shoot me through Jessica's bedroom window wouldn't go away as I excused myself and went into the bathroom. I needed to do something normal. I washed my face and brushed my hair, forcing myself to focus on those two tasks. My hair color was fading, I could see that in the mirror. I needed a touch-up, maybe even a change.

Rich had always liked me as a blonde but since he may've just tried to shoot me, it was my call now. Auburn? Chestnut brown with blonde highlights? Lots of time to decide, I thought as I brushed on some of Jessica's blush. I checked my watch--1:15--and looked in the mirror again. Not too bad, all things considered.

"Okay, you saw those empty shells," Jace said when I came out. "She found some footprints, too, men's size 11. Does that mean anything to you?"

"Rich wears an 11, but—"

"It's a common size. She'll take the shells in, but they looked like they came from a small handgun."

I began to ask him if he could tell anything else about that gun when Melissa's phone rang. She went out to take the call and came back a few minutes later. "Domestic on Oaktree Drive," she said. Jace nodded. She turned and went out, then. I waited till I heard the door close before I offered him coffee.

"Only if you'll have some, too."

"I nodded Might as well. No way would I ever get to sleep tonight. I showed him Jessica's single-cup coffeemaker and the cartridge holder next to it. He came up next to me and chose a nice strong Colombian. He didn't plan to get much sleep tonight either, apparently.

I was about to put the cartridge in when he put his arms around me. They felt so strong and comforting, I put it down, turned to him and hesitated before I gave in to the temptation to lay my head on his chest.

"It's over. You're safe," he said softly. We kissed, then, warm and deep. "If anything ever happened to you..." He pulled me closer.

How would you feel, if anything ever happened to me?

I was disappointed when he let me go and took a few steps back. “I never thought I’d feel this way after… y'know...” He frowned. “My divorce felt like it took forever. Diane fought me every step of the way, acted like it was all my fault.” He sighed. “I did my part, I admit it, but... we've been separated three years, now and I still…” He frowned as his voice trailed off.

I fought the urge to smooth that frown away. “I haven’t filed yet. I know it'll be hard.”

He nodded. “It's just, tonight? I had no right...”

I so want to give you that right. Not that I was ready to say that. “I can’t believe someone tried to shoot me.” *Do something normal.* I slipped in his cartridge and pressed the button.

He sat down at Jessica’s table, half a room away. “You did the right thing, calling me.“

And you did the right thing, kissing me.

Not that I needed to say that. I was pretty sure he knew I wanted him. He confirmed that when he stood up, crossed the room, took me in his arms and kissed me again. Wonderful, until he pulled away. “I don’t have any business—”

Kissing me, making love with me? Why not, when I want you to? Could I ever work up the courage to say that? Probably not. Rich had never hesitated to tell me how mediocre I was between the sheets. Jace was probably used to younger women, too, women with tighter, better-toned bodies. Women who were better in bed.

The coffeemaker beeped.

“Guess we could both use some coffee,” he murmured as he began to run his hands down my back. “I need to stop…”

I don't want you to stop.

"There are guidelines, here. I have no right—" He stopped, then, pulled me closer and kissed me with enough passion for me to respond to him in a way I'd never responded to Rich. I kissed him back, returning all his heat and passion in kind.

"If you don't stop—" He frowned.

"What'll you do if I don't stop?"

"You'll force me to—"

"Arrest me?" I giggled. Did I really just say that?

"Take you to bed," he replied "Definitely not procedure," he added breathlessly.

I smiled and ran my fingers gently over the fullness of his bottom lip, enough for him to kiss me again. "I'd never tell."

He took a few steps back and put his hand up. "Time out."

I hesitated before I nodded, turned away and helped myself to a bottle of San Pellegrino, the sparkling water Jessica favored, as he took his coffee cup out of the machine.

He took a few sips of Colombian and nodded his approval before he looked me in the eye. "Want to tell me why you're staying here tonight?"

I was afraid I was next on Rich's hit list. I believed in my heart Rich had killed Wendi even though I had nothing in the way of proof. Tell him? Maybe not. I could also tell him what Helen and I saw tonight when we'd done our peeping Tom number. Not a good idea. For all I knew, it might even be against the law.

Begin at the beginning. "Rich served me with divorce papers today."

"I'm sorry. I know how that feels."

I'm not sorry, I'm relieved. "I called Teresa. She suggested we counter file ASAP."

He nodded. "Good idea. Those DVDs should help."

"Yes." I hesitated. "Things haven't been good between us, not for a very long time." *Not ever.*

He flashed me a half-smile. "I know how that feels, too."

"Then, tonight?"

"What happened?"

I took a moment to center myself. I didn't want to blurt. "After I got served, I went over to Helen's. We ended up going out to dinner." *Where we saw Cliff and Burt practically doing it right there in the restaurant and I couldn't eat a thing.* "When we got home and Rich's SUV wasn't in the driveway, Helen decided to, um, drive over to Paige and Jim's house." I hesitated. "She didn't ask if I was okay with it. It was all her idea," I added, in case it was illegal.

He just nodded. "What happened then?"

"When no one was home at Paige and Jim's, she drove over to Pete and Monica's."

"And?"

"We looked in their windows. That wasn't my idea, either. I should never have gone along, but Helen can be so—"

"Controlling?" He smiled. "I couldn't help but notice. Okay, you looked in their windows and—"

I took a deep breath. "They were at it again. It shouldn't have surprised me, but..." *It was awful, so awful,, I'm still upset.*

He ran his fingers through his hair. "I'm glad you're filing for divorce."

"Me, too. Rich was just watching tonight, but Jim, Monica and Paige?" I shook my head. "It doesn't matter."

"It does if it upset you. Want to tell me about it, just for the record?"

"Okay." I felt myself start to blush. "Paige and Monica were in bed together, wearing this sexy silk underwear. As for the men? They were mostly just watching."

"Then what happened?"

I hesitated. "You think you could use your imagination?"

He nodded, then got up and put his arms around me. I shivered as he brushed the back of my neck with his lips. Too soon, he let me go.

I turned to face him. "Y'know, Rich and I have led separate lives for a while now. And…" *Don't say it..*

"What?"

He always says I'm lousy in bed.. I hesitated. "It's just, I mean, I didn't meet his expectations...sexually."

I was surprised when he smiled, actually smiled. "Been there, done that. According to Diane, I worked too many hours, didn't bring home enough money and made her so unhappy she had no choice but to turn to other men. And liquor."

How many men, how much liquor? Ask him? Sometime, maybe, not tonight. "I'm sorry." I wished I could kiss his pain away.

"When I watched those DVDs? It was hard for me to set my feelings aside and concentrate on the case." He pulled me closer. "This must be terrible for you."

"I didn't tell Rich about the DVDs." *Because I was afraid he'd kill me too.* Why did

I feel so sure it was Rich who'd murdered Wendi and tried to shoot me tonight?

"We're still keeping an eye on the victim's house," he said quietly.

"Has anyone tried to get in there?"

"No. I went back yesterday and checked the closet myself." He sat down at the table, picked up his coffee and took a few sips.

Tell him about the copies Helen made? I wrapped my arms around myself. "Helen offered to make copies of those DVDs before we put them back. She said it'd be a good idea, in light of the divorce."

"She made those copies before she ever told me about that secret compartment, didn't she?"

I nodded slowly. "I guess she's not as good an actress as she thinks she is."

"You're blushing."

"It happens at lot. I hate it."

"It's cute. Sweet," he added as he stood up, came over and stroked my lips with his fingers before he kissed me there, slowly, tenderly. "I made a major mistake on a case once, back in the city. You might've read about it."

I nodded. *It wasn't your fault.*

"A killer went free because I screwed up, in terms of the search warrant parameters." He sighed softly. "The day Helen told me about the DVDs, the warrant for the vic's house was already in place. If she'd told me any sooner..." He shook his head and frowned.

I wish we'd never found those DVDs.

"You might know how warrants work, from all those cop shows on TV."

Warrants, focus on that. I nodded. "You mean now when we find the killer, we can include those DVDs at their trial, right?"

He raised an eyebrow. "We?"

“Just a figure of speech.”

“It'd better be.”

I tried not to smile. “Find anything else that day?”

He nodded. “Enough clothes for a village, including a couple of those funky outfits the vic wore on those DVDs, what do they call them?”

“Bustiers?”

He nodded. “Five of them, all top quality leather. When we brought them in? This vice squad guy said they looked custom-made.”

I nodded. They were expensive, too. Had Rich paid for them? I knew for a fact that he'd enjoyed them. “I just keep wondering if Rich knew about those DVDs.”

“Hard to say. From everything we've learned about the vic, it feels like she might've arranged to have them shot herself, planning to blackmail him and all the others.”

“But isn't it possible that someone else shot them, planning to blackmail everyone in them, including Wendi?”

“We considered that possibility, too, more so after we interviewed the people who claimed to have hated her. Hard to figure out which of them had the strongest motive.” He frowned. “As far as any concrete evidence goes? We've got *nada.*”

I remembered the day I told him about all the Women’s Club members who’d hated her, the same day I found out someone had told him about my fantasy of strangling her with that purple pashmina.

Not my finest hour.

“The DVDs complicate everything. If they got out, it’d destroy some lives for sure. And now, with someone slashing your tires, then taking a couple of shots at you? I don’t like it.”

“You don't think it was a coincidence?”

“Do you think it is?” I knew that wasn't really a question as he took my hand. “Who knew you were sleeping here tonight?”

“Just Helen.”

“Could Warren have seen you go in?”

“He was probably watching TV, but I guess it’s possible.”

“I’ll question him tomorrow, but...” His frown confirmed all my worst fears. I flashed back to that shattered water glass and my heart began to race. It slowed down when he pulled me close again and I kissed him. Hard to resist the temptation, after all those years with Rich. I needed something. Someone. *I need you, Jace. I don’t care if I’m no good in bed. I have to have you, even if it's only for tonight.*

I had mixed feelings when he pulled away, went back to the table, picked up his empty coffee cup and put it in the dishwasher. Refreshing, after all those years with Rich. Until he turned to me. “As for tonight…”

Was I thankful he wasn’t kissing me again? I knew I should be.

“I don't want you staying here alone.”

I pictured the Welcome Inn and frowned.

“I can stay with you. I’ll take the couch,” he added. “I keep a change of clothes in my car, no problem.”

I smiled. “You could take the couch, but the bed would be a lot more comfortable.” Did I really just say that?

Yes! My spirits soared when he smiled and kissed me again.

Chapter Eighteen

I was alone in bed when I opened my eyes the next morning and caught the scent of fresh-brewed coffee. It smelled wonderful, but I didn't get up till I relived last night.

Hard to believe Jace's ex hadn't thought much of him, in or out of bed, apparently. I had to take issue with that. I didn't know what it'd be like to live with him, but I could attest to the fact that the man knew how to take his time. We'd spent almost an hour making love.

I pictured it as I turned on my side, hugged his pillow, breathed in his scent and smiled. An hour of the best lovemaking ever, enough to tempt me to go out to the kitchen and tell him exactly how wonderful he was.

I thought about all those years with Rich and all the doubts I'd had about my sexuality. Last night put every last one of them to rest. Rich was the one who was mediocre between the sheets, not me. I knew that now. I smiled as I sat up, stretched and felt some aches and pains in places where I'd never felt them before. Fine with me, I loved the way my body responded to his last night.

I showered and got dressed before I joined him at Jessica's kitchen table. He was wearing jeans this morning with a dark green shirt, sipping a cup of coffee and jotting down some notes. I took a hazelnut cartridge from the rack and popped it in.

He stood up and kissed me. His face was smooth and he smelled like that fresh, woodsy aftershave. He'd taken the time to shave. I missed that shadow, and the way it'd felt against my skin last night.

“Your husband left around 6:30 this morning, early for him?”

I kissed him again before I replied and was thrilled when I felt him shiver, slightly. “A little. He usually leaves around seven.” We were sharing another kiss when his phone rang. He let me go and checked the caller ID. "It'll wait," he murmured as he watched me fix my coffee. “Warren took some pictures this morning, too.”

”Pictures?”

“Photos. Of my car.” He pointed to his Toyota, parked at the curb in front of Jessica’s house. “Any idea why he’d do that?”

I shook my head.

“We'll wait, see what happens.”

Wait to see if he tries to shoot me again? I wrapped my arms around myself and shivered.

He stood up and gave me a hug. “Calm down, sweetheart.”

“Sweetheart?” Did he really just say that?

“Sweetheart.” He kissed me again. “You okay with that?”

Wonderful. I proved it by kissing him back. I was disappointed when we stopped, and I flashed back to those gunshots last night. “You think Rich was the one who shot at me through the window last night?”

He shrugged his shoulders. “Whoever it was, don't worry. We'll keep you safe.” He took my hand as I sat down at the table and smiled at him.

But the vision of Rich shooting at me wouldn't go away. “Maybe he thought if he could prove I was with another man, he’d do better in the divorce. You think that's possible?”

He shook his head. “You were alone when it happened. And after those DVDs get out? Nothing will help.” He smiled, slightly.

I didn't smile back. “I wish I knew if he has any idea they exist.” I took s sip of coffee. "I have to wonder if he saw me come in here last night.”

“Think back, did you see him by the window?”

“No, but I wasn’t looking. I couldn't stop thinking about what Helen and I had just seen, that, and how much I didn’t want to go home.“

“Someone saw you.” He frowned. “The lab results won’t be back for a while, depending on what else they've got down there.” He popped in another coffee cartridge. “Can you think of anyone else who could've wanted to harm you?”

I hesitated. “I’ve just got a feeling it was Rich.”

“Women’s intuition?” He smiled.

“Whatever it is, it’s been right on target, at times. And it was strong last night.” I braced myself for the same kind of negative comments I’d always gotten from Rich, when it came to my intuition. I was relieved when Jace just nodded. “Maybe he saw me and thought I was here with another man.”

“Then got angry enough to shoot you and risk getting caught? Doesn't make sense, especially in light of his own-- activities." He hesitated. “Any way he might’ve known you found those DVDs and watched them? Take your time, now, think about it.”

I nodded. It wasn't long before I reached a conclusion. “Honestly? I don't think he knows about them." I made myself another cup of coffee. “When I saw them in action last night?

It was just so awful." A sigh escaped me. "I guess I should call Teresa."

He nodded. "I can pick up some stuff for breakfast while you do that."

"Let's check the fridge first." I went over, opened the door and looked around. "She's got eggs. I make great scrambled eggs."

"Great! I'm okay on the grill, but my scrambled eggs never come out right." He opened some cabinets, found a pan, held it up and smiled.

I smiled back. A man who liked to help? Every woman's dream, especially mine, after all those years with Rich. I was breaking the eggs into a bowl, trying not to flash back to those gunshots, and the terror I'd felt last night, when he spoke again.

"You think your husband could be the killer, don't you?"

I stopped whisking the eggs. "I don't have any proof."

"I know that. Why do you suspect him?"

I thought it over. "It's just, he's always been aggressive, especially when it comes to money. He can be secretive, too." I managed a smile. "Well, obviously."

"Obviously," he agreed. He smiled, then, enough to ease a little of that anxiety.

"I couldn't help but notice how forceful he was, too, on those DVDs, more forceful than anyone else, except maybe Wendi."

Jace nodded. "Determined to get what he wanted no matter the cost, that's how it looked to me. Assuming he wanted the victim dead—"

"I can't imagine why. They were lovers." Something that should've hurt me. It didn't, though. Had I stopped caring? I hoped so.

He nodded. "It's possible he's the killer."

I poured the eggs in the pan and turned to face him. “But I was thinking, what if he wanted her in some, y'know, peculiar way?”

He looked confused

“What if he wanted to, like, possess her? Wendi would never have gone along.” The silence stretched out between us as I waited for him to reply. *Rich was never possessive with me.* Say that, why would I? I pictured Wendi. “Wendi would've never have allowed him or anyone else to tell her what to do.”

“Assuming that’s true, and from what we've found out about her, I'm sure it is-- she would’ve rejected him. That'd give him good, strong motive.”

I stirred the eggs. They were almost done and they smelled delicious, especially when I hadn't had dinner last night. I put them on plates, gave one to Jace and watched as he tasted them. “Delicious.”

I sat down with him. I’d just begun to eat mine when he went on. “I meant to ask you, about that Amex receipt, was it just out in the open?"

I hesitated. “Not exactly.”

He put his fork down and looked me in the eye. “Where was it, *exactly*?”

“In his nightstand drawer.”

“You went through his drawers?”

I stopped eating. “I just wanted some answers. I never went through his things before, I swear it.” Not that I should have to swear it...

“Okay.” I was relieved when he started eating again.

Till something else occurred to me. “What if he knows I found those DVDs and watched them? If he also realized, somehow, I found that knife? You think that'd scare him enough to try to kill me?" A scenario that sounded melodramatic even to me, but I still thought it was possible.

"I took a look at the bullets before Melissa brought them in. They came from a .22. We won't know the specifics till they work them up in the lab, but--"

"You think they'll be able to find out anything about the shooter?"

"Maybe, if they find some fingerprints. I didn't see any, but they could still be there." He stood up, went over to the sink, rinsed off his plate and put it in the dishwasher. "Assuming it was your ex? We've got to be grateful he didn't come over here last night."

"Yes. I thought that was strange, too, with that police car outside."

"Whatever the reason, I'm glad. If he found us together…"

I blushed as I pictured what he would've seen if he'd found us together. I looked at Jace, a man who made the best love in the world, helped with breakfast the next morning and even cleaned up after himself. Enough to make me feel good, till I flashed back to those gunshots again.

"What's wrong?"

I hesitated. "I was just thinking how Rich did all that kinky stuff on those DVDs. You think maybe that kind of thing could've, like, changed him?"

"Maybe." He hesitated. "But I've got a feeling catching you with another man and saving himself big bucks in the divorce settlement would be a lot more important to a man like Warren."

"Important enough to shoot me?"

I watched his muscles flex as he shrugged his shoulders. “Can’t rule it out.”

“It’s just so…” *Scary…*

He put his arm around me and kissed the back of my neck. “Don’t worry, sweetheart, I’ve got your back.”

What to say, thanks? It meant so much more. He meant so much more. He stopped, went over to the frig, took out a tube of crescent rolls, held them up and smiled. “Almost missed these. I’m a whiz at baking these things.”

I smiled. *I'm a whiz at eating them.*

He popped the package open. “I got that invitation from your gallery.”

“I hope you can make it.”

He smiled. “Free wine and cheese? Wouldn't miss it.”

I smiled back. A sense of humor, too. Did Rich ever have a sense of humor? If he did, I couldn’t remember it.

“We could drive in together,” he suggested as he found a baking sheet, laid out the crescents and put them in the oven.

“I’d like that.“ He set the timer and turned to me.“So tell me, how many of those DVDs did you watch?”

“Four, only enough to see who was in them. Helen fast-forwarded them a lot, too. I was relieved when she offered to watch the last two herself.”

He nodded. “What stood out most, when you watched them?”

I shuddered slightly as I pictured them. “One of them, the third? It sort of starred Rich.” A good enough answer?

No, as it turned out. "What'd he do that stood out most?”

I felt myself blush. “It was just so bizarre.” *So upsetting.*

He patted my shoulder. “I had a hard time watching them myself.”

I looked in his eyes. He’d watched them with someone else. A woman, I knew that, somehow. I hesitated before I asked him.

He shrugged his shoulders. “Tough to watch them alone."

"So, I mean, someone did watch them with you.”

He nodded. "A female colleague who was there that night. Rachel's married. Happily," he added. "With three kids." He sighed. "She only made it through one of them."

“You watched the rest of them alone?”

“Not much choice. It is my case. I fast-forwarded them, too, not that it helped.” The oven timer sounded. He took out the crescents. "Perfect," he murmured as he picked up two of them with a paper towel and gave them to me, then looked at the clock and frowned. "Didn’t realize the time. I should call in.” He went out of the room to do it while I pretty much inhaled the crescents, glad Rich wasn’t around to make me feel fat. And guilty.

“They postponed my meeting. Gives me a little more time.” He glanced at my empty plate and pointed to the baking sheet. “There's more.”

I shook my head even as I eyed the baking sheet longingly.

He took two crescents of his own and polished them off as quickly as I did. “Guess we both worked up an appetite last night.”

I smiled.

He smiled back.

I stopped smiling when I thought about what I needed to do today. “I've got to go back to my house. Can you come with me?" *I hate to be a wuss, but I don't want to go in there alone.*

"No problem." He gave me another kiss.

I kissed him back. It was almost good enough to put my world back in order, at least for now.

In my house a few minutes later, I packed enough for a few days. I was glad he was there but I still didn't want to linger. He did, though, long enough to look at my two new paintings "Mesas and canyons? Doesn't look like the Jersey shore."

"It's Arizona. Rich and I went out there a few years ago. He had this conference in Phoenix. I drove up to Sedona, red rock country? It was so beautiful, I shot all these photos. It took a while, but I finally turned this one into a painting."

He smiled. "Well worth the wait." He pulled me close, then, and gave me a hug.

He loves my paintings. Enough to make me happy, till I imagined Rich coming in and finding us here. He seldom came home during the day. On the other hand, he'd never filed for divorce before.

"You sure you're okay to come back here to finish them?"

"All they need is a few final touches." *I'll work fast.*

He nodded, then took out his phone and called in again. I couldn't hear what he was saying, but he was smiling when he came out. "We've got another hour or so. Let's go back to Jessica's, talk about the case.

I was quick to agree.

***

A half hour later, he looked at his notes and frowned. “Okay, we've got the vic, her stepdaughter Steffi, Warren, Paige and Jim, Pete and Monica and Harvey and Cliff? They were all on the DVDs.”

”Don’t forget Burt Davidson. Helen feels sure he and Cliff are involved.”

"I know." He still made a note of it. “He appeared in two of them, right?”

“I think so. With Cliff.”

“Harvey, too, if memory serves.” He shrugged his shoulders. “To each his own.”

“Burt’s playing the lead in the Players’ next production. Helen thinks he got the part because he and Cliff are—”

“Intimate? I figured that out.”

I hesitated before I nodded. And blushed. It didn't bother me, though, not when he thought it was cute.

“What do you think?” His voice brought me back.

About what?

He sighed softly. “Richardson and the dentist?”

“I thought they looked close, when we saw them together at the Main Street Grill. But Helen's known Cliff a lot longer than I have. If she feels so sure that they're involved, I trust her judgment. That’s why I asked her to go with me to a rehearsal.” I pictured that rehearsal, and my slashed tires, and wrapped my arms around myself.

“What's wrong, sweetheart?”

“Just thinking--”

“About your tires?" He hesitated. “What else can you remember about that rehearsal?”

“Just what I told you, Paige ran out of there crying and Cliff asked if I was interested in playing that little part. I thought it over before I said yes. It's not many lines, but it's been fun."

"Really?"

No. Not that I said that. Not that I had to. When I looked in his eyes, I felt sure he knew.

"To get back to the case—" He looked over his notes again. "When I watched those DVDs, it occurred to me that just because they were the only ones we found doesn't mean there aren't others. For all we know, they might even feature different people."

"I don't know, Paige, Monica and their husbands were Wendi's closest friends, if you could call them that. She always referred to them as her Inner Circle."

He pursed his lips. "I wish we could find out if she left them anything."

I debated telling him what I'd seen the night I'd looked at her will. I hated to admit I'd swiped a copy, but it was the right thing to do. "Remember the night you stopped by Wendi's house? I wasn't really there because Rich got a phone call."

"No kidding?" He smiled.

"I'm a terrible liar, always have been."

"Not necessarily a bad thing." He took my hand and began to stroke warm circles on my palm. Seductive. Also enough for me to tell him what he wanted to know. "You use this interrogation technique often?"

"Depends, how is it working?" He removed his hand. "Why were you there?"

"I got angry when Rich said he'd revised Wendi's will."

"Couldn't have been much of a surprise. You did say the two of you had grown apart."

"I was still upset."

He nodded. "You're sure he didn't tell you?"

"Positive. I also wanted to find out if Wendi left him anything. Oh, and I thought her will might provide some clues about who could've killed her."

He frowned. Not good, but least he wasn't telling me to butt out again. "Then, when you rang the bell and he got up to open the door—"

"You swiped a copy and shoved it under your shirt, didn't you?"

"You saw that?"

He just smiled. "What'd you find out?"

"I was too tired to read the whole thing that night, but I did take a quick look."

"How quick?"

"She left most everything to the shelter, as far as I could see."

He made a note of it. "You remember any specifics?"

"Her gold and diamond Rolex and the Nigel Blakely bronze?"

"The one she was using as a coffee table base?"

I nodded. "She left them both to the shelter."

He jotted it down. "Anything else?"

"She left a few pieces of jewelry to Rich. Men's jewelry, her late husband's, maybe?"

"And?"

"I would've expected her to leave something to Paige and Monica but if she did, I didn't see it. Strange."

"How strange?"

"They were close." I pictured her will. "I didn't get to read the whole thing. I hid it between my mattress and box spring that night. The next night? It was gone.

"Only one person who could've taken it." He frowned. "A shame you didn't get to read it all. The more we know, the better." He glanced at his notes. "She leave anything to you?"

"No, not that I would've expected it. She didn't like me any better than I liked her. She only invited me to those soirees because I was married to Rich."

"You didn't like her parties?"

"I hated them."

"But you went because of your husband."

I went because I still thought I owed him. Tell him about Danny? Sometime, maybe. Not now.

"Amanda?"

"I didn't want to go, but Rich could be so—"

"Controlling?" He didn't wait for an answer. "Don't blame yourself."

Who else can I blame? "I should've stuck up for myself. I didn't like Wendi or her friends, but if Rich expected me to go…"

He nodded. "My ex had some friends I could've done without."

I let my breath out slowly. "Rich has always been controlling. After Katie started school, he expected me to get a full-time job. A real job, that's how he put it. He knew how much I'd always wanted to paint and he was making enough money for me to give it a shot." *After I supported him through law school,* something else I didn't care to tell Jace right now. "I had a terrible time trying to get him to understand."

"He didn't want you to become an artist?"

"Teaching, graphic arts or charity work, that's what he thought I should be doing. But my painting has always just meant so much to me."

He took my hand. "I'm glad you stood up for yourself. Your paintings are wonderful."

I felt myself blush— again. "Thank you."

He looked in my eyes, enough for me to feel something so intense, I couldn't even begin to describe it. Too soon, he moved away. "Back to those DVDs, no way could you have known, or even suspected what that group was really about, unless-- they ever invite you to join them?"

"No, but even if they had? I could never—"

I was glad when he patted my shoulder. "Back to the vic." He frowned. "I hate to ask you this again, but before you watched those DVDs, you had no idea…"

"What Rich was doing in his spare time? No clue! Spending time with Wendi and her friends bored me beyond belief. All they ever talked about was things: cars, jewelry, shopping, vacations. At some point, I began to suspect Rich and Wendi might've been intimate, but I never imagined..."

"But you did suspect he was sleeping with her."

I nodded. "He talked about her a lot, how beautiful she was, how special. He'd done the same thing with a few other women, over the years." *More than a few,* something else he didn't need to know.

"He was a serial womanizer?"

I tried not to flinch, but I couldn't help it.

"I'm sorry. I thought—"

"I knew?" I sighed. "I should've, but there was never any proof, not till I found that Amex statement." *And the world fell out from under me.*

He glanced at his notes again. "The Ocean Winds and the Borgata? They went first class." He looked at me, waiting for a reply?

I didn't have one.

"Sorry." An apology, something else I never got from Rich. "Anything else you can think of?"

I hesitated. "Just, whenever Rich talked about how petite and delicate Wendi was? It drove me crazy. He knew it, too, and he still kept doing it."

He shook his head and smiled. "Barracudas are more delicate than that one!"

What about beautiful? I was about to ask when he took my hand. "As for beautiful? Everyone always said how beautiful Diane was. But living with her? It was hell."

I would've loved to hear more about Diane, but I knew he'd tell me, in his own time. And we would have more time together. I needed to believe that.

"To get back to the vic—"

"Wendi? She looked so good at Women's Club meetings, it intimidated me. I can only imagine how Helen and her friends must've felt."

"You don't have to imagine, they told me. I get it, too. Diane always looked perfect, even after she'd downed most of a bottle of vodka."

I wanted to know more, but I wouldn't push. I sighed as I pictured Wendi, Paige and Monica in all their pricey, designer label glory. "Jessica always said Wendi and her friends would be happier if they could wear their labels on the outside."

"Sad."

Was his ex a designer groupie, too?

"Back to the case. And the will. If there's anything else you remember…"

"I was just so surprised when I didn't see anything she'd left to her friends. As far as I could see, she cut Steffi out, too, not that they got along that well. Really, Steffi had just started coming around to see her."

He made a note of it. "What about Jim and Pete? How well do you know them?"

I shrugged my shoulders. "Not too well."

"Did they ever say or do anything that would've led you to suspect they'd engaged in group sex in front of a camera? And, sorry to ask you this again-- are you absolutely sure they never invited you to join them?"

I took a sip of coffee and choked on it.

"I'll take that as *no*." He began to go on when his phone rang. He took the call in the living room and came back a few minutes later. "They need me." He looked around. "You're staying here the next few days, I hope."

I nodded. "I just need to go back to finish those two paintings. I'll be fine," I added. "Rich never comes home during the day." I wished I felt as sure of that as I sounded.

But Jace didn't seem to notice, as he nodded and looked off into the distance, picturing Rich and the others in those DVDs? I was almost about to ask when he went on. "Those two paintings you're working on? They're fantastic!" He kissed me again, then, a kiss that held all kinds of promise.

I wrapped my arms around myself after he left. Going back to what used to be my house was the last thing I wanted to do, but the sooner I finished those paintings, the sooner I could move on. That's what I told myself as went over there, unlocked the door and forced myself to go in.

I took a quick shower, packed a few more things and called Jessica, but she didn't answer. I left a message before I got dressed and put on a little makeup. I smiled at my reflection in the mirror as I thought back to last night. Jace made me happy, happier than I'd been in years.

It wasn't just him, though. I'd been through a lot, enough to change me, something that might not have happened if Wendi was still alive, if I'd never seen those DVDs, if Rich had never filed for divorce. That's what I was thinking when the phone rang.

I stiffened, until I checked the caller ID. It was Teresa. "We're missing your signature on a few documents. I've got an opening at 2:15. Can you come in?"

"No problem."

"We need to discuss strategy, too. I still think it'll be cut and dry, but since your husband is an attorney, we need to consider all the variables."

"But I thought, those DVDs…"

"We'll talk about it when you come in," she replied smoothly. Too smoothly, was she worried? *Deal with it later. Right now? Paint.*

Time passed quickly as I put the final touches on those two paintings, cleaned up and got ready to go. When I checked the time, I was glad to see I had an hour to spare.

I'd always put Rich's wants, needs and desires first except when it came to my painting. *No more,* I told myself as I opened the front door and saw Jessica pulling in. I met her in her driveway. "I'm so glad you're back!"

She got out, gave me a hug and asked if I could help bring her bags in.

"No problem." She handed me some shopping bags, then, and I followed her in. She looked around. "Do I smell coffee?"

I put her bags down by the door. "I, um, needed a place to stay last night. Since I had your key... I hope you don't mind…"

"Of course not." She looked around. "It just feels like something else happened here last night, too."

I hesitated.

"Tell me! Everything."

I took a deep breath before I did. I began with the gunshots and moved on to—Jace. "I hope you're okay with, y'know…"

"I'm not okay with someone shooting at you, but you and Jace having hot sex in my guest room? Wow!" She grinned. "After all those years with Rich, you deserve it!"

"But I'm still married, technically, at least."

"Technically," she agreed.

"You don't think I cheated on Rich?"

She shook her head. "I can't believe you'd worry about cheating on a man who had sex with Wendi and her friends and recorded it for posterity."

"That still doesn't make it right."

"We all have needs." She sat down on the sofa. "Stay here as long as you'd like. I'm not sure how I'd feel about Jace coming over every night, but--" She smiled and shrugged her shoulders.

"It's just so hard for me to go back to that house."

"Don't worry, I'll go with you. I can go to the lawyer's with you today, too, if you want. Been there, done that."

"If you're sure you're up to it."

"No problem."

Chapter Nineteen

I took the scenic route down to Teresa's office just as I always did, but with Jessica in the car, it felt like an adventure. I was glad she was doing so well. I could tell by the way every bistro, café and boutique we passed seemed to just, well, fascinate her. "Beachy Keen? Great name, and just look at all those sundresses! We've got to stop there on the way home."

"Okay."

"Thongs? Cute name for a store, even if all they sell is—"

"Skimpy underwear?"

She smiled. "Thong sandals. Get your mind out of the gutter!"

"That'll be hard, after watching those DVDs."

"Sorry I missed them."

"I wish I'd missed them." We both began to laugh, then, easing some of my anxiety.

"I'd love to stop there, too, on the way home," she was saying as I tuned back in.

"Okay." I was okay with it, too, until I realized the reason she wanted to stop into those boutiques: she was planning to move down to the Outer Banks and open one of her own.

"I'm glad we don't have to get home in time to cook dinner."

"Me, too." Deep down, though, I was surprised to realize how mixed my feelings were about the daily routines that can make or break a marriage. Rich had seldom come home in time for dinner. I'd gotten used to a long, long time ago. I frowned as I realized just how many of his unacceptable behaviors I'd gotten used to.

"Not forever." Jess was saying as I pulled up in front of Teresa's office.

"What's not forever?"

"Everything. Here today, gone tomorrow." Was she thinking about Tomas? I was trying to come up with the right thing to say when I glanced at my watch and realized we were late.

***

A half hour later, Teresa handed me yet another set of papers. "These papers authorize me to serve your husband."

I signed them quickly, the same way I'd signed all the other papers she'd given me.

I'd phoned her first thing this morning to tell her about the gunshots. What I didn't tell her was how anxious and fearful I'd been ever since. I didn't mention Jace's name, either, nor had she asked about any police involvement.

Not that this meeting was over...

"I don't imagine you want to talk about what happened last night, but it'd probably be a good idea to get it down for the record. Are you up to doing that right now?"

I glanced at Jessica. "Best to get it over with."

I hesitated before I nodded my agreement.

"I requested a copy of the police report, but that can take a while." She took out a recorder, then and recorded my name, the date, the time and the fact that she was interviewing me here in her office. "Whenever you're ready."

As ready as I'll ever be.

***

An hour later, we'd gotten it all down—everything except the fact that I'd slept with Jace last night.

"If the police find any connection between last night's incident and your husband, that'll give us some extra insurance, if we do end up in court." She put the recorder away. "One more thing we need to discuss."

"What's that?"

"I'll get right to the point-- your husband is charging you with adultery."

"Me? He was the one—"

"I know that, and we have all the proof we'll ever need to prove he cheated on you. But I still need to ask if there's any basis in fact for that charge."

I thought it over. I needed to lie and I needed to do it well enough so she'd believe me. "After being with Rich all these years? I can't tell you how wonderful it feels to be alone." It was the truth, too, at least in one sense. I'd never expected another man to come into my life. That'd happened pretty much on its own.

I watched closely as she nodded and made a note of it. "I'll take that as *no*. But I also need to tell you, the man he claims you had sexual relations with is the detective assigned to the case, Jason Connolly."

The same detective I slept with last night?

"If you have had, or are having any kind of personal relationship with this man, it could come out, if we should end up in court."

"I thought you said that'd never happen."

"I don't believe it will, but the fact that your husband is an attorney? It does leave a little room for doubt. So if you're having any kind of relationship with Connolly—"

"I met him last year at an exhibit we did at Brook Haven's new Civic Center. He bought one of my prints. Then, the day they found Wendi's body and he came out to investigate, we talked. That's all we did." *Until a few weeks later, when he kissed me and last night, when we made love.* I was flashing back to it when she spoke again.

"Talking was only the beginning, according to his statement."

Did he see us through the window last night-- after he tried to kill me? I squared my shoulders and shook my head.

"In light of the DVDs, his accusations shouldn't hold much weight, but we still need to counter file." She handed me another set of papers. "This is a statement that denies you have, or have ever had any such relationship with Connolly. Read it over and sign it." She paused. "Unless you're having second thoughts."

"No second thoughts." I proved it by signing on the dotted line.

"I'll phone your husband's attorney today to set up a meeting."

"We really have to meet with him?" That was not something I wanted to do.

She nodded. "We do. First, I'll inform his attorney that the DVDs exist. I need to watch them, by the way, especially the ones that include him. I hope that's all right with you."

Fine, when I have no choice. I nodded.

"I just need to see enough to jot down some details for his attorney. She needs to know we're telling the truth."

His attorney was a *she?* I began to ask her name until I remembered Teresa was waiting for an answer. What was the question? *Permission to watch the DVDs.* "I understand. It's just, Rich and I? We were married for such a long time..." *And I feel like I was such a fool.*

I felt a little better when Jessica patted my shoulder. “I felt the same way when I found out about Dennis and Tara. You'll get over it, trust me.”

Doing my best.

“Only natural you'd be upset,” Teresa agreed. “Right now, you need to focus on the goal, divorcing him with a fair settlement. In this case? I’m sure you’ll get one."

I so wanted to believe that.

***

I felt better when we were back on the road. We made two stops on the way home, one at Thongs, the other at Beachy Keen. I enjoy shopping as much as the next woman, but picking out a sundress and a pair of sandals was the last thing I felt like doing after meeting with Teresa.

But I was still glad to see how much better Jessica was feeling as I watched her pay for three sundresses and four pairs of sandals, one of them a pair of gold metallic thongs with three inch heels for me.

“When would I wear them?”

“Think about it, you'll figure it out.”

I blushed as I imagined wearing them for Jace.

“You’re blushing. I love it!” She smiled as the clerk wrapped my sandals. “Always remember, in a divorce? The better your poker face, the better you come out in the end.”

I thought back to the night Rich said I’d never make a poker player. That was then, this is now, I told myself as we pulled up in front of The Beachcomber, a trendy little café by the bridge back to Brook Haven. I checked my watch-- 5:25. Early for dinner, I thought, until I heard my stomach rumble, reminding me that I hadn't eaten since breakfast. With Jace.

After they'd seated us at a table by the windows overlooking the beach, Jessica gestured around the café. “This is the look I have in mind for my café on the Outer Banks.”

She was really going to move down there and leave me behind. I was sad until I imagined moving down there myself, someday. With Jace. *Crazy!*

A pretty blonde server in shorts and a Beachcomber tee shirt came up to take our drink orders. Moments later, we were sipping icy macchiados and perusing the menu. Salads, wraps, paninis and quesadillas, the perfect menu for a beach cafe. I looked out at the beach, let my breath out slowly and almost succeeded in putting Rich, the DVDs. even the divorce out of my mind.

Jessica pointed to the menu. “Remind me to ask for a copy.”

I nodded. She's really going to do it, I thought, then: if she can make changes, so can I. I held on to that idea till we got home. I was relieved when Rich’s SUV wasn’t in the driveway. I pulled in and sat in my car for a moment, thinking about last night, Rich's adultery charges and the divorce. I would find a way to come to terms with it, all of it.

“You’re staying at my house tonight, I hope.” Jessica reached over and shut the engine.

I nodded. “I just need to put the final touches on those last two paintings.” I went on to tell her how I planned to drive them up to Chloe’s New Jersey gallery tomorrow.

She smiled. “I know, I'll go with you. We can have lunch, do some shopping, make a day of it.”

“Sounds good.” I hoped her coming with me would allay the case of nerves I'd had, since we'd left Teresa's office. I flashed back to the awful sound of that water glass shattering the other night as we went into my house and looked around. It was fine until we went into the three-season room and I stopped cold. Someone had broken in, ransacked my studio and slashed those last two paintings.

I began to head in there when Jessica stopped me. “We need to call the police.”

Jace. I need to call Jace. I took his card out and gave it to her. The knowledge that I could turn this crisis over to him made me feel a little better—until I took another look at my studio and those two paintings. They'd both been slashed neatly down the middle, not unlike Wendi's purple pashmina.

I couldn’t take my eyes off them as Jessica phoned him. I looked down at the floor, then, and saw the tackle box that'd held my supplies. The intruder had overturned it, scattering my paints and brushes all over the floor, splattering the walls with paint. My mermaid clock wasn't in its spot on the wall, either. I looked down. It was on the floor, smashed to smithereens.

Was Rich the one who'd done it? Hard to believe he’d take that kind of risk until I thought back to Forestville: *I did it because I can.*

I was glad when Jessica took me into the kitchen and told me to sit down, then pressed a glass of ice water into my hands and told me to drink it. Jace arrived what felt like minutes later, a crime scene team right behind him.

I stayed in the kitchen, the same room where I'd prepared all those breakfasts, lunches and dinners, meals I'd generally ended up eating alone. Jace and his team were in my studio now. I stood up, ready to go in there, when Jessica stopped me.

Jace came in, then, and put his arms around me. "Calm down, sweetheart. We need to finish up this scene and take some photographs and samples. I'll be back. Promise."

No choice but to agree. But I still couldn't stop thinking about my two ruined paintings.

"I'll help you clean up, when you're ready." I heard Jessica's voice as if from a distance. I tried to put a response, any response together, but nothing came to mind. *Focus,* I told myself, but it didn't help. Nothing could help...

"Give her some brandy," I heard Jace telling her. When had he come back? Not that it mattered. He was going back in my studio now.

Jessica sat down next to me. "Why don't we go back to my house?"

I hesitated before I agreed. Helen was waiting at the door when we got there. "What are all those police cars doing at your house?"

I began to tell her what happened when Jessica shook her head and miraculously, Helen got quiet. Minutes later, we were in Jess' living room and I was sipping brandy from one of her Waterford snifters. "I'm glad the Waterford was in the wine cellar the night Grace & Company came over," Jessica said as I held it up and watched the light refract off the design before I took another sip and closed my eyes.

I didn't wake up till Jace showed up at 10:45, according to Jess' wall clock. Helen was gone, and Jessica excused herself as he sat down, put his arms around me and kissed me.

“Did Rich come home?” Why did it matter, why did I care?

“Jessica didn’t tell you?”

I shook my head. “I guess I dozed off.”

“Good.” He took my hand and gave it a comforting little squeeze. “Looks like he moved out. His clothes are gone, his laptop, too, even his golf clubs.”

I nodded. That should’ve made me happy. Why didn't it? Why couldn't I seem to feel...anything?

“We also found evidence to suggest he was planning to leave the country. I got an APB out. They picked him up at Newark Liberty Airport an hour ago, before he could board a flight to Grand Cayman."

“Grand Cayman?” I flashed back to our wedding on St. Thomas. A lifetime ago.

“Great place to hide money," Jace went on. "Don't worry, sweetheart, he’s not going there or anywhere else. They're interrogating him down at the station right now.”

“Has he been charged with... anything?” *Was he the one who slashed my paintings?* He of all people knew how much they meant to me.

“Not yet, but he had a large amount of cash on him.” Jace didn’t volunteer any more details and I didn't ask. “I’ll question him myself a little later. If he says anything that might connect him to the vandalism—”

“Or those gunshots last night?”

He nodded. “No hard evidence on that one yet, but they're doing their best.” He looked in my eyes and frowned. “If you need anything from your house, tell me now. I don’t want you going in there alone.”

“I don't want to go in there. Ever.” He moved in closer, put his arms around me and held me for a few moments, calming me enough to picture the house and ask myself if I needed to go back there. “I don't need a thing from my house.”

He nodded, let me go and stood up. I was cold, suddenly. Freezing. He leaned down and took my hand. “We'll find out who did this. Promise,” he added as he kissed me gently on the cheek. “We did find a little something. It isn't much.”

“What?”

“There were all these nice, clear footprints outside. Could be the perp’s. Women’s athletic shoes. With a real distinctive tread.”

I wanted him to tell me more, but I couldn’t seem to get the words out.

“One of the techs recognized the tread. His wife has shoes like that. They're Swedish imports. Aerobicas. Ever heard of them?”

“Aerobicas?” I'd seen them, where?

“They're only sold in spas and fitness centers. They sell for $150 and up.”

Wendi would buy shoes like that. If she had, Paige and Monica would've followed suit. I managed to tell him that somehow.

“We’ll call the pro shop, see what they have to say.” He looked around. “You're staying here tonight?”

“I can’t go home.” *Ever.* I looked over at the house that'd never felt like home through Jessica's windows and began to shiver again. He helped me up and took me in his arms.

“You could stay at my place, but I don't know how late I'll be and I don't think you should be alone."

His place? Yes. Alone? Not tonight.

“You also need to call your lawyer tomorrow, tell her what happened.”

I nodded. “I thought Rich might’ve done it. But those footprints…”

He shook his head. “Warren was at the airport. He'd already checked in for his flight." He sighed softly. "Don’t worry, sweetheart, we’ll get it done.” He leaned down and gave me another kiss. “Talk to you in the morning, okay?”

I nodded, even though I desperately wanted to be with him tonight. Jessica came in after he went out. “Helen thinks you should cancel your part in *Born Yesterday.* She says Cliff will understand.”

Especially if he knew about the break-in. Or helped with it. Or Wendi’s murder, or Harvey’s disappearance. I wasn’t sure why I suspected he'd been involved, but that feeling wouldn’t go away. The footprints outside my house may have been made by a woman, but when it came to Wendi’s murder, I still believed it'd been a man who'd done it.

“Try to relax. Don’t think about anything but getting a good night’s sleep.” I was glad when Jessica’s voice brought me back.

I nodded. I didn’t think I’d ever get to sleep, but an hour later, I crashed the minute I closed my eyes, awakening only when I heard a terrified scream, then sat up and realized it came from me.

Jessica rushed in. “What’s wrong?” she asked as I followed her gaze to the clock on the nightstand--2:19. AM.

I sat up and wrapped my arms around myself. I was shivering again. If I could just warm up, I'd feel better, I thought as she went out. A minute later, I heard her talking on the phone. I pulled the quilt back up, lay back down and closed my eyes again, just for a minute.

It was 3:43 when I opened them and found Jace in bed with me. I sat up slowly. He opened his eyes and propped himself up on his elbow. He looked exhausted.

"I'm sorry Jessica called you."

He shook his head. "I'm not."

"You're exhausted."

He shrugged his shoulders, then pulled me close. "I got here as soon as I could."

I'm glad, thank you? I debated what to say. But in the end, I just nodded.

"Okay, sweetheart, I'm giving you two choices."

I nodded even though I didn't want him to talk. I wanted him to hold me, kiss me, make love with me.

"I can stay here with you tonight or we can go to my place. What'll it be?"

I don't care, as long as we're together. I was about to say that when he kissed me lightly on the lips. "Better if I stay here."

Better than that if Jessica wasn't in the next room, I thought as I pulled him closer and reveled in the feel of him against me--until he backed off, got up, took my clothes from the top of the dresser and tossed them on the bed. "Get dressed."

I was confused but not for long. We were going to his place tonight. Together.

***

Fifteen minutes later we were in his car when Rich came to mind. If he'd tried to shoot me, then destroyed my paintings, he might well be the one who'd murdered Wendi, slashed her pashmina and stuffed her body into her designer trash can.

Harvey came to mind, too. Was he still alive? Assuming he was, where was he? Had Rich done anything to help his disappearance along? "About Rich..."

Jace stifled a yawn. "We had to let him go a couple hours ago but we're holding his passport. They'll check on him, make sure he doesn't go anywhere in the near future." He flashed me a tired little smile.

I tried to come up with a reply. It didn't surprise me when I couldn't.

"We'll go back to your house tomorrow, see if anything's missing."

It was never my house, not really. I would've told him that, if I wasn't so tired. He was pulling up in front of his condo now, where we'd sleep together, maybe even make love.

That didn't happen, though, not tonight. Moments after we got in bed, we fell asleep. I didn't wake up till after ten the next morning, when I followed the scent of fresh-brewed coffee into the dining el, where one of my other prints was hanging on the wall. He was sitting at the table. He'd just finished his coffee, and most of what looked like an Upper Crust Danish.

He looked up from his laptop. "Saved you a croissant. Chocolate." He smiled, crinkling the corners around those crystal blue eyes, clear blue, this morning, as he got up, gave me a kiss and pointed to the coffee cartridges. "What's your pleasure?"

You're my pleasure. I almost said that but we both knew this wasn't the time. I'd make my own coffee this morning, but I couldn't forget how good it'd felt when he made it for me. *He'll make you coffee again.* I was sure of that, somehow. "Any French vanilla?"

He nodded. Moments later, I was enjoying my coffee and devouring that croissant— who doesn't like chocolate? I felt almost, well, normal, till I flashed back to last night, and those two slashed paintings.

He took my hand. "We will find out who did this."

I wanted to believe him, as I picked up the last piece of my croissant, put it back down and frowned.

"It'll be okay." He hesitated. "Why don't you get dressed?"

I nodded, then showered and did so quickly. Too soon, we were back in my studio. I'd never paint in there again, but I needed to get it back in order before I could move on with my life.

"I can't tell you how sorry I am about this." He frowned. "We'll leave this room alone for now, we're not done with it yet. But we can check the rest of the house, see if anything's missing."

He was calm about it, a good thing, when I felt like I was almost about to jump out of my skin. I took a deep breath before I began to look around. I couldn't disappoint him or myself by falling apart. What felt like hours later, I discovered that despite the way my paintings had been slashed, nothing had been taken from the living room, dining room or kitchen.

It was another hour before I realized some of my jewelry was missing, including the diamond wedding ring set I'd never wanted. Not that I'd planned to wear it again, I told Jace, explaining how Rich had replaced my simple gold band with "a proper set," as he'd climbed the ladder that ultimately led to a Senior Partnership at the firm.

"Lots of rumors going around the office," Rich said the night he brought it home. "Everyone says I'm about to make partner. A partner's wife cannot wear some tacky little gold wedding band."

Tacky or not, my simple gold band was a reminder of how he'd cared enough to marry me. Not that I told him that the night he gave me the new set, not when I still felt like I owed him. I thanked him as I put it on and told him how lovely it was. I knew he thought of the three carat, emerald-cut diamond complemented by two wedding bands set with smaller stones as my reward.

"When was the last time you wore it?" Jace was asking me now.

"Wendi's funeral."

"How 'bout the other pieces?" A sapphire and diamond necklace I'd worn twice and the diamond tennis bracelet Rich insisted I had to have me were gone, too. I hadn't worn the tennis bracelet more than five or six times.

"A tennis bracelet? I don't play tennis," I'd pointed out the night he brought it home.

"Tennis is trendy. Sign up for lessons at the club," he said as he slipped it on my wrist. "Wear it to the benefit tonight," he added. We were always going to one benefit or another back then.

"What about the other pieces? Take your time," Jace added softly.

I'm making him crazy. "I'm sorry—"

He shook his head and pulled me close. "I understand." He proved it by giving me a sweet, gentle kiss. "No rush, sweetheart."

I heard myself sigh. "Rich bought me all those pieces. I would never have chosen them myself. He had this vision of how I should look whenever we went out together."

Jace frowned.

"I'm not sorry they're gone, especially the ring set, even if it cost a fortune." Another sigh escaped me. "I thought I'd give it to Katie."

"Any idea how much it cost?"

"$41,000, I think that was the appraisal figure we got last year." Rich insisted on having all our jewelry appraised every few years for insurance. He always got those appraisals in writing, too. "The appraisal's here somewhere. I can look." Not that I wanted to.

He shook his head. "We've got time for that. Just tell me, do you remember the last time you saw those other pieces?"

I closed my eyes. "The day—"

"Of the victim's funeral?"

I nodded. Wendi's funeral, the end of my marriage, the gunshots, Tomas' death-- they all ran together in my mind. I felt better when he pulled me close and began to massage my neck and my shoulders gently. Wonderful, until his voice pulled me back. "We'll get through this. You're going to be okay."

I wanted to believe him, needed to believe there were good, maybe even great things in store for me, a happy, productive rest-of-my-life with a man who loved me for the woman I was, not the woman he wanted me to be.

Chapter Twenty

Jace and I were having coffee the morning after my second night at his place. I'd loved falling asleep in his arms. That print of my favorite painting on the wall where we could both see it from the bed made it even better.

I still felt guilty about sharing his bed. I'd been through a lot, the slashed tires, those gunshots and the two vandalized paintings. Enough to justify sleeping with a man who wasn't my husband? I couldn't seem to get there yet, but last night confirmed something: Rich was wrong about my sexuality. I was a vital, responsive woman, with the right man.

"What's that smile about?" Jace asked.

"Last night." I kept smiling as I remembered how perfect it'd been. Did he feel the same way? He'd separated from his ex three years ago, but his divorce had been finalized only a few months ago. What if he wasn't ready for a relationship? What if he felt guilty, too?

"Last night was..." He smiled and took my hand across the table. "I hope you don't feel guilty."

"A little, but I'm working on it."

He smiled. "Keep right on doing that, sweetheart." He leaned over to kiss me before he got serious. "You were right about the vic's friends, by the way. They followed her every move." He indicated his laptop. "Heavenly Bodies is the only place that sells Aerobicas between here and Manhattan. They sold five pairs in the past six weeks, one to that technician's wife, four more to the vic, her stepdaughter and her friends." He hesitated. "They all have the same tread as the footprints we found outside your house."

A shiver ran down my spine as I pictured Paige, Monica, maybe even Steffi vandalizing my studio and slashing my paintings. "Paige, Monica and Steffi were the other three women who bought them, right?"

He nodded.

"High time I got something right."

He looked in my eyes "Oh, you get lots of things right." He picked up his cinnamon raisin Danish, broke off a piece and offered it to me. I'd finished my own, but I took it and ate it anyway, savoring the taste and texture, not the least bit embarrassed by the way he was watching me eat.

"Glad your appetite's back."

I wasn't. I'd been eating too much lately. "I know. Time to start watching myself again."

"Watching yourself do what?"

"Rich always said—"

"What, he thought you were fat?"

I nodded. "He was always comparing me—"

"To the vic?" He frowned. "You won't have to worry about her anymore."

"Won't have to worry about Rich, either, after the divorce is final." Or would I? I flashed back to that awful night with Danny. Had I really put it to rest? If I had, why wasn't I ready to tell Jace about it?

"We brought Paige, Monica, Pete and Jim in this morning and questioned them separately," he said as he made himself another cup of coffee. "If they even mention Warren's name, that'll give us enough to bring him back in."

"I hope they do." I sipped my coffee as he glanced at the clock.

"They should be there by now. You need to stay here today, okay?"

"I can do that." No place else I'd rather be. A few kisses later, he went out the door.

The hours passed quickly as I phoned Chloe to tell her about my paintings and the insurance company to file claims for the damage and the stolen jewelry. I checked in with Teresa after that, then took a break for lunch before I called Jessica and Helen to reassure them I was all right. I was surprised when I realized it was true. I felt a lot better today, something that had everything to do with Jace.

It was after four when I began to wonder when he'd be home. Make dinner or order out? Since he didn't know when he'd be back and there wasn't much food in the condo, I opted for takeout. I'd spotted a stack of menus in a basket on the counter. I was glad when I saw Golden Siam's on top. I forced myself not to think about what might be happening down at the station until after I'd placed my order and made myself some tea.

The phone rang, then. I was glad when I saw it was Jace. "The vic's friends didn't implicate Warren, exactly but—"

"What?"

"I can't say too much, but his name came up in several different contexts. The good news? We've got enough to bring him back in."

"Rich is there now?"

"Got here 15 minutes ago. One of my colleagues is interrogating him."

I waited for him to volunteer more information. "And?"

"That's all I can say. Sorry about dinner. I know there's not much in the house."

"I ordered in. Golden Siam."

"Could you call in some shrimp Pad Thai for me? Spring rolls, too. I'm not sure when I'll be home."

Home. That sounded wonderful. I called in his order a few minutes later. Takeout was no problem for Jace, apparently. It'd been a huge issue for Rich. The minute he'd made partner, he'd informed me takeout was no longer an option, not that it made much difference, when he was seldom home in time for dinner.

I'd finished my Pad Thai, enjoying every bite, by the time Jace came in. I heated up his takeout and forced myself not to ask questions. It wasn't nearly as hard as I might've expected, I was that glad to see him.

"I guess you want to know what happened."

"Yes." I put his Pad Thai on a plate and gave it to him.

"We were all hoping Warren wouldn't lawyer up," he began as he picked up his spring roll and dipped it in Golden Siam's sauce, a luscious blend of honey and spices, took a bite and smiled. "Delicious…"

A man who liked Thai as much as I did? Perfect. "Rich brought in another lawyer?"

He nodded. "As full of himself as he is, it surprised us."

"Who'd he bring in?" I imagined it'd been one of his Duncan Fitzgerald Kaufman colleagues. I'd met many of them, over the years.

I was surprised, and a little annoyed, when Jace didn't answer me directly. "He wouldn't have brought her in if he wasn't worried." He finished his spring roll and moved on to his Pad Thai. "This one? She's so high-profile, she's almost a celebrity."

"She?"

He nodded and kept on eating. He didn't think the fact that Rich's lawyer was a woman was nearly as important as I did. "That search warrant could come through as early as tomorrow morning. I'd love to clear this case."

And charge Rich with murder? Not pretty, but oh so satisfying. As for Rich's lawyer, he still hadn't told me who she was. "His attorney, she was from Duncan Fitzgerald Kaufman?"

He shook his head. "Ever hear of Maggie Parsons?"

Maggie Parsons of the long legs, great body, long, jet black hair, beautiful brown eyes and intellect as sharp as a steel trap? I'd heard more about her than I ever wanted to. Not that I was about to share that with him. "She was his intern when she first started out."

"Good to know. She's a big criminal lawyer these days. Came all the way down from Basking Ridge."

Of course she would, assuming she and Rich had been lovers.

"You ever meet Ms. Parsons?"

"Once or twice, years ago." Right around the same time that Rich, who'd just made Senior Partner, couldn't stop talking about her, something else Jace didn't need to know.

"Remember that murder trial three years ago, the doctor who killed his wife up in Montclair? That trial really made her."

"I read about it." I'd seen coverage of it, and Ms. Parsons, on TV, too. If I'd expected the years to dull her good looks, I'd been crushed when she'd looked better than ever on TV.

"*Jersey Trends* magazine named her the highest-profile female attorney in New Jersey that year," Jace was saying now.

"Rich showed me the article." *I hated it!* A sigh escaped me. "He talked about Maggie and that trial..." *Forever.*

"She's the best, in criminal law."

That's when it hit me. She specialized in criminal law, but Rich had also retained her to represent him in the divorce. Surprising, when he loved to tell me, lecture me, really, on all the differences between civil and criminal law.

Maggie Parsons had chosen to work in criminal law. She'd made an exception when she'd agreed to represent Rich in the divorce. Only one reason she'd do that, I thought as I pictured Rich in bed with her and went on to imagine him in bed with Wendi, Paige, Monica, Steffi, Cliff, Harvey, Burt the dentist-- and heaven only knew who else!

"I was questioning him myself, not getting much, when Ms. Parsons came in. After that?" He shrugged his shoulders.

"I get that." Had Rich continued to see, and sleep with the delectable Ms. Parsons, all these years?

"But really, he didn't tell us much even before she got there." I looked at Jace. Sexy, the way he was eating, so sexy, I couldn't wait to get him into bed. I didn't feel guilty, either, not tonight. The image of my soon-to-be-ex faded quickly as I began to get warm all over.

"We'll do a more thorough search of your house and his office as soon as the search warrant comes through. That should help us find out more about his affairs."

His affairs. I felt like crying, suddenly. Could he see it?

"His financial affairs." He reached over, put his hand on my cheek and stroked it gently. He knew how I felt. I was glad until he stopped, stood up and went to rinse off his plate.

"There's more tea."

"Good." He refilled both our cups. "How was your Pad Thai?" he asked, something else Rich never did.

I smiled. "Delicious." *Even better when Rich wasn't here to tell me Thai wasn't his favorite, add up the calories and try to make me feel guilty for finishing the whole thing.*

"Good." He leaned down and kissed me again. He'd helped me to my feet, and we were beginning to go from there when my phone rang. I checked the caller ID--it was Chloe.

"I just wanted to make sure you're all right. I feel terrible about what happened last night."

"I'm trying not to let it get to me." I heard Jace's phone ring as I reassured her I was all right. Not the whole truth, but I did feel a lot better here in Jace's condo. "I'm not going to have time to do any more paintings."

"Don't worry about it. I love the pieces we have. Really, it'll be fine. If you need me to come down to help you clean up, just say the word."

"Thanks. I think it'll be okay, but I'll let y you know." Maybe it would be okay, I thought as we ended the call. Just for tonight, I felt a little stronger. I wasn't sure how I'd feel when I had to go back there, but I was glad I wouldn't be alone. Jessica and Helen both offered to help.

Jace came back a few minutes after I ended the call. "One case down," he murmured. "Remember Reverend Willard Bailey? You must. You did visit him in jail. Brought him some baked goods, if I remember correctly." He raised an eyebrow.

"You know about that?"

"I know about everything." He smiled, taking his time and enjoying it, too. "The Feds finally got enough on him to put him away."

"What about his son?"

"They're working on it. He's not Wendi's son, either, by the way."

"He's her stepson, I know."

"I guess you would." I was glad when he seemed all right with that. "They both have an airtight alibi for the day of the murder, too. They were driving up here, with toll and gas receipts that prove it."

"It does narrow the field."

"I wish it narrowed it enough." He frowned.

I gave him a kiss, then we headed into his bedroom, where we made love before we fell asleep in each other's arms. It felt good, almost good enough for me to let go of Rich, and Danny, and that last little twinge of guilt.

His phone didn't ring again till he was almost out the door the next morning. I'd planned to go home today, not that it felt like home, not that it ever had. I still had to clean up my one-time studio before I could move on. Unfortunately, though, as Jace just told me, that room, along with the entire house, was a crime scene. I couldn't set foot in there without him, let alone begin to put my studio back in order, not till they'd finished going over it.

Jace was on his way to the station to check on the search warrant. "Assuming the judge signed off on it, we'll start this morning," he said before he kissed me goodbye.

***

"I've got to clean up that room!"

Jessica, Helen and I were having coffee at Helen's house. My phone was on the table because I was hoping Jace would call. My heart beat a little faster when it finally rang. I was disappointed when it turned out to be Jessica's phone, not mine. Hal was calling to let her know Grace upped the ante on her lawsuit.

He asked if she could come in ASAP, not a bad thing. Really, I didn't have it in me to hear about anyone else's problems today. I let Helen convince me to run some errands with her after Jessica left. I looked over at my house when we got back. I was crushed when no one was there.

When my phone rang a few minutes later, I hoped it was Jace. I was disappointed when Jessica's name and number came up. "I just got back. You think you could come over? I need to talk."

"On my way."

Jess told me more about Grace's demands over the sandwiches we made for lunch. I couldn't seem to eat, but I did my best to just, well, listen. Difficult, when I couldn't stop thinking about the vandal, or vandals who'd destroyed those two paintings and made a total mess of my one-time studio.

Jessica made us some coffee, decaf this time, as I imagined strangling Rich with a different one of Wendi's pashminas. The teal blue with the metallic gold embroidery came to mind. I was into that soul-satisfying vision when the doorbell rang and Helen came in and joined us in the kitchen, bearing some of Elaine's home-baked toll house cookies.

She shook her head when Jessica offered her coffee. "I just wanted to tell Amanda, last night? Steffi stalked out of the rehearsal. She said she's not coming back, too. She also told everyone

Cliff and Burt are lovers-- right in front of Burt's little blonde trophy wife!" Helen glanced at me, hoping I'd ask for more details. How could I disappoint her? "What happened then?"

"Kayla burst into tears and ran out. Monica went after her."

"Monica?" All I'd ever seen Monica actually do was wear designer clothes and brag about the stores where she'd bought them.

"Monica's close to Kayla? I didn't realize..." Jessica frowned.

Helen nodded. "Closer than that! I'd put money on it after seeing them together last night." She shook her head and smiled.

Jessica looked surprised. "You mean—"

Helen paused, for effect, no doubt. She did love, well, drama. "They looked like more than friends last night, a lot more."

I thought it over. "After seeing Monica on those DVDs, anything's possible." She'd gone both ways in at least two of them. Did I really want to know if she and Kayla Davidson were lovers? I hesitated. "You really think the two of them may be involved that way?"

Helen just rolled her eyes as Jessica laughed. Assuming Kayla was involved with Monica and she knew Monica was on those DVDs, that'd make her one more person with motive.

As for Monica, she probably had enough physical strength to murder Wendi, especially if Kayla helped her. Monica wasn't a trainer like Steffi but, just like Wendi, she worked out at Heavenly Bodies three or four times a week.

Helen got up and made herself some coffee. "I was thinking Kayla could've been involved in the murder, too. She wasn't on those DVDs, but assuming she and Monica were, y'know..."

“It gives her, what do they call it, motive?” Jessica said.

Helen nodded. And frowned. That's when I realized she had no idea who the killer was either.

“I was thinking maybe Steffi did it. I only met her once or twice, but she was just so cold, and, like, hard.” That from Jessica.

I began to agree when Helen cut in. “Steffi was pretty detached when she walked out last night. Distant, too." She shook her head. “I didn't expect that, as close as she is to Cliff.”

She also owns a pair of Aerobicas. Not that Jace would want me to tell them that.

“I wish I knew what was going on with the Players.” Helen sighed. “With Steffi out of the picture, I can’t imagine who else can play the lead.”

“Isn’t there an understudy?” I asked.

“Meghan Russo, but she can hardly remember her lines. I wouldn’t be surprised if Cliff canceled the production.”

Easy come, easy go. Not that I hadn't enjoyed my little part, but there was a lot on my plate right now. I was debating whether or not to say that when we heard some noise outside. I got up and looked out the window, An unmarked black sedan was pulling up in front of my house, followed by two Mediterranean blue-and-whites.

He got the warrant.

***

“What do you mean I can’t go in there?” Jace and I were in front of my house as his team brought in equipment. Lots of it.

“C'mon now, sweetheart, you know exactly I mean,” he said, much too calmly. “That room, and the rest of your house? It’s a crime scene.” He took my hand. “I just heard Helen invite you over. You could wait at Jessica’s house or even my condo, if you feel like driving over there.” He put his hand on my shoulder. “Your call.”

“Jessica’s got an appointment.” A manicure and pedicure appointment she made when she got back from Hal's, not that he needed to know that. “C'mon, Jace, you know I don’t want to stay there or anywhere else." I didn't want to whine, either, but I couldn't seem to help it.

“I’m sorry you can’t come in, but you know there's nothing I do about that." He reached out to smooth my hair, condescendingly? “I don't make the rules, here,” he added.

"What if you find something important?”

“I’ll tell you. Promise.”

I hesitated before I nodded my agreement. He leaned down, about to kiss me, when two of his team came up. “Ready?” one of them asked. A sigh escaped me as he nodded and followed them inside. I waited until they closed the door before I headed back to Helen’s.

***

“What if they find something important and he doesn’t tell me?” I asked her a little later. He promised he would. Why couldn't I believe him? *Because you were married to Rich all those years.*

“I'm sure they'll find out who vandalized your studio. After that? You can move on,” she replied evenly. “Everything will be okay, you’ll see.” She took my hand and gave it a reassuring little squeeze.

I smiled and nodded, but really? I didn't believe her, not for a minute.

"He'll find out who killed Wendi, too," she said a short while later, in the den. "After that? It'll all fall into place."

"You really think so?"

She began to reply when her phone rang. She took the call in her bedroom. I heard her talking, but I couldn't make out the words.

"That was Steffi," she said when she came back.

"I didn't think you knew her that well."

"I don't. I was surprised when she called, even more surprised when she told me some things I think Jace needs to know."

"Oh?"

She nodded. "First? She feels sure Cliff will cancel the production. She thinks he might even dissolve the group, with Harvey still MIA and Kayla making all that fuss about Burt's indiscretions."

Fuss? Not the word I would've used, not that there was any point in going there. "Indiscretions, is that how she put it?"

Helen nodded. "Not that Kayla would do anything to hurt Burt's career. Straight, gay or AC/DC, the man makes a good living. And according to Steffi, he ended it with Cliff after Kayla threatened to call a friend of hers at the *Brook Haven Banner*."

Interesting. "You really think he'd dissolve the group? He seems so dedicated."

"True, till that Hollywood producer he met with last year called a few days ago and asked him to come back to California. Steffi says Cliff can't wait. And with Harvey gone? No one else could run that group, except me, maybe. Not that anyone's asked me, or even suggested it."

A pity. She'd do a great job. I began to say that when she cut in.

"She also hinted at the fact that, how can I put this?" She took a deep breath. "She and Rich might've spent some time together." She frowned. "She didn't mention the DVDs, either."

The DVDs? They were the last thing I wanted to think about. "What did she say about Rich?"

She hesitated. "It sounded like she was kind of, I mean the two of them were—"

"Intimate?"

"Don't get upset, now." She sighed. "But she said she's in love with him."

Why wasn't I surprised? "You're sure she didn't say anything about the DVDs?"

She shook her head. "I don't think she knows about them."

She wouldn't, though, if someone else had shot them secretly, planning to blackmail them all, including Wendi? If that was the case and Wendi found out about them and tried to cut herself in, that'd make the blackmailer one more person with motive. Strong motive. "You didn't tell her about them?"

"Of course not. We both suspected they may've been shot secretly, remember?" She didn't wait for a reply. "Steffi also insists she's the one Rich really loves. And wait till you hear the rest!"

"There's more?" I felt torn between wanting to hear it and wanting to run out of there screaming. I felt sure Rich had been in love with Wendi. If he'd told Steffi the same thing, he'd lied. A good possibility-- he'd never had a problem telling lies.

"Steffi thinks Cliff is in love with her, too. She said he was just using Burt to get the best performance out of him, to say nothing of all that free cosmetic dental work."

"You think she could be right?"

Helen smiled. "As egotistical as he is? The dental work might've come first."

I nodded, about to agree, when she went on.

"But the most important thing she said—"

My heart sank. "Tell me."

"She knew Wendi'd been strangled with that purple pashmina. She also referred to the fact that it was slashed, along with the fact that the killer, or killers had stuffed her body in that trash can." Helen smiled. "Apt, the way her body ended up in a trash can."

"A designer trash can." Almost enough to make me smile, until I flashed back to how the purple pashmina looked when the garbage men dumped it on the curb. The pashmina was all I'd seen. I'd assumed Wendy's body was underneath it, but I hadn't actually seen it.

Nor had the police released the cause of death, let alone the way the purple pashmina had been slashed. Jessica was there; she'd seen it herself. Helen and John would've seen it, too, from their porch. But Steffi? No way could she have known about the purple pashmina unless she'd done it, or helped the person, or people who had.

"We need to tell Jace." Helen's voice brought me back abruptly.

I had to agree.

***

"The footprints around the house? Women's, size eight and a half." The crime scene tech looked almost as tired as Jace.

"Call that pro shop again. We can hope only one of those women wears that size." He turned to us as the tech nodded and went off. "Ladies?"

Ladies, how condescending is that?

He was looking at me with interest and pretty much ignoring Helen until she began to tell him what Steffi had said, talking so quickly, it made my head spin.

He glanced at me. "Did you hear it, too?"

I shook my head.

"We'll check it out." He signaled one of the uniformed officers. "Have someone pick up Steffi Willis and bring her in."

He nodded. "How soon will you be there?"

"I think I'll finish up here first, give her a some time to think things over." He turned back to us and looked almost surprised to see us there. He recovered quickly, though, and smiled at Helen. "Thanks," he said. I was gratified when this time, she was the one who blushed.

He was about to say something else when the tech came back. "We caught a break. Only one of those gals wears an eight and a half."

"Which one?"

"Paige Morgan."

Chapter Twenty-One

"You mean Paige was the one who vandalized my studio?"

Jace frowned. "Looks that way." He put his hand on my shoulder. "Wanna' go back to Helen's while we finish up here?"

I was almost about to tell him I wasn't going anywhere when Helen touched my arm and nodded. I'd turned to leave when one of the crime scene techs came up. "Something you should see."

Jace nodded and went off with him.

"Come on, Amanda. We'll go back to my house and relax for a bit."

I didn't have much choice. But after we got to her house, I was still upset.

"Hard to believe it was Paige." Helen shook her head. "You've got to watch the quiet ones. That's what I always say," she added as we sat down in the den.

I thought it over, but no matter how I looked at it, Paige vandalizing my studio made no sense, unless I factored Rich into the equation. I turned to Helen. "Okay, we know Rich was involved with Wendi. Steffi swore he said he loved her, too. What if he told Paige the same thing?" *And Monica. And God only knows who else?*

Helen struggled not to laugh.

"You think it's funny?"

"Sorry." She shrugged her shoulders. "But your ex? He has quite the energy level. You've got to give him that."

I don't have to give him anything. I would've said that, too, if it didn't sound so, bitter. I was wondering what I could say when I heard the key in the lock. John was home. He looked upset as he said hello and gestured Helen into the kitchen. More bad news? Maybe, if he didn't want me to hear it.

I'll close my eyes, just for a minute. I didn't realize I'd dozed off till Helen and John came back a good half hour later. They both looked upset.

"What's going on?" Not that I really wanted to know.

"John and Ed went over the books again," Helen began.

John nodded. "The good news? We finally figured it out. The bad news…" His voice trailed off weakly.

"Tell me."

Helen frowned. "Your husband Rich, I mean, your ex?"

"He may have taken some money." John said softly.

Money he needed because someone was blackmailing him? Why else would he need it? I flashed back to the Young Republicans: *I took that money because I can.* Had Rich kept right on taking other people's money all these years just for the thrill of it? Sick...

John sat down. "Sad to say, we've got everything we need to press charges. But we do plan to speak to him first."

"We need to tell Jace," Helen added.

I nodded and turned to John. "How much money are we talking about, here?"

He hesitated. "Ed didn't want me to tell you, but I think you're entitled to know, especially now that you're filing for divorce."

Helen took John's hand. "I told him. I hope that's okay."

I nodded and turned to John. "How much?" I repeated.

He hesitated a little longer, this time. "$87,000, give or take."

I felt myself go numb as I flashed back to Forestville again. Embezzlement was a crime in the eyes of the law, but it had always been just a game to Rich— until now. I looked up as the doorbell rang. It was Ed Cullen. I could see how upset he was. "Amanda, I didn't realize you were here."

"It's okay," John said. "I told her."

Helen turned to Ed. "I can't tell you how happy I am that she's divorcing that—"

Ed turned to me and frowned. "You had no idea about the money?"

"No." *Not that it surprises me..*

He nodded. "I need to ask you this: how would you feel if we pressed charges?"

"I'm okay with it." Maybe not, I decided as all this nausea hit me. Nothing new, I told myself. Rich had been making me sick for years, but this time? It was all so--real. Too real.

When I looked up, Ed was going outside with Helen and John. I watched as they crossed the street to my house, where Jace and his team were still at work. I hoped they'd found a few more clues. I took a deep breath to center myself before I stood up.

Call Teresa. I took out my phone, entered her number and hoped she'd answer. I hated to bother her again, but embezzlement? That had to be important.

I was relieved when she answered, then offered her sympathy. Again. "This makes it more important than ever to stay focused, Amanda. The divorce is going to happen, probably without incident. Your ex is in no position to put up a fight. Although there has been another new development."

My heart sank. "What's that?"

She hesitated. "Maggie Parsons sent some paperwork over this morning. Your husband is suing you for half the money you earned from your paintings. He claims you could never have succeeded as an artist without his support."

The rage surged up, suddenly, from the depths of my soul. I was glad Teresa couldn't see it. "Try not to worry about it," she went on. "It was a longshot at best, but in light of the embezzlement charges? I can't imagine any judge would take it seriously."

Good news. Focus on that. I did my best to release the dark visions of Rich in bed with Maggie Parsons. I'd only met her once, but I'd never forgotten how beautiful she was. I sighed as I flashed back to that night, and the way she'd touched his hand when they spoke, while I tried to convince myself there was nothing to be jealous of.

"Oh, and I wanted to ask if you'd told your daughter about the divorce."

I didn't tell her I slept with Jace.

"Amanda?"

"I haven't said much. She knows I plan to divorce her father, but I haven't given her any details. Now, with Rich about to be charged…"

"Think it over. Let me know if you want me to get a statement from her."

Think? I wish I could. "I'll let you know." We ended the call, then, and I threw myself down on the recliner and closed my eyes. I didn't wake up till John and Helen came in with Jace. I glanced out the window, relieved that it was still light out. I checked my watch—4:55. I took a moment to orient myself: the search warrant, the embezzlement, Maggie Parsons, adultery…

When I looked up, I knew they were waiting for me to say something. I tried to do that, but--nothing. I wished I could put the words together as Jace perched on the armrest next to me, put his hands on my shoulders and began to massage them gently. It felt so good, I closed my eyes again.

"I'm glad you dozed off for a little while," he said softly.

"I didn't mean to." I sighed. "What—" *What did you find out? Who killed Wendi? How many women did Rich sleep with? How many did he say he loved…*

"Hard to know where to start," he began.

"Start with the break-in, and that— Paige!" Helen said. She looked so upset, I was glad when John took her into the kitchen.

Jace waited until they were gone before he sat down on the loveseat next to me and took my hand. "Okay, let's start with Paige's footprints. There were lots of them outside. Her fingerprints were all over your studio, too. We arrested her. She's being processed right now, down at the station."

"Hard to believe. She was always so quiet."

He nodded. "That's the way it goes, sometimes." He frowned. "The vandalism was about her, by the way. You were just the target." He stood up and frowned. "The sexual stuff they were doing? It couldn't help but cause problems, as I'm sure you must realize."

I nodded. "I knew Rich and Wendi had been together. Steffi just told Helen he swore he was loved her, too. If he said the same thing to Paige—"

He nodded. "Your ex talked the best game in town. Looks like he backed it up, too."

I didn't want to hear the details, but on some level, I needed to know. "Who else was there with him and Wendi, when they went down to Atlantic City?"

He sat down across from me, steepled his hands and frowned.. "We made some phone calls. One of the front desk agents at the Ocean Winds remembered three couples who generally came down together."

"Paige and Jim, Monica and Pete and Wendi and Rich?"

He nodded. "Cliff, Harvey, Steffi and Burt joined them from time to time." He dropped his voice. "I'm so sorry, sweetheart."

Not as sorry as I am. "No sense looking back."

He stood up, helped me to my feet and put his arms around me. "Harvey was also involved. We're making a special effort to find him right now. We've got a few questions for him."

"You still don't know where he is?"

"No." He hesitated before he let me go. "And what with those embezzlement charges along with everything else? We'll be busy, down at the station."

"Have you made any other arrests?"

He smiled weakly. "Full house!"

"But we still don't know who murdered Wendi, or where Harvey is." I couldn't imagine why Rich would've embezzled all that money either, not that I was about to go there right now.

Jace frowned. "I was thinking, in terms of the embezzlement money? Maybe Warren thought he'd need it for blackmail payments."

It made sense. "Have you found any evidence of that?"

"Not yet, but we're still working on it." He was about to go on when his phone rang. He went outside to take the call as Helen and John came back to check on me. He looked upset when he returned a few minutes later and turned to Helen and John instead. "Keep a good eye on Amanda, okay?"

I can take care of myself. I started to say that when he cut in. "Steffi and your ex are both in lockup right now, but they could make bail. Ordinarily, it'd take a while, but with Maggie Parsons representing them? Anything's possible. We strongly suspect the two of them were involved in the murder and maybe Malden's disappearance as well."

Disappearance, or murder? A chill ran down my spine as I envisioned Harvey's dead body. "What about Paige?"

"Looks like she's ready to deal."

"You mean she's going to turn in her friends so she can end up with an easier sentence?"

"Maybe. I won't know for sure till I talk to her." He glanced at his watch. "I need to get down there. You can stay here or at my place—your call."

"Your place."

He turned to Helen and John. "If you could drive her over?"

Helen nodded—while I tried not to just, well, panic. "I have to stay there alone?"

He took my hand. "You'll be fine till I get home."

Home. That had such a nice, comforting ring to it, I could almost believe that at some point, it would all work out.

"We'll stay with her till you get back." Helen said.

“We’ll keep a good eye on you, too, honey. Don’t worry.” John added softly.

Jace glanced at me. “Or you could hang out, here with Helen and John. I’ll be back as soon as I can.” He gave my shoulder a comforting little squeeze.

I hesitated. "It's just, don’t want to be alone, but..." I didn't want to be a wuss, either, the way I’d been with Rich, all those years. I should’ve put that night with Danny behind me, should’ve divorced Rich before he got involved with group sex, embezzlement, maybe even murder.

“Don’t blame yourself.” Jace leaned down and kissed me.

“Doing my best.” I took a deep breath. “I need to see how this turns out. I want to come with you.”

He shook his head. “C’mon, sweetheart, I just want you safe."

“No place safer than the police station.”

“I’d feel better if you stayed at my place.”

“I need to know,” I repeated. *After all this grief, I’m entitled to know.*

"Let me put a call in, see who's down there right now. Maybe I can work it out..." He frowned as he turned away to make that call.

He was on the phone for what felt like a very long time before he came back. “Okay, just this once. You'll have to stay out of the way, too.“

“No problem.” I put my arms around him and gave him a kiss.

It didn’t make him any happier.

***

Brook Haven’s police station looked the same as it did the day I visited Willard Bailey. I wasn’t sure why I expected something more dramatic, a shootout, maybe? “Don’t be silly.” Not that I'd meant to say that out loud...

“What?” Jace frowned.

I shook my head and smiled. He didn’t smile back. Ten minutes later, he'd seated me in a spot where I could watch him interrogate Paige through a one-way mirror. I forced myself to breathe as I focused on the small, gray, windowless room. Jace, Paige, a well-dressed man who was probably her attorney and a young woman getting it all down on her laptop sat around the table. I was glad Maggie Parsons wasn't there, although the man in the suit could've been one of her associates.

I focused on Paige. And Jace, who was promising to ask the judge for leniency if she cooperated, She turned to her lawyer, who nodded slightly, then took a deep breath before she began to speak. “I kept asking myself, why should Wendi have Rich? Wasn’t it enough that she always ran the show? She always found a way to get everything she wanted, at our expense! She didn't care who got hurt, either.” Paige shook her head tearfully. “As for Rich? She used him the same way she used all of us. I was the one who really loved him. She knew it, too, but she didn’t care.”

Jace leaned in closer. “It upset you when he put her first?”

“It upset Monica, too.” Paige sighed. “The sex helped. It leveled the playing field, if you know what I mean."

He frowned. "I'm not sure..."

If I was waiting for her to explain it, she didn't. “I still can’t believe I went along.” She pursed her lips. “I never wanted to do that kind of thing. never planned it...”

"No? Then what made you do it?" he asked.

"I had to, to be part of the group." She looked off into the distance. "It was the best when Rich and I were alone together. When we made love, just the two of us? I knew he loved me just as much as I loved him. But when Wendi was around, she always came first."

You thought Rich loved you? How could he, when he doesn't know what love is? I felt the tears well up as I flashed back to our wedding on St. Thomas. How stupid had I been to believe he loved me!

"I didn't know he'd told Monica the same thing until this one night down at the Borgata, when she mentioned it to me," Paige was saying now. "A few days later, Steffi said he told her he loved her, too. I felt sure she was lying. We all knew how little time he spent with her." Paige looked like she was beginning to calm down as she went on about Rich, what a horrible person he was and how much she loved him anyway.

"So what you've said is that the group revolved around Warren, is that correct?" Jace asked as I glanced at my watch. I was surprised to see I'd only been here 15 minutes. It felt so much longer.

I forced my attention back to little gray room, and Paige, again. "Rich was important, but he wouldn't have been, not without Wendi. The group business? That was all her idea. She spoke to Rich privately first, to enlist his support, then the two of them talked the rest of us into it." She sighed. "Not that I don't love my husband," she remembered to add, afraid Jim would file for divorce if she went to prison? Although as far as I could see, he could end up in prison, too.

Complicated.

"Jim and I lost sight of our marriage, there, for a while. Thirty-six years is a long time." She sighed. "When Rich kept telling me how beautiful I was, how perfect, how much more sensitive than Wendi? I really wanted to believe him. Then, when he swore he loved me..." Her voice broke, then, and she began to cry. Her lawyer handed her some tissues as the court reporter leaned back in her chair, yawned and stretched.

"You're saying you and Warren both managed to overlook the fact that you were married," Jace frowned.

"His marriage? That was a joke! He was forced to marry that woman after he knocked her up and she wouldn't have an abortion. He never loved her, never!"

I was glad Jace couldn't see me flinch.

***

"And those DVDs, were they a joke, too?" Almost an hour later, Jace looked like he was ready to call it a night.

Paige shook her head, confused. "DVDs?"

"Someone shot DVDs of your group's—activities. You didn't know?"

"DVDs?" She blushed furiously. "I would never—in front of a camera?" Her voice broke again and she began to cry.

Jace frowned as her lawyer handed her more tissues and I wondered if she was telling the truth. Maybe someone did shoot them secretly, planning to blackmail them all.

"I had no intention of doing the group thing till Rich took me aside one night, down at the Borgata. He said I'd do it if I loved him."

Jace glanced at his notes. "Now you're saying Warren lured you into it? A half-hour ago, you said it was the victim who'd pressured you to join in."

She shook her head. "You don't understand. Rich and Wendi? They did it together. They both pressured me, all of us, really. And now you're telling me there are DVDs of us? Are you sure, I mean, did you see them?"

"Yes."

Paige frowned. "I'll bet Rich and Wendi were in it together."

"How 'bout Warren's wife? Do you think she had any idea what was going on?"

"Amanda? Never! She didn't mean a thing to him, I told you that."

I clutched my purse . I had no idea why Jace had just asked that question. I didn't care, either, as I imagined myself strangling Rich. *Focus!* Difficult, but I gave it my best shot.

Jace leaned back a bit in his chair. "Okay, you confessed to vandalizing Amanda Warren's studio and destroying her paintings. Was that your idea or Warren's?"

Paige shook her head. "It wasn't his fault."

He raised an eyebrow. "You're under oath, here, you know."

She hesitated. "Rich didn't care enough about her or those precious paintings of hers to do anything. We never understood why he went home to her every night. I asked him once how he could make love with me then go home to her." A shiver ran down my spine as I watched her lips curl into a nasty snarl.

Jace leaned in closer. "If we could get back to the victim..."

Paige nodded. And smiled. "Monica and I? We'd call her Winona sometimes. She hated it!"

He nodded, encouraging her to go on.

"But she was such a controller! Wherever she went, whatever she did? We all had to follow." Her blue eyes darkened with a hatred so deep, I would never have thought she had it in her.

Jace glanced at his notes again. "Okay, you say the victim and Warren were the ringleaders. That being the case, didn't you think he might have feelings for her, too?"

She nodded tearfully. "I tried to accept it, but Wendi? She just kept getting worse. Always telling us what to say, what to do, what to wear, where to go. So when Rich said I was the one he really loved, I realized being with him would be the best way to defy her."

"You really believed he loved you?"

She nodded. "Until I found out he said the same thing to Monica and Steffi. That made me feel so awful, I just wanted to die."

"Wanted to die, or wanted to kill Wendi?"

And Rich? I was waiting for her reply when her lawyer touched her arm and frowned. I was glad when it didn't stop her. "Rich is blameless in all this! Wendi's the one who's responsible. She didn't care who got hurt!"

"Is that why you killed her?" Jace asked calmly.

She sighed deeply. "I wanted to kill her, planned to do it. I'm not sure I would've gone through with it, but..."

"What?"

Paige frowned. "Someone got there first."

"If you can tell us who? It could help, down the road."

"I'd tell you in a minute, if I knew." She began to twist the tissues in her hands, then glanced at her lawyer, who nodded. "Steffi, that's my best guess."

"Why?"

"Steffi resented Wendi a lot more than I did. She thought Wendi was responsible for her father's death. But she still used to watch everything Wendi did. She was trying to learn from the master, that's what Monica said." She sighed. "Then, one night, when Steffi told us Rich said he loved her…"

"Did you believe her?"

When she didn't respond, Jace looked at his notes again. "Okay, first you said Warren and Wendi were inseparable. Then you said Steffi told you how much she loved him, right around the same time Warren told you and Monica he loved you, separately--correct?"

Her face fell. "I was thrilled when said he loved me. But when I found out about Monica and Steffi, I realized he didn't know what love is. In the end? He was just as cold and calculating as Wendi." She began to cry again, enough for her lawyer to ask for a break.

A good thing when I needed one myself. Badly. I took a deep breath to try to hold back the tears as I thought about the marriage I'd stayed in out of guilt, all those years.

He doesn't know what love is. Why did it take me so long to see it?

***

"You think Rich and Steffi could've murdered Wendi together?" I asked Jace as he grilled the chicken breasts and I made a salad. It was a pleasure it was to cook with him, after all those years with Rich.

"At this point, I feel fairly sure the homicide was Warren's idea. Steffi might've egged him on, maybe Paige and Monica did, too. Paige did think Steffi wanted to assume the vic's position in the group."

"I don't think that ever would've happened." Really, I didn't think anyone could've replaced Wendi, as strong a personality as she was.

He turned the chicken. "Maybe Steffi didn't know that, and as far as motive goes? All we have to look at is the fact that her father died shortly after he married Wendi."

"I didn't know."

He nodded, then began to brush more barbeque sauce on the chicken. It was his own recipe. It was also delicious. "What's that smile about?"

"You've got your own recipe for barbeque sauce."

"I've got a few recipes. Most of 'em could use some work, but I think I got this one right." He covered the grill and turned to me. "I assume your ex was not acquainted with the working end of a kitchen?"

"He never came in there at all." Rich also believed that all meals should be served— by me—in the dining room. I was about to say something, well, bitter about that when I changed the subject instead, as we sat down in the dining el, where one of my other prints was hanging on the wall and I could see the full moon rising in the cloudy night sky through the window. Lovely...

"Now, Malden's disappearance? That's a whole 'nother story. We still have no idea where he is, or even if he's still alive." Jace helped himself to the salad I'd made.

"But you're still looking for him, aren't you?"

He nodded. "The homicide is a lot more important, though. Malden's missing with no sign of foul play. For all we know, he could've just decided to up and leave. If that's the way it happened, we can't even consider him a missing person."

"I doubt that's what happened. He and Cliff went all the way up to Vermont to get married. Harvey loved directing plays, too." I waited for him to reply, but he just kept eating. "You think Rich could've been involved in Harvey's disappearance, too?"

"No idea, unfortunately." He put his fork down. "But we do think it was Malden who shot those DVDs. He worked in TV production for almost ten years," he added.

"He said something, once, about working on this cable series back in 2006. If he shot those DVDs, then planned to try to blackmail the others—"

"It's possible."

"But there's no proof."

"Not yet." He stood up, went out to check the grill and brought in more chicken. "I thought I'd bring Cliff in again, lean on him harder."

"You think he'd know if Harvey shot those DVDs?"

"I can't imagine he wouldn't."

"When are you going to bring him in?"

"Since he's leaving for California in the day after tomorrow. tonight's is as good a time as any." He took out his phone, called in and made the arrangements in front of me, for once. "I'll be there in an hour," he said before he ended the call and my breath caught in my throat. I still wasn't ready to be alone.

“Don’t worry, sweetheart.” He took my hand. “The suspects are all behind bars.”

“For now.”

“It's possible a few of them might make bail tonight, with Maggie Parsons on it. But if you just stay here, you'll be fine.”

I nodded, even though I was not completely convinced. I helped myself to another piece of chicken before I realized my appetite was gone.

A half-hour later, he gave me a kiss as he was leaving. “It'll all work out, sweetheart, you’ll see.”

Right...

Chapter Twenty-Two

“I wouldn't mind coming over, really," Jessica said when I called her later. Jace had been gone over an hour, now. I’d tried meditating, watching TV, listening to music. Nothing allayed my fears.

“It's okay, Jess,” I replied. “I’m sure he’ll be home soon.” *Not!*

“Home? Sweet!” I could almost hear her smile. “I've got to get over to the mall right now, but listen, if you need anything, just call, okay?"

“I will.” I ended the call and went back in the kitchen, where I wiped down the already clean countertop. I was wishing Jace was here when my phone rang. I glanced at the caller ID. *Unknown.*

“Amanda Warren.” I'd just identified myself when I shouldn't have answered. Not smart.

“Amanda? This is Liz O’Brian, Chloe’s new assistant. She said she was going to tell you about me?"

"Tell me about you? No..." I was almost about to apologize for that when I forced myself not to. I hadn't spoken to Chloe today, but she didn't say a word about any assistant when I spoke to her yesterday.

“She's been so busy," the woman on the other end replied.

No busier than usual, I thought. "I know, but--"

"It doesn't matter. We have a problem," she went on. "Chloe asked me to finalize the program for your next show and I just realized I don't have your bio. If you could get a copy out to me tonight..."

I could if I was home. I frowned. "Chloe has it in her files. Just ask her—"

"I called, but it went straight to voicemail. I hope you can get it out to me tonight."

"Tonight will be difficult, but I'll do it first thing tomorrow morning, when I'm at home." I'd just told her I wasn't home, a terrible idea, when there was no way to confirm who she really was. If Chloe did hire an assistant, I felt sure she would've told me.

"That'd be okay with me, but we've got a tight deadline and she specifically asked me to take care of it tonight. Since I'm a new hire, I need to get it right."

Understandable. I was about to say, well, something when she went on. "Oh, and she also asked me to be sure to use the same bio as last time. She said it was in her files, but they're in rough shape." She hesitated. "Not that I'm complaining, that is why she hired me."

I thought it over. Chloe overextended herself sometimes but I'd never known her to be particularly disorganized. Trust this woman or not?

"Amanda?"

"Sorry." *Don't apologize!* "I know, I can write up a new bio and get it out to you tonight."

"I don't know, Chloe insists she wants to use the old one. Isn't there any way you could stop by your studio and pick up a copy?"

I promised Jace I'd stay right here. How could I tell that to someone I'd never met? "If you're sure you really need it."

"It would be a big help, huge!"

I glanced at the clock— 8:07 PM. My house was ten minutes away. My studio was still a mess, but I'd made a point of putting my laptop in my bedroom. I could drive back to my house, go in, e-mail her my old bio and be back without Jace ever knowing I'd left. "I guess..."

"Wonderful! I'll never be able to thank you enough."

Really, I thought back to that phone call and realized the woman's voice had sounded vaguely, well, familiar. What if the woman had been lying?

Just call Chloe. I pulled over and entered her number, but it did go straight to voicemail, just as that woman said. It didn't occur to me to call Jace until I'd pulled into my driveway. I wasn't surprised when that call went straight to voicemail, too.

He was busy. This wouldn't take long, either. I'd go in, do what I had to do and get back with time to spare.

Maybe Jessica could come in with me. I glanced at her driveway, then remembered she'd gone to the mall. I checked John and Helen's house. It didn't look like they were home either.

Don't be a wuss, I told myself as I opened the garage door with my remote and went in. I was startled to hear it come down. I was about to press the button again when I felt someone come up behind me.

Then everything went black.

***

I was in my studio, still a disaster, when I opened my eyes, sat up and began to stretch, until I realized my hands were bound. I looked around. The only light in the room was the moonlight coming through the window. I was alone. I was a little dizzy, too, but I wriggled my wrists anyway to try to get free. It didn't take me long to realize that wasn't going to work.

There was enough light for me to see one of my palette knives on the floor a few feet away. It wasn't sharp but if I could get over there, maybe I could use it to get free. I'd begun to inch my way over when I heard the footsteps. A moment later, the room was flooded with light.

"You're awake." I looked up at... Cliff?

You're supposed to be at the police station with Jace. I almost said that, until I realized it'd be smarter to keep my mouth shut.

"You thought you could stick your nose into other people's business and get away with it, didn't you?" He shook his head and laughed dramatically. No surprise, he did everything dramatically. Even killing Wendi? Was he the one who'd done it?

"It's just, I was there when her body, um, turned up." I looked up into his cold gray eyes and shivered. Could he see how terrified I was?

"Curiosity killed the cat." He laughed again. "Now, curiosity is about to kill you."

"Did you kill Wendi?" The more I talked, the more questions I asked, the more time I could buy. If I could just hold him off long enough for Jace to realize I was here, and in trouble, maybe it'd keep me alive.

Cliff shrugged his shoulders. "Wouldda,' couldda,' shouldda…' I was going to but someone beat me to it."

The same thing Paige said. "Rich?" I ventured.

He rolled his eyes. "Don't know, don't care."

"Not even if it was Harvey who did it?" A scenario that made no sense, as enamored of Wendi as everyone said Harvey had been.

Cliff frowned. "Harvey, the man who vowed to be my life-partner, then betrayed me with that cheap seductress? Harvey, who thought it'd be fun to shoot those goddamn DVDs and blackmail us all?" He sighed. Dramatically, of course. "When Wendi told Harvey she loved him? He was fool enough to believe her. Big mistake! It took him a while to realize she just wanted to own him, the same way she wanted to own us all. He apologized, swore he'd never stray again but it was late for that!" Cliff looked sad, now, almost tearful.

He can't murder me if he's crying.

I was disappointed when he calmed down quickly. "When Wendi told Harv she wanted him to shoot those DVDs? He didn't hesitate. They were going to split the proceeds, including the money they thought they'd get from me." His added, his voice devoid of emotion.

Not good. I felt cold, suddenly, so cold, I started to shiver. I was glad when he just shrugged his shoulders. "Doesn't matter now. I'll take care of you, then it's off to LA and my real career, the one my life-partner resented so much, he couldn't stand it." He laughed again, while I tried to come up with some way, any way I could hold him off.

He was reaching into the back of his waistband, now, pulling out a small handgun.

There was a dark corner behind me. No choice but to try to get myself over there. Anything get away from him and his gun! I began to half-crawl, half-roll, but it didn't take me long to realize it wasn't going to work. Nothing would help me now, I thought as I closed my eyes and saw my life flash before me—till someone kicked in the door.

Jace, please let it be Jace!

I was crushed when I opened my eyes and saw Rich, taking out his own gun. About to shoot me? Not when he was aiming it at Cliff. He indicated Cliff's gun. "Drop it."

Cliff hesitated before he did.

"Now get down on the floor." Cliff did that, too, as I watched, afraid to move, afraid even to breathe. Rich didn't shoot him, though, not right away. He came over and knelt down next to me instead, close enough so I could feel his breath on my face before he brushed the barrel of the cold metal gun across my cheek.

"I thought you were in jail." If I was going to die tonight, I wanted to know who'd murdered Wendi and why. If I could just buy a little more time, maybe Jace would realize I was in trouble. A few more minutes might also give Cliff time take Rich down.

Rich followed my gaze as I glanced at Cliff, just lying there across the room. I let my breath out slowly as Rich looked around and took a few steps back, away from me.

A chill ran down my spine as he looked me in the eye. "I can't believe your boyfriend thought he could keep me in jail. Didn't you tell him I was the best-connected attorney, down here in the boonies?"

I shook my head, then sensed Cliff beginning to get up. Rich did too, unfortunately. I knew that when he stood up and kicked him hard in the ribs, then turned back to me and smiled. "I didn't play golf with Judge Robertson because I enjoyed it. Arrogant bastard, but I knew he'd come in handy someday. But then, you know how good I am at making all the right connections. At least you should know."

I nodded and wished I could steal another glance at Cliff, but I didn't dare, not when Rich was aiming his gun at my forehead. “Connections I made myself. " he went on. "Want to know why?”

No choice but to nod, even if the last thing in the world I cared about right now was his connections.

“I made those connections alone, managed my career alone, achieved my position alone because all you ever cared about was yourself, you and your art!” He frowned. “I saved you from that goddamn rapist and what do you do? Get yourself pregnant, force me to marry you, then bury yourself in your art.” He waved his gun around the studio and laughed. “Well, tonight's the night you get your wish, my *wife*. Tonight's the night you really get buried in your art.” I was horrified when I heard the *click* as he released the safety.

I sensed rather than saw Cliff reach out, grab Rich’s ankle and take him down, not fast enough to stop Rich from firing the gun, though, hitting him in the shoulder. Cliff still managed to wrestle Rich to the floor even as he clutched his shoulder to stem the bleeding.

I tried to get up, impossible with my wrists bound. I watched them go at it, then, not that it mattered, not when they both wanted me dead. They were still wrestling when the security lights come on outside. Jace? I was crushed when Harvey came in, his clothes rumpled, his left shoulder bandaged, a gun in his hand.

“You’re alive?” Cliff looked shocked as Harvey aimed, released the safety and shot him twice in the chest. Rich turned to fire at Harvey, then, while I flattened myself against the floor.

Harvey dodged the bullet. Rich was turning to fire again when Jace rushed in, his gun pointed at Rich, a backup team right behind him. “Drop your weapons and get down on the floor!”

Harvey dropped his gun first. Rich hesitated before he did the same. Two of the backups moved in to cuff them and read them their rights as Jace knelt down and checked Cliff’s pulse. He took out his phone, then, made a call and spoke to someone so softly, I couldn’t hear a word.

I was still tied up. Jace was coming over to me now, but not making a single move to untie me. *Untie me!* That’s what I wanted to say, what I would’ve said, if I could put those two words together. I glanced at Cliff again, just lying there, his eyes closed.

“He’s still alive,” Jace said softly—as the room began to swirl around me. *Strong, modern women don’t faint*. That’s what I was thinking when everything went black for the second time that night.

***

I was in the living room, my hands free, when I came to. Jace was handing me a glass of water, telling me to drink it and checking my pulse as I forced myself to take a sip. I was only marginally aware of the EMT’s taking Cliff, or his body, out on a stretcher.

“Is he—”

Jace shook his head. “The EMTs say he’ll make it.” He sat down and put his arms around me but then, too soon, he backed off and frowned. “I thought you promised you'd stay at the condo tonight.”

“I was going to, till I got this phone call.” I took another sip. “I should never have gone.” I took a deep breath. ”It was stupid…”

"Stupid? That's the least of it. You could've been killed."

I nodded, then started to shiver. Then, to my horror, I started to cry. He sighed and pulled me close. "Wanna' tell me about that phone call?"

I did, but I couldn't seem to do it. "Cliff. Tell me about Cliff."

"We didn't have enough on him to hold him." He frowned. "Had to let him go right around the same time I found out Warren had been released on bail. I called to warn you. When you didn't answer, I called Jessica, who said she was at the mall. Then I called Helen. She and John had just come in. When she looked out the window and saw your car, I knew I had to get over here." He let me go, squared his big, broad shoulders and looked me in the eye. "Your turn."

I took a deep breath. "I wasn't going to leave the condo till this woman called. She said she was Chloe's new assistant. I thought it was a little suspicious, but..." *I was crazy to believe her.*

He leaned in closer. "What did she say?"

"She introduced herself as Liz O'Brian. She said Chloe had just hired her and she needed my bio, my old bio, right away." I frowned as I asked myself why Chloe would've asked her to use my old bio. *What was I thinking?*

"Your old bio?" His voice brought me back.

I nodded. "She said Chloe wanted to use it for that show we're doing next month. I offered to write up a new one and send it over, but she insisted Chloe wanted the old one." I sighed. "It was here on my laptop." I took another deep breath. "I can't believe…" *I was so stupid.* Enough to make the room start swirling again.

Jace put his arm around my shoulders, to keep me from keeling over? Maybe. "I was terrified when you didn't answer your cell." He looked so upset, I felt even worse.

"Chloe's always saying she needs an assistant. I thought maybe…" I heard myself sigh as if from a distance. "I should've known."

"Yes. You should've."

I felt the tears well up. I bit my lip and tried to hold them back.

"Calm down, sweetheart."

I wished I could.

"Anything else can you tell me about that phone call?"

"When the caller ID said *unknown?* I knew shouldn't have answered it. If Chloe really did hire an assistant? She would've told me."

Jace nodded and gave me his phone. "Call her."

I checked the time— 11:15. "It's late—"

"Call her anyway. For me," he added.

I nodded and did so quickly. She answered on the first ring and assured me I didn't wake her. "An assistant? We both know how much I need one, but I never seem to have time."

"So the name Liz O'Brian doesn't ring a bell?"

"No..." Chloe asked me another question, then. I was trying to answer when Jace pointed to the phone and shook his head. I said I'd call her tomorrow, ended the call and turned to him. "Is there any way you can find out who called me?"

He nodded, got up and went over to the liquor cabinet, where he took out a bottle of brandy, then, poured some into a shot glass and handed it to me. "Drink."

I hesitated before I took that first warm, comforting sip. “I can’t believe you took a call from a perfect stranger, then agreed to come over here to meet them.”

“I wasn’t supposed to meet anyone here,” I replied, not that it mattered. “I know I should never have left the condo. But at least I found out what happened." *Maybe.* Only then did I realize I still didn’t know who'd killed Wendi, or even where Harvey might've fit in.

“Where’s your phone?”

"In my purse. I had it in the garage…” *When Cliff came up and hit me from behind.*

He turned to go in there. I wanted to go with him, but I was still so dizzy. I closed my eyes. I didn’t open them again till he came back with my purse. He opened it, took out my cell and slipped it in his pocket. “I'll take it in, see what they can find out.”

I nodded. “I didn't tell you what Cliff said.”

He sighed softly as he sat down and took my hand. "Want to tell me now?"

“Okay, first, he said Harvey was in love with Wendi. That was why he killed him.”

Jace frowned, confused. “But Malden was here tonight. Alive.”

I nodded. “Cliff was surprised. He thought he’d killed him.”

“Okay, you're saying Cliff tried to kill Harvey because Harvey was in love with the vic? Strange, in light of the fact that he was married. To a man.”

I shrugged my shoulders. “I didn't say I could explain it, but Cliff? He was so angry.”

“Angry enough to murder the vic?”

I shook my head. “He said he was planning it when someone got there first.” I took another sip of brandy and relished the warmth as it went down.

"Exactly what Paige said." He frowned. "He didn't say, or even suggest who the killer might've been?"

"I'm not sure he knows. But he did tell me Wendi was the one who asked Harvey to shoot those DVDs. They were going to blackmail all the others."

He nodded thoughtfully. "But Malden appeared in some of them. That's why we didn't suspect him."

"He could've set the camera to shoot remotely."

He nodded. "They were going to blackmail Cliff, too?"

"Apparently." I took another few sips of brandy. Soothing…

"Don't make me sorry I gave you that brandy. Back to the vic— you were here with Harvey, Cliff and Warren and none of them said anything that would've indicated who killed her?"

"Cliff thought Rich might've done it."

"What did he say, do you remember?"

I shook my head. "I was terrified. He knocked me out and tied me up. Rich came in right after I came around. He pointed his gun at Cliff first. Then he came over to me..."

"And said he was going to shoot you?" Jace had the grace to give me a sweet little kiss on the cheek. Comforting, but I needed more. He knew it, too. "Later," he murmured. "You think you're up to going down to the station to give us a statement? It could wait till tomorrow, but—"

"It'd be better to do it now, when it's fresh in my mind, right?"

He nodded. And frowned. "Right."

I hesitated. “I'll give it my best shot. Not like I'm going to get any sleep tonight.”

"If you're sure..."

I nodded. I didn’t think to ask about Rich’s gun till we'd reached the station. “Did you get Rich’s gun?”

Jace rolled his eyes and held up a brown paper evidence bag.

“You think it’s the same gun those bullets came from, the other night?”

“Ballistics will check it out. It could take a while, but I’ve got a hunch it’ll match.”

I pictured Rich pointing his gun at me and shuddered. “I'm pretty sure he planned to kill me and Cliff tonight.”

“Till Malden showed up and all hell broke loose.”

I nodded. "You got there just in time.” I managed a smile as he pulled me closer and kissed me.

An hour later, I’d almost finished giving my statement when a young man in jeans and a tee-shirt came in with my cell phone and handed it to Jace along with a slip of paper. “Peter Woodruff, 26 Elm Circle. It's in that fancy new development, Brook Haven Acres?”

Jace nodded. “Thanks," he replied as he handed me back my phone.

"Pete and Monica?” *Pete is an insurance guy. Maybe he wrote a policy on Wendi.* I began to mention that to Jace when he cut in.

“We know Pete’s in insurance. And yes, he did write a policy on the vic.”

“He and Monica were the beneficiaries?”

He shook his head. “Steffi. Maybe she was working with them.”

Strange. “You'll question her too?”

"You think she could've been the one who called you?"

"It didn't sound like her, or Monica, for that matter, but I guess it's possible."

"Okay," he said slowly. "You just said there was more?"

"It's a little thing, but Rich? He loved to brag about his relationship with this judge, Edgar Robertson."

Jace wrote down the name. "I've been in his courtroom a couple times. Seemed like an okay judge."

"Rich made a point of telling me it was Robertson who'd released him on bail."

"I'll check it out."

"There's more-- Rich played golf with him, but behind his back? He always called him—"

"What?"

"An arrogant bastard. His words." I didn't blush when I said that, either. Progress.

"Judge Robertson just might like to know that." Jace smiled.

I giggled, suddenly. Was it the brandy, or all that stress? I forced myself to focus while Jace called someone in to review my statement, then made a second call. "Peter and Monica Woodruff, 26 Elm Circle. Pick them up and bring them in. Oh yeah, bring Jim Morgan in, too. The address is on file."

It's almost over, I told myself as they asked me to review my statement one more time and sign off on it, something I needed to do so I could close this horrific chapter of my life.

***

It was almost two A.M. by the time we got back to Jace's condo. He'd offered to have someone drive me back after I'd reviewed my statement and signed off on it, but staying there, or anywhere else by myself was not something I was willing to do. Not that it mattered. After everything that happened tonight, I couldn't imagine I'd ever get to sleep.

It was hard not to flash back to the way I'd been knocked out, tied up and almost killed tonight as I brushed my teeth. I was wearing one of Jace's tee shirts over my panties. Not my lingerie of choice, but it was soft cotton and it smelled like coconut fabric softener and Jace, giving me a nice, safe feeling. He was checking his messages when I got in bed.

"What's going on?" I asked. The fact that we still hadn't ID'd Wendi's killer did not make me happy. "Did they find out who did it?"

He nodded. "It's bizarre." He sat down on the bed. "Okay, so we know how much Paige wanted Wendi dead."

"Yes."

"A lot of rage there, but as it turned out? She didn't like Monica and Pete or Cliff and Harvey much, either."

"Hard to believe when she always, like, went along."

He nodded. "Until she fell in love with Warren."

I swallowed hard as he went on. "So here it is, Paige decides she's going to kill Wendi. She's thinks with Wendi dead, she and Warren will ride off into the sunset together."

Pain shot through me as I pictured Rich with Paige, and Wendi, and all the other women he'd been with. *Paige, focus on Paige.* "What about Jim?"

Jace smiled. "Even more bizarre, as it turns out. Jim had his eye on a very different sunset. He pictured himself riding off with Harvey."

Enough to take any thought of Rich out of my mind. "Did Harvey feel the same way?"

Jace nodded. "Harvey did love Wendi at one time, but she'd become too much for him,. From what he told us? He felt such a strong connection with Jim, he couldn't help but feel they belonged together. They were about to go public with that when Cliff found out."

"And killed Harvey, or thought he did."

"Right. Bottom line? Paige wants Wendi dead. So do Warren and Monica."

"So Rich tells one of them to go ahead and do it, right?" *Which one?*

"You'd think so, but according to Paige? Warren thinks he can do it better himself."

"Sounds like Rich."

Jace nodded. "He's got it all planned when Steffi gets involved. She's in love with Warren, too. And just like the others, she believes he loves her back."

"I guess she didn't realize the only one he could ever love is himself." Not that I could fault her for that, after all the years it took me to get there.

He shook his head. "Not a factor."

It is for me.

He understood. I knew that when he leaned over and pulled me closer. "Sorry, sweetheart."

"It's not your fault." *Rich and I are over. I will not cry, I refuse to cry.*

"It was never your fault. Warren ran the best con in town."

I let my breath out slowly. If only I'd known...

"Want to know who killed her?"

"Of course I do."

"Monica, only because she got there first. After she was done? Steffi showed up and went ballistic when she found out Wendi was already dead."

"So she settled for slashing the purple pashmina?"

"That comes later." He sighed softly. "Back to the scene. Steffi and Monica are trying to dispose of the body when Paige shows up. Paige had also planned to kill Wendi, but she knew she couldn't move the body herself. Since Jim had been complaining about the vic for a while, she asked him to help. He agreed. He brought his knife along, too, just in case.

"So Steffi takes his knife and uses it to slash the purple pashmina."

He sighed. "You got that right. While she's doing that, Pete was running his SUV across your property, destroying that, what'd you call it?"

"Pampas grass. But why?"

"Monica made the mistake of telling him she was in love with Warren."

"He did it for revenge?"

Jace nodded. "Lame, but as I'm sure you can understand, he wasn't thinking too clearly at the point."

I nodded. "Back to Wendi. She's dead, now. Pete helped move the body, then ran over our grass—"

He nodded. "While Steffi was busy slashing the pashmina with his knife."

"Then she gave the knife to Rich, who hid it in our garage." I shook my head. "What a story."

"That it is."

"I'm glad you found the killer." *I'm glad we found the killer.* "But now, I mean, who's going to jail?"

"Monica, Paige, Jim and Steffi for sure. It was Steffi who called you, by the way."

"I thought her voice sounded familiar."

He nodded. And frowned. "Pete helped move the body. That makes him an accessory."

I took a deep breath. "What about Rich?"

"He definitely motivated the others, even though they all blamed the vic for that, too. The fact is Wendi'd become so controlling, most of her so-called friends wanted her dead."

"Will Rich be charged?"

"Only for what happened when he threatened you, but attempted murder? Should be enough to get him some time. Along with those embezzlement charges..."

"John told you?"

He nodded. "I was hoping we could get him on possession of an unregistered firearm, too, but as it turns out? He did have a permit." He leaned over and kissed me softly, sweetly on the lips, then backed away and frowned.

"What is it?"

He frowned. "One more thing. Try not to get too upset, now, sweetheart." He hesitated. "It was Warren who encouraged Paige to vandalize your studio."

A chill ran down my spine. "Will she go to prison for it?"

"If that was all she did, as a first time offender, she'd probably just get probation. Factor in her complicity in the homicide, though, and she should get some time. She'll have to make restitution for your paintings, too."

"That can't bring them back."

“I know, but she should get some time behind bars,” he repeated as he lay down next to me.

Almost enough to ease my mind. “What about Harvey?”

“He knew what they were planning and he didn’t try to stop them.”

“He shot Cliff, too. Isn’t that attempted murder?”

He nodded. “You saw that one yourself.”

I sighed. “It’s just, Rich? I hope he spends a long time in prison.”

“I don’t know about that, but I do have a little good news on that front.” He smiled. “No guarantees, but Judge Robertson may be the one who hears the case-- after I make sure he finds out what Warren’s been saying about him behind his back.”

“You’re going to tell him?”

“Not directly, but we'll get it done.” He shrugged his shoulders. “Slip of the tongue.”

“Your tongue?”

He smiled. “Does good work. C’mere, I’ll show you.” He shut the lights, then, and proceeded to do just that.

Much later, I fell asleep in his arms and slept till noon the next day. Only then did I realize he hadn't given me any idea when the trial would be.

He was down at the station now, having a busy day. Frustrating to wait till he got home, but I didn’t have much choice.

***

“Any idea when it'll go to trial?” I asked Jace when he came in. I’d planned to wait till he'd finished dinner, but I'd run out of patience, so much, I was frustrated when he didn't answer me directly. "Okay, so we know Warren aided and abetted."

"By telling all those women he loved them, right?"

He nodded. "But we didn't have anything to prove he was physically involved in the actual murder."

"\Doesn't the aiding and abetting count?"

"It's better than nothing but not by much. The good news? The attempted murder at your house that night, along with all that money he embezzled should definitely get him some time." He looked at his plate, still on the counter. "Dinner?" he asked.

"My pleasure." I put the food on his plate and set it down in front of him. I was surprised when he didn't start eating. He stood up, instead, took me in his arms and kissed me. "I thought I was hungry, but—"

"What?"

"It's just, not for food." He ran his thumb lightly over my lower lip, then began to kiss me.

I indicated his plate. "It'll reheat."

He grinned. "Later."

Chapter Twenty-Three

It was the week before Christmas and Jace was putting my bags in the trunk of his Toyota.

"We're going away for seven days. You must've packed for a month."

"Good thing you're such a big, strong, macho guy." I put my arms around him and kissed him.

He kissed me back before he turned to shut the trunk. "You're wearing jeans, too." He smiled. "I love a woman who looks great in jeans."

"That's good. I love to wear them." More so, after all the years I spent listening to Rich complain about them.

"I still don't understand why we're not taking your Beamer," he said. "It's a lot more comfortable."

"The Beamer reminds me of Rich, the divorce, Wendi and everything else."

"That's why you're trading it in?" he asked as we got in.

I nodded. "I need to move on."

"Good idea." He started the engine. "What happened when you told your daughter what happened?"

"Katie? She was—"

"Surprised?"

I shook my head. "The hardest part was finding time to talk to her. She's been busy, at school."

"I guess those MBA courses must be pretty demanding."

"It's not that. She's become involved with that visiting professor, Kevin Patterson? He's a TV personality, a financial guru, according to the media. Katie? She's just, well, taken with him. It worries me."

"I watched his show a few times. Arrogant guy, but he was popular, till he gave out these bad stock tips, companies that tanked big time after he recommended them."

"Katie thinks he's perfect."

"You think he might try to take advantage of her?"

"A definite possibility, the way she always talks about him. I'd hate to see her get hurt, after Andrew." I'd told Jace all about what a slime Andrew had been since they'd separated.

He shrugged his shoulders. "Her ex? I know he's a piece of work. But at her age, she is responsible for her own choices."

"I realize that, but her father wasn't much of a role model. He wasn't home often, for one thing, and they didn't get along when he was."

"Maybe that'll help her accept the fact that he'll be away for a while."

I nodded. "One good thing." Just as Jace had predicted, Rich had been tried and convicted of attempted murder. Along with the embezzlement charges and the fact that Judge Robertson, who did hear the case, had opted for maximum jail time, Rich could be away as long as fifteen years. But when I'd looked into it on the Net, I was dismayed when I found out as a first time offender, he could serve as little as five years before he made parole. Enough time? It'd have to be.

"She really wasn't upset?" I was glad when Jace's voice pulled me back.

"She was blown away at first, but she got over it. She also told me she'd always wished I'd leave him."

"Always?"

I nodded. “He wanted her to major in early childhood education or nursing when she went to college.”

“She thought you should divorce him for that?”

“Not just that.”

He glanced at me questioningly as we stopped for a red light.

“He might’ve said something about wishing he had a son, every now and then. And when Katie filed her business administration major? He went ballistic.”

Jace shook his head and laughed, something else Rich seldom did. “I’m glad she’s okay with the fact that he's going to prison.”

“*Nothing I can’t handle*, that’s what she said.”

“I know you’re okay with it, too.” We were approaching the Interstate now, on our way to Jessica’s house in Corolla, on North Carolina’s Outer Banks. When she offered to let us use it over the holidays, we were quick to accept. We were going to stay there through New Year’s Eve.

“I’m looking forward to seeing my daughter in Chapel Hill, too,” Jace said the night we planned the trip. I was surprised when he told me how she’d chosen to stay with Diane's parents over the holidays. “Makes sense, with Diane in rehab. Again." He sighed. "She stuck with Alcoholics Anonymous almost a year, this time."

“And now she's in rehab--that's good, isn't it?”

"Better than nothing." He sighed “Her parents have had a hard time of it, all these years, another reason I thought we'd visit then while we’re down there.”

"Should help." Having their granddaughter with them would help even more, I thought.

"A lot of things don't work out the way you think they will, but everything passes, sooner or later," he said as he pulled onto the Interstate.

I hoped he was right. I still felt blown away by the murder, all those arrests and the fact that I'd come so close to getting killed. But I could be grateful for the way Teresa had taken it all in stride--and the fact that my divorce would be final within the next few weeks.

"Just a matter of time," she told me last week. "You're also exceptionally well-positioned to get most of what's left after they collect what he owes in restitution."

As for Katie, she was in the process of moving into her own place. "It's a lot smaller," she said of her new and very modest two-bedroom garden apartment. "But it'll be my place, mine and Corey's. I might even have a little dinner party," she added.

"New friends from school?"

"Sort of." She'd blushed, the same way I do. "I invited Kevin Patterson to dinner. I was thrilled when he said yes."

Kevin Patterson. I tried not to worry, but no matter how old Katie was, she'd always be my little girl. I was glad she'd scheduled her first appointment with Teresa the Wednesday after New Year's. "I'm not ready to file, but Kevin thinks it'd be a good idea to find out more about my options," she told me when I spoke to her yesterday.

Her absolute faith in the man disturbed me, but I managed to keep that myself, as I told her more about my divorce. "Teresa doesn't foresee any problems. She was the one who suggested I get away for a few days."

Exactly what we were doing, I thought as Jace switched over into the middle lane. Nothing new with Rich or the rest of the gang, he said as we approached the Delaware Memorial Bridge. "He reports to prison the day after Christmas."

I can't wait. The idea of Rich spending time behind bars didn't make me happy, exactly. Vindication was more like it. As for the others, Cliff was out of the hospital now, in jail awaiting trial. Robertson remanded him without bail for his attempt on Harvey's life and mine, too.

Paige and Steffi's attorneys were both in the process of trying to negotiate plea bargain deals, but Monica was negotiating from her jail cell. Robertson had remanded her without bail, too. The rest of the gang was out on bail, but they'd turned in their passports and been ordered not to leave the state until the trial, which could take a while, according to Jace.

Helen called me yesterday. She'd driven by Paige and Monica's houses. "They're both up for sale." She was happy about that, and thrilled about the fact that she'd just begun to reorganize the Haven Players. She was looking forward to her first production, *Our Town,* the perennially popular play written in 1938 and performed countless times by so many theatrical companies.

I would not be part of that production. I'd be busy putting my house up for sale, for one thing, something I hadn't been ready to tell her. Teresa helped me find the house of my dreams, an cute, white oceanfront bungalow in Seaview Pines recently renovated for year-round use. I'd signed a rental lease last week with the option to buy. I had every intention of doing that, assuming it worked out as well as I expected.

The ocean view would've been enough, but I knew I had to have it when I saw the big addition with floor-to-ceiling windows and skylights, a perfect place for my studio, the studio where I'd prepare for my next show, a one-woman show in April.

"Helen must've been disappointed when you talked to her yesterday. I know how much she wanted to be in on it when we found the killer." Jace's voice brought me back to the Interstate, and the prospect of spending a nice, private, romantic week at the beach.

"She was horrified when she found out I almost got killed. But she was glad we found the killer."

"Figured that one out together." He glanced at me and smiled.

"Not that you wouldn't have figured it out on your own."

"Hard to say. If you ask me, everything pointed to your ex. But with no proof…" He shrugged his shoulders and flashed me a sexy smile.

I smiled back. "If you keep doing that, we might have to stop."

"Tempting, but I was hoping we'd get there today. As for Helen—"

"The good news? She's reorganizing the Haven Players. She's going to run it herself."

He smiled. "She's good at running things." He put in a CD, then, a soothing instrumental. He wasn't much on news or sports, thank goodness. He also knew how to cook, or at least grill. Enough to make me happy. That's what I thought as I closed my eyes let myself drift off.

***

"Jessica's house reminds me of my rental. I have an option to buy it, if it works out as well as I think it will," I told Jace as we watched the moon rise over the ocean from her deck. It was cold but not uncomfortable, with the fire burning in her fire pit.

"This house reminds me of one I grew up in. It was small, but living by the water? I loved it."

I glanced at him, then looked out at the ocean and breathed in the fresh, tangy salt air. *I'd love to live with you in a house by the water. With you.* Say that?

Why not? You love him.

If only I trusted that feeling. If only I could trust any of my feelings. I was healing, not fast enough for me. I looked up and saw him just, well, watching me. Did he know what I was thinking? How much did it matter, I asked myself as I moved closer and kissed him.

It wasn't long before we went inside, made love, then talked for a little while. At some point, I glanced out the French doors that went out to the deck. "I've wanted a house by the ocean all my life."

"But you never had one before, did you?"

I shook my head. "I was glad I could move my furniture in there before we left." I'd finish moving in when we got back. I pictured the little beach house, smiled and snuggled close enough to feel his heartbeat. "But sometimes? It makes me sad that I waited so long."

"That's all in the past. You could leave it there, you know," he added we turned to gaze at the full moon over the water.

"Beautiful," I murmured.

"Your life will be beautiful, too." He hesitated. "Our lives will be beautiful."

Our lives? Did he want to move in with me? I was almost about to ask him when he sat up, wrapped a towel around his hips and began to get out of bed.

I wrapped the sheet around myself and followed him out to the patio, where he checked to make sure the fire was out. "The fire was nice."

He looked in my eyes and smiled. "We made some fire of our own, too. Even better."

I nodded, and felt myself blush.

He shrugged his shoulders. "No reason we can't make more, y'know, fire." He kissed me, then.

How could I say no?

We generated lots of fire over the next few days. The weather stayed mild for December. It was quiet on the island, too, off-season. Perfect.

A few days later in Chapel Hill, I was pleasantly surprised when his daughter and her grandparents welcomed us to this wonderful southern style Christmas dinner: deep-fried turkey with homemade cornbread dressing, fresh biscuits and sweet potato pie. I ate too much and enjoyed every bite. I was feeling well-fed in all kinds of different ways by the time we left.

I was particularly happy when his daughter Kim seemed to accept me. She was a beautiful young woman, tall and slim, with Jace's black hair and crystal blue eyes. I could see how intelligent and well-spoken she was, too. I felt sure she'd get along with Katie, if and when our relationship reached that point.

"A perfect day," I told Jace as we headed back to Jessica's house.

He smiled. "I have a lot to be grateful for."

Rich was never grateful for anything, I thought as I realized every last one of those doubts, fears and guilt I'd burdened myself with, all those years, had had everything to do with my marriage, a marriage I'd stayed in far too long. Now that the divorce was almost final, I hoped to leave them there and never look back.

As for Jace, I wasn't surprised when he volunteered a little more information about Kim's issues with her mother. Diane's drinking problem was the main reason she'd chosen UNC over Rutgers and two other New Jersey colleges that had accepted her. I didn't ask for more information than he wanted to tell me. Everything in its own time. That was the way I always wanted it to be, between us.

***

It was December 31st, our last day on the island, when I woke up, stretched and glanced at the clock— 11:15. I'd slept almost ten hours. A lot more than usual, but I felt wonderful-- till the phone rang. I looked at the caller ID. It was Katie, calling to wish us a happy new year, most likely.

"Mom? I hate to bother you—"

No *happy new year*? Strange. "It's okay. Happy new year, honey."

"Oh. You, too." I heard her sigh. "I know how much you needed this vacation, but—"

"What is it?"

"I hate to upset you, but—"

"What's wrong? Has Andrew been giving you more grief?" I hoped not, but whatever it was? We'd deal with it.

"Andrew's just being Andrew. I'm used to it by now." She hesitated. "Remember Kevin Patterson? I told you about him."

Dozens of times. I knew how attracted she was to him, because he was a TV celebrity? Maybe. I felt sure she didn't realize that in his private life, he was just another 50-something guy with a divorce or two under his belt and a couple of grown children.

"Mom?"

"Kevin Patterson. I remember." *Impossible to forget. He's all you talk about.* Did she sleep with him yet? Did I really want to know?

"We were at this big fundraiser last night when he sort of, um, passed out." Her voice pulled me back abruptly.

"What happened, is he all right?"

"I called 911 as soon as it happened, but by the time they got there, he wasn't breathing. And now…" I could hear her voice break.

"What happened, Katie, tell me!"

"He's dead. I just can't believe it."

"He had a heart attack?"

"I don't know. They're supposed to do the autopsy today, but in the ER last night? I overheard one of the doctors say something about poison."

"They think he was poisoned?" *Murdered, like Wendi?*

"Then this morning? This horrible detective woman from Seaview Pines showed up at my door to bring me in for questioning. I had to call Andrew to get Corey and take him to school. He was awful about it, really, really arrogant." She hesitated. "I'm so upset."

I struggled to process it. "A Seaview Pines detective brought you in for questioning?

"The fundraiser was in Seaview Pines, in that elegant new place on the ocean?"

"Sea Island?" *What difference does it make?*

"That's the one. I can't believe Kevin's, like, dead." I listened as she began to cry.

"I'm so sorry, honey."

"That's not the worst of it! Since I was with him last night, that awful detective woman thinks I must've had something to do with it. After they drove me down to the station—in a police car—she kept asking me all these questions, the same ones over and over again. I hate to ask you to come home early, but I need you, mom."

"We were going to drive back tomorrow. No problem to leave today. I'll just tell Jace." Watching me and frowning, right now. He gestured to the phone. "He's right here, Katie. Why don't you tell him what happened."

She hesitated. "Okay."

I handed him my phone and listened to his end of the conversation until I got so upset, I went out to the patio. I was trying to calm myself when he joined me there. "The sooner we get home, the better," he said.

***

Two hours later, we were on the road. "I called Lori Malone."

"Lori Malone?" The name sounded familiar, somehow, but I couldn't place her.

"Seaview Pines' lead detective. Patterson's death? It's her case," he added.

I nodded, then remembered how she and one or two of her cases had been front page news in the *Brook Haven Banner* this year.

"Lori's the reason we need to get up there ASAP," he added as he pulled onto Interstate 95.

"Why?"

"She's a good cop, but she can go off, a little, at times."

"Something you know—how?"

"She was NYPD." He hesitated. "We spent ten months as partners. Lori lives to clear cases, a little too quickly, sometimes." He frowned. "I've seen her jump the gun more than once. And with your daughter involved—"

I nodded. I knew he could see how worried I was. I also knew he was aware of the way I was picturing the two of us clearing this case together. *My next murder.* Not that I was about to tell him that.

Not that he didn't know.

"Just because you got lucky the last time out, almost getting yourself killed in the process, don't think for a minute I'd ever let you do it again. You are not to interfere with this investigation," he added as he picked up speed and swung into the passing lane

Giving me orders? Not acceptable, not that it'd be a good idea to tell him that, at the moment. For Katie's sake as well as my own, I needed to keep the peace.

"I understand."

"Yeah, right!" He rolled his eyes.

I smiled. He didn't smile back, not that it mattered. If Katie was in trouble, I was already involved.

I looked at him closely. From the way his jaw was set, I could tell he knew it, too.

The End